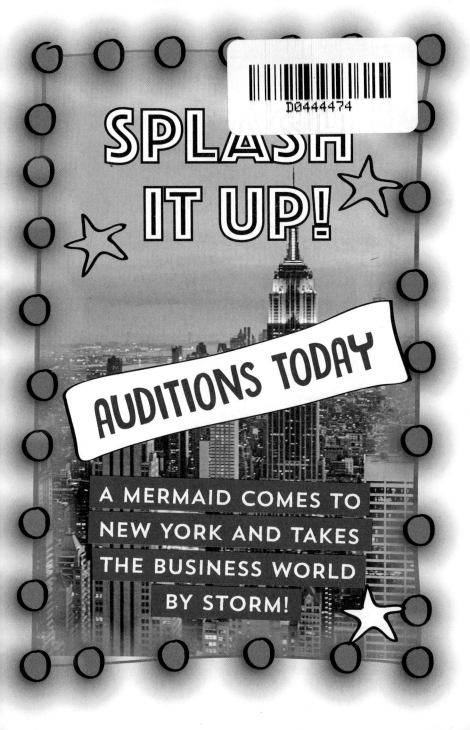

SPLASH IT UP!

AUDITIONS TODAY

A MERMAID COMES TO NEW YORK AND TAKES THE BUSINESS WORLD BY STORM!

To Gillian Sore and Clare Whitston
(The Queens of Storyland); Alex McNabb and Iain Martin
(Chief Glitterers); Tracy Donnelly, Annabel Kantaria,
Lucy Strange, and Charlotte Butterfield
(Cupcake Decorators); Wayne Jordan and Jack Cheshire
(Rainbow Polishers); and Abbie, Darius, Emily, and
Kelsey (Unicorn Racing Enthusiasts)

Copyright © 2017 by Rachel Hamilton
Illustrations copyright © 2017 by Oscar Armelles

All rights reserved. Published by Scholastic Inc., 557 Broadway, New York, NY 10012,
Publishers since 1920. SCHOLASTIC and associated logos are trademarks and/or registered
trademarks of Scholastic Inc.

First published in the United Kingdom in 2017 by Oxford University Press,
Great Clarendon Street, Oxford, OX2 6DP.

The publisher does not have any control over and does not assume any
responsibility for author or third-party websites or their content.

ISBN 978-1-338-05518-4

10 9 8 7 6 5 4 3 2 1   18 19 20 21 22

Printed in the U.S.A.   23
First Scholastic printing 2018

All photographs copyright © Shutterstock

UNICORN IN NEW YORK

LOUIE
MAKES
A
SPLASH!

RACHEL HAMILTON

Illustrated by Oscar Armelles

SCHOLASTIC INC.

Chapter One

Greetings

Greetings, humans. It's me, Louie the Unicorn, and I'm back once again to say, "LOVE ME!"

Oops. Sorry. Bit over-excited. What I *meant* to say was . . . Greetings, humans. It's me, Louie the Unicorn, and I'm back

once again to say, "LISTEN TO ME!" Because I'm here to share another thrilling tale of drama, destiny, and DIVAS (that would be you, Miranda the Mermaid) from the New York School of Performing Arts.

This time, our adventure began outside the John Feelgood Theater, lining up to audition for *Splash It Up!*—the hottest new show in town from the world-famous musical theater producers Andrew Velvet-Curtains and Tim Dry-Ice.

Splash It Up! was creating a huge buzz in the entertainment world and an even bigger buzz in Miranda the Mermaid's tank as we read the audition poster aloud for the thousandth time:

Splash It Up!

☆ A mermaid comes to New York and takes the business world by storm.

"It's perfect!" Frank the Troll burped with delight and pirouetted on the spot. "This part could have been written for you, Miranda."

I clapped my hooves in agreement. "There is only one superstar, super-singing mermaid in this city. You were born to make a 'splash,' Miranda."

3

"♩ Oooh ♩," Miranda trilled, flicking her tail with glee. "This could be the big break I've been waiting for my whole life." She smiled dreamily, and then added, "I'm sure there'll be roles for the rest of you, too."

"Not for me," Danny the Faun sighed. "I'm just lining up for support. They already have an award-winning director—the magnificent Trevor Phatt-Bunns—but it's a great opportunity for you, Miranda."

"I'm still not sure I've picked the right scene for my audition," Miranda said. "I'd have made a lovely, if soggy, Juliet from *Romeo and Juliet*. Or perhaps I should have chosen the dying swan scene from *Swan Lake*?" Miranda paused and then sang, "♩ Qua-a-a-a-ck! Aaaargh ♩."

"Dur! Fish for brains!" heckled Arnie the Unicorn, who'd managed to get a spot ahead of us in the line and kept reminding us about it. "Swans don't quack."

"Don't they?" Miranda asked us.

We shook our heads.

"Maybe they do when they're dying," Miranda yelled at Arnie. "Don't be judgy."

"Whatever," Arnie harrumphed, with a toss of his tail. "Mermaids are so stupid."

"Tell that to the producers of this *mermaid show*," Miranda retorted. "You big bully."

"Ignore him, Miranda. You'd make a great dead swan," Danny reassured her. "But since they're looking for a mermaid and you *are* a mermaid, it makes sense to do a scene with a mermaid in it."

"I should have chosen the scene from *Peter Pan* where the mermaids try to drown Wendy," Miranda replied. "With Arnie playing Wendy."

"Miranda!" I protested. "You can't drown Arnie. He's my friend and fellow unicorn."

"I wouldn't really hurt him. Well, not much." Miranda sighed at my expression. "OK, OK, no messing with Arnie. Boooring."

"Stop worrying about your audition," Danny told her. "Ariel from *The Little Mermaid* is the perfect choice."

"Of course it is!" I cheered. "I make a fabulous Sebastian the Crab. Check out my funky plastic crab claws."

"Louie!" Danny narrowed his eyes at me. "Remember what we agreed? This is Miranda's audition."

"It's OK," Miranda said. "I want my friends involved. Louie IS a fabulous Sebastian. And Frank . . . well . . . Frank would make a fantastic King Triton." She beamed up at him and sang:

"♪ **So big, so powerful, so . . .** ♪"

"I don't want to be Triton!" Frank growled. "I want to be Flounder the Fish."

"Yes, we know!"

We giggled as we looked at Frank. Despite being six feet tall and six feet wide, he had squeezed his wide warty face and hairy troll body into a tiny yellow-and-blue fish

costume. Even in a line of crazily dramatic auditionees, a troll dressed as a fish was attracting attention—in particular, since he was accompanied by a faun, a mermaid in a tank on wheels, and a unicorn wearing crab claws.

"You make a lovely Flounder, Frank," Miranda assured him with a giggle. "Come on, let's practice our group audition. ♫ We'll knock their socks off ♫."

I jumped up and down. "We are having ALL the fun. Can you believe I found such realistic pincers on such short notice?"

"**YES, I CAN!**" Frank yelled. "Because you keep pinching my bottom with them. And that will stop being funny very quickly now that we're stuck in the longest line in history."

Chapter Two

Buffalo Bob

Frank wasn't exaggerating about the length of the line. Well, not much. People had come from all over the world to audition, and they were trying all sorts of tricks to get into the theater ahead of the rest of us.

Girls in tutus said they felt faint and needed to get inside to cool down, only to recover miraculously when offered a ride home. Boys in tap shoes claimed to be on guest lists that didn't exist. And angry mothers insisted they had friends waiting for their children inside—except they couldn't remember their names.

The bouncers were having none of it, and everyone who tried to push in got sent straight to the back of the line. "No special cases," they insisted.

"That's a good thing," Frank said. "But we're still never going to get in. There are thousands in front of us."

I pinched him with a crab claw again for being negative, but he had a point. The only thing moving in this line was a strange, shouty man wearing a Stetson hat, a gold leather tie, and a pair of shiny

pointed cowboy boots, who wandered up and down the line, stopping every now and again to peer at anyone who caught his eye. His grin was as shiny as his boots.

He stopped in front of us and clapped his hands when he saw Miranda. "Magnificent costume! I can hardly see where the tail's attached. You'd almost pass for a genuine mermaid!"

"♫ I AM a genuine mermaid ♫," Miranda protested.

"That voice! She sings, too!" The man rocked back on his cowboy-boot heels and whistled. "You're going to be a huge star, little lady. Just follow me and let Buffalo Bob Parker be the brains behind your success." He strode toward the front of the line, pulling Miranda behind him.

"My friends, too?" Miranda asked.

"As you wish, baby. With me as your manager, your every wish will be granted."

"*Baby?*" I stared at Miranda. She didn't look like any baby I'd ever seen.

"♩ **Manager?** ♩" Miranda trilled, and when she looked at Buffalo Bob Parker, I could almost see the stars in her eyes.

"Wait," Danny protested. "If we move, we'll lose our place here. It's not a great spot but there are thousands of people behind us and the bouncers are sending everyone who tries to push in to the back of the line."

"You heard my cowboy manager," Miranda said, giving Arnie a little wave as she passed him. "♪ I can have whatever I want ♪."

"Yeah, baby," I said with a giggle, prancing to the front with Miranda.

Danny sighed, but he and Frank followed along behind us.

Chapter Three

A Real-Life Mermaid

The bouncers glanced up grumpily. It was a long, hot afternoon. They were sweaty. And their sweat smelled of impatience with a hint of sulkiness.

Before we even reached them, one raised his arm, exposing a very sweaty armpit, and pointed to the back of the line.

Buffalo Bob Parker grabbed at the

bouncer's raised hand and shook it heartily. "No need to thank me, young man. Just let us through."

"No special treatment. Everyone waits in line. The boss says so."

Buffalo Bob Parker continued pumping the bouncer's hand. "Can you imagine how impressed 'the boss' will be when you tell him you've found a REAL-LIFE MERMAID for his show?"

The bouncer used his free hand to push his sunglasses up so he could study Miranda more closely.

"You're seriously telling me this is a genuine mermaid?" the bouncer asked, pulling his other arm free.

"♪ Ahem ♪," Miranda coughed. "I am here, you know. And yes, genuine mermaid."

"Prove it," the bouncer said.

"Just look at that divinely radiant tail," Buffalo Bob said. "Beautiful, magical . . ."

Miranda beamed at the compliments, until Buffalo Bob added, "Tug it. You'll see it's real."

"♪ Hey! ♪" Miranda protested as the bouncer reached toward her.

"I have an idea!" I blurted as Miranda prepared to wallop the bouncer with her "divinely radiant tail." "Go underwater for five minutes, Miranda. No human could do that without coming up for air."

"Uh, actually they could," Danny said.

"There's a Swedish man who can hold his breath underwater for over twenty minutes."

"Impossible!" I turned to Miranda. "Isn't it?"

"No idea. But if you want proof, then watch this." Miranda did an underwater

somersault in her tank, then emerged from the water and combed her perfect tresses.

"It's dry!" The bouncer stared in disbelief. "Your hair's dry."

"♫ **Mermaid magic** ♫," Miranda sang.

"Convinced?" Buffalo Bob asked.

The bouncer nodded, murmuring, "A real-life mermaid. Wow! I can't wait to tell my mom about this." He waved Miranda through.

"What about us?" Frank bellowed.

The bouncer looked at me, Frank, and Danny. He didn't seem quite as impressed. "A horse with a shiny horn and crab claws, a big ogre thing, and a . . . what exactly are you?" He prodded Danny the Faun. "Some sort of goat boy?"

"They're with me," Miranda said. "So if you want me, then you have to let them in, too."

"Already issuing diva demands?" Danny asked, half laughing, half frowning.

"You heard my cowboy manager." Miranda gave a toss of her magical mermaid hair and a harmonious warble. "♩ **What I want, I get, baby!** ♩"

Chapter Four

The Audition

We followed Miranda into the theater, where people dressed in black whisked us up onto the stage.

"♩ **Hello** ♩," Miranda sang. "♩ **What can I perform for you today?** ♩"

"Do you always sing everything?" asked a voice in the darkness.

"Not always." Miranda tried to take the song out of her voice and failed.

"♪ Sorry ♪."

"Don't be sorry. And don't stop!"

"♪ OKAAY ♪," Miranda trilled. "♪ I am so excited to be here today ♪." She paused and did a couple of somersaults in her tank. "Getting this role would be my dream come true. How can I convince you I'm right for the part?"

"I think you already have. You can sing. You've got the tail, the hair, and you even come with your own tank. How can any actress—however great—make as good a mermaid as a real-life fishy female?"

"Um, I like what you're saying," Miranda said carefully. "But I'm going to object to the term *fishy female*."

"Apologies, Miranda the unfishy female.

You're in! Leave your contact information and we'll be in touch."

"♪ **Oooh** ♪." Miranda clapped her hands with glee. "Can my friends have parts, too?"

"I'm sure we can find a little something for them to do."

"Should we audition now?" Frank asked.

"No need," said the voice in the dark.

We were ushered off the stage and back

out onto the street as Miranda stayed behind to fill out all the paperwork.

"Why no need?" Frank asked. "They have to see what we can do to give us the right parts."

"I am sure everything will work out swimmingly," I said, grinning. "See what I did there? That was a mermaid joke! Fear not, Frank, our *tail* will have a happy ending. Tail like a mermaid's tail. See what I—"

Frank grabbed me by my crab pincers. "Yes, I see what you did there. Don't do it again."

"Frank! You're hurting me on *porpoise*. Ha-ha! Get it? Porpoise, like the sea crea-ture? See what—?"

"GRRRR!" Frank was starting to look less like his normal cuddly self and more like the kind of troll who likes to eat unicorns for breakfast.

Luckily, Miranda reappeared. Frank released my pincers and told her he was worried about the lack of auditions.

"♩ Don't worry ♩." She patted him on the shoulder. "They don't need you to audition. They only gave you the part because I asked them to."

Frank went quiet after that.

Chapter Five

Miranda's Marvels

Splash It Up! was the talk of the town, so the teachers at the New York School of Performing Arts were thrilled one of their pupils had the starring role. Obviously not as thrilled as Miranda, who looked ready to explode with excitement.

I was ecstatic for her, so I didn't mind my principal and favorite teacher, Madame Swirler, replacing the photos from our recent national dance competition (including several very flattering pictures of me performing the Leaping Champion jump) with posters of Miranda.

I did mind a little bit when Miranda moved my "special commendation" ballet certificate from the main hall bulletin board to the back of the bathroom door so she could make room for newspaper clippings about her being the "next big thing." But I cheered up when Danny pointed out people spend far more time in the bathroom than by the main bulletin board.

Arnie *definitely* minded Miranda moving his pictures. His response was to change the spelling of "Miranda the Mermaid" to "Miran-DUR the MEH-maid" on the *Splash*

It Up! posters. (Don't tell Miranda, but I thought that was funny.)

Miranda didn't find it funny at all. She punished Arnie by offering to swap any of his fans' "Arnie's Army" T-shirts for a brand-new "Miranda's Marvels" T-shirt. Buffalo Bob, her cowboy manager, had created them and they were super shiny, with a special sparkly mermaid tail you could attach with Velcro at the back.

"ARGHnie is just jealous," Miranda told the crowd that had started appearing everywhere she went when the huge billboard posters of her face popped up across the city. "He must feel like a loser because the *Splash It Up!* team wouldn't even let him audition. Ha-ha."

The crowd of "Miranda's Marvels" laughed. I didn't. They hadn't let me audition, either. And Frank and I still hadn't heard anything about our roles.

Meanwhile, Miranda had been sent a rehearsal schedule, so we crowded around it in the dorm.

"They want you almost every day!" I cheered. "You're a big star now, Miranda. How will you fit in your classes here?"

Miranda shrugged. "I guess I'll learn on the job."

"Wow!" I bounced. "This is all sooooo exciting!"

Frank studied Miranda's schedule and burped with pleasure. "Awesome. Look! You're free for the whole day on my birthday! The four of us can do something fun."

"♫ **Can't think of anything I'd like more** ♫," trilled Miranda. "I don't want my new role to change what we do as friends."

"Why would it?" Danny asked.

"♪ **No reason** ♪," Miranda sang breezily. "You guys run on to class. I just need to call Buffalo Bob. You know, my *manager*, dahlings."

Chapter Six

Rehearsals

Frank and I accompanied Miranda to the first rehearsal at the theater. I couldn't wait to find out what roles they'd given us.

The minute we arrived, everyone swooped on Miranda and tried to lift her onto their shoulders, chanting, "The next big thing," like in the newspaper clippings. It all got a little damp and slippery, like a group of people trying to hold on to a large, slithery fish. Frank caught Miranda as she whooshed between the hands of two lighting engineers toward the first row of seats. She gave him a grateful smile as he dropped her back into her tank and placed her on the stage.

I followed behind and addressed the theater crew. "Greetings. I am Louie the Unicorn and this is Frank the Troll. We wondered where you wanted us to stand?"

No one replied. Instead, they trampled Frank and me in their rush to get on stage and talk to Miranda.

It's hard to trample a troll, so you can imagine how much they wanted to see her.

The preshow publicity meant that everyone was super excited.

I told myself being ignored might be a good thing. Madame Swirler always said you shouldn't spoil talented people, because they won't realize they have to work for success if everyone acts like they've already made it.

So, maybe this was a good sign. No one was acting as if I'd already made it. No one was acting as if I even existed. They must *really* want me to succeed.

"Hello?" I tried again. "Hello?"

Nothing. The rehearsal had begun and everyone was noisily cheering every note Miranda sang.

It was very different from Madame Swirler's shouty method of teaching. All the whistling and clapping certainly made Miranda smile more, but Madame Swirler's snapping and criticism did make you try harder.

Anyway, no need for *me* to worry about it. No one was clapping and cheering for me. When Frank finally managed to make himself heard to ask what we were supposed to be doing, he was told they'd figure out what to do with us later, if it made Miranda happy.

Frank picked his nose, which was usually a sign he'd forgotten he was calmer and nicer than the average troll.

I tried to cheer him up. "That's good news, Frank. It *will* make Miranda happy if they give us roles. So they *will* figure out what to do with us."

That didn't help. Frank just moved his warty finger from his nose to his mouth. Ewww. I moved away and watched Miranda prepare for stardom.

She had a wonderful voice and got the songs down quickly. She wasn't as comfortable with the talky bits, maybe because the

lines of the play were a little strange. They were all about being pretty and popular, and I was surprised they thought that was enough to take the business world by storm in the way the audition poster described.

But Miranda was clearly enjoying herself. As a uniquely dashing actor myself, I was proud of the unusual approach she was taking to the craft. Sadly, those of us with original acting skills are doomed to be mocked by those who don't understand. A couple standing behind us snickered every time Miranda spoke, and muttered things like, "That mermaid sings like an angel, but couldn't act

her way out of a puddle—wearing an inner tube."

When they got quiet, I assumed they'd been won over by the power of Miranda's acting. But when I turned around, I saw that Frank had his hands over their mouths.

I squeaked and tugged his arms away. It was right to support Miranda—she was our friend and no one should mock her—but Frank couldn't just stop people from breathing! The girl critic's face had turned slightly blue and the boy's throw-uppy expression suggested Frank's troll hands might still be covered in boogers.

When Frank released them, they fled backstage to the dressing rooms. I know because I saw them there later when we went to find Miranda during her break. Luckily, Frank didn't spot them since they ducked behind a large bouquet of roses when they saw him coming.

We found Miranda talking to the director. Frank had sent her a note earlier asking her to find out about our roles.

Miranda's manager, Buffalo Bob, was sitting with them, and as we approached, I heard him mutter, "Ditch the flying horse and the ogre, baby. They're dragging you down."

"Oooh! Did you hear that?" I poked Frank. "Maybe those guys will want to be friends."

Frank kicked a costume rack and sent twenty sparkly tutus shooting across the room.

"Frank!" I said. "Stop kicking and start listening. Miranda's manager says there's a flying horse and an ogre here. They might want to hang out with us."

"There's no flying horse, Louie. And you're looking at the ogre. That horrible man couldn't even be bothered to get our species right."

"I don't understand."

"No, I don't suppose you do." Frank patted my shoulder. "Life is probably nicer that way." He paused by a bowl of purple M&Ms, ate a handful, and then threw the rest at Buffalo Bob, who ducked and glowered at us.

Chapter Seven

Frank's Birthday

I was so excited about Frank's birthday. Our friend Victoria Sponge at the Sunshine Sparkle Dust Café had made a giant cake with pictures of Frank, Danny, Miranda, and me on the top, and Frank had promised we could all eat ourselves later!

But first we were going to do a mini birthday show to celebrate how FUNTASTIC our lives had been since we left Story Land

and arrived in New York in search of adventure. Our first performance together had been in the Sunshine Sparkle Dust Café, and I was looking forward to reliving our famous conga-through-the-cupcakes there later.

After that, Frank and I planned to do a repeat performance of our starring roles as the Handsome Prince (me) and the Scary Giant (Frank) in the rescue scene from *The Handsome Prince and the Princess Pointlessly Stuck in the Tower* we'd performed on Broadway two semesters ago.

Miranda pointed out, several times, that had been a one-off school performance, not a "real show" like *Splash It Up!* But we'd still been the talk of the city . . . OK, the talk of a little bit of the city . . . OK, OK, the talk of Frank and me. But we lived in the city, so that still counted. Whatever! It was going to be great to do our favorite scene all over again.

To finish the show, each of us planned to do our own special number. For me that would be my Leaping Champion jump from the national dance competition. After all, it was worthy of a "special commendation," as anyone who'd been to the bathroom recently and seen my certificate on the back of the door would know.

The main thing was we'd all be together. FRIENDSHIP WAS FUN, and we had a whole day to celebrate it. We hadn't seen enough of Miranda lately. Even when she was with us, she was busy signing autographs and shaking hands, so we didn't have time to talk.

But she'd be all ours today. We'd been talking about Frank's birthday for weeks and none of us would dream of missing it. I couldn't wait!

I was still smiling when I entered the dorm room. My grin faded slightly when I found Miranda ordering Frank to give her a manicure and Danny to clean the inside of her tank.

"♪ Louie! ♪" she sang. "Thank goodness you're here."

I beamed. She'd obviously missed me as much as I'd missed her.

"You're just in time to scrub my tail."

"Hmm," I murmured. "Perhaps another time. I've got my special rainbow-tastic disco outfit on, ready for Frank's birthday celebration. I don't think I'm supposed to get the flashing lights and sequins wet."

Miranda scowled as her new cell phone buzzed. She pulled her hand away from Frank's to answer the call, smudging the nail polish he'd been carefully applying.

She giggled into the receiver, tossing her hair as she sang, "♪ **Who, me? Yes, me! Oh yes, I am rather wonderful** ♪." She finished the conversation with, "Yes! Oh yes! Of course I will. I'd love to."

She dropped the phone back into its waterproof bag and waved at Frank.

"Frank, dahling. Take me down to reception."

"Please!" Danny reminded her.

"Please what, Danny?" she asked. "Ah, you want to continue cleaning my tank? Of course you can, sweetie. *Mwah, mwah.* You'll just have to wait until later."

"No," Danny replied. "I don't particularly want to clean your tank, Miranda. What I meant was, you should say 'please' to Frank, instead of giving him orders."

"Frank doesn't mind, do you, dahling? It's his birthday, so I'm letting him treat me." Miranda gave Frank a little tickle under his chin, which made him sneeze. Miranda withdrew her hand quickly. Troll snot is not a pretty thing.

"I'm not sure whether I mind or not yet,"
Frank replied, wiping his nose on his sleeve.
"Who was that on the phone, Miranda?
And what would you love to do?"

Miranda blushed. "It's nothing, really,
Frank. It was just Buffalo Bob. My cowboy
manager," she added unnecessarily.

"We know who he is," Frank said with a
giant snort. "What does he want you to do?
ON MY BIRTHDAY?!"

"Only a teeny little meeting, sweetie.
Won't take a second. It's just . . . the film
star Andromeda Jolene is in New York and
Buffalo Bob thinks it might be nice for me
to spend some time with her, and of course
be *totally* surprised when the paparazzi
turn up."

"It might also be nice for you to spend some time with us," Frank growled. "ON MY BIRTHDAY."

"Of course, sweetie, I'll be with you on your birthday. ♪ **Happy Birthday to yooooooooooou** ♪. But it's not all day, is it?"

"Well, yes," Danny pointed out. "That's the point of birthdays. They are all day, aren't they? Birth-day. All-day. Plus, Frank has spent ages making sure today will be perfect."

"I know, sweetie, dahling—*mwah*—but you wouldn't want me to miss the opportunity to meet Andromeda, would you?"

Frank's and Danny's faces suggested they definitely would like her to miss that opportunity. But I understood why Miranda was excited. Andromeda Jolene could find lost treasure in tombs, perform incredible feats of kung fu as a tigress, and fly—at least she could until they chopped her wings off. Hmm. On reflection, perhaps she could only do these things in films. But it would still be thrilling to meet her.

"Why don't we let Miranda get on her way to meet this super-famous lady?" I suggested. "I'm sure she won't be more than a few minutes. We've all been looking forward to your party for weeks, Frank, and Miranda would obviously rather be with us."

Miranda nodded, although I noticed she kept glancing at her phone.

"She can meet us at Sunshine Sparkle Dust Café for the show, in an hour. We're going to have so much fun together."

A horn beeped below. I looked out of the window and saw Buffalo Bob Parker peering up from a truck that had "Miranda the Magnificent Mermaid" painted on the side.

"Looks like your ride is here."

"♪ Door, dahling ♪," Miranda trilled at Frank, who just stared at her. Miranda stopped preening for a moment and looked more like her old self. "Please, Frank, would you mind helping me into the truck?"

He grunted, but did as she asked. I heard her telling him not to worry, she'd be back in plenty of time for the show, dahling.

*   *   *

Five hours later, Frank and I were doing our final bows on the café-counter-slash-stage and thanking Danny for his brilliant direction. The huge crowd in the café cheered, but I heard lots of them mumbling things like, "I thought Miranda the famous mermaid would be here. That's the only reason I came."

I know Frank heard them, too, because he scratched his armpits and forgot to say "Pardon me" after a bottom burp. But he was pretending it didn't matter.

He kept up his slightly scary birthday smile until everyone else had gone and the three of us were sitting around the counter enjoying the super-delicious birthday cake. Frank ate fondant Frank. Danny gobbled up fondant Danny. And I devoured fondant Louie. Mmm. Only a quarter of the cake remained. The quarter of the cake with Miranda on it.

A fly landed on her beautifully iced face. None of us brushed it away.

Chapter Eight

Getting Our Skates On

The atmosphere in our dorm was sticky after Frank's birthday, and not just because we forgot to wash our hands and hooves after eating all that cake. Everyone was still upset about Miranda's disappearance on Frank's birthday and about the fact she'd told Frank and me—BY TEXT—there were no longer roles for us in the *Splash It Up!* show.

Danny ordered Miranda to apologize to Frank. She did, but she didn't sound at all sorry: She sounded more like she was angry with us for bothering her when she was so busy and important.

We hardly saw her anymore. It made me sad and left a Miranda-size hole in my life. And that was a big hole. A mermaid-in-a-tank-size hole.

I never stopped trying to include her in everything we did—inviting her to parties and school events and trips to the shops or the café, but she was always busy.

Finally, though, I thought of something fun to do on one of Miranda's rare free evenings. Go to a roller disco! We had always talked about going to one of those together, so I spent all week in the school's prop department making a special pair of flashing wheels to stick on the bottom of her tank and a glitter ball to hang inside it.

Miranda said she was grateful, but gave a large yawn. "I don't think I'll be able to make it, Louie. I'm sooooo tired. It's all 'schedule this,' 'rehearsal that.' I need to rest."

I felt disappointed, but I understood. She'd been working so hard, no wonder she just wanted a quiet night in bed.

Before we left for the roller disco, I set up the glitter ball on the dorm ceiling, decorated the room with twinkling lights, and persuaded Danny to set up a speaker system that would pump disco music into the room. When I was confident I'd done

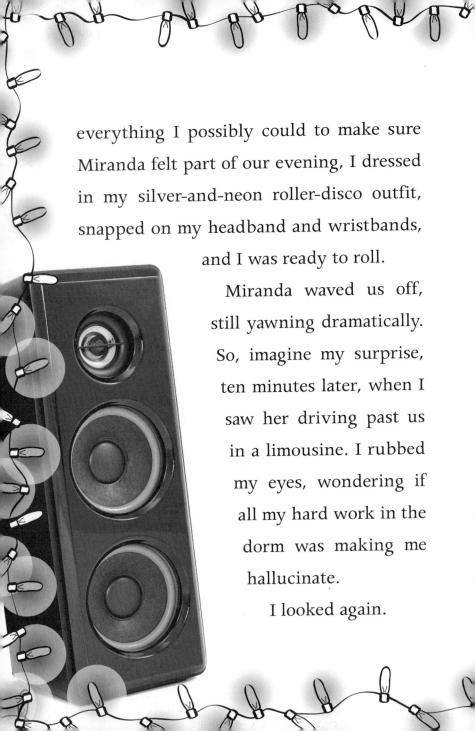

everything I possibly could to make sure Miranda felt part of our evening, I dressed in my silver-and-neon roller-disco outfit, snapped on my headband and wristbands, and I was ready to roll.

Miranda waved us off, still yawning dramatically. So, imagine my surprise, ten minutes later, when I saw her driving past us in a limousine. I rubbed my eyes, wondering if all my hard work in the dorm was making me hallucinate.

I looked again.

No. There was no mistake. The limousine had been customized to allow her tank to stick out of the top so her hair could blow in the breeze. Buffalo Bob sat alongside her and they were both drinking pink fizzy stuff, their heads thrown back with laughter.

I turned indignantly to tell Danny and Frank. But I stopped when I saw how happy Frank

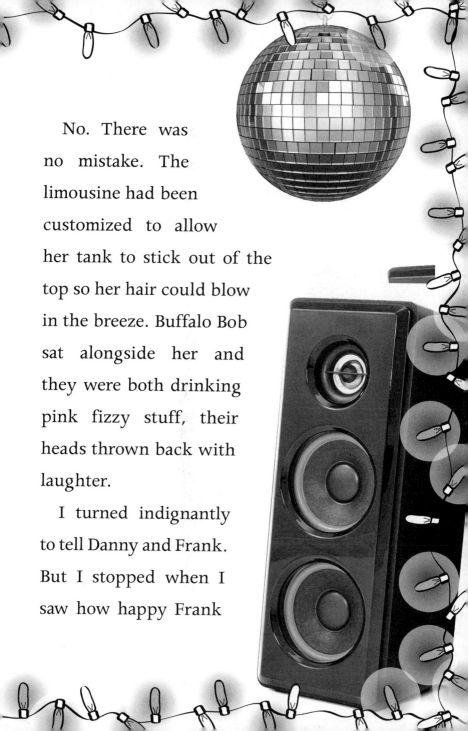

and Danny looked, chatting about the moves we were going to do at tonight's roller disco. I didn't want to upset them with my disturbing news.

My horn twitched uneasily as I realized

that, not only was Miranda lying to me; she was also stopping me from telling the truth to my best friends.

This had to stop. This was not the unicorn way.

Chapter Nine

Moving On

The roller disco was a fun-filled extravaganza of sparkling lights, shiny costumes, and killer dance moves, but I couldn't stop thinking about Miranda's betrayal all evening. I tried to talk to her the following morning, but she wouldn't listen.

"You're killing my buzz, Louie. I expected you of all people to be more supportive."

"Buzz?" I asked in confusion. "Are you learning to talk to insects? Cool! I bet bees are fun to chat with."

"Don't be silly, dahling. It's something Buffalo Bob told me . . ." She smiled when she mentioned his name and it made me want to poke him with my horn. " 'Killing your buzz' is what people do when you become famous, because they're jealous. People tell me my acting sucks because it's so great. They want to be me, but they can't, so they try to kill my buzz."

"Huh? So when people say your acting is bad, what they actually mean is it's super-spectacularly good?"

Miranda nodded.

This put a new spin on Madame Swirler's

comments in dance lessons. I must be the most amazing student that ever lived. Nice!

One thing still confused me. "How am *I* killing your buzz?"

"By saying it was wrong of me to go out on the night of the roller disco."

"But it *was* wrong of you." I was finding this conversation confusing. "So if I'm telling the truth about this, maybe Madame Swirler is telling the truth when she says I need to practice more and maybe the people who say your acting is bad are . . . Oh."

I stopped when I saw the look on Miranda's face, but it was too late. In her head I'd already said it.

"You think I can't act," she wailed.

"No. I don't think that. I didn't say that.

I didn't even *nearly* say that. What I *nearly* said was other people might think you can't act. But I didn't mean it. I didn't even *nearly* mean it."

Miranda wasn't listening. "Buffalo Bob is right. You're all jealous. I shouldn't listen to anyone."

"You can't ignore everyone. What about your director? The acting coaches?"

"Negative, negative, negative," Miranda waved her hand dismissively. "Laters, haters."

"I'm not a hater. I'm your best friend."

Miranda covered her ears with her hands. "Not listening. ♫ **La la la** ♫. My cowboy manager is right. I don't belong here anymore. I need to move onward and upward.

I need support. I need positivity. I need to feel the ♫ la-la-looove ♫."

"But that's what you get from us," I said. "Well, the stuff at the beginning. I don't know about all this la-la-looove business."

"He says you bring me down and he's right," Miranda continued. "You yell at me for having fun. You tell me I can't act." She ignored my protests. "Well, my *manager* has found me the perfect apartment, right next to the theater. He says I need space to be creative, to express myself, to prepare for my big role."

With that, she flung open the dorm room door and ordered the group of Miranda's Marvels waiting outside to pack her stuff up so she could leave for her new life.

I didn't want things to end on such a bad note, so I told Miranda to come back in an hour after I'd made sure the speakers and the glitter ball were still working and I'd put my neon outfit back on. Then we could have a nice big good-bye party and send her off with a bang.

She did go out with a bang.

The bang of Danny and Frank slamming

the dormitory door. Because Miranda didn't even bother to show up.

"I'm sure she's very busy," I said quietly.

"Enough is enough, Louie," Danny told me. "She can't even be bothered to come to a party you've organized in her honor. That has to tell you something. I've had enough of that mermaid. I'm not going to her silly *Splash It Up!* show. Especially now that you and Frank aren't even in it. Besides, have you seen the price of the tickets?"

"Yes, but don't worry, Danny. Arnie says the main actors get three free tickets. I'm sure Miranda will give hers to us."

"I'll believe it when I see it," Danny growled.

Chapter Ten

Tickets

Miranda must have had a good reason for not giving us her free tickets. I'd just have to find another way to get some. Friendship was friendship and she had always been there for all of my performances. But how was I going to get the money for a ticket?

Fortunately, Victoria Sponge had a solution.

"This is perfect timing," she said, wiping

icing sugar from her cheeks. "We're having a huge promotional doughnut-eating contest here at the Sunshine Sparkle Dust Café next week and I've always said that horn of yours is the perfect doughnut-hole-punch. If you're happy to help me out by horn-punching holes in doughnuts, I can give you the money for a ticket. Tickets for doughnuts. Win-win."

The only challenge left was convincing Danny and Frank to buy tickets, too.

"I know you're angry," I said. "But we're best friends, and best friends support each other no matter how silly the other best friend is being." I opened the box of chocolate-filled and chocolate-sprinkled doughnuts Victoria Sponge had given me

earlier as a thank-you for agreeing to help her out with the contest. "Plus, if you buy a ticket, I'll give you a doughnut."

"No, Louie," Danny said. "If Miranda had wanted us to be there, she'd have sent tickets." He made a gesture at Frank that I didn't understand until they both dived on my doughnuts and started stuffing their faces. "Besides, best friends support each other *with doughnuts*, no matter what!"

I tried to protest, but I got the giggles and grabbed a handful of doughnuts for myself. "So," I mumbled through a mouthful of chocolate icing and chocolate sprinkles, "are you saying you'd go if Miranda sent tickets?"

"'Spose so," Danny muttered.

"What if I could get tickets from somewhere else?"

Frank scratched his armpit thoughtfully, but Danny was firm. "No. If Miranda doesn't invite us, we're not going."

Bah! I knew they wanted to go. But now Danny had made a big deal about it, there was no changing their minds, and it didn't look like Miranda was going to send tickets any time soon.

I tried talking to Arnie about it. He yawned. "Boring. Just buy the stupid tickets and pretend Miranda sent them."

"Lie?" I whinnied in horror. "I can't lie! That is not the unicorn way."

Arnie harrumphed scornfully. "Did your father ever ask your mother if his bottom looked big with a newly fashioned tail style?"

I nodded.

"And what did she say?"

"She always said his bottom looked lovely."

"But did it sometimes look big behind his tail?"

I didn't answer.

"There you go. You're always telling me your mother is the most wonderful unicorn in Story Land. Well, she says you should lie to your friends."

"Um. No she doesn't. *You* say I should lie to them."

"Whatever. I have given you a solution. It's up to you whether you use it."

Much as I loved Arnie, I'd learned it wasn't always wise to follow his advice, so I checked with Victoria Sponge.

"I can certainly give you enough work to pay for three tickets," she said. "We're very busy this week because of the contest, so that's not a problem."

"But is Arnie right? Should I lie to my friends?"

"I have an idea." Victoria Sponge pulled up a chair and handed me a brownie. "Sit down, hear me out, and see what you think."

Two days later, I raced up to the dorm room, ignoring Miranda's empty bed.

"She sent them!" I cheered. "The tickets are here! We're going to *Splash It Up!*"

"Miranda sent us tickets!" Frank grinned, reaching for them.

I followed Victoria Sponge's advice and didn't explain that "she" was in fact the ticket lady from the kiosk where I'd bought the tickets.

"Really?" Danny emerged from the bathroom, toothpaste still on his chin.

I let Frank answer for me. "Yes, Danny," he said. "Look! Here! Three tickets for the show. Isn't that amazing?"

"AMAZING, ASTOUNDING, MARVEL-OUS, AND MIRACULOUS! You are coming, right?" I checked, wincing as I spoke. My horn still ached from several late-night sessions of doughnut-punching.

"Guess so," Danny said, trying not to look too pleased about it, but I could tell he was thrilled.

Chapter Eleven

The Performance

There was an excited murmur as everyone took their seats for the opening night of *Splash It Up!* The line to get in had been almost as long as the audition line on that hot afternoon all those weeks ago.

The curtain rose, revealing Miranda surrounded by a crowd of briefcase-wielding, suit-wearing businesspeople in front of a huge backdrop of the Manhattan skyline. People were still gossiping among themselves. No critics had written any advance reviews for the show and people were wondering why. It usually meant a show wasn't good, but that was obviously impossible with all these famous producers and composers and directors involved.

Except it wasn't impossible.

As the show went on, the audience fell silent apart from embarrassed giggles, a few "yikes," and some unkind booing and hissing. The script was very strange—all about how brilliant and beautiful the mermaid was, and nothing else. And while Miranda's singing *was* beautiful, people didn't seem to "get" her acting.

An entire row got up and left after twenty minutes and lots of people followed shortly after. Hardly anyone came back after the intermission and by the end of the show Frank, Danny, and I were three of only about twenty people left in the theater.

We tried to talk to Miranda afterward, but she ran away, and we couldn't find her no matter how hard we looked.

The following morning, the newspapers ran with nasty headlines:

THE DAILY DOUGHNUT

Mermaid Tanks!

SHOWBIZ ON SUNDAY

LITTLE (TALENT) MERMAID

THE FAIRY TALE TIMES

MAID TO
FAIL

SHOWBIZ NEWS

SPLASH IT UP!
A WASHOUT

THE GOLDEN GLOBE

FISH FARCE
BATTERED

THE DAILY NEWS

Mermaid
Tanks!

During the week, we all tried to get a
hold of Miranda. We tried calling, we
tried texting, we tried emailing, someone

even suggested sending a pigeon. I think they were joking, but you can never tell. However, Miranda refused to speak to anyone.

By the weekend, the big announcement was:

THE MUSICAL MAIL

"MERMAID'S TALE" TO BE PULLED

The reviews had been so critical and the crowds so small that the producers decided to close the show after just two weeks.

THE PERFORMANCE

We went over to Miranda's new apartment building and tried shouting up at her, but she wouldn't come to the window. We tried sneaking in, but the lobby was full of actors and actresses managed by Miranda's cowboy manager, Buffalo Bob, and they weren't very nice to us.

To be honest, they weren't very nice to anyone. No one said thank you to the pizza delivery man who came while we were there, and we watched in shock as a group of dancers let the door slam on a plumber. They didn't even apologize when it made him drop his toolbox on his toe.

"They don't even look at these people," Danny said. "It's like they're not there."

I felt my horn tingle. "That's it! That's

how I can get into the building! If I dress up as some kind of salesperson, they won't even look at me. It will be easy to get in."

Frank and Danny clapped. I bowed happily. I deserved the applause. It *was* a good idea.

We returned to school and raided the costume closet. I emerged in a work shirt and overalls with a cap balanced on my horn and a tool belt around my waist.

"WHAT DO YOU THREE THINK YOU'RE DOING?" Madame Swirler appeared out of nowhere. How did she always know when you were doing something wrong?

"HOW DARE YOU MESS AROUND WITH MY COSTUMES!"

I lowered my horn in shame. Unicorns do not sneak around. (We generally prance.)

Frank and Danny were less embarrassed.

"It's a rescue mission," Danny declared. "Louie is going to sneak in and save Miranda, dressed as a handyman."

I waited for Madame Swirler to yell something like, "Off with the unicorn's head."

She didn't. Instead she said, "Wait here." She ducked into the prop closet and came out brandishing a

large wrench. "Here. Your costume is now complete. Go get her, Tiger."

"Thank you. But I think you're confused, Madame Swirler. I'm a unicorn, not a tiger. You may have been tricked by my disguise." I lifted my cap. " 'Tis I, Louie."

Madame Swirler raised the wrench over my head, and for a moment I thought she was going to wallop me with it. But she just growled and handed it to me as she shoved me out the door. "Might be best not to speak on this mission, Louie. Just hurry up and bring Miranda back where she belongs."

Chapter Twelve

Breaking In

The costume worked perfectly. None of the divas in Miranda's apartment building paid any attention to a lowly handyman—not even one with a horn—so I made it through the main entrance and up the stairs with no difficulty. The problem came when I arrived at Miranda's door. I could hear splashes inside, but she refused to answer.

"Open up," I ordered. "I am a handyman

and many things in your apartment need, um, handy-ing."

Nothing.

"I have a wrench."

Still nothing

"It's a really big wrench."

Silence.

Hmm. Honesty might be the best policy.

"OK, I'm not a handyman," I confessed. "Shh, don't tell anyone, but it's me, Louie. Please let me in, Miranda." I heard movement and guessed she'd come to peer through the peephole.

Still no answer.

I remembered my disguise and lifted off the cap. " 'Tis I, Louie." Then, just in case I still wasn't recognizable, I added, "Louie the Unicorn."

Still no answer.

I couldn't give up now. Not after we'd gone to all this trouble. Madame Swirler was expecting me to succeed. No way was I going to let one apartment door stop me. I bashed it with my wrench. It didn't budge but the wrench squished slightly. Stupid fake tools! I shuddered at the thought of telling Madame Swirler I'd damaged one of her props. No more wrench-bashing.

What next?

Kick the door down?

Maybe my back legs were stronger than my front ones? It was worth a try. I did a handstand on Miranda's doormat and kicked as hard as I could. I thought I felt something move, but it must have been something inside me, since the door stayed stubbornly shut.

To make it worse, a group of performers I recognized from *Splash It Up!* came dancing up the stairs just as my hat fell off! What if they realized who I was and made me leave?

I dropped down onto my rear legs, quickly placed the cap back on my head, and nodded at them in a handyman kind of way. "Greetings, dramatic people. I am just a humble handyman. Pay no attention to me while I make sure all the doors are working properly. Carry on up the stairs. Nothing to see here. Definitely no unicorns."

They giggled into their hands, but kept walking up to the next floor.

I glared at Miranda's door. I wouldn't be able to force my way through it without resorting to desperate measures.

"Come on, Miranda. Please let me in. Don't make me do something I'll regret."

I'd heard that phrase on television and it usually worked. I hoped it would be enough to convince Miranda to open up.

It wasn't. The time had come for the horn of last resort.

"Step away from the entrance, Miranda," I whinnied as I got a running start and leapt at her apartment door.

My horn was magical. It could get through anything. And it did. It pierced the heavy apartment door with no trouble at all. The problem was the rest of me, which was stuck on the other side, dangling in the air.

"Um? Miranda? A little help?"

I heard a heavy sigh and finally the sound

of a key turning in the lock. I entered the
room swinging around in a horn-stuck-in-
the-door sort of way.

"Louie, what are you doing? Can't you take a hint? I don't want to see anyone. And I certainly don't need a new unicorn-shaped door knocker," Miranda said.

"Perhaps you could, um, help me down?"

Miranda moved closer and let me rest on her tank while I loosened my horn.

"Anyway, where was I? Oh yes, we miss you and we want you to come home."

"Home?" Miranda sniffed.

"Yes," I said as I slid off her tank. "You belong at school. Madame Swirler says so. It'll always be your home."

Miranda wouldn't look at me and the music had vanished from her voice. "What if I don't want it to be?"

"I know you're a big star now, with

your name on posters and everything"—
I pointed at the promotional pictures
on Miranda's apartment walls—"but it's
always nice to have friends."

Tears started to trickle down Miranda's
face and as I looked closer I saw she'd drawn
little moustaches and pointy ears on her
pictures.

"I'm not a star, Louie. I'm a laughingstock. A wet, fishy laughingstock."

"You're a star to us, Miranda. You always
will be. You have a beautiful, twinkly voice
and you are a nice, twinkly person. Well,
most of the time. Now, what about making
yourself into a shooting star and whooshing
back to school?"

Miranda reached out of her tank and

flung her arms around me. "I'd love to, Louie. If you really mean it." We stayed like that for a while. I wasn't sure whether the water trickling down my neck was from Miranda's tears or her tank. Eventually she pulled away. "But you're always kind, Louie, and you forgive everyone—you've had all that practice with Arnie! Everyone else must hate me."

"Don't be silly," I said. "They'll probably whine and moan—I wouldn't mind having a chat about moving certificates to bathrooms at some point—but best friends forever means best friends forever." I pulled up her apartment window and waved at the two figures below. "Frank! Danny! Up here! Miranda is coming home."

Frank whooped and hollered and roared with glee and Danny looked quietly pleased. I buzzed them both into the apartment.

"What about Buffalo Bob?" Danny asked, pushing up his sleeves and looking around as if he expected to find Buffalo Bob lurking in a closet. "Do we have to fight him?"

"He's gone," Miranda said sadly. "Along with the limousine and the flowers and his promises of whatever I wanted. Buffalo Bob says he doesn't do losers."

"We'll show him who the loser is," Frank growled, picking up Miranda's tank as if it weighed nothing and skipping all the way down two flights of stairs.

Chapter Thirteen

The Finale

Back at school, Miranda was quieter than normal, but we slowly slipped back into our old routines and the song slowly slipped back into her voice. However, her face always fell when the car came to pick her up for that night's show.

"Just try to enjoy it." I told her. "Don't let the critics kill your buzz."

"Ha. Thanks for your support, Louie!"

Miranda smiled. "Seriously! And not just now. Always. Victoria Sponge told me how hard you worked to get the tickets for the first night's show and I feel terrible. I could have gotten you free tickets. But I didn't know. Buffalo Bob took my tickets and sold them."

"I knew you'd have sent them if you could!" I punched the air triumphantly, then whispered, "Don't mention this to Frank and Danny. I tricked them and I feel bad about it—unicorns aren't supposed to lie."

"Idiot!" Frank appeared behind me with a loud *BURRRRP*. "We already figured it out and we're grateful, not mad."

"Yeah," Danny agreed. "You wouldn't have had to lie if I hadn't been an idiot."

"You're all idiots," Miranda agreed with a grin. "But you're my idiots. And I have free tickets for the final show . . . Not just three this time. LOTS! . . . I guess there are some advantages to no one wanting to see the show," she said sadly, her grin disappearing. "Anyway, I'd love it if you came. It would mean a lot to have my friends in the audience. Actually, it would mean a lot to have *anyone* in the audience."

"We'll be there!"

The lines were shorter than they had been for the opening night, but there were still quite a few people in the theater for the last night of *Splash It Up!*

Listening to them talk, as we waited to

take our seats, it seemed most of them had come just to see how bad it could really be.

"I hear it's a disaster. Most of the original cast have refused to perform."

"Oh, that poor creature. Looks like she mer-made a terrible decision when she took this role. Ha-ha."

"Not funny," I muttered under my breath. Poor Miranda. It must be hard to show up every night for crowds like this. I had to help her.

So I cheered at the top of my lungs when she came on stage, and then cheered louder and louder with every song that she sang.

At first Danny told me to shush, but when people started grumbling about how awful the show was and walking out of the theater, he took a deep breath and joined in. So did Frank, and Frank was LOUD.

Before long, Frank, Danny, and I were leaping up and dancing around every time Miranda did anything.

A small group of children behind us joined in, and by the time Miranda began

her "Singing in the Drain" number, there were at least fifty of us on our feet, singing along as best we could.

Miranda waved across at us and ignored the tuts and the frowns. It was time for the final song, but she paused before it.

"♫ **Hello, final night's audience!** ♫ " she trilled. "I want to dedicate this last number to my friends," Miranda declared. "They supported me when I was on the way up, even when I didn't have time for them. And they are still supporting me— ♫ **loudly** ♫ —on the way back down. It's when things go wrong that you can really tell who your friends are. So this song is for you, Louie, Danny, and Frank—'I Want to

Hold Your Hand.' Or hoof. Or, er, hairy knobbly thing with claws."

The orchestra began and Miranda burst into song. After looking at one another uncertainly, the other actors on stage started to slowly join in. After a few lines, they were all involved and looked like they were having fun for the first time in the entire performance.

Miranda gestured for us to come up and join her on stage.

Danny ummed and aahed and stood up and sat down. I laughed and clambered over the top of him to canter down the aisle. I'd never say no to a chance to be on a Broadway stage. I beckoned to Frank, who

jumped to his feet, flung Danny over his shoulder, and joined me.

The audience wasn't quite sure how to react. A lot of people had already left and more were heading for the exits, but our fifty or so new friends were on their feet clapping and cheering and so were others dotted around the theater.

There was also a big group at the front throwing things at us.

"Aww, look," I said. "They love us."

"Um, Louie," Danny snorted. "That's not love. That's what is known as 'unfriendly fire.'"

"Pah! What nonsense. Don't be such a gloomburger, Danny. When people like

you, they throw flowers and teddy bears onto the stage," I explained.

"Yes. But this group is throwing tomatoes. And eggs."

"And rocks. Ow!" yelled Frank as one bounced off his head.

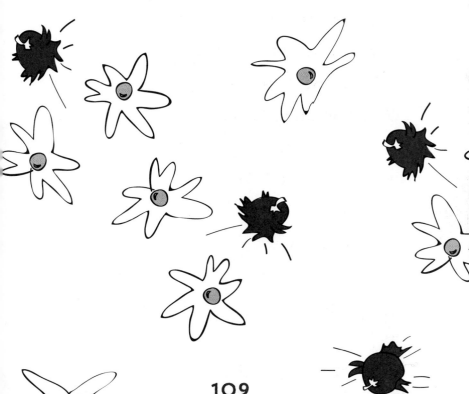

"I'm sure they mean well," I said, ducking to avoid a particularly squishy-looking tomato. "Wait a minute!" I peered at the group, who'd paused to collect more ammunition. Some of them looked familiar. "No way! It's Arnie's Army!"

And sitting right in the middle wearing a very large hat and dark glasses . . .

"**ARNIE!**" I yelled in delight, thrilled to see that he'd come after all. "How marvelous!" I held out a leg toward him and sang, "I want to hold your hooooooooof."

THE FINALE

Arnie sank down into his seat, and tipped his hat further over his eyes, obviously overcome with joy.

"Join us," I cried, reaching out for Arnie.

He seemed to be struggling to get up, but fortunately our fifty new friends danced down the aisle and helped lift him up onto the stage, where he stood awkwardly, obviously a bit stage-struck.

I gave him a huge hug. "Isn't this perfect?" I said. "All us best friends together?"

Miranda looked at Arnie and laughed. "At least your 'army' won't throw things at us while you're on stage. And nothing can spoil the feeling of having my friends up here with me. ♫ BEST FRIENDS FOREVER! ♫ "

Danny, Frank, and I joined her in a group hug and sang, "🎵 **BEST FRIENDS FOREVER!** 🎵"

When Miranda released us, I grabbed Danny and Frank, and like a team of not-very-synchronized synchronized swim-mers, we all leapt into Miranda's tank, cheering and yelling, "We'll make sure you go out with a SPLASH!"

Frank was last to dive in. He got squished at the top and wedged us all into the tank.

It made it hard to bow, but fortunately, the stagehands managed to pry us out just in time for Miranda to receive her first standing ovation.

Greetings, beloved parents,

Hope you are well and life in Story Land is full of cupcakes and rainbows.

Everything is marvelous here in New York. As you know, all my friends are stars to me, but this semester, my friend Miranda the Mermaid became a real-life superstar, with her face on posters, her tail on T-shirts, and her life plastered all over the magazines and newspapers. Although that last one is far less fun than you might think. Newspapers can be mean and the news is not always the same as the truth.

I learned it's sometimes hard to be a good friend. It can leave you smelling like tomatoes, or dangling by your horn from a fancy apartment door. But it's always worth it. There is nothing more important than friendship.

My new theory is that friendship is like a pencil case. You need glue to stick together in the tough times. You need colored pencils to create the good times, and you need Wite-Out to delete any bad parts from your mind. I tried to share this theory with my friends, but they told me to stop talking and set up the glitter ball for our next party, because that's what friendship is really all about.

They are probably right.

Love you more than cake,
xoxo

Louie

Rachel Hamilton studied at both Oxford and Cambridge and has put her education to good use working in an ad agency, a high school, a building site, and a men's prison. Her interests are books, films, stand-up comedy, and cake, and she loves to make people laugh, especially when it's intentional rather than accidental.

Rachel divides her time between the United Kingdom and the United Arab Emirates, where she enjoys making up funny stories for kids.

Oscar Armelles was born in Spain, and almost from day one, he could be found with a pen and a paper in his hand. He loved to draw—anything and everything. As soon as he was old enough he collected all his crayons and moved to America where he studied commercial art.

After graduating he relocated to London, and now he spends his time coming and going between London and Madrid.

He works mainly in digital format . . . although he is quite handy with watercolors, too.

LOOK OUT FOR EVERY ADVENTURE WITH LOUIE THE UNICORN.

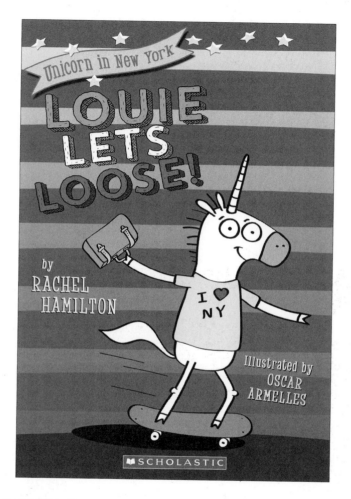

Unicorn in New York

LOUIE
LETS
LOOSE!

by
RACHEL
HAMILTON

I ♥ NY

Illustrated by
OSCAR
ARMELLES

SCHOLASTIC

LOUIE THE UNICORN LEAVES STORY
LAND TO BEGIN HIS SEARCH FOR
STARDOM IN NEW YORK CITY. FIRST
STOP, PERFORMING ARTS SCHOOL!

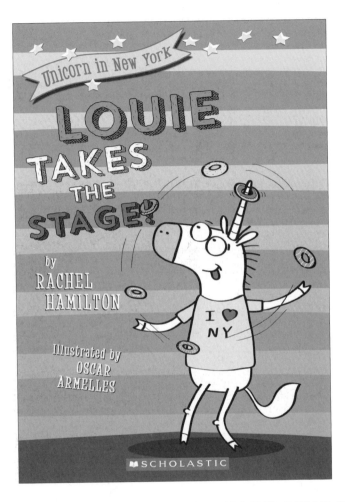

Unicorn in New York

LOUIE TAKES THE STAGE!

by
RACHEL HAMILTON

Illustrated by
OSCAR ARMELLES

SCHOLASTIC

LOUIE JOINED THE NEW YORK SCHOOL
OF PERFORMING ARTS IN SEARCH OF
STARDOM, BUT HE'S YET TO LAND ANY
STARRING ROLES. WITH A BIG AUDITION
COMING UP, IS IT FINALLY TIME FOR THIS
UNICORN TO SHINE?

LOUIE'S DANCE MOVES ALWAYS END IN
DISASTER, SO WHEN HE MISTAKENLY
GETS ENTERED INTO A NATIONAL
DANCE CONTEST, HE'S GOING TO
HAVE TO GIVE IT HIS ALL IF HE WANTS A
CHANCE TO WIN.

Welcome to the
ENCHANTED PONY ACADEMY,
where dreams sparkle and magic shines!

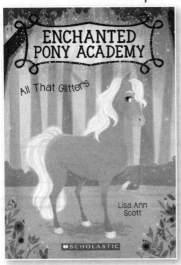

ENCHANTED PONY ACADEMY

All That Glitters

Lisa Ann Scott

SCHOLASTIC

ENCHANTED PONY ACADEMY

Wings That Shine

Lisa Ann Scott

SCHOLASTIC

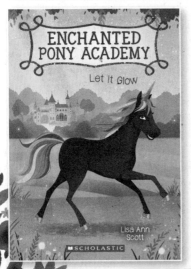

ENCHANTED PONY ACADEMY

Let It Glow

Lisa Ann Scott

SCHOLASTIC

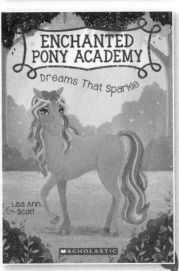

ENCHANTED PONY ACADEMY

Dreams That Sparkle

Lisa Ann Scott

SCHOLASTIC

UNCLE JOHN'S POLITICAL BRIEFS

Articles in this edition have been included from the following books: *Uncle John's Absolutely Absorbing Bathroom Reader* © 1999; *Uncle John's All-Purpose Extra Strength Bathroom Reader* © 2000; *Uncle John's Supremely Satisfying Bathroom Reader* © 2001; *Uncle John's Ahh-Inspiring Bathroom Reader* © 2002; *Uncle John's Unstoppable Bathroom Reader* © 2003; *Uncle John's Bathroom Reader Plunges Into the Presidency* © 2004; *Uncle John's Slightly Irregular Bathroom Reader* © 2004; *Uncle John's Bathroom Reader Colossal Collection of Quotable Quotes* © 2004; *Uncle John's Fast-Acting Long-Lasting Bathroom Reader* © 2005; *Uncle John's Bathroom Reader Plunges Into Hollywood* © 2005; *Uncle John's Curiously Compelling Bathroom Reader* © 2006; *Uncle John's Bathroom Reader Wonderful World of Odd* © 2006; *Uncle John's Bathroom Reader Quintessential Collection of Notable Quotables* © 2006; *Uncle John's Triumphant 20th Anniversary Bathroom Reader* © 2007; *Uncle John's Bathroom Reader Plunges Into Music* © 2007; *Uncle John's Unsinkable Bathroom Reader* © 2008; *Uncle John's Certified Organic Bathroom Reader* © 2009; *Uncle John's Endlessly Engrossing Bathroom Reader* © 2009; *Uncle John's Heavy Duty Bathroom Reader* © 2010; *Uncle John's Bathroom Reader Plunges Into Canada* © 2010; *Uncle John's Bathroom Reader History's Lists* © 2010; *Uncle John's Bathroom Reader The World's Gone Crazy* © 2010; *Uncle John's Bathroom Reader Plunges Into New York* © 2011; *Uncle John's Bathroom Reader Tunes Into TV* © 2011; *Uncle John's 24-Karat Gold Bathroom Reader* © 2011

For information, write:
The Bathroom Readers' Institute, P.O. Box 1117, Ashland, OR 97520
www.bathroomreader.com • 888-488-4642

Cover design by Michael Brunsfeld, San Rafael, CA (*Brunsfeldo@comcast.net*)

ISBN-13: 978-1-60710-560-2 / ISBN-10: 1-60710-560-8

Library of Congress Cataloging-in-Publication Data

Uncle John's political briefs.
        p. cm.
ISBN 978-1-60710-560-2 (pbk.)
1. American wit and humor. 2. United States—Politics and government—Humor. I. Bathroom Readers' Institute (Ashland, Or.)
    PN6231.P6U53 2012
    818'.60208—dc23

2012009288

Printed in the United States of America
First Printing: March 2012
1 2 3 4 5 16 15 14 13 12

Uncle John's
POLITICAL
BRIEFS

By the
Bathroom Readers'
Institute

Bathroom Readers' Press
Ashland, Oregon

INTRODUCTION

THE PUBLIC DISS-COURSE

T "Politics make me sick!" Sounds like something you might hear on the radio or at the dinner table, but that proclamation was made more than a century ago by President William Howard Taft. And who could blame him? After all, he *was* surrounded by politicians all day. Thankfully, the rest of us can just sit back and be entertained by these "public servants."

That's what *Uncle John's Political Briefs* is about—poking fun at peculiar politicians from all political persuasions. But it's more than that. You'll also find out how things got to be the way they are today, starting with the rise of democracy in the Western world (thanks to the Magna Carta) and continuing through the American Revolution to the rise of the Donkeys and Elephants. You'll also learn how various governments govern in other countries.

We chose the very best politics articles from the *Bathroom Reader* series, many of them updated with current information. There are also a few all-new articles and a ton of new facts. You will be briefed on…

• The president who accidentally gave the pope the wrong set of the Ten Commandments, the president who fell victim to a voodoo curse, and the president who survived two assassination attempts…in one month

• The British PM who taxed wigs, the Canadian PM who held policy meetings with his dog, and the Japanese PM who held President George H. W. Bush's head while he threw up all over himself

• The origins of the Pledge of Allegiance and "Hail to the Chief," the stories behind the most impactful U.S. Supreme Court decisions, and that world-class hypocrite Benjamin Franklin

• Scathing barbs from Maher, O'Reilly, Limbaugh, and Colbert; plus embarrassing goofs on news-ticker crawls; and Dan Rather's home-spun election-night expressions, such as, "This race is spandex-tight!"

• The woman who lost a local election because she forgot to vote…for herself; the candidate who confused a movie star with a serial killer; and dogs, pigs, and other animals who ran for office

• Secret plots from past and present: poisoning the skies with chem-trails, feeding human embryos to unwitting consumers, and a weird presidential assassination theory—not JFK, but…Lincoln?

• The only woman who got to vote for giving women the right to vote, the "Conservative Conservationist," and a real political party called Party! Party! Party! (All they want to do is party.)

• Why 300 angry Canadians mooned the United States, and why an old man from India released cobras in a government office

In closing, I would like to thank my poo-litical operatives for putting this all together: Supreme Chancellor Newman; the Honorable J. A. Altemus; and Angie, Queen of Facts. So have fun, and don't forget to hold your elected representatives accountable for their looney actions…unless, of course, you happen to live in a dictatorship or an absolute monarchy, in which case—good luck!

And as always, go with the Flow!

—Uncle John, Felix the Dog, and the BRI Staff

BUREAUCRACY IN ACTION

We start this book off with a few tales of government spending.

The *Hindustan Times* reported in 2005 that the city of New Delhi employs 97 paid rat-catchers. What's odd about that? They haven't caught a single rat since 1994. (And, according to the *Times*, there are a *lot* of rats in New Delhi.)

• In October 2005, the U.S. Department of Homeland Security awarded a $36,300 grant to the state of Kentucky. Purpose of the grant: to prevent terrorists from using bingo halls to raise money.

• Father Anthony Sutch had to call an electrician to change four light-bulbs on the 40-foot ceiling of St. Benet's Church in Suffolk, England. In the past he used a local firm to do it and paid them £200 ($370), which he thought was pretty steep for changing four bulbs. But government safety regulations now prohibit the workers from using a ladder—they have to erect scaffolding instead. Result: The church had to spend £1,300 ($2,450) to change the bulbs.

• In 2003 Congress agreed to subsidize the Alaska Fisheries Marketing Board, a salmon industry trade organization. The AFMB used the money to paint an Alaska Airlines 737 jet to look like a salmon (the jet's nickname: "Salmon-Thirty-Salmon"). Cost: $500,000. The subsidy was proposed by the late Senator Ted Stevens, whose son, Ben Stevens, happened to be the chairman of the AFMB.

• The Youth Outreach Unit of Blue Springs, Missouri (pop. 48,000), received $273,000 from the government to combat teenage "goth culture."

• In 1981 the U.S. Army spent $6,000 in federal funds in order to create a 17-page manual for government agencies. The subject: how to properly select and purchase a bottle of Worcestershire sauce.

• What did the U.S. government spend $24.5 billion on in 2003? Nobody knows. According to the General Accounting Office, that's how much the federal government couldn't account for that year.

FARMER BILL DIES IN HOUSE

Our all-time favorite political flubbed headlines. They're all real.

RALLY AGAINST APATHY
DRAWS SMALL CROWD

*Legislators Tax Brains
to Cut Deficit*

California Governor Makes
Stand on Dirty Toilets

*Reagan Wins on Budget,
but Moore Lies Ahead*

Obama: Gays Will Be Pleased by
the End of My Administration

Legalized Outhouses
Aired by Legislature

MASSACHUSETTS WOMAN
HAS EYE ON KERRY'S SEAT

*ELIZABETH DOLE HAD NO CHOICE
BUT TO RUN AS A WOMAN*

Brawl Erupts at Peace Ceremony

**U.S., China Near Pact
on Wider Ties**

Intern Gets Taste of Government

Carter Plans Swell Deficit

MPs Seek Answers on Nutt Sacking

RED TAPE HOLDS
UP NEW BRIDGE

William Kelly Was Fed Secretary

SANTORUM BLASTS OBAMA
DURING CUMMING RALLY

NATION SPLIT ON BUSH AS
UNITER OR DIVIDER

**Hotel Cancels Jihad Conference,
Citing Safety Reasons**

IRAQI HEAD SEEKS ARMS

HILLARY CLINTON ON WELFARE

**Marijuana Issue Sent to
Joint Committee**

*L.A. Voters Approve Urban
Renewal by Landslide*

Louisiana Governor Defends
His Wife, Gift from Korean

Mayor Parris to Homeless: Go Home

COUNCIL TO EXAMINE
IMPOTANT PROBLEMS

U.S. Ships Head to Somalia

MAYOR SAYS D.C. IS SAFE
EXCEPT FOR MURDERS

Ten Commandments:
Supreme Court Says
Some OK, Some Not

In 1999 a record 70 million viewers watched Barbara Walters interview Monica Lewinsky.

ON POLITICS

We found a bunch of quotes about politics that weren't cynical, but these are more fun.

"Whenever a man has cast a longing eye on office, a rottenness begins in his conduct."
—**Thomas Jefferson**

"If Thomas Jefferson thought taxation without representation was bad, he should see how it is *with* representation."
—**Rush Limbaugh**

"Get the fools on your side and you can be elected to anything."
—**Frank Dane**

"To become the master, the politician poses as the servant."
—**Charles de Gaulle**

"We may not imagine how our lives could be more frustrating and complex, but Congress can."
—**Cullen Hightower**

"We live in a world in which politics has replaced philosophy."
—**Martin L. Gross**

"Put a federal agency in charge of the Sahara Desert and it would run out of sand."
—**Peggy Noonan**

"American politics is like fast food: mushy, insipid, made out of disgusting parts of things—and everybody wants some."
—**P. J. O'Rourke**

"Our elections are free. It's in the results where eventually we pay."
—**Bill Stern**

"Politics is the gentle art of getting votes from the poor and campaign funds from the rich—by promising to protect each from the other."
—**Oscar Ameringer**

"Today's public figures can no longer write their own speeches or books. There's some evidence they can't read them, either."
—**Gore Vidal**

"Just because you do not take an interest in politics doesn't mean politicians won't take an interest in you."
—**Pericles**

"Good thing we've still got politics—the finest form of free entertainment ever invented."
—**Molly Ivins**

Mussolini's Fascist Party slogan: "Me Ne Frego!" Translation: "I don't give a damn!"

IF ELECTED,
I PROMISE TO...

Sometimes politicians come up with strange campaign promises. It rarely gets them elected, but it does make for good bathroom reading.

POLITICIAN: Andrew Uitvlugt, running for mayor of Kelowna, British Columbia, in 2005

PROMISE: Free crack cocaine for anyone who volunteers to pick up trash

BACKGROUND: Uitvlugt's reasoning: The town had too many crack addicts and too few garbage collectors. So why not let the crack addicts pick up the trash? The work, said Uitvlugt, would be so satisfying that they wouldn't even want the crack anymore. (He also proposed moving all of the city's homeless people to the local landfill, where they could learn to manufacture products out of the trash.)

RESULT: Uitvlugt lost (he finished fourth out of five candidates).

POLITICIAN: Silvio Berlusconi, Italian prime minister, running for reelection in 2006

PROMISE: To abstain from sex until after the election

BACKGROUND: At a campaign rally, Berlusconi was blessed by Massimiliano Pusceddu, a famous Italian televangelist, who congratulated the conservative prime minister for his strong stance on "family values." To show his appreciation for the blessing, the 70-year-old Berlusconi, who is married to actress Veronica Lario, proclaimed, "Thank you, dear Father Massimiliano, I will try not to let you down and I promise you two and a half months of complete sexual abstinence until the election."

RESULT: No word on whether Berlusconi kept his promise, but he lost the election.

POLITICIAN: Jackie Wagstaff, who calls herself "J-Dub," running for mayor of Durham, North Carolina, in 2005

PROMISE: To form a "hip-hop cabinet" full of "streetwise teens"

The FDA puts the value of a human life at $7.9 million; the EPA says it's $9.1 million.

BACKGROUND: Running on the "Gangsta" platform, the 46-year-old former city councilwoman acknowledged that because most of her support came from young African Americans, that was the demographic she was targeting. To prove her street cred, J-Dub bragged about her checkered past of run-ins with the law (although she wasn't alone in this: 8 of the other 17 mayoral candidates also had criminal records). J-Dub said she wanted to get drug dealers off the street and into her cabinet because "they already have some business skills."

RESULT: J-Dub lost (she received less than 5% of the vote).

POLITICIAN: Percy, running for U.S. Congress in 2002
PROMISE: "Ruff ruff. Bark bark. Bow wow."
BACKGROUND: Percy, a dog, challenged Katherine Harris in Florida's Republican congressional primary. "No one has a realistic expectation that a dog can get elected," said Wayne Genthner, Percy's owner and campaign manager. "But plenty of people will be willing to vote for a dog to represent their discontent with the political system." He then added that, if elected, Percy promised to be obedient. "Don't you wish your representative in Washington could do that?"

RESULT: Percy never got the chance to run: The Florida election board ruled that he was ineligible (because he's a dog), so Genthner ran in his place...and lost.

POLITICIAN: Jacob Haugaard, running for parliament in Denmark in 1994
PROMISE: Better weather, and tail-winds for Danish bicyclists
BACKGROUND: Haugaard is the founding member of the "Party of Conscientiously Work-Shy Elements." He's also a stand-up comedian and admitted that he was only joking when he announced his candidacy (and then spent all his campaign money on beer).

RESULT: Haugaard won, becoming Denmark's first independent legislator in 50 years. "I don't know anything about politics," he said, "but now I get an education...with full salary!"

*　　　*　　　*

"I never vote for anybody. I only vote against." —**W. C. Fields**

Since its independence from Spain in 1825, Bolivia has had almost 200 governments.

THE ONLY PRESIDENT TO...

You may know that Richard Nixon was the only U.S. president to resign or that Grover Cleveland was the only president to serve two nonconsecutive terms. Here are a few more unique presidential anomalies.

The president: Jimmy Carter
Notable achievement: Only president to write a children's book. Carter wrote *The Little Baby Snoogle-Fleejer*, which was illustrated by his daughter Amy, and published in 1995. The plot: A disabled boy named Jeremy meets a repulsive sea monster, who turns out to be quite friendly.

The president: Abraham Lincoln
Notable achievement: Only president to earn a patent. In 1849 Lincoln invented a type of buoy. Lincoln is also the only U.S. president to have worked as a bartender.

The president: Theodore Roosevelt
Notable achievement: Only president to be blind in one eye. Roosevelt took a hard punch to his left eye in a boxing match. It actually detached the retina, leaving Roosevelt blind in his left eye for the rest of his life. The boxing match occurred in 1908, while Roosevelt was president.

The presidents: George H. W. Bush and George W. Bush
Notable achievement: The Bushes are not the only father and son who both served in the Oval Office (the Adamses did as well), but they're the only father-son presidents who were fighter pilots in their younger days.

The president: Gerald Ford
Notable achievement: Only president to survive two assassination attempts in the same month. In September 1975, former Charles Manson follower Lynette "Squeaky" Fromme tried to shoot Ford when he reached out to shake her hand in a public meet-and-greet. She pulled the trigger, but the gun's chamber was empty. Just three weeks later another woman, Sara Jane Moore, fired on Ford in a similar crowd situation, but a bystander knocked her arm away.

Pat Buchanan, Ben Stein, and William Safire all wrote speeches for President Nixon.

NO GERM VENT

These anagrams—words or phrases that are rearranged to form new words or phrases—don't really speak well of their subjects.

THE COMING PRESIDENTIAL CAMPAIGN *becomes…*
DAMN! ELECTING TIME IS APPROACHING!

DEMOCRAT PARTY *becomes…*
RAT-TRAP COMEDY

THE REPUBLICAN PARTY *becomes…***ELEPHANT CRAP! BURY IT!**

GOVERNMENT *becomes…*
NO GERM VENT

SENATOR *becomes…***TREASON**

RONALD WILSON REAGAN *becomes…* **RAN ON ALL WRONG IDEAS**

BILL AND HILLARY CLINTON *becomes…* **CAN ROT IN HILLBILLY LAND**

GEORGE W. BUSH *becomes…*
HE GREW BOGUS

BARACK HUSSEIN OBAMA *becomes…* **I, ARAB SHAM, BECKON U.S.A.**

ELECTION PROMISES *becomes…*
STEEP, MORONIC LIES

SARAH PALIN *becomes…*
LAS PIRANHA

NANCY PELOSI *becomes…*
ALIEN CON SPY

RUSH LIMBAUGH *becomes…*
UH, GALS RUB HIM

ARLEN SPECTOR *becomes…*
RECTAL PERSON

ERIC CANTOR *becomes…*
ERRATIC CON

RUDY GIULIANI *becomes…*
GAUDILY I RUIN

HARRY REID *becomes…*
HAIRDRYER

JAMES RICK PERRY *becomes…*
SCARY PRIME JERK

MICHELE BACHMANN *becomes…* **A CALM BI-HENCHMEN**

WILLARD MITT ROMNEY *becomes…* **A RIMMED WINTRY TROLL**

ELECTION RESULTS *becomes…* **LIES! LET'S RECOUNT!**

In 2008 Silverton, Oregon, elected Stu Rasmussen as America's first transgender mayor.

WHAT *IS* DEMOCRACY?

At the BRI, democracy consists of us telling Uncle John that we all voted unanimously for him to hire a professional catering service to provide us with lunch and snacks. Uncle John, sadly, is a snackless dictator. Here are what some other folks have said about democracy.

ARISTOTLE: "The real difference between a democracy and an oligarchy is poverty and wealth. Wherever men rule by reason of their wealth, whether they be few or many, that is an oligarchy, and where the poor rule, that is a democracy."

E. B. WHITE: "Democracy is the recurrent suspicion that more than half of the people are right more than half the time."

WOODROW WILSON: "Democracy is not so much a form of government as a set of principles."

H. L. MENCKEN: "Under democracy one party always devotes its chief energies to trying to prove that the other party is unfit to rule—and both commonly succeed and are right."

SAM SHEPARD: "Democracy's a very fragile thing. You have to take care of democracy. As soon as you stop being responsible to it and allow it to turn into scare tactics, it's no longer democracy, is it? It's something else. It may be an inch away from totalitarianism."

KARL MARX: "Democracy is the road to socialism."

ABBIE HOFFMAN: "You measure democracy by the freedom it gives its dissidents, not the freedom it gives its assimilated conformists."

HELEN KELLER: "Our democracy is but a name. We vote? What does that mean? It means that we choose between two bodies of real, though not avowed, autocrats. We choose between Tweedledum and Tweedledee."

TOM STOPPARD: "It's not the voting that's democracy; it's the counting."

Late bloomers: On January 30, 2005, Iraq held its first-ever democratic elections.

WINSTON CHURCHILL: "Many forms of government have been tried, and will be tried in this world of sin and woe. No one pretends that democracy is perfect or all-wise. Indeed, it has been said that democracy is the worst form of government except all the others that have been tried."

THOMAS JEFFERSON: "A democracy is nothing more than mob rule, where 51 percent of the people may take away the rights of the other 49."

VLADIMIR PUTIN: "A legal electoral system alone will not guarantee full-fledged democracy unless it is incorporated into the real democratic institutions of society as a whole."

MARGARET THATCHER: "Whether it is in the United States or in mainland Europe, written constitutions have one great weakness. That is that they contain the potential to have judges take decisions which should properly be made by democratically elected politicians."

GEORGE ORWELL: "It is almost universally felt that when we call a country democratic we are praising it; consequently, the defenders of every kind of regime claim that it is a democracy, and fear they might have to stop using the word if it were tied down to any one meaning."

JOHNNY CARSON: "Democracy is buying a big house you can't afford with money you don't have to impress people you wish were dead. And, unlike communism, democracy does not mean having just one ineffective political party; it means having two ineffective political parties. Democracy is welcoming people from other lands, and giving them something to hold onto—usually a mop or a leaf blower. It means that with proper timing and scrupulous bookkeeping, anyone can die owing the government a huge amount of money. Democracy means free television, not good television, but free. And finally, democracy is the eagle on the back of a dollar bill, with 13 arrows in one claw, 13 leaves on a branch, 13 tail feathers, and 13 stars over its head—this signifies that when the white man came to this country, it was bad luck for the Indians, bad luck for the trees, bad luck for the wildlife, and lights out for the American eagle."

BILL MOYERS: "Democracy may not prove in the long run to be as efficient as other forms of government, but it has one saving grace: It allows us to know and say that it isn't."

Q: Which U.S. politician coined the term *lunatic fringe*? A: Teddy Roosevelt.

TICK...TOCK...BROKE

Round and round it goes! Where it stops—nobody knows!
Here's the story of the National Debt Clock.

GROWING PAINS

In the winter of 1980, a New York real estate developer named Seymour Durst wanted to communicate his concerns about the ballooning national debt to elected officials in Washington, D.C. So he sent them New Year's cards that read "Happy New Year! Your share of the national debt is $35,000." No response—so Durst went to a sign maker and asked if it was possible to make a billboard with a numeric display that showed the national debt growing in real time—a doomsday clock for the American taxpayer. It *wasn't* possible: That year, the debt was growing at a rate of about $13,000 per second, and the computers of the day weren't fast enough to operate a numeric display at that kind of speed. It took eight years for technology to catch up with Durst's vision, and in 1989 the first National Debt Clock was installed on a Durst-owned building near Times Square. Cost: $100,000. (No word on whether Durst went into debt to pay for the clock.)

TAKES A LICKING

Each week Durst called the U.S. Treasury to get the latest national debt figures and updated the sign via modem so that the continuously changing numbers were as accurate as possible. He continued updating the clock until his death in 1995, after which the sign company assumed the responsibility. In 2000 the national debt stopped growing, and for the next two years it actually *shrank*. That created a problem for the sign, which wasn't designed to run backward. On Durst's birthday in 2000, the sign was switched off and covered with a red, white, and blue banner in the hope that it would never be uncovered.

But the debt soon started rising again, and in July 2002 the sign was switched back on. It was replaced with a new, improved sign in 2004, but the new sign wasn't "improved" enough: When the national debt hit $10 trillion in 2008, there weren't enough digits to display all the debt, and the "$" had to be converted to a 1. Plans are in the works to add another two digits to the sign. (Every American's share of the national debt, as of 2012: $49,044...and climbing.)

There's nothing in the law to prevent a convicted felon from becoming U.S. president.

FAMOUS FOR 15 MINUTES

The political world has played a big part in helping Andy Warhol's prophetic statement come true: "In the future, everyone will be famous for 15 minutes." (Even dogs.)

THE STAR: Lisa Gebhart, a 25-year-old fund-raiser for the Democratic Party

THE HEADLINE: *Pushy White House Intern Proves a Picture is Worth a Thousand Words…and Then Some*

WHAT HAPPENED: In 1996 Gebhart went to a fund-raiser for President Bill Clinton. She wanted to shake hands with the president, so she made her way up to the front of the rope line just as he was approaching. "I was all beaming," she says, "just ten feet away from him. Then someone pushed me from behind, trying to get in there, very rude….I had seen Monica Lewinsky around, but I didn't know her. She couldn't wait to get to Clinton." Lewinsky got a hug; all Gebhart got was a handshake.

When news of Clinton's affair with Lewinsky broke in 1998, footage of the 1996 hug, with a smiling Gebhart standing next to Lewinsky, became one of the most famous images of the Clinton presidency.

THE AFTERMATH: By the time the scandal broke, Gebhart had met a Welshman named Dean Longhurst over the Internet and was communicating with him by email. Longhurst asked what Gebhart looked like. "I emailed him, 'Watch the news.'"

"When I saw her in real life," Longhurst told reporters in April 2001, "I thought she was even more beautiful." The two eventually met, fell in love, and got married.

THE STAR: Michael Brown, 49, head of the U.S. Federal Emergency Management Agency (FEMA) from 2003 to 2005

THE HEADLINE: *Dubious Endorsement from Dubya Leaves FEMA Head Treading Water*

WHAT HAPPENED: "Brownie, you're doing a heck of a job." That's

---

In 1807 Pres. Henri Christophe of Haiti declared all gourds the property of the state.

what President Bush said to Brown on September 2, 2005, four days after Hurricane Katrina caused major devastation along the U.S. Gulf Coast. Because the federal government was facing criticism for its slow response to the catastrophe, Brown became an example of the cronyism in the Bush administration—which was accused of appointing friends and business associates to positions for which they were unqualified.

Case in point: Before being hired to run the nation's disaster response team, Brown was chairman of the International Arabian Horse Association, a post he resigned in 2001 amid allegations of corruption. Even more damning for Brown: His emails to staffers were leaked to the press. On the day Katrina made landfall, Brown wrote, "Can I quit now? Can I go home?" In another email (sent while there were still corpses floating in New Orleans), he complained about the tacky suit he had to wear. "Call the fashion police!" Dozens of other petty emails were sent, all while his office took four days to respond to an urgent request for medical supplies.

AFTERMATH: Brown resigned from his FEMA post on September 12, stating that all the attention was hindering his agency from doing its job. He accused the press of making him a scapegoat for the administration's botched response, and added that most of the blame lay on the shoulders of local Louisiana officials. His biggest mistake, he claimed, was "underestimating" their incompetence.

Brown made news again in 2007 when he was hired by Cold Creek Solutions, a company that specializes in data storage for big businesses, as their "Disaster and Contingency Planning Consultant." Said the company's CEO, "With Michael's experience and his unique view into what possibly could go wrong when looking at a plan, we can truly help clients be prepared for the unexpected." Brown is currently hosting a conservative radio talk show in Colorado.

THE STAR: Blanco, a white Collie
THE HEADLINE: *First Dog Is Second Rate*
WHAT HAPPENED: When President Lyndon Johnson moved into the White House in 1963, he brought along his beagles—Him and Her. The dogs made headlines on April 27, 1964, when LBJ picked them up by their ears. A photographer got a shot of Him and Her yelping in pain. The White House was deluged with letters from angry dog lovers.

Her died in November 1964 after swallowing a stone, and Him died the following June, run over by a car while chasing a squirrel across the White House lawn. It made national news, and dozens of people wrote the White House offering the president a new dog. LBJ said no, but eventually, he gave in. Johnson chose a white collie named Blanco. Bad choice: When Blanco arrived at the White House, she began biting every dog and most of the people she came in contact with.

THE AFTERMATH: Blanco was kept on tranquilizers for the rest of LBJ's presidency, and according to one account, "When Johnson left office, he was finally persuaded to give Blanco away."

THE STAR: Fawn Hall, a 27-year-old, $20,000-a-year government secretary assigned to Col. Oliver North the National Security Council in 1987

THE HEADLINE: *She Stood by Her Man...and He Fed'er to the Shredder*

WHAT HAPPENED: Colonel Oliver North was one of the key figures behind the Iran-Contra scandal, a plan to sell arms to Iran in exchange for the release of U.S. hostages, then divert the profits to the Contras in Nicaragua—a direct violation of U.S. law.

As word of the scheme began leaking to the press in mid-1986, North, assisted by loyal secretary Fawn Hall, began altering and destroying incriminating documents. After North was fired from his post, Hall continued the shredding on her own. When Hall testified about her role in the cover-up before a nationally televised congressional hearing, she became a celebrity overnight.

THE AFTERMATH: Hall tried her best to keep a low profile; she even turned down several lucrative endorsement offers (including one from Revlon to become part of the "America's Most Unforgettable Women" campaign). "I was so out of my league," she says. "One day you're just a normal girl walking down the street; the next, they want to put you in movies."

Hall worshipped North as "a hero." At the conclusion of her congressional testimony she let his friends know she "wanted to hear from him." But according to Hall, North never spoke to her again, not even to thank her for the risks she'd taken on his behalf. Hall later married a former producer of the Doors, and became addicted to crack cocaine in the 1990s. She's now clean, and at last report was working at a trendy bookstore in West Hollywood.

THE RHINOCEROS PARTY

Who says government has to be stodgy and humorless? Not Canada.

PLAYING POLITICS

In the early 1960s, Quebec was wracked by violent protests against the federal government and the Anglo-Saxon establishment that dominated the province. In the midst of this turmoil, Dr. Jacques Ferron, a physician and writer, launched a new political party—a satirical alternative "to serve as a peaceful outlet for disgruntled Quebecois." And he chose the rhinoceros as the party's symbol. Why a rhino? Ferron said it epitomized the professional politician—"a slow-witted animal that can move fast as hell when in danger."

It lasted for only 30 years, but the Rhinoceros Party "put the 'mock' back in 'demockracy.'" And for a fringe group, it attracted a surprising number of votes. Here are some of their more creative campaign promises:

• They vowed to sell Canada's senate at an antiques auction in California.

• They promised to plant coffee, chocolate, and oranges in southern Ontario, so Canada could become a banana republic.

• In the 1980 election, the Rhinos promised to break all their promises and introduce an era of "indecision and incompetence."

• Fielding candidates with names like "Richard the Troll" and "Albert the Cad," the Rhinos ran on a platform of "sex, drugs, and rock 'n' roll" for the masses.

• Other parties talked about a guaranteed annual income; the Rhinos vowed to introduce a "Guaranteed Annual Orgasm" and to sell seats in Canada's senate for $15 each.

• In 1988 they made national headlines by running a candidate named John Turner against the incumbent opposition leader…John Turner. Turner was not amused (everyone else was).

• They promised to repeal the law of gravity, provide free trips to bordellos, and nationalize all pay toilets.

• When the Canadian government was trying to decide where to locate its embassy in Israel, the Rhinos proposed to locate it in a Winnebago,

Don Rumsfeld was the youngest, and oldest, U.S. secretary of defense. (He served twice.)

which could travel continuously between Jerusalem and Tel Aviv.

MORE PROMISES AND PROPOSALS

• As an energy-saving measure, the Rhinos proposed larger wheels for the backs of all cars, so they would always be going downhill.

• They proposed legislating a lower boiling point of water (another energy-saving measure).

• They also proposed moving half the Rockies one meter to the west, as a make-work project.

• They promised to make bubble gum the currency of Canada and to provide tax credits for enthusiastic sleepers.

• They promised to spend $50 million on reform schools for politicians.

• The Rhinos pledged that "none of our candidates will be running on steroids."

• Another promise: to have the Rocky Mountains bulldozed so that Alberta could get a few extra minutes of daylight.

• They promised to turn the parliamentary restaurant into a national franchise operation.

• One Rhino candidate proposed "to create a cartel of the world's snow-producing countries, call it Snow-pec, and export snow to cool down the Middle East conflict."

• They promised to bring back "the good old English system of driving on the left-hand side of the road, but in the first year only, buses and trucks will drive on the right-hand side."

THE PARTY'S OVER

When the Canadian government passed a law in 1993 requiring a $50,000 deposit from every party in a national election—essentially killing off the Rhinoceros Party—the Rhinos asked Canadians to write their own names on the ballot and vote for themselves.

"We cannot fool all of the people some of the time or even some of the people all of the time," said Charlie McKenzie, the party's general secretary, "but if we can fool a majority of the people at election time, that's all the time we need."

How do they know who to vote for? In Norway, political ads are banned from TV.

DUBYA

*In the long history of the BRI, no president has been
more fun to quote than George W. Bush. Here's
the first of two pages of his best one-liners.*

"I think if you know what you believe, it makes it a lot easier to answer questions. I'm not gonna answer your question."

"You know, there are all these conspiracy theories that Dick Cheney runs the country, or Karl Rove runs the country. Why aren't there any conspiracy theories that I run the country? Really ticks me off."

"I just want you to know that, when we talk about war, we're really talking about peace."

"I would still invade Iraq even if Iraq never existed."

"Well, I think if you say you're going to do something and don't do it, that's trustworthiness."

"More than two decades later, it is hard to imagine the Revolutionary War coming out any other way."

"I promise you I will listen to what has been said here, even though I wasn't here."

"It'll take time to restore chaos."

"And Karen is with us—a West Texas girl, just like me!"

"My job is a decision-making job. And as a result, I make a lot of decisions."

"See, in my line of work you got to keep repeating things over and over again for the truth to sink in, to kind of catapult the propaganda."

"Reading is the basics for all learning."

"I think that the vice president is a person reflecting a half-glass-full mentality."

"It would be a mistake for the United States Senate to allow any kind of human cloning to come out of that chamber."

"Public education is where children from all over America learn to be responsible citizens and learn to have the skills necessary to take advantage of our fantastic opportunistic society."

"As you know, my position is clear—I'm the Commander Guy."

ALTERED STATES

*Think it's hard to remember the names of all 50 states? If lawmakers
had had their way, there could have been even more.*

CUBA

When the U.S. won the Spanish-American War in 1898, Spain
ceded control of Puerto Rico, Guam, the Philippines, and Cuba.
The first three were considered to be in the developing-colony stage, so
they became U.S. territories. Cuba was far more established and was
granted independence (although the U.S. reserved the right to intervene
in Cuban affairs at any time). Things were fine until 1906, when opponents of Cuban president Tomas Estrada Palma accused him of voter
fraud in his successful reelection. The protests that erupted created an
instability that made the U.S. nervous, and a small congressional delegation proposed annexing Cuba and making it a state—the easiest way to
quell any uprisings. Ultimately, the cultural differences between the two
nations were seen as too great, or, as Representative John Sharp Williams
of Mississippi said, "We have enough people of the Negro race."

GREENLAND

In 1945 Secretary of State James Byrnes offered Denmark $100 million
for the gigantic, ice-covered Arctic island. Why? For its strategic location.
This was at the very beginning of the Cold War, and Greenland was situ-
ated much closer to the Soviet Union's major cities than any current U.S.
land, making it an ideal place for a missile-defense system. The Danish
government did not entertain the offer.

FRANKLIN

When the U.S. established its constitution in 1787, the 13 former
colonies became the new nation's first states. There could have been 14.
In 1785 a group of citizens in an isolated, sparsely populated mountainous
region of western North Carolina proposed creating their own state, pred-
icated on one idea that doctors and lawyers were too highbrow, not representative of the common man, and thus unfit to serve in the legislature.
Despite that weird premise for independence, 7 out of 13 states voted yes.

Chevron owns an oil tanker named the *Condoleezza Rice*.

Franklin was denied statehood, but by only two votes. Nevertheless, Franklin's leading proponents acted like they *had* been granted statehood and proceeded to form a basic government: electing lawmakers (but no doctors or lawyers), establishing a court system, and assembling a small militia. All that local power wasn't enough to prevent attacks from local Indian tribes, who saw Franklin residents as easy targets. Because they'd behaved like a rogue state, North Carolina and the federal government left them to their own devices and offered no protection. In 1796 Franklin was absorbed into Tennessee.

JACINTO

When the independent republic of Texas was annexed by the United States in 1845, it retained a right to split into as many as five separate states whenever and for whatever reason the state government saw fit. The Texas legislature entertained the idea in 1850, when the state's congressional delegation introduced a bill to divide the state in two, right along the Brazos River. The western portion would still be called Texas, while the eastern part was to be named Jacinto, commemorating the 1836 Battle of San Jacinto, which was decisive in Texas gaining its independence from Mexico (and lasted only 18 minutes). However, the bill never gained enough support to make it to a vote, but the idea of partitioning Texas into multiple states wouldn't go away—it resurfaced six more times over the next 120 years.

GREAT BRITAIN

In the peacetime years that followed World War II, Senator Richard Russell Jr. of Georgia made a bizarre proposal to the news media: The United States should annex England, Scotland, Ireland, and Wales—at the time, the whole of Great Britain—as four new American states. His reasoning: The British had been ravaged by the war, and the U.S. military needed some strategically located sites in Europe. Russell argued that it was a win-win situation: The U.S. would get military bases, and the U.K. would receive an influx of American revenue that would be beneficial to both countries. The British government quickly dismissed the idea, and half-jokingly reminded Senator Russell that his home state of Georgia still owed England the money back that it had borrowed a century earlier during the Civil War.

Former 3rd-party candidate Ross Perot plays the accordion...and is worth $3.4 billion.

HEY—THAT'S MY NAME ON THE BALLOT!

As people pay less attention to elections, candidates have to focus more on name recognition. That can lead to some confusion—as it did in these elections.

RUSSO FOR CONGRESS!

Story: In 1946 Joseph Russo, a popular Boston city councilman, decided to run for a seat in the U.S. Congress. At first his only opponent in the Democratic primary was a young World War II veteran named John Fitzgerald Kennedy. But at the last minute, another candidate appeared on the ballot: a second Joseph Russo.

Who was this new challenger? Turns out he was a family friend of the Kennedys. It's widely believed that JFK's father got Russo #2 into the race to confuse voters and ensure his son's victory.

Outcome: It worked. Joseph Russo and Joseph Russo split the Russo vote; JFK won the primary by a landslide.

JOHN F. KENNEDY FOR STATE TREASURER!

Story: Kennedy had just been elected a U.S. senator in 1952; what was he doing running for state treasurer in 1953? It was John *Francis* Kennedy. He was not related to JFK, wasn't rich, didn't attend Harvard, and wasn't even a high school graduate. This Kennedy had quit school at the age of 14 and was working as a stockroom supervisor at the Gillette Razor Blade Company when he decided to cash in on his popular name and run for office. The incumbent treasurer, John Hurley, resigned in 1953, and "JFK" ran in the special election to replace him. His qualifications? "I got a good name," he said in an interview, "I know a lot of people at Gillette to say 'hi' to, and I want to make money and get ahead in life."

Outcome: Kennedy lost the 1953 race…but never underestimate the power of a name. When he ran again in 1954, he won. Total campaign expenses: $100, most of which was spent to throw an election-night party. Kennedy served six years as state treasurer. In 1960—the year the more famous JFK was elected president—he ran for governor, and lost.

In 1630 Massachusetts governor John Winthrop introduced the fork to America.

CAROL MOSELEY-BRAUN FOR ALDERMAN!

Story: In 1998 a 21-year-old woman named Lauryn K. Valentine asked a court to allow her to change her name to Carol Moseley-Braun. It had nothing to do with politics, she said—it was a tribute to the first African American woman to serve in the Senate. Valentine claimed that Moseley-Braun "had encouraged me to stay in school when I was considering dropping out." The judge granted her request.

Surprise! In December 1998, the new Carol Moseley-Braun filed papers to run for Chicago city alderman. The real Moseley-Braun and another candidate for alderman both filed legal challenges.

Outcome: When the judge found out that Valentine had entered the race, her name change was disallowed. She dropped out.

WARNER FOR SENATE!

Story: In 1996 John Warner, the incumbent U.S. senator from Virginia, ran for reelection against a multimillionaire businessman named... Warner. The challenger's first name was not John; it was Mark. But under Virginia law, the ballot did not identify which Warner was the incumbent, or even which one was the Republican (John) or the Democrat (Mark). "Although some analysts figure the name problem will make no real difference in the end," the *Washington Post* reported, "others envision a chaotic scenario in which thousands of votes could be cast unwittingly for the wrong man. Mark Warner figures, at least half seriously, that he could gain a couple of percentage points simply by winning the drawing to determine who will be listed on the ballot first."

Outcome: No contest—John Warner was reelected.

OTHER RACES

Taylor vs. Taylor. "In 1886 two brothers named Taylor ran against each other for governor of Tennessee, a battle that became known as the 'War of the Roses' because their mother had given each candidate a different color rose." (*San Francisco Chronicle*)

Hansen vs. Hansen vs. Hanson. A candidate named George V. Hansen gained more votes over incumbent Orval Hansen in the 1974 Republican primary for a seat in Idaho's state legislature. Then in the general election that fall, George V. Hansen gained more votes than his Democratic rival, Max Hanson.

LATE-NIGHT ZINGERS

*Who says politicians aren't "job creators"? Without their buffoonery,
talk-show hosts (and their writers) would be out of work.*

"President Obama was in Disney World to introduce a new plan to boost tourism. And also because the Mickey Mouse ears fit perfectly over his real ones."

—Jimmy Kimmel

"There is a power struggle going on between President Reagan's advisers. Moe and Curly are out. Larry is still in."

—Johnny Carson

"A new poll says 84% of Americans disapprove of Congress' job. The other 16% weren't aware Congress was doing one."

—Jay Leno

"Santorum says Gingrich is too hot, Romney is too cold, but he's the 'Goldilocks candidate.' Nothing gets voters excited like comparing yourself to tepid porridge."

—Craig Ferguson

"Today, the rapper Snoop Dogg endorsed Ron Paul for president. Snoop said he likes Paul's positions on everything from legalizing pot…to legalizing pot."

—Conan O'Brien

"Mitt Romney is quite a guy. At one point he and his wife bought a zoo and fired all the animals."

—David Letterman

"Sarah Palin's not running for president, which is good news for Palin haters, but bad news for the moose population."

—Jimmy Kimmel

"Newt Gingrich and Hillary Clinton are very similar. Both spent the '90s trying to figure out who Bill was sleeping with. And they have the same tailor."

—Craig Ferguson

"Several Fox News hosts criticized SpongeBob SquarePants for pushing a global-warming agenda. Then things got really ugly when they demanded to see Dora the Explorer's immigration papers."

—Conan O'Brien

"Steve Jobs gave Obama an iPad last year. Unfortunately, it broke when Joe Biden thought it was an Etch-A-Sketch and started shaking it."

—Jimmy Fallon

Only Supreme Court justice pictured on currency: Salmon Chase (the defunct $10,000 bill).

SONG-WRONGERS

Politicians don't commission original campaign songs anymore. Instead, they like to use well-known songs, often without offering payment or getting permission. Here are some song stealers who got caught.

Infringer: Bob Dole
Song: "Soul Man"
Story: During the 1996 presidential campaign, Sam Moore, a member of the popular 1960s R&B duo Sam and Dave (who also wrote the theme song from *Shaft*), rerecorded one of the duo's biggest hits, "Soul Man," for the presidential campaign of Bob Dole, changing the lyric "I'm a soul man" to "I'm a Dole man." The song was originally written by Isaac Hayes and David Porter, and they were not happy with Moore's version. "People may get the impression that David and I endorse Bob Dole," Hayes told the *New York Daily News*, "which we don't." And Rondor Music International, the music publishing company that owned the song, threatened to sue for $100,000 for every unauthorized use of "Soul Man." The campaign immediately stopped using the song, and no lawsuit was filed. But the Dole campaign hadn't learned its lesson—they started using Bruce Springsteen's "Born in the USA," again without permission. Ronald Reagan had done the same in 1984, and, just as he had done with Reagan, the Boss (and his lawyers) forced Dole to stop. After that, Dole's aides finally *asked* a songwriter for permission, and Eddie Rabbitt allowed them to use "American Boy" as their campaign song.

Infringer: Joe Walsh
Song: "Walk Away"
Story: In January 2010, Illinois Republican politician Joe Walsh, who was running for a seat in the U.S. House of Representatives, changed the lyrics to the 1971 song "Walk Away," written by guitarist Joe Walsh in his pre-Eagles days, and used it in a campaign video on his website. Musician Walsh's lawyer, Peter Paterno, wrote to the campaign: "Given that your name is Joe Walsh, I'd think you'd want to be extra careful about using Joe's music in case the public might think that Joe is endorsing your campaign, or, God forbid, *is* you." Walsh the politician's response: The song was parody and therefore permitted under copyright

law, and "I am not backing down on this." A month later he backed down, and the video was pulled.

Infringer: Barack Obama

Song: "Hold On, I'm Coming"

Story: In 2008 Sam Moore was back in the news when the Obama campaign used another Sam and Dave hit, "Hold On, I'm Coming," as one of its theme songs without asking permission. Although Moore didn't write the song, he sent them a letter asking them to stop, and the campaign complied. Eleven months later, Moore performed at one of Obama's inaugural balls. (He sang "Soul Man.")

Infringer: Charles DeVore

Songs: "The Boys of Summer," "All She Wants to Do Is Dance"

Story: Most unauthorized users of songs apologize and promise to never do it again, and that's usually the end of it. But sometimes they fight back. Charles DeVore's campaign for the 2010 Republican senate primary in California used a knockoff of "The Boys of Summer" by Don Henley in a video mocking Barack Obama. (It was called "Hope of November.") Henley complained, and the video was pulled. But then DeVore did it again, ripping off Henley's "All She Wants to Do Is Dance" for a song called "All She Wants to Do Is Tax" about his opponent, Democratic Senator Barbara Boxer. (DeVore actually wrote both parodies himself.) Henley had enough, and he filed a lawsuit against DeVore for copyright infringement. DeVore fought back, claiming the songs were parodies and therefore protected by free speech. In June 2010, a judge ruled that DeVore was wrong: Parody involves mocking the thing being parodied, in this case Henley's songs. DeVore's songs didn't do that; they were used to comment on something else entirely—Barack Obama and Barbara Boxer—which made them *satires*, not parodies. Henley won the case, making him the first musician to successfully sue a politician for stealing a song. (No word on how much DeVore had to pay, but he lost the election.)

Infringer: Newt Gingrich

Songs: "Eye of the Tiger"

Story: From 2009 to 2011, Survivor's rock anthem—made famous in the

1982 film *Rocky III*—was played to introduce Gingrich at the Conservative Political Action Conferences (CPAC). Gingrich also used the song in online campaign ads. In 2012 Frank Sullivan, who co-wrote the No. 1 hit, sued Gingrich, claiming he never asked for permission. In the suit, Sullivan points out that Gingrich should have known better: He's a published author who guards his copyright very closely. The suit also points to Gingrich's arguments against the Stop Online Piracy Act, in which the former Speaker of the House said, "We have a patent office, we have copyright law. If a company finds it has genuinely been infringed upon, it has the right to sue." So Sullivan and his company, Rude Music, did just that. "It is not for political reasons," said Sullivan, "it is strictly an artist protecting their copyright."

Gingrich's supporters argued that the Republican National Committee had purchased a venue-based "blanket license" from the American Society of Composers, Authors, and Publishers to use at the conference. (Abbreviated, that goes: The RNC paid ASCAP to use the song at the CPAC.) Sullivan acknowledged that fact, but countered that Gingrich did not have permission to use the song in online campaign ads. As the lawsuit wallowed in legal limbo in early 2012, Dave Bickler, the original singer of the song, appeared on Comedy Central's *The Colbert Report* to perform his own bit of copyright infringement: He sang passages from Newt's book *A Nation Like No Other*…to the tune of "Eye of the Tiger."

*　　　*　　　*

HOW A SMALL PIECE OF TAPE CHANGED HISTORY

In the early morning of June 17, 1972, an $80-a-week security guard named Frank Wills was patrolling the parking garage of an office complex in Washington, D.C., when he noticed that someone had used adhesive tape to prevent a stairwell door from latching. Wills removed the tape and continued on his rounds, but when he returned to the same door at 2:00 a.m., he saw it had been taped again. So he called the police, who discovered a team of burglars planting bugs in an office leased by the Democratic National Committee. This "third-rate burglary"—and the coverup that followed—grew into the Watergate scandal that forced President Richard M. Nixon to resign from office in 1974.

New Hampshire state lawmakers earn $100 per year. California lawmakers earn $99,000.

WHAT WON'T THEY TAX?

*They say the only certainties are death and
taxes. Death may be the better option…*

PAY UP
Oliver Wendell Holmes referred to taxes as "the price we pay for
civilization." But civilization, it seems, comes at a cost, and few
things provoke more outrage in citizens than having to pay taxes. Today,
we hear about the Tea Party, which stands for "Taxed Enough Already,"
but the fight against unfair "negative dividends" goes back millennia. The
first recorded tax evader was imprisoned by the Roman emperor Constan-
tine in AD 306. The greatest revolt in English history occurred in 1381
when Richard II imposed a poll, or "head," tax. The first armed rebellions
against the newly formed United States were Shay's Rebellion in 1786
(by New England farmers against property taxes) and the Whiskey Rebellion of 1791 (against a liquor tax). During the French Revolution in
1789, all tax collectors were rounded up and sent to the guillotine. And
despite all that, governments persist in extracting revenue from their
reluctant citizenry. Here are some of the more peculiar examples of taxes
throughout the centuries:

• **URINE TAX.** Imposed by the Roman emperor Nero around AD 60.
Why urine? The contents of public toilets were collected by tanners and
laundry workers for the ammonia, which was used for curing leather and
bleaching togas. Nero slapped a fee on the collectors (not the producers)
and it proved to be such a great way to raise funds that Nero's successor,
Vespasian, continued the tax. When his son, Titus, complained about the
disgusting nature of taxing urine, Vespasian is reputed to have held up a
gold coin and declared, *"Non olet!"* Translation: "This does not stink!"

• **SOUL TAX.** Peter the Great, czar of Russia, imposed a tax on souls in
1718—meaning everybody had to pay it (it's similar to a head tax or a
poll tax). Peter was antireligious (he was an avid fan of Voltaire and other
secular humanist philosophers), but agreeing with him didn't excuse anyone from paying the tax—if you didn't believe humans had a soul, you
still had to pay a "religious dissenters" tax. Peter the Great also taxed

Cheney got a $34-million payout when he left Halliburton to become Bush's running mate.

beards, beehives, boots, basements, chimneys, horse collars, hats, food, clothing, all males, as well as birth, marriage, and even burial.

• **BACHELOR TAX.** Are you an unmarried man? Pay up. The bachelor tax is a strategy that many governments have imposed to encourage population growth (and raise money at the same time). Augustus Caesar tried it in 18 BC. The English imposed it in 1695. The Russians under Peter the Great used it in 1702, as did the Missouri legislature in 1820. The Spartans of ancient Greece didn't care about the money—they preferred public humiliation. Bachelors in Sparta were required to march around the public market in wintertime stark naked while singing a song making fun of their unmarried status.

• **WIG POWDER TAX.** In 1795 powdered wigs were all the rage in men's fashion. Desperate for income to pay for military campaigns abroad, British prime minister William Pitt the Younger levied a tax on wig powder. Although the tax was short-lived due to the protests against it, it did ultimately have the effect of changing men's fashions. By 1820 powdered wigs were out of style.

• **WINDOW TAX.** Pitt the Younger also tried a chimney tax, but found that windows were easier to count. People paid the tax based on the number of windows in their home. Result: A lot of boarded-up people boarded up their windows.

• **LONG-DISTANCE TAX.** On June 30, 2006, the U.S. Treasury Department stopped collecting a 3% federal excise tax on long-distance calls—familiar to bill payers as one of a list of taxes tacked onto every phone bill. The purpose of the tax? To help the government pay for the Spanish-American War...in 1898. Phone service was so rare at the time that the tax was intended to impact only the wealthiest Americans. But the tax persisted for more than a century after the war ended, and every American household that had phone service ended up paying it. "It's not often you get to kill a tax," Treasury Secretary John Snow said after the tax was repealed, "particularly one that goes back so far in history." Taxpayers were told that they could file for a refund for the last three years that the tax existed—but not for the previous 105. (Note: There's still a 3% excise tax on *local* phone calls.)

It takes the average American 129 workdays to earn enough money...

THE WRATH OF AGNEW

As vice president under Richard Nixon, Spiro T. Agnew (1918–96) served as a mouthpiece for the administration, saying the things that Nixon couldn't. His role was to throw verbal darts at the liberal establishment—intellectuals, hippies, and the press—anyone who disagreed with the administration. His remarks were antagonistic, outrageous, controversial…and very quotable.

"I have often been accused of putting my foot in my mouth, but I will never put my hand in your pockets."

"A spirit of national masochism prevails, encouraged by an effete corps of impudent snobs who characterize themselves as intellectuals."

"Some newspapers are fit only to line the bottom of birdcages."

"An intellectual is a man who doesn't know how to park a bike."

"Ultraliberalism today translates into a whimpering isolationism in foreign policy, a mulish obstructionism in domestic policy, and a pusillanimous pussyfooting on the critical issue of law and order."

"In the United States today, we have more than our share of nattering nabobs of negativism."

"Yippies, hippies, yahoos, Black Panthers, lions and tigers alike—I would swap the whole damn zoo for the kind of young Americans I saw in Vietnam."

"The lessons of the past are ignored and obliterated in a contemporary antagonism known as the generation gap."

"If you've seen one city slum, you've seen them all."

"They have formed their own 4-H club: the hopeless, hysterical hypochondriacs of history."

"Perhaps the place to start looking for a credibility gap is not in the offices of the government in Washington but in the studios of the networks in New York."

"Three things have been difficult to tame: the oceans, fools, and women. We may soon be able to tame the oceans; fools and women will take a little longer."

THE UNFINISHED MASTERPIECE

Even if you're not an art lover, you've probably seen the best and most famous picture of the first U.S. president, George Washington, painted by Gilbert Stuart—it's the one on the dollar bill. But did you know that it was never finished? Here's the story.

PRESIDENTIAL PORTRAITURE

Before photography, sitting for a portrait was a long, tedious process. George Washington never liked it, and by the time he retired from the presidency, he'd vowed never to do it again. He routinely refused requests from artists who wanted to capture his likeness one more time for posterity. But in 1796, he got a request he couldn't refuse: His wife Martha wanted them both to pose for portraits to be hung together in a central place in their home.

The painter Martha had in mind was Gilbert Stuart—a celebrated artist in both Britain and America and the portraitist of choice for hundreds of politicians and dignitaries. George agreed with her decision; he'd already posed for two other paintings with Stuart and found him relatively easy to sit for.

STUART'S STORY

Stuart didn't feel the same way about Washington. He thought the ex-president was too stiff, and complained to friends about his stony countenance, his foul teeth, and the dead look in his eyes.

But Stuart still took Mrs. Washington's assignment gladly. Alcoholism and exorbitant spending had put him in debt, and he needed cash. Besides, he'd made quite a bit of money from his first two Washington portraits:

• He sold the first one to a wealthy merchant for a tidy sum, but before delivering it, quickly painted and sold at least 15 copies. (One was later used for the image on U.S. quarters.)

• The second painting—a full-length portrait this time—was so well received that Stuart was able to sell dozens of copies before delivering it to the banker who originally commissioned it.

Aware of Stuart's past duplicities and not wanting to spend months waiting while the artist copied her paintings, Martha Washington made a careful deal: She insisted that Stuart agree to deliver the portraits the moment they were finished.

WORKING WITH GEORGE

The sitting with Washington began much like the previous efforts. Stuart was relieved to see that the president was wearing a new set of false teeth that made his face look more natural. But he was exasperated when, once again, Washington's face turned to stoniness the minute he sat down.

Stuart told jokes and anecdotes, trying to capture an engaging, interested look. It didn't work, but in the middle of the sitting, Washington's face momentarily lit up with a pleasant expression. Stuart began drilling him to find out what had happened…and discovered that Washington had seen a horse trot by outside.

Stuart began talking horses—anything and everything he could think of. Then he talked about farming, and anything to do with rural life. Washington's entire demeanor changed: He became more natural, more lighthearted, and his face became brighter.

CREEP OR GENIUS?

The result was the best portrait of the first president ever painted. In fact, Stuart was so pleased that he immediately began trying to figure out a way to keep it. If he could just get out of his deal with Mrs. Washington, he could make more than just a dozen hurried copies—he could do *hundreds* at his leisure and finally get out of debt. But how could he pull it off?

Then he hit on a plan. He stopped a few brushstrokes short of completing the painting, leaving a little canvas peeking through where Washington's collar should have been. Then he told messenger after messenger sent from an impatient Martha Washington: "Sorry, it's not finished yet."

SECOND-RATE ART

Even a visit from the former president couldn't shake the painting loose. Instead Stuart sent along one of his copies of the original. Mrs. Washington hung it up, but told her friends: "It is not a good likeness at all."

The presidential retreat Camp David was originally named Shangri-La.

In fact, not many of the copies were. Stuart was interested in speed, not quality. According to one of his daughters, on a "good day" he could pump out a copy every two hours. Many had little or no resemblance to Washington at all. An acquaintance of Stuart's wrote, "Mr. Stuart told me one day when we were before this original portrait that he could never make a copy of it to satisfy himself, and that at last, having made so many, he worked mechanically and with little interest."

Regardless, the portrait became a wildly popular commodity and Stuart dashed off more than 200 copies, calling them his "hundred-dollar bills." But he still couldn't completely rid himself of debt. Ironically, in the end there were so many inferior copies of the unfinished portrait (by other artists as well) that they actually did significant damage to Stuart's reputation. When he died in 1828, he still owed considerable money, and his youngest daughter, Jane—also a portrait painter—had become the breadwinner for the family.

BY THE WAY

The original paintings, still technically "unfinished," never were delivered to the Washington family. The Boston Athenaeum wound up owning them, and today they're shared part of the year with the Boston Museum of Fine Arts and the National Portrait Gallery in Washington.

*   *   *

BLOVIATED (REAL) POLITICAL TERMS

- **Flugie:** A rule that helps only the rule maker
- **Speechify:** To deliver a speech in a tedious way
- **Bloviate:** To speechify pompously
- **Roorback:** An invented rumor intended to smear an opponent
- **Bafflegab:** Intentionally confusing jargon
- **Gobbledygook:** Nonsensical explanation; bafflegab
- **Snollygoster:** A politician who puts politics ahead of principle
- **Boondoggle:** A wasteful or crooked government-funded project
- **Mugwump:** A political maverick

Clint Eastwood's 1st act as mayor of Carmel, California: legalize ice-cream parlors.

BEFORE THEY WERE INFAMOUS

*Great leaders make choices early in life that pave the way
for their illustrious careers. But what about the world's
worst tyrants? Here's a look at the early lives of
some rotten apples in the history barrel.*

JOSEPH STALIN (1879–1953)

Place in History: Soviet ruler from 1924 to 1953. Fueled by a mad paranoia, Stalin is responsible for the murder and mass starvation of millions of Soviet citizens. His forced collectivization of Soviet agriculture starved as many as 5 million people from 1932 to 1933; the political purges that followed from 1936 to 1938 may have killed as many as 7 million more. His diplomatic and military blunders leading up to World War II contributed mightily to the 20 million Soviet military and civilian casualties during the war.

Before He Was Infamous: Born Iosif Vissarionovich Dzhugashvili, young Joseph entered a Russian Orthodox seminary in 1894, but he was kicked out at the age of 20. He went underground, became a Bolshevik revolutionary, and later adopted the pseudonym Stalin, which means "Man of Steel." Between 1902 and 1913, the man of steel was arrested and jailed seven times, and sent to Siberia twice. In 1917, he became the editor of *Pravda*, the Communist Party newspaper. Stalin did not play a prominent role in the communist revolution of November 1917, but in 1922 he was elected general secretary of the Communist Party, a post that became his power base. Vladimir Lenin died in 1924, but it wasn't until after six years of maneuvering against opponents that Stalin emerged as Lenin's unrivaled successor in 1930.

MAO TSE-TUNG (1893–1976)

Place in History: Leader of the Chinese Communist Party (1935) and founder of the People's Republic of China, which he ruled from 1949 until his death in 1976. Under such disastrous programs as the Great Leap Forward (1958–60) and the Cultural Revolution (1966–76), more than

---

Flight of fancy: *Air Force One* costs taxpayers $40,243 per flight hour.

30 million people starved to death or were murdered outright by Mao's government and its policies.

Before He Was Infamous: At 13, this child of peasant farmers left home to get an education. He tried police school, soap-making school, law school, and economics before settling on becoming a teacher. He attended the University of Beijing, where he became a Marxist and in 1921, at the age of 27, a founding member of the Chinese Communist Party. In 1927 he alienated orthodox Marxists by arguing that peasants, not workers, would be the main force in the communist revolution. It wasn't until 1935, following the 6,000-mile "Long March" to escape the Chinese government's brutal campaign against the communists, that he emerged as the party's leader.

ADOLF HITLER (1889–1945)

Place in History: Elected German chancellor in 1933 and ruled Nazi Germany from 1933 until his death in 1945. The Nazis murdered an estimated 6 million Jews and other people it considered inferior, including Gypsies, Jehovah's Witnesses, communists, and homosexuals. Hitler also started World War II, which killed as many as 55 million people.

Before He Was Infamous: As a small boy, Hitler dreamed of becoming a priest, but by age 14 he'd lost his interest in religion. As a young man he enjoyed architecture and art and dreamed of becoming a great artist, but when he applied for admission to the Academy of Fine Arts in Vienna, he was turned down—twice—for lack of talent. He bummed around Vienna until 1913, living off an orphan's pension and what little money he made from odd jobs like beating carpets, and from selling paintings and drawings of Viennese landmarks. When World War I broke out in 1914 he was living in Munich, where he volunteered for the Bavarian army and was later awarded the Iron Cross.

Germany lost the war in 1918; the following year Hitler joined the German Workers Party at a time when it had only about 25 members. He soon became its leader, and in 1920 the party changed its name to the National Socialist German Workers' Party—better known as the Nazis.

POL POT (1925–1998)

Place in History: Leader of the Cambodian Khmer Rouge guerrilla movement, which seized control of the Cambodian government in 1975

What do Fiji, Chile, and Egypt have in common? You can be jailed there for not voting.

and ruled the country until January 1979. On Pol Pot's orders the cities were emptied and the urban population forced out into the countryside to work on collective farms that became known as "killing fields." Nearly 1.7 million Cambodians—20 percent of the entire population—were starved, worked to death, or murdered by the Khmer Rouge.

Before He Was Infamous: Born Saloth Sar, Pol Pot lived in a Buddhist monastery for six years, and was a practicing monk. He worked briefly as a carpenter before moving to Paris at the age of 24 to study radio electronics on a full scholarship. While there he joined the French Communist Party. He later lost his scholarship and returned home in 1953, the same year that Cambodia won independence from France. Over the next decade Sar rose through the ranks of the Cambodian Communist Party (the Khmer Rouge), and in 1963 he became its head. In the mid 1970s he adopted the pseudonym Pol Pot.

IDI AMIN DADA (1924–2003)

Place in History: Ugandan dictator from 1971 to 1979. In those years he expelled the entire Asian population of Uganda (more than 70,000 people) and is believed to have murdered as many as 400,000 people during his eight-year reign of terror. In 1979 he invaded the neighboring country of Tanzania; when the invasion failed and the Tanzanians counterattacked he fled into exile, eventually settling in Saudi Arabia. He died there in August 2003.

Before He Was Infamous: Amin, a member of the small Kakwa tribe of northwestern Uganda, was born in 1925 and raised by his mother, a self-proclaimed sorceress. As a child he sold *mandazi* (African doughnuts) in the streets. In 1943 he joined the King's African Rifles of the British colonial army and went on to serve in the allied forces' Burma campaign during World War II. After the war he became a boxer and was the heavyweight champion of Uganda for nine years (1951–1960).

Amin continued his rise through the ranks of the military, and by the time Uganda became independent of England in 1962 he was one of only two African officers in the entire Ugandan armed forces. The nation's president, Milton Obote, appointed him head of the army and navy in 1966; five years later Amin seized power in a coup and declared himself president for life.

Eleanor Roosevelt once held a toga party to poke fun at FDR's "Caesar-like" reputation.

POLITICAL WORD & PHRASE ORIGINS

If it looks like a word-origins page, acts like a word-origins page,
and reads like a word-origins page, then—well, you know.

POLITICS
Meaning: The activities associated with the governance of a region
Origin: Despite comedians and talk-show hosts joking that *politics* is derived from *poly*, meaning "many," and *tics*, meaning "blood-sucking parasites," that's not the true origin of the word. It comes from the Greek *politika*, used by Aristotle to mean "affairs of the city," which was also the name of his book about governing.

FILIBUSTER
Meaning: The use of prolonged speeches to obstruct legislative action
Origin: First used in English in the 1850s to describe a pirate of the Caribbean (not that one), the word comes from the Spanish *filibustero*, which means "freebooter" (derived from the Dutch *vrijbuter*). These so-called filibusters took part in illegal expeditions against Cuba, Mexico, and Central America in order to set up local governments that would apply to the United States for annexation. The word was adopted by the U.S. Senate in the late 1800s.

POLITICALLY CORRECT
Meaning: Language that seemingly goes out of its way to not offend anyone, often so far as to obfuscate its meaning
Origin: This term dates back more than two centuries to a 1793 U.S. Supreme Court decision in *Chisholm v. Georgia*. Justice James Wilson argued that it is the people, not the states, who held the real power in the country. He wrote: "To 'the United States' instead of to the 'People of the United States' is the toast given. This is not politically correct." In the late 1960s, pinko hippie commies, err…socially minded, progressive activists revived the term.

Herb poll: 68% of liberals like cilantro. Only 59% of conservatives do.

SENATE

Meaning: A representative body in a republic or democracy

Origin: Early clans that predated the Roman Empire would send their eldest, wisest men—who were originally called *senex*—to meet with each other. The Latin word *senatus* came later, meaning "a gathering of old, wise men." It has kept its basic meaning to this day—except now there are a few women, too (and the "wise" thing is debatable).

GERRYMANDER

Meaning: To redivide a state or county into election districts so as to give one party a majority

Origin: The term was coined in 1812 when Massachusetts governor Elbridge Gerry redrew Congressional lines in order to give his Democrat-Republican party an advantage over the Federalists. A Boston newspaper ran a political cartoon showing that one of Gerry's new districts looked a lot like a salamander. The word *gerrymandering* was born, and the bad publicity cost Gerry the election.

IF IT LOOKS LIKE A DUCK, WALKS LIKE A DUCK, AND QUACKS LIKE A DUCK, IT'S PROBABLY A DUCK.

Meaning: Don't look beyond the obvious when trying to determine someone's true nature.

Origin: It's generally credited to Walter Reuther, the American labor leader during the McCarthy witch hunts of the 1950s. Testifying at a hearing before the Senate Committee on Labor and Public Welfare in 1953, he used this phrase to illustrate that someone who acted like a communist was probably a communist.

GOBBLEDYGOOK

Meaning: Unnecessary jargon that's used when simple words will do

Origin: U.S. Representative Maury Maverick (D-TX)—grandson of Samuel Maverick, from whom we get the word "maverick"—once compared his fellow lawmakers to turkeys: "They're always gobbledy-gobbling and strutting around with ludicrous pomposity!" While chairman of the Smaller War Plants Corporation in 1944, Maverick sent out a memo: "No more gobbledygook language! Anyone using the words 'activation' or 'implementation' will be shot!"

DON'T LEAVE HOME WITHOUT IT

*What happens when a big-time politician tries to pay for something
just like us regular folks...and can't? Here are three news items
we first printed in* Uncle John's All-Purpose Extra-Strength
Bathroom Reader *that show what happens when it's
time to pay the piper (or the cashier, as it were).*

CHEAP WILLIE

"President Bill Clinton was visiting Park City, Utah. He picked out several books at Dolly's Books and handed over his American Express card for the $62.66 bill—only to be informed it had expired the day before." He paid cash.

—**Medford, Oregon,** *Mail Tribune*

CHECK OUT THE IRON LADY

"In April 1997, former British Prime Minister Margaret Thatcher tried to purchase $40 worth of groceries with a check. The clerk wouldn't accept it. "I can't override the system, so there was no way I could take her check," said cashier Shirley Taylor. "She was very good about it, tore the check up and paid cash. It was a bit embarrassing for her, I think."

—**Wire service reports**

SAVED BY THE BUCK

"In 1979 Treasury Secretary Michael Blumenthal found himself in an embarrassing situation in Beethoven's, an expensive San Francisco restaurant. Blumenthal was confronted with a sizable dinner bill, an expired Visa card, and a waiter who wanted proof of signature to back up an out-of-town check. Blumenthal solved his predicament in a way that only he could: He produced a dollar bill and pointed out his own signature, 'W. M. Blumenthal,' in the bottom right-hand corner. The signatures matched, and Blumenthal's personal check was accepted."

—*The Emperor Who Ate the Bible,* **by Scott Morris**

GOVSPEAK

Who actually talks like this? Only politicians.

"I haven't committed a crime. What I did was fail to comply with the law."
—**David Dinkins, New York City mayor**

"As we know, there are known knowns. There are things we know we know. We also know there are known unknowns."
—**Donald Rumsfeld**

"I have opinions of my own—strong opinions—but I don't always agree with them."
—**Pres. George H. W. Bush**

"The private enterprise system indicates that some people have higher incomes than others."
—**Jerry Brown, California Governor**

"All of 'em. Any of 'em that have been in front of me over all these years."
—**Sarah Palin, when asked what newspapers she reads**

"I do not like this word 'bomb.' It is not a bomb. It is a device which is exploding."
—**Jacques Le Blanc, French ambassador, on nuke testing**

"It was not a strip bar, it was an erotic club. And what can I say? I'm a night owl."
—**D.C. Mayor Marion Barry**

"Every week we don't pass a Stimulus, 500 million Americans lose their jobs."
—**Rep. Nancy Pelosi (D-CA)**

"A billion here, a billion there, sooner or later it adds up to real money."
—**Rep. Everett Dirksen (R-IL)**

"We are not without accomplishment. We have managed to distribute poverty equally."
—**Nguyen Co Thatch, Vietnamese foreign minister**

"I don't really know much about 'Americanism,' but it's a damn good word with which to carry an election."
—**Pres. Warren G. Harding**

"I believe in an America where millions of Americans believe in an America that's the America millions of Americans believe in. That's the America I love!"
—**Mitt Romney**

More American Revolution battles were fought in So. Carolina than in any other colony.

TICKER SHOCK

Breaking News: Fire destroyed by home **(Fox 5)**

Bernanke on the Housing Market: BLAH blah BLAH blah BLAH blah
BLAH blah BLAH blah **(CNN)**

3,0000 pupils sat maths exams for 1976 **(BBC)**

Space Shuttle traveling nearly 18 times speed of light **(CNN)**

Will high gas prices cost your kids their eductaion? **(Fox News)**

Experts Agree: Al Qaeda Leader is Dead or Alive **(CNN)**

dsfgdfgfsfgdf sdfgsdfgsdfgsdfg **(Fox News)**

Authorities are reminding everyone to now allow impaired drivers to get
behind the wheel **(CNN)**

Breaking News: Many words should fit on this sentence bar. Do not try
to type in a paragraph to tell story **(KDKA 2)**

Fight over N.Y. Mosque Shits to D.C. **(CNN)**

Tiger Woods Takes Leave From the Game of Golg **(CNN)**

Los Angeles Lakers vs. Boston Knicks **(ESPN)**

Norah O'Donnell - The White Ho **(MSNBC)**

Sara Palin (R) Former Presidential Candidate **(CNN)**

Memorial Day Weekend: Buckle up,
Slow down & Drink & Drive **(KARE 11 News)**

JOIN THE PARTY:
THE FEDERALISTS

American politics is—for better or for worse—entrenched in a two-party system.
But the Founding Fathers never even intended for there to be political parties.
Here's the first part of the story of how we got the Dems and the Repubs.

PARTY POOPERS

For all the diversity of opinion among the Founding Fathers in the 1770s, there was one thing that virtually everyone agreed upon: Political parties were a very bad idea.

In his farewell address as president, George Washington referred to political parties as "the worst enemy" of democratic governments, "potent engines by which cunning, ambitious, and unprincipled men will subvert the power of the people." Alexander Hamilton equated political parties with "ambition, avarice, and personal animosity." And Thomas Jefferson could hardly agree more: "If I could go to heaven but with a party," he wrote, "I would not go there at all."

ENGLISH LESSONS

The Founding Fathers' abhorrence of political parties was in response to the partisan politics that characterized England's House of Commons. The Commons was supposed to serve as a check on the power of the monarch, but successive kings had been able to use their vast wealth, power, and control of public offices to create a party of royalists. Thus, it had been reduced to members fighting among themselves instead of working together to advance the common good.

This was what the Founding Fathers were trying to avoid in the United States: warring factions that would pursue selfish interests at the expense of the nation.

But what exactly was the national interest? And if the Founding Fathers couldn't agree on what the national interest was, who among them got to decide? These fundamental questions caused the first factions to form in American political life.

Henry Kissinger complained that he came off as a "slimeball" in the 1995 film *Nixon.*

FIRST FEUD: THE ARTICLES OF CONFEDERATION

Bringing the original 13 colonies together to form the United States had not been easy. The Founding Fathers drafted the first U.S. Constitution, the Articles of Confederation, in 1777, but it was flawed. The Americans had just won independence from one central government—England— and they were reluctant to surrender the power of the individual states to a new central government, so they intentionally made that government weak.

But it soon became obvious that the federal government established by the Articles of Confederation was too weak to be effective at all. The most glaring problem was that it had no power to tax the states, which meant that it had no means of raising money to pay for an army to protect its territories from encroachment by Britain and Spain. In 1787 a constitutional convention was held in Philadelphia to draw up an entirely new document.

It was during the debates over the creation and ratification of the new constitution that some of the first and most significant political divisions in American history began to emerge. Those who supported the idea of strengthening the federal government by weakening the states were known as "Federalists," and those who opposed the new constitution became known as the "Anti-Federalists."

The Federalists won the first round: 9 of the 13 states ratified the U.S. Constitution, and Congress set March 4, 1789, as the date it would go into effect. Elections for Congress and the presidency were held in late 1788. George Washington ran unopposed and was elected president.

TROUBLE IN THE CABINET

Washington saw the presidency as an office aloof from partisan divisions and hoped his administration would govern the same way. But by 1792, Washington's cabinet had split into factions over the financial policies of Alexander Hamilton, the secretary of the treasury.

Perhaps because he was born in the British West Indies and thus did not identify strongly with the interests of any particular state, Hamilton was the foremost Federalist of his age. He strongly believed in using the power of the federal government to develop the American economy. In 1790 he proposed having the government assume the remaining unpaid Revolutionary War debts of the states and the Continental Congress.

Pork queen: Rep. Mazie Hirono (D-HI) sponsored 67 earmarks in '10, worth $150 mil.

This would help establish the creditworthiness of the new nation, albeit by enriching the speculators who bought up the war debt when most people thought it would never be repaid. Hamilton's plan also meant that states that had already paid off their war debt would now be asked to help pay off the debts of states that hadn't, which added to the controversy.

Secretary of State Thomas Jefferson supported the new Constitution but had Anti-Federalist leanings. He grudgingly agreed to support Hamilton's plan, on one condition: Hamilton had to support Jefferson's plan to locate the new capital city on the banks of the Potomac River. Hamilton agreed.

Hamilton got his debt plan, and in return Jefferson got Washington, D.C. (Jefferson later regretted the deal, calling it one of the greatest mistakes of his life.)

A BATTLE ROYAL

Then in December 1790, Hamilton proposed having Congress charter a Bank of the United States as a means to regulate U.S. currency. This time Jefferson thought Hamilton had gone too far. He vehemently opposed the idea, arguing that a national bank would benefit the commercial North more than the agricultural South (Jefferson was a Southerner), and would further enrich the wealthy while doing little to help common people.

Hamilton's financial policies, Jefferson said, were intended to create "an influence of his [Treasury] department over the members of the legislature," creating a "corrupt squadron" of congressmen and senators who would work "to get rid of the limitations imposed by the Constitution [and] prepare the way for a change, from the present republican form of government, to that of a monarchy, of which the English constitution is to be a model."

Like Jefferson, Hamilton deplored political parties. But he and his supporters were also adamant about chartering a national bank and strengthening the powers of the federal government. Faced with the determined opposition of Jefferson and his allies, they began to organize what became known as the Federalist Party. The young nation had its first political party, but another one was right on its heels.

Go to page 97 to find out how Jefferson created the Democratic-Republican Party, which became the Republican Party, which looked more like today's Democrats. (It's not quite as complicated as it seems.)

TAKING THE LOW ROAD

Anything can happen in an election. Here's proof.

CANDIDATE: Mike Rucker
OFFICE: County commissioner in Tallahassee, Florida
CAMPAIGN: One morning in 2002, Rucker was putting up "Vote for Rucker!" lawn signs when he noticed that someone had removed a sign he'd put up just minutes earlier. Rucker installed a new one (he had permission from the homeowners) and continued on his way. A few minutes later he drove by the house again—the new sign had disappeared. Miffed, he rang the doorbell but got no answer. So he went into the backyard...and found the missing signs. About that time, coincidentally, Rucker felt the call of nature, so he relieved himself—right in the backyard. The owners witnessed the offense and told the papers about it, and his "pee of revenge" ended up in the national news.
OUTCOME: His campaign petered out and he lost the election.

CANDIDATE: Arnold Schwarzenegger
OFFICE: Governor of California
CAMPAIGN: During the 2003 campaign to recall California governor Gray Davis, several women accused Schwarzenegger of touching them inappropriately during his acting career. One of them—Rhonda Miller, a stunt double in *Terminator 2*—made the claim just one day before the election. Within hours, Schwarzenegger's press secretary, Sean Walsh, sent an e-mail press release to reporters and editors pointing to the L.A. Superior Court website. There, he said, anyone who typed in the name "Rhonda Miller" would find that Miller had a long rap sheet, including four convictions for prostitution, three for drug possession, and one for forgery. Conservative talk shows and Internet sites jumped all over the story, bringing Miller's credibility into serious question.
OUTCOME: Schwarzenegger won the election, but the next day an interesting fact emerged: The Rhonda Miller on the court website was *not* the Rhonda Miller who had made the accusations. A simple background check would have shown that the two women had different birthdays. But the damage had been done—Miller the stunt double had to endure

being labeled a drug addict and prostitute. "When I turned on the TV set," she said, "oh my God. I was in shock. What they were saying about me was horrible. I just stood there and cried."

Radio stations and websites issued retractions, but the press secretary claimed he had nothing to apologize for. "We did not make any allegations," Walsh explained. "I wrote that memo myself. I wrote it very, very carefully."

CANDIDATE: Howard Metzenbaum

OFFICE: U.S. senator of Ohio

CAMPAIGN: During the 1974 Ohio Democratic primary, incumbent senator Metzenbaum was running against famed astronaut John Glenn. Metzenbaum accused Glenn of being a lifetime "government employee" and "never holding a real job." What was Glenn's government job? He served for 23 years in the Marine Corps, fought in World War II and the Korean War, and went on to become the first American to orbit Earth. Glenn responded to the insult by giving the "Gold Star Mother" speech. He asked Metzenbaum to look any "Gold Star Mother"—a mother who had lost a son in combat—in the eye and tell her that her son had not held a "real job."

OUTCOME: The speech made national news and Metzenbaum looked like a buffoon. Glenn won the primary by more than 100,000 votes and then went on to win the November election.

CANDIDATE: Ernie Eves

OFFICE: Premier of Ontario, Canada

CAMPAIGN: During the Conservative premier's 2003 reelection campaign, one of his staffers sent an e-mail to media representatives attacking Eves's opponent, Liberal candidate Dalton McGuinty. The e-mail ended with the statement: "Dalton McGuinty. He's an evil reptilian kitten-eater from another planet." When asked by reporters if he really ate baby cats and was a space alien, McGuinty smiled and said, "I love kittens, and I like puppies too." Eves, the incumbent, refused to apologize and blamed the release on a staffer who "had too much coffee."

OUTCOME: The kitten-eater won.

Dick Cheney's dog Dave was banned from Camp David for attacking Bush's dog Barney.

COLBERT'S RETORTS

Comedy Central's Stephen Colbert is so good at parodying arrogant news hosts that it makes you wonder if he's really pretending.

"I'm not a fan of facts. You see, facts can change, but my opinion will never change, no matter what the facts are."

"Do you know you have more nerve endings in your gut than you have in your head? You can look it up. Now, I know some of you are going to say, 'I did look it up, and it's not true.' That's 'cause you looked it up in a book. Next time, look it up in your gut."

"I believe democracy is our greatest export. At least until China figures out a way to stamp it out of plastic for three cents a unit."

"All God's creatures have a soul. Except bears. Bears are godless killing machines."

"It's never okay for men to cry. Man holds it in until his eyeballs swell to the size of baseballs, his throat feels like it's about to explode, and his gut just aches like there's a snake wrapped around his heart. That's why we die earlier, but it's worth it. At least we don't look weak while we're alive."

"I've never been a fan of amphibians. They are nature's fence-sitters. Come on, amphibians, which is it? Water or land? Pick one!"

"Like any good newsman, I believe that if you're not scared, I'm not doing my job."

"Just because the Pope is infallible doesn't mean he can't make mistakes."

"If these foreign newspapers have nothing to hide, how come they don't print them in English?"

"Why must we wait for elections? Why not have every elected official have electrodes implanted in their chest? If they don't please us, every morning, we stop their hearts."

"America has a simple deal with the wealthy: We cut their taxes and in return they inspire us with their golden toilets and trophy wives."

"There's nothing wrong with stretching the truth. We stretch taffy, and that just makes it more delicious."

THE PLEDGE OF ALLEGIANCE

The origin and controversy behind an American tradition.

CELEBRATION DAY

As the 400th anniversary of Columbus's voyage to the New World approached in 1892, the nation planned to honor the date with a World's Fair in Chicago. Editors at the magazine *The Youth's Companion*—the *Reader's Digest* of its day—jumped on the bandwagon and became sponsors of the National Public School Celebration for Columbus Day, 1892. Their goal: to get every public school in the U.S. to honor the occasion by raising a U.S. flag and reciting a flag salute. This meant, of course, that they needed an official flag salute.

Assigned to write it was an editor named Francis Bellamy, a former Baptist minister who'd been forced out of his Boston church for delivering socialist sermons. The pledge he composed—which was recited by an estimated 10 million schoolchildren on Columbus Day in 1892—is slightly different than the one we know now:

> I pledge allegiance to my Flag
> and the Republic for which it stands,
> one nation, indivisible,
> with liberty and justice for all.

According to historian John W. Baer, Francis Bellamy "considered placing the word 'equality' in his pledge, but knew that the state superintendents of education…were against equality for women and African-Americans."

REVISIONS

Bellamy's pledge quickly became part of America's culture. But people couldn't leave it alone. In 1923 and 1924 the National Flag Conference, under the leadership of the American Legion and the Daughters of the American Revolution, changed "my Flag" to "the Flag of the United States of America." Bellamy protested this change, but was ignored.

In 1942, a decade after Bellamy died, what had been known as the

---

In 1965 President Johnson issued the first Medicare card. The recipient? Harry Truman.

"Bellamy Salute" also changed. Until then, Americans pledged with their arms outstretched toward the flag with their palms facing down. Sound familiar? It's the same salute that the dreaded Nazi Party was using in Germany. So, just like it was with the U.S. national anthem, the gesture was changed to placing the right hand over the heart.

The next big change came in 1954 when Congress—after a campaign by the Knights of Columbus—added the phrase "under God." It was in response to the infiltration of "godless communists" in America. (According to Bellamy's granddaughter, he would have resented this change because he'd grown disillusioned with the church.) But the change stuck, and the Pledge of Allegiance achieved its final version:

> I pledge allegiance to the flag of the United States of America,
> And to the Republic for which it stands, one Nation under God,
> indivisible, with liberty and justice for all.

But is it really the *final* version? Or are there more changes to come?

CHURCH V. STATE

In the 21st century, about half of U.S. states require the pledge to be recited each day in public schools. Most of the other states do so voluntarily. But anyone who follows current events knows that the pledge has become a centerpiece of the debate over the separation of church and state. A few recent high-profile court cases have brought up some tough questions: Because the Pledge of Allegiance uses the phrase "under God," does that make it a prayer? And if so, should it not be recited in schools? Or should the phrase "under God" be removed from the pledge altogether?

So far, the U.S. Supreme Court has refused to hear any of the cases, leaving it up to the states and lower courts to decide. In 2010, after several controversies surrounding students who were berated as "unpatriotic" for refusing to recite the pledge (mostly on religious reasons), a U.S. appeals court ruled that the pledge is indeed *not* a prayer, but a recitation of a "ceremonial and patriotic nature." What does that mean? Basically, the words "under God" will stay in, but any student who does not feel comfortable reciting that phrase, or the entire pledge, cannot be forced to do so by their teacher. What would it take to change it? The U.S. Flag Code specifies that any alterations have to be made with the consent of the president. That would be a risky move for a president from either party, so expect the Pledge of Allegiance to stay as is for the time being.

IT'S A CONSPIRACY!

*Loyal readers know that Uncle John loves a good (and unbelievably wacky)
conspiracy theory. We had fun looking through our old books for the best
politically themed examples. There were so many, it's kind of scary.*

THEORY: George W. Bush was the inspiration for Curious George,
and was willing to commit murder in order keep that a secret.

THE STORY: Little George Bush was a curious child who was
constantly getting into trouble. Margret and H. A. Rey, friends of Bush's
parents, wrote a series of books about a mischievous monkey whom they
named Curious George after the mischievous boy. The books were
immensely popular, but Bush didn't learn that he was the inspiration for
the character until 2006, when he was already president of the United
States (his father told him). Facing low approval ratings and a public
perception of being dim-witted, Bush was embarrassed and outraged. To
prevent the information from leaking out, he ordered the Reys killed.
When he found out they'd both been dead for years, Bush ordered the
murder of Alan Shalleck, owner of the movie rights to *Curious George*
and producer of the 2006 *Curious George* film.

THE TRUTH: It's impossible for Bush to have been the inspiration for
Curious George. The Reys never met the Bush family, and they wrote
their first book in 1939, seven years *before* Bush was born. Alan Shalleck
was indeed a real person: He wrote several episodes of a *Curious George*
TV series in the 1980s, but he wasn't a producer on the feature film. And
he was in fact murdered, but not by Bush. Shalleck was found dead in his
Florida home in February 2006, the victim of a botched robbery.

THEORY: Reggae superstar Bob Marley was a voice for political change
in Jamaica. But when he opposed the puppet government in place there,
he was murdered…by George H. W. Bush's son Neil Bush.

THE STORY: In 1980 the U.S.-backed International Monetary Fund
(IMF) was offering loans to Third World governments. Jamaican president Michael Manley turned it down because he thought it would make
him a puppet of American business interests and the CIA. The CIA was
furious, so it worked with American-born Jamaican politician Edward
Seaga to force Manley out of office. But an outspoken critic of the IMF

The U.S. president and VP are not allowed to travel together.

plan was Jamaica's *other* most influential voice: Bob Marley. One night as Marley slept, two of Seaga's goons went to the singer's home in Kingston and shot him. But Marley didn't die—he went to a mountain retreat to recuperate, where he was interviewed by a reporter from *Rolling Stone*. When Marley's manager called the magazine a few days later, editors told him they hadn't sent a reporter. So who *had* been there? Neil Bush, CIA operative and son of former CIA director George Bush. While Marley was asleep, Bush injected him with a syringe of "something," and a few months later, in May 1981, Marley died at age 36 of cancer.

THE TRUTH: Manley rejected the IMF loan, but he wasn't over-thrown—his party simply lost power in 1980. As for Bob Marley, he was diagnosed with cancer far earlier, in 1977, and died four years later. He was never shot and never went to a mountain retreat, so he never had a chance to "get" cancer from Neil Bush.

THEORY: As a POW during the Vietnam War, Senator John McCain was brainwashed by the Viet Cong. They can "flip the switch" in his brain and turn him into a spy, or worse…anytime they want!

THE STORY: McCain, a naval pilot, was shot down over Saigon in 1967 and was held captive in a military prison for six years, subject to physical and psychological torture. The Vietnamese hypnotized him, brainwashed him, and implanted a chip in his brain. McCain was released in 1973, but the Vietnamese used the chip to force him to run for the U.S. Senate and eventually president. As president, McCain would have been the helpless puppet of the communist government of Vietnam.

THE TRUTH: Sound familiar? It's the plot of the book (and movie) *The Manchurian Candidate*—conspiracy theorists just modernized it by adding "the chip," which they borrowed from UFO conspiracy theories. The theory probably stems from McCain's controversial efforts to normal-ize diplomatic relations with Vietnam in the 1980s. This enraged many veterans and POWs, who felt that Vietnam was still the enemy. From there the rumors took off, first turning McCain into a collaborator and then into someone with a chip in his head. The story gained traction dur-ing his unsuccessful run for the presidency in 2008.

Similar charges arose when Barack Obama took office; he was accused of—either knowingly or unknowingly—being a Manchurian Candidate for the Muslim Brotherhood (who brainwashed him as a child in Kenya).

24% of male politicians have made their first run for office by age 30.

POLITICAL ENTERTAINERS

Some people just can't get enough of fame, and the world offers no better stages than entertainment and politics. Here are some celebrities who became prominent political figures.

1. Clint Eastwood: Actor with attitude turned mayor of Carmel, California (1986–88)

2. Frederick L. Grandy: Lovable *Love Boat* Gopher turned Iowa congressman (1987–94)

3. Ben Jones: Greasy *Dukes of Hazzard* mechanic turned Georgia congressman (1989–92)

4. Al Franken: *Saturday Night Live* funnyman turned U.S. senator from Minnesota (2009–)

5. Jesse "the Body" Ventura: Pro wrestler turned Minnesota governor (1999–2003)

6. Sonny Bono: Cher's hubby turned mayor of Palm Springs turned California congressman (1995–98)

7. Alessandra Mussolini: Fascist Italian dictator's granddaughter turned actress and model turned member of the European parliament (1992)

8. Tina Keeper: TV Mountie turned member of Canada's House of Commons (2006–08)

9. Shirley Temple Black: Precocious child star turned delegate to the U.N. (1969–70), turned U.S. ambassador to Ghana (1974–76) and Czechoslovakia (1989–92)

10. Arnold Schwarzenegger: Bodybuilder who won Mr. Universe five times and Mr. Olympia six years in a row (1970–75) turned actor turned California governor (2003–11)

11. Glenda Jackson: British Academy Award winner turned member of Parliament in Labour Party (1992–)

12. Ronald Reagan: Actor turned California governor (1967–75) turned 40th U.S. president (1981–89)

Reversing the Order: A politician who became a celebrity…

13. Jerry Springer: Cincinnati, Ohio, mayor (1977–78), who, after a failed bid for governor, turned daytime talkshow host

---

In 2004, 170 college campuses ran campaigns to get John Cusack to run for president.

THE PRESIDENCY

*It's important for the president to take his job seriously—
after all, it's the most important job in the world.
But the rest of us don't have to.*

"When I was a boy, I was told that anybody could become president. I'm beginning to believe it."
—**Clarence Darrow**

"Anyone that wants the presidency so much that he'll spend two years organizing and campaigning for it is not to be trusted with the office."
—**David Broder**

"Any man who says he wants to be president is either an egomaniac or crazy."
—**Dwight D. Eisenhower**

"A female president—maybe they would start calling it the 'Ova Office.'"
—**Brett Butler**

"In my White House, we will know who wears the pantsuits."
—**Hillary Clinton**

"The only reason I'm not running for president is I'm afraid no woman would come forth and say she's slept with me."
—**Garry Shandling**

"The office of the presidency is such a bastardizing thing—half royalty, half democracy—that nobody really knows whether to genuflect or spit."
—**Jimmy Breslin**

"Take our politicians—they're a bunch of yo-yos. The presidency is now a cross between a popularity contest and a high school debate, with an encyclopedia of clichés the first prize."
—**Saul Bellow**

"Anyone who is capable of getting themselves made president should on no account be allowed to do the job."
—**Douglas Adams**

"If you were to go back in history and take every president, you'll find that the numerical value of each letter in their name was equally divisible into the year in which they were elected. By my calculations, our next president has to be named Yellnick McWawa."
—**Cliff Claven, *Cheers***

Looney law: In Texas it is illegal to carry a sword or spear to the voting polls.

THE NEW DEAL

A massive government effort to get people back to work and restart the economy, the New Deal had its detractors, then and now. But it remains one of the most popular and effective government programs in American history.

CRASH AND BURN

In October 1929, during the first year of Herbert Hoover's presidency, the U.S. stock market crashed. By 1933 unemployment had climbed from 4 percent to 25 percent, plunging the nation into the Great Depression. Hoover, a Republican, took a lot of the blame for it and was beaten by a landslide in his 1932 reelection bid by the Democratic candidate, former New York governor Franklin D. Roosevelt. FDR promised Americans a "New Deal"—sweeping government intervention to revive the economy, and new laws to make sure the collapse was never repeated. His legislation was quickly passed through the Democrat-controlled Congress.

Although heavily criticized at the time as socialism or even communism, the New Deal put millions of Americans back to work, provided security to senior citizens, and in the process helped to stabilize the American economy. Most importantly, it gave Americans hope. Here's a look at some of the many agencies created in the New Deal to institute Roosevelt's reforms.

Federal Emergency Relief Administration. The first relief agency of the New Deal, it provided emergency welfare and aid. More than $3 billion was allocated to states and cities for homeless shelters, soup kitchens, and vaccinations, as well as literacy training and free childcare for job-seeking parents. FERA also provided temporary work for as many as 20 million people—construction and maintenance jobs, such as repairing public buildings, laying sewer pipes, and raking leaves for $15 per week. The agency was terminated in 1935, and its projects were absorbed into other programs.

National Recovery Administration. The aim of the NRA was to stimulate economic recovery by asking businesses to set a 40-cents-per-hour

---

India is the world's largest democracy, with 620 million voters.

minimum wage and standardizing the work week at 40 hours for white-collar jobs and 36 for blue-collar. More than 23 million people worked under NRA-abiding companies, but violations of the code were common. Also, participation by firms was voluntary, so the agency really didn't have a lot of authority. In 1935 the Supreme Court declared the NRA unconstitutional because the federal government had overstepped state labor laws. Nevertheless, minimum-wage and work-hour laws were later passed by Congress.

Civilian Conservation Corps. Not only did the CCC raise awareness of the importance of preserving natural resources, but in doing so it created 250,000 conservation, forestry, and land-improvement jobs in 2,600 locations. Nicknamed by workers "Roosevelt's Tree Army," CCC workers planted more than three billion trees from 1933 to 1942, accounting for half of all organized planting in American history. But "conservation" meant a lot of things for the CCC—workers constructed fire towers, built 100,000 miles of fire roads, fought and prevented wildfires, pre-served wildlife habitats, controlled floods, and prevented soil erosion. One clever element of the CCC was how it reallocated labor surpluses to areas where there were labor shortages. American cities had far too many needy workers, so the CCC moved them to sparsely populated rural areas, where there was work to be done and few to do it.

Public Works Administration. In one of the first New Deal programs enacted in 1933, the government allocated $4 billion for the construction of what was ultimately 34,000 projects, including airports, highways, air-craft carriers, bridges (including San Francisco's Golden Gate Bridge), hospitals, and schools. By June 1934, the PWA had planned all of its projects and allocated all of its money. So in 1935 Congress created a new agency called the Works Progress Administration to develop more civic construction and job-creation programs in the same vein.

Works Progress Administration. Picking up where the PWA left off, the WPA employed 8.5 million people between 1935 and 1943 at an average wage of $2 per day for civic construction projects such as roads (650,000 miles), bridges (78,000), buildings (125,000), and 700 miles of airport runways. The WPA was the nation's largest "employer" at the time, and the largest New Deal agency—it spent $11 billion over its life span. Some WPA projects still in existence: Dealey Plaza in Dallas (where John F.

The U.S. Secret Service was first established to combat counterfeiting.

Kennedy was shot in 1963), LaGuardia Airport in New York, Timberline Lodge in Oregon, and the presidential retreat Camp David (which was initially a resort for all federal employees). One notable branch of the agency was the Arts Program, which hired thousands of artists, musicians, actors, photographers, and writers to use their talents for public works. For example, future major authors Saul Bellow and Ralph Ellison wrote state guidebooks, and painter Jackson Pollock produced murals.

Federal Deposit Insurance Corporation. During the Depression, consumers lost faith in banks. Many had failed and closed suddenly, and their customers' money was irretrievably lost. But banks are an important part of the financial system—no modern economy can function without them. Created by the Glass-Steagall Banking Reform Act of 1933, the FDIC restored faith in banks with a government-backed insurance policy on deposits. If a bank failed, a consumer's account was insured up to $5,000. (Today the guarantee is $250,000.)

Agricultural Adjustment Administration. In order to increase the market price of crops and livestock, and thereby make farms financially stable again, there had to be either a greater demand or less supply. The AAA paid farmers a subsidy to grow less. The AAA opened in May 1933, by which point the year's crops were already planted. Since it was too late to pay farmers not to plant, the agency destroyed existing stockpiles and reduced the size of livestock herds. Twenty-five percent of the nation's cotton fields were razed, and six million piglets and 220,000 pregnant cows were slaughtered. Destroying crops while so many Americans struggled to put food on the table made the AAA very controversial. Besides, it didn't work—large farms benefited most; they simply evicted tenant farmers and sharecroppers, let the land go fallow, then collected a fee from the government. And by 1937, wholesale food prices hadn't changed much from before the AAA went into effect.

Federal Housing Administration. During the Depression, home mortgages were mostly short-term—about three to five years, as opposed to the 30-year standard of today. The FHA, born out of the National Housing Act of 1934, regulated interest rates and mortgage terms so home ownership was more within reach for middle- and low-income families. The agency also helped to ensure that enough affordable housing existed for purchase by offering loans for home-building companies, which had

---

The term "weapons of mass destruction" was coined in 1937 during the Spanish Civil War.

suffered greatly in the economic downturn.

Securities and Exchange Commission. Fraud, deception, and insider trading contributed to the stock market crash, so in an attempt to make sure it never happened again, Congress passed the Securities Exchange Act in 1934. In addition to requiring disclosure of a company's financial information and dealings to investors, it made securities (stock) fraud a crime and established the Securities and Exchange Commission. Its five commissioners are appointed by the president to police the financial world.

National Labor Relations Board. Created by the National Labor Relations Act of 1935, the board's purpose was to protect and enhance the rights of workers to organize into unions and collectively bargain for better wages and better working conditions.

Farm Security Administration. Formed by the Resettlement Administration Act of 1935, this agency delivered aid to the nearly one million farm families who'd fled the Dust Bowl agricultural disaster in Arkansas and Oklahoma for California, as well as those evicted by farm bosses after AAA subsidies. The FSA purchased ruined farms from victims of the Dust Bowl and relocated the farmers to 34 government-owned group farms, where they grew food for themselves while learning modern techniques from agriculture scientists. The FSA also set up refugee camps for farmers and provided educational grants to farm families. But the most famous project of the FSA was its photography branch—it sent out photographers, most notably Gordon Parks and Dorothea Lange, to document the plight of the Depression-era farmers.

Social Security Administration. The SSA provided financial assistance for single mothers, a free food program for children of low-income families, and unemployment insurance. But most famously, the SSA created and managed a federal pension system for retired people. Not only did it allow aging citizens to retire from the workforce (without starving), it also opened up their jobs to new workers. Social Security payments were financed by a payroll tax, and they still are: It remains in effect today, covering 40 million people and accounting for a quarter of the federal budget.

GOVERN-MENTAL

Five-time presidential candidate Eugene McCarthy said, "The only thing that saves us from the bureaucracy is inefficiency. An efficient bureaucracy is the greatest threat to liberty." (Looks like our liberty is safe.)

SECRET TREASURE

Did you receive a piece of junk mail in the spring of 2008, addressed to "Resident" and labeled "National Household Travel Survey"? Don't remember? Then you probably threw it away, as did thousands of others who received the mailer from the Department of Transportation requesting that you take part in a survey about your travel habits. If you'd opened the mailer, you would've found a crisp $5 bill inside (a "token of appreciation"). Had the DOT sent out *checks* for $5, they could have tracked how many people cashed them and canceled all the checks that weren't cashed. But because they sent out cash, there was no way to trace how many people got the money...or how many $5 bills ended up in the trash.

GATOR AID

According to the book *Great Government Goofs*, compiled by Leland Gregory, "Members of the Georgia State Game Commission were fiercely debating the pros and cons of regulating 'alligator rides' when one alert member noticed a typographical error on the agenda—the commission was actually supposed to be discussing whether or not they should regulate 'alligator hides.'"

KICKED THE BUCKET

From 1999 to 2005, the USDA awarded more than $1 billion to farmers who were no longer living. Farm families are eligible to receive money for two years after the head of the household dies in an effort to help them get back on their feet. After an investigation, however, the Government Accountability Office discovered that the USDA has no steps in place to *stop* the payments— families continue receiving payments until an heir of the deceased farmer informs the USDA to stop. According to the GAO's findings, few of the dead farmers' families have contacted the USDA...so most continue receiving checks to this day.

GOING POSTAL

As part of the 2008 economic stimulus package, the IRS decided to inform citizens that their checks were coming, so they sent out letters to 130 million taxpayers. Cost of sending the letters: $42 million. A few weeks later the IRS spent that amount again to send the real checks.

ME ME ME!

In 2007 Rep. Charlie Rangel (D-NY) requested funds for three construction projects at City College of New York. They include the "Charles B. Rangel Center for Public Service," the "Rangel Conference Center," and the "Charles Rangel Library." Cost to taxpayers: $2 million. When freshman congressman John Campbell (R-CA) railed against the politician for naming buildings after himself while still in office, Rangel, who's been in Congress since 1971, responded, "I would have a problem if you did it, because I don't think that you've been around long enough to inspire a building." The library, incidentally, will only display memorabilia that pertains to Rangel. According to a CBS News report, "It's kind of like a presidential library, but without a president."

NAMING WRONGS

As president, Ronald Reagan preached smaller government and less spending. So why not name one of the biggest and most expensive projects in government history after him? The Ronald Reagan Building and International Trade Center opened in Washington, D.C., in 1998, and it's the largest federal building in D.C. (The only larger federal building is the Pentagon, located in Virginia.) And at the time, the Ronald Reagan Building boasted the heftiest price tag for a single structure in U.S. government history: $768 million. (Another ironic naming fact: In 1981 the nation's air-traffic controllers went on strike—and President Reagan fired them all. In 1998 National Airport in Washington was renamed...Ronald Reagan National Airport.)

LONG-DISTANCE TAXI SERVICE

In 2008 an accused thief named Mark Bailey was being arraigned in Northampton, England. After a brief hearing, the judge ordered that Bailey be sent to the magistrate's courtroom—located in a building across the street—to plead his case. One problem: The prisoner transport van wasn't available (it had "gone on to do other things"). So police officers offered to escort Bailey to the courthouse, about 200 yards away, on foot. Court officials said that the public walk would "violate Bailey's human rights," so they were forced to call for another van...the closest one being in Cambridge, nearly 60 *miles away*. Two and a half hours later, the van showed up, and Bailey took the 30-second trip to the courthouse. The van then drove the 60 miles back to Cambridge. "I've never heard such nonsense," said Conservative MP Brian Binley. "Why we should have to suffer such ludicrous incompetence, and pay for it, is beyond me."

THE TIP OF THE ICE CUBE

In the aftermath of Hurricane Katrina in 2005, the Federal Emergency Management Agency (FEMA) purchased 112,000 tons of ice for $24 million. Unfortunately, they were unable to distribute all of it to those in need, so they stored the unused ice in cold warehouses. Two years later, the ice was still in storage—and the cost to keep it cold all that time totaled more than $11 million, nearly half of what it cost to purchase. Even more embarrassing, it was announced that because FEMA didn't know the "shelf life" for ice, the stockpile couldn't be reused and had to be melted. The cost of the melting operation: another $3.4 million. (FEMA subsequently announced that they are no longer in the business of buying and storing ice for disasters.)

NO MORE MR. NICELEY

In 2012 Tennessee state congressman Frank Niceley became upset when one of his constituents—a 39-year-old nurse named Meredith Graves—was arrested while visiting the Ground Zero Memorial in New York City. Why? Because she brought a loaded pistol. Although Graves had a permit to carry in Tennessee, it's illegal to bring a gun to Ground Zero. Nicely drafted an official motion in the Tennessee Legislature admonishing New York City officials for their lack of "common sense." But what put the motion in the news was the final sentence: "Be it further resolved that we remind the citizens of New York City to drive carefully through the great State of Tennessee, paying extra attention to our speed limits." New York mayor Michael Bloomberg viewed it as a not-so-veiled threat that traveling New Yorkers would be singled out and pulled over. Bloomberg retorted: "Common sense also includes checking gun laws before traveling." Nicely said he was just kidding about the speeding-ticket threat: "You've got to inject a little humor to get attention." Mission accomplished.

LOONEY LAWS

Sometimes lawmakers make laws that make no sense.

- In Providence, Rhode Island, it's illegal to sell toothbrushes on Sundays. (Toothpaste is okay.)

- It's against the law in Washington State to pretend that your parents are rich.

- Women in Corvallis, Oregon, are not legally permitted to drink coffee after 6:00 p.m.

- By law, Washington drivers must carry an anchor to be used as an emergency brake.

- In Christiansburg, Virginia, it's a crime to imitate the sound of a police whistle.

- It's against the law in Iowa to charge people to watch a one-armed pianist perform.

- In Missouri, men are legally required to have a permit to shave.

- It's a crime in Long Beach, California, to curse while playing miniature golf.

- It's against the law in Oklahoma to display a hypnotized person in a window.

- In Israel, it's illegal to pick your nose on the Sabbath.

- In Florida, widows may not skydive on Sunday afternoons.

- It's illegal for a woman in Joliet, Illinois, to try on more than six dresses in one store.

- It's okay to wear a fake nose in Aberdeen, Scotland, but only if it doesn't conceal your identity.

- Richmond, Virginia, prohibits anyone from flipping a coin to determine who will pay a restaurant tab.

- A man may not legally wear a strapless evening gown in Miami.

- In Devon, Colorado, it's illegal to walk backward, but only after sunset.

- In Connecticut, it's against the law to play Scrabble while waiting for a politician to speak (other games are okay).

- It's illegal to run a three-legged race for money in British Columbia.

- Eating soup with a fork is against the law in New York.

- It's illegal to sell used confetti in Detroit.

1900 presidential campaign slogan of William McKinley: "Let Well Enough Alone."

MOUNT PELÉE

We first ran this article in Uncle John's Supremely Satisfying
Bathroom Reader, *published in 2000. However, new research has
surfaced in the past few years that tells a slightly different story
than the one told in history books. Here's our update.*

R**UMBLE RUMBLE**
In late April 1902, Mount Pelée, on the island of Martinique in
the Caribbean Sea, began smoking and shaking. Only four miles
away lay the town of St. Pierre, the cultural and commercial capital of the
French West Indies. More than 30,000 people lived there. They were
wary of the rumbling volcano, but it wasn't the first time it had acted up.
Since the French had settled the island in the 17th century, Pelée had
burped a few times, but always calmed right back down. No one had any
reason to believe it would be any different this time, so they stayed put.

But in early May, scalding mudflows began pouring down the slopes
and ash fell in the town faster than it could be swept away. Many people
changed their minds about leaving and urged the town leaders to start
evacuation measures. They didn't. Why? No one knows for sure, because
a few days later, nearly everyone in St. Pierre was dead.

ABSOLUTE POWER

Over the past century, historians and geologists alike have tried to piece
together the events that led up to the eruption of May 8, 1902. The most
common version: The death toll was so high because of politics. The
island's elections were only a few days away. St. Pierre mayor Roger
Fouché and Martinique governor Louis Mouttet were more concerned
with keeping power than with keeping their constituents safe. Their
biggest concern: the growing popularity of a radical political party—led
by a black candidate—that stood for equal rights and threatened the
white supremacy of the island.

With their support starting to slip, Mayor Fouché and Governor
Mouttet refused to allow anything to delay the election even a single day.
To reassure the people that the mountain would calm down, they planted
a story in the local newspaper that a team of "volcano experts" had studied the mountain and deemed there was no danger to the town.

Elle **magazine once dubbed John Edwards "the sexiest man in politics."**

But Pelée didn't calm down. On May 4, a giant mudslide obliterated the sugar mill on the edge of town, taking 23 workers with it. It caused a tsunami that drowned the seafront district, killing dozens more. As the frightened citizens began packing to leave, they were ordered to stay home. The mayor even told his men to spread rumors that the outskirts of town had been taken over by swarms of poisonous centipedes. Those citizens who did try to leave St. Pierre were met at the borders by armed militia men who turned them back. Only a few people made it out.

LEVELED

At dawn on election day, a colossal cloud of superheated gasses, ash, and rock erupted from Mount Pelée…and headed straight for St. Pierre at more than 100 mph. Within three minutes, the entire city was gone. Even ships anchored offshore were set ablaze, killing all those aboard.

Only two people in St. Pierre were left alive. One was a prisoner who was being held in an underground cell with one small window facing away from the volcano. He was horribly burned, but survived and later toured with the Barnum and Bailey Circus as a sideshow attraction. The other survivor was the town cobbler, a religious fanatic who had been hiding in his cellar. He went insane after venturing outside to discover the charred remains of everyone he knew.

THE TRUTH

Dozens of books published since the catastrophe tell this same basic story, but recently historians have been able to piece together a more accurate version of events: It seems that the governor wasn't quite as concerned about the election as previously thought, and there's no evidence that he and the mayor spread false rumors and forced people from leaving. Even the volcano experts knew Pelée would erupt, but they figured that when it did, townsfolk would have plenty of time to escape the river of lava flowing down the mountain. It *was* four miles away, after all.

But no one at the time had ever witnessed what is now known as a *pyroclastic flow*—a wall of gas, ash, and rocks that can travel many miles and instantly consumes everything in its path. So while St. Pierre's leaders were perhaps corrupt (all too common in colonies), their biggest fault was actually ignorance. They simply didn't see the danger.

If any good has come out of Mount Pelée's eruption, it's that political leaders now take the threat posed by volcanoes much more seriously.

Do the cancan: Bush's '04 slogan: "Yes, America Can!"; Obama's in '08: "Yes We Can."

A PEACH OF AN ELECTION

*The strange events surrounding the 1946 Georgia
gubernatorial election may read like the plot of a
Marx Brothers movie. But this really happened.*

IT ENDS IN A DEAD HEAT

In November 1946, Democrat Eugene Talmadge won a fourth (non-consecutive) term as governor of Georgia, defeating the unpopular incumbent, Ellis Arnall. But on December 21—a month before he was supposed to be sworn in—Talmadge died of cirrhosis of the liver. As of January 1947, Georgia would have no governor…or perhaps it would have three.

Governor #1: Herman Talmadge. Eugene Talmadge's son, Herman, knew before the election what the public didn't—his father was dying. Herman wanted his father's job, so he had organized a write-in campaign for himself in the 1946 election. He knew that if his father won and then died before taking office, there'd be a runoff election between the next two highest vote getters. Herman aimed to finish in the top three and then win the runoff based on public love and sympathy for the elder Talmadge. It worked: He came in second to his father.

Governor #2: M. E. Thompson. In many states, when a governor dies, the lieutenant governor assumes the executive office. Georgia had only created the post of lieutenant governor in 1945 and the first lieutenant governor was to be elected in the 1946 general election. The winner: Talmadge rival M. E. Thompson. His position was that even though he hadn't yet been sworn in as lieutenant governor, technically he was next in line for the governor's job.

Governor #3: Ellis Arnall. Arnall, who lost to Eugene Talmadge, actually was the sitting governor, and as such, refused to vacate his office until the Georgia Supreme Court could decide who the new governor would be.

THERE OUGHTA BE A LAW

But it wasn't up to the Georgia Supreme Court; it was in the hands of the Georgia General Assembly (the legislature), which had the constitutional authority to decide contested elections. When the assembly met in January 1947, the majority of members were against the idea of having another election—they favored giving the governorship to Herman Talmadge because he'd finished second in votes. Furthermore, Talmadge supporters argued, the new lieutenant governor, M.E. Thompson, had no claim to the office because he hadn't yet taken office himself, and therefore couldn't be a successor.

Thompson wasn't going down without a fight. His supporters plied pro-Talmadge legislators with drinks that were laced with knockout drops. Thompson figured that if the Talmadge faction fell asleep, they couldn't very well vote for Talmadge, giving Thompson backers an easy win. But the vote never took place. It was prevented when Talmadge supporters found out about Thompson's scheme and stormed the capitol building. "There were several thousand people there, 90 percent of them my friends—some of them armed," Talmadge later recalled. "And some of them drunk."

MINOR SETBACK

Meanwhile, ballot recounts showed that Herman Talmadge hadn't finished second in the election after all. He'd actually finished third, making him ineligible for any claim at governor. Did that eliminate him from the running? Nope. Later that week, a bunch of ballots from Telfair County (Talmadge's home county) were suddenly "discovered" and sent to the capitol. That put Talmadge back into contention for what looked to be a runoff vote with Arnall. (Historians later found that all the late ballots were written in the same handwriting and cast in alphabetical order by deceased voters.)

Amazingly, the assembly opted against a runoff and hurriedly appointed Talmadge governor on January 15, 1947. The only problem: The incumbent, Ellis Arnall, refused to acknowledge Talmadge's appointment. He locked himself inside the governor's office and would not leave...until a Talmadge mob stormed the office, broke the door down, and forcibly removed him. As Arnall later recalled, "The lock splintered with a crash and the mob poured into the office. A pathway opened in the crowd, and the young son of the dead governor-elect of Georgia was led through the office on the arm of his chief advisor. Behind them trailed a committee of legislators and a giant professional wrestler who had been the strong-arm man for the faction."

BACKROOM BARGAIN

As the mob escorted Arnall from the governor's office, he changed his plan. He would no longer focus on remaining governor, but on unseating Talmadge. Still declaring himself the acting governor, Arnall worked out a deal with the now sworn-in lieutenant governor, M.E. Thompson: Arnall would "resign" and Thompson would become governor. Now the number of potential governors was down to two…and Arnall would get what he really wanted: The debacle would be decided by the Georgia Supreme Court.

At this point, Talmadge and Thompson each claimed to be the rightful governor. But who actually was the governor? Georgia Secretary of State Ben Fortson didn't know, but he wasn't taking any chances—he began sitting on or sleeping with the state seal, which was needed by the governor (whoever it was) to make certain documents legal. With neither man able to perform the functions of the job, they took the fight to court.

DISORDER IN THE COURT

In March 1947, the Georgia Supreme Court declared Thompson acting governor. Their reasoning: The general assembly had acted improperly in its January sessions. According to the court, they should have declared Eugene Talmadge the governor-elect, even though he was dead. That would mean the next in line, the lieutenant governor–elect, Thompson, would be the successor.

Or would he? The court also ordered a special election to be held in 1948, mostly to avoid any more Talmadge-organized mobs and riots. Thompson would serve until then. The legitimate winner of the 1948 election was Herman Talmadge. In the final analysis, all three men vying for the office—Talmadge, Thompson, and Arnall—served as governor of Georgia.

Although the controversy seems comical today, at the time it was a great embarrassment for Georgia, and it still ranks as one of the weirdest political moments in American history.

Single largest expenditure of a presidential campaign: TV ads.

DON'T CALL ME LIZ

*In 2009 a lobbyist from JP Morgan Chase emailed the office of Rep.
Jim McDermott (D-WA) requesting a meeting. The recipient was
Elizabeth Becton, the congressman's scheduler. After a week,
she still hadn't responded. So the lobbyist wrote her again,
and made one crucial mistake. Here's the exchange.*

From: [Name redacted—we'll call him "Chase Lobbyist."]
Hi Liz, Just checking in on whether the Congressman is available
next week. Thank you! Best, Chase

From: Elizabeth Becton

Who is Liz?

From: Chase Lobbyist
Hi Elizabeth, I thought you went by Liz, apologies if that's incorrect.
Best, Chase

From: Elizabeth Becton
I do not go by Liz. Where did you get your information?

From: Chase Lobbyist
Hi Elizabeth, I'm so sorry if I offended you! I thought you'd gone by
Liz at Potlatch [a paper company]. My mistake. Best, Chase

From: Elizabeth Becton
NEVER. I hate that name.

From: Chase Lobbyist
Hi Elizabeth, I'm so sorry if I offended you! I must have mis-heard.
My mistake! Best, Chase

From: Elizabeth Becton
Chase, if I wanted you to call me by any other name, I would have
offered that to you. It's rude when people take all sorts of liberties

with your name. This is a real sore spot. My name has a lot of "nicknames" which I don't use. I use either my first name or my last name because I row with a lot of other women who share the same first name. Now, please do not ever call me by a nickname again.

From: Chase Lobbyist

Hi Elizabeth, I'm so sorry I offended you! My mistake! Best, Chase

---

From: Elizabeth Becton

Chase, sounds like you got played by someone who KNOWS I hate that name and that it's a fast way to TICK me off. Who told you that I go by that name? They are not your friend…

From: Chase Lobbyist

Hi Elizabeth, Again, I am sincerely sorry for offending you. I don't want to cause trouble as I clearly must have mis-heard the person. It was in no way my intention to make you upset. Best, Chase

---

From: Elizabeth Becton

I REALLY want to know who told you to call me that.

From: Chase Lobbyist

Hi Elizabeth. Again, I am sincerely sorry. I don't recall who I over-heard. It was in no way my intention to upset you. Best, Chase

---

From: Elizabeth Becton

Let me put it this way, they don't know me and perhaps they were PRETENDING to know me better than they do. They did YOU a disservice. You should be VERY careful about such things. People like to brag about their connections in DC. It's a pastime. It's also dangerous to eavesdrop, as you have just found out. Quit apologizing and never call me anything but Elizabeth again. And correct anyone who attempts to call me by any other name but Elizabeth. Are we clear on this?

EPILOGUE: After the email exchange was leaked to the press, a spokesman for McDermott apologized for Becton's behavior: "This is not reflective of the way we do business in this office."

"Washington, D.C., is 12 square miles bordered by reality." —Andrew Johnson

CROOKED AS A DOG'S HIND LEG

These New York politicians tried to buck the system...and got caught.

REDEFINING NONPROFIT

Who: State senator Pedro Espada Jr. (D-Bronx)

What he did: The unraveling of Senator Espada began in 2009, when he and fellow senator Hiram Monserrate defected to the Republican side of the aisle, taking majority control of the state senate away from the Democrats. A five-week legislative deadlock ensued, after which Espada agreed to rejoin the Democratic fold, but only in exchange for being named majority leader.

This kind of coercion doesn't play well in Albany (New York's capital) and runs the risk of retribution. Attorney General Andrew Cuomo investigated Espada, and there was plenty to find. Cuomo filed a civil suit accusing Espada of draining $14 million from a group of nonprofit health clinics that he owned in the Bronx and using the money for personal expenses (including $20,000 worth of sushi delivered to his Westchester home). Another lawsuit accused Espada of running a bogus job-training program that let him pay janitors at the clinics only $1.70 per hour, far below the minimum wage. He was also being investigated by the federal government and the IRS for his connection to a consulting firm allegedly involved with tax fraud and money laundering. And the Bronx district attorney was after him too...for not actually living in the Bronx.

Result: In the September 2010 Democratic primary, a 34-year-old unknown named Gustavo Rivera defeated Espada. Rivera said that the choice between the two candidates was between "ethics or indictments, and the people of the Bronx made the right choice." Rivera went on to win the November election.

THE CONSULTANT

Who: Senator Joseph L. Bruno (R-Rensselaer and Saratoga Counties)

What he did: In 1995 Bruno became majority leader in the Republican-

---

The light above Big Ben's clock face is only lit when Parliament is in session.

controlled state senate. He was a powerful force who channeled billions of public dollars to the Albany region. It all went bust in 2008 when he resigned in the face of a federal investigation into his business dealings. Bruno was charged with several crimes, including receiving lucrative consulting fees from companies that were either seeking business from the state or in need of assistance with state regulators, and for failing to disclose his conflicts of interest. The investigation probed into 15 years of Bruno's activities as a consultant for more than a dozen firms, during which he earned about $3.2 million in fees.

Result: In January 2009, Bruno was indicted on eight felony counts of corruption, including mail and wire fraud. In December, he was convicted on two of the counts, acquitted on five, and got a hung jury on the last count. A federal judge sentenced him to two years in prison, and Bruno had to pay $280,000 in restitution to the State of New York, the amount of money he made in the two felony counts on which he was convicted. "I can say to you honestly," he insisted, "as honestly as I can: In my heart, and in my mind, I did nothing wrong."

RETIREMENT PLAN

Who: State Comptroller Alan Hevesi (Democrat from Queens)

What he did: Hevesi had a PhD (his doctoral dissertation: "Legislative Leadership in New York State"), and had been a professor of political science at Queens College and a longtime veteran of the state senate. He aspired to higher office, and was elected New York City's comptroller in 1994. He tried for the mayoral nomination in 2001, but that was a no-go, so in 2002, he ran for state comptroller and won. He then decided to run for a second term. But in September 2006, just before the election, his Republican opponent called in a tip (to the hotline Hevesi himself had set up for citizens to report fraud and corruption), revealing that Hevesi had been using a state worker as chauffeur and errand boy for his ailing wife.

What started as a minor infraction turned into a very big deal, apparently, because the inquiry sparked a much wider investigation that revealed a pattern of fraud, bribery, and what Attorney General Andrew Cuomo called a "culture of corruption."

Result: Hevesi still won the 2006 election, but was forced to resign almost immediately. He then pleaded guilty to charges of defrauding the

Lyndon B. Johnson was the only president to take the oath of office on *Air Force One*.

government. The state's pension fund (third largest in the country) was worth $125 billion, and it had apparently become a moneymaker for Hevesi—his top political consultant had been acting as a middleman, steering pension-fund investments to Hevesi's friends and political associates—and getting kickbacks for his efforts. By the time the investigation was over in 2010, Hevesi pleaded guilty to directing $250 million in state pension funds to an investment company that gave him $75,000 for travel expenses for himself and his family, $380,000 for other expenses, and $500,000 in campaign contributions.

HELPFUL COP

Who: Bernard Kerik

What he did: In 1994 Bernie Kerik was an NYPD detective assigned to Mayor Rudy Giuliani's "protective detail" as bodyguard and driver. The mayor trusted Kerik so much that he appointed him as head of the Department of Corrections and then, in 2000, promoted him to NYPD commissioner. Kerik was the commissioner on September 11, 2001, and happened to meet—and impress—President George W. Bush at the disaster site. In 2004 Kerik was tapped by the Bush administration to become the next Secretary of the Department of Homeland Security.

Kerik, a highly decorated police officer, had always been a tough guy and a bit of a loose cannon, but when he was vetted by White House officials about his career, he assured them he was squeaky-clean. He wasn't: A New Jersey construction company had paid for $255,000 of renovations on Kerik's Bronx home in the hopes that Kerik would help them get a New York City building license, and Kerik had contacted city officials on the company's behalf.

Result: Kerik was convicted and sentenced to prison after pleading guilty to eight felony charges, including tax fraud and lying to White House officials. His plea agreement recommended a maximum of 33 months in jail, but the angry judge slapped him with 48, calling him a "toxic combination of self-minded focus and arrogance."

*   *   *

"Is the country still here?"

—President Calvin Coolidge, waking from a nap

In 1969 author Norman Mailer ran for NYC mayor with the slogan: "No more bullsh*t."

BILL O'REALLY?

Fox News pundit Bill O'Reilly speaks his mind and doesn't apologize for it.

"You gotta look people in the eye and tell them they're irresponsible and lazy. Because in this country, you can succeed if you get educated and work hard. Period. Period."

"Public misbehavior by the famous is a powerful teaching tool."

"Winston Churchill said that democracy was the worst possible form of government, except for all the others. Maybe we can say the same about capitalism. For all of its faults, it gives most hardworking people a chance to improve themselves economically, even as the deck is stacked in favor of the privileged few. Here are the choices most of us face in such a system: Get bitter or get busy."

"Unfortunately, many of our leaders are not being honest about the new world. Machines are changing everything from labor to emotions to behavior. This is not your grandfather's country anymore."

"Hate speech is hate speech, whether it's being spewed by some nut wearing a Nazi armband, or by some gnome hunched over a keyboard."

"In a country of 300 million, I'd say 15 percent of us are evil."

"Here's the bottom line: If you're offended by Christmas, you have a problem. See somebody or tough it out."

"My advice to homosexuals, whether they're in the Boy Scouts, or in the army, or in high school: Shut up, don't tell anybody what you do. Your life will be a lot easier."

"I've said 'shut up' six times in 12 years. They all deserved it. They were either bloviating, filibustering, or lying."

"I just wish Katrina had only hit the United Nations Building and just flooded them out, and I wouldn't have rescued them."

"The children of America have seen that liars can win and cheats can prosper. They know our nation will accept venal behavior and reward it with tremendous wealth and power. So why wouldn't kids lie, cheat, and steal?"

"Lots of people want to hurt me. That's the price you pay for being a big mouth."

Youngest active system of governance: communism—introduced in 1848.

INCIDENT AT HAVERING

A sheepish tale of political intrigue from the United Kingdom.

BAAACKGROUND

In September 2005, a zoning meeting took place in the town hall of the East London borough of Havering. The meeting concerned a proposal to convert an exotic horse and sheep farm into a mobile home park. To do so would require a zoning change and the council would have to approve it. Such zoning changes are commonplace throughout the world, but this one was different. Councilman Jeff Tucker, who represented the area where the proposed mobile home park would be built, got up to speak in favor of the idea. And that's when the trouble started.

Somebody in the room apparently did not agree with Tucker. The anonymous adversary began making loud, sheeplike "baa" noises whenever Tucker tried to talk, drowning him out. Despite the fact that there were only a handful of people in the room—including just five city council members—nobody could figure out who made the noises…and nobody would own up to it.

BAAAD FORM

Councilman Tucker was enraged (and the proposal failed). He lodged a complaint with the Standards Board for England, an oversight agency for governmental disputes. The board didn't think it worthy of their time to determine who made the sheep noises and why, so they referred it back to the Havering council. The Havering Standards Hearings Sub-Committee began an investigation. They narrowed down the source of the "baa"-ing to four culprits, all of them city councilors. One of the suspects, councilor Denis O'Flynn, called the process "an extremely expensive example of the worst kind of bureaucracy" and "the height of stupidity."

Fourteen months later, the Havering city council issued a 300-page report, the result of an investigation that cost £10,000 (about $20,000). What did they find? The source of the sheep noises was Denis O'Flynn. The punishment: nothing. By the time the investigation was completed, O'Flynn was no longer a city council member…and no longer subject to any disciplinary action.

Tennessee's constitution forbids priests and atheists from holding public office.

"A GOOD EXAMPLE IS THE BEST SERMON"

Benjamin Franklin: Founding Father, renaissance man, and...world-class hypocrite? His advice in the pages of Poor Richard's Almanack *is timeless—but did Dr. Franklin always practice what he preached?*

What Poor Richard Said: "God helps those who help themselves."

What Franklin Did: It probably wasn't what he meant, but Franklin wasn't above helping himself to the work of others. One of the things Franklin is best known for is *Poor Richard's Almanack*, which he wrote and published for 25 years. What's less wellknown is the extent to which Franklin "borrowed" from the works of others: He appropriated his journal's title from his own brother James, publisher of *Poor Robin's Almanack*, and took the pen name Richard Saunders ("Poor Richard") from a dead astrologer and doctor of the same name.

• Only a handful of Franklin's most famous quotes are his ("Experience keeps a dear school, yet fools will learn in no other" is one example); the rest he lifted without permission, compensation, or apology from *Lexicon Tetraglotton, Outlandish Proverbs*, and other popular journals of the day. "Why should I give my Readers bad lines of my own, when good ones of other People's are so plenty?" he liked to joke. And with no copyright laws in place to stop him, there was nothing the other writers could do.

• To his credit, whenever possible, Franklin tried to improve upon the writing he stole from others, either by making it more to the point ("God restoreth health and the physician hath the thanks" became "God heals and the doctor takes the fee"), or by adding coarse references to sex, flatulence, or bodily functions. ("He that lives upon hope, dies farting," "The greatest monarch on the proudest throne is obliged to sit upon his own arse," and "Force sh*ts upon reason's back.")

What Poor Richard Said: "Dally not with other folks' women or money."

The president of the United States has an annual entertainment budget of $12,000.

What Franklin Did: Franklin had a lifelong habit of engaging in "foolish intrigues with low women," as he put it, a tendency that began in his teenage years and continued through his married life. He amazed friends and associates with the number and variety of his conquests; it wasn't unusual for visitors to happen upon Franklin in a compromising state with a parlor maid, cleaning girl, or someone else who had consented to the great man's advances. According to legend, when he was young and short of funds, he got his rent lowered by taking his elderly landlady as a lover.

• Why settle for one woman at a time? When Franklin lived in London, he became close friends with the postmaster general of England, Sir Francis Dashwood, with whom he coauthored a revised edition of the *Book of Common Prayer*. But Sir Dashwood also had a naughty side—he was the founder of the Order of St. Francis, a society of orgiasts better known as the Hellfire Club. The club met regularly at Dashwood's country house in Buckinghamshire, and its proceedings usually began with blasphemy, usually a black mass or some other obscene religious ceremony, before turning to fornication, which usually involved women dressed as nuns.

• To be fair, there's no proof that Franklin ever went to a single Hellfire Club orgy. But "it is certainly known that he was a frequent, not to say eager, visitor to Dashwood's house," Bill Bryson writes in *Made in America*, "and it would take a generous spirit indeed to suppose that he ventured there repeatedly just to discuss postal regulations and the semantic nuances of the *Book of Common Prayer*."

What Poor Richard Said: "One good Husband is worth two good Wives; for the scarcer things are, the more they're valued."

What Franklin Did: Technically speaking, even Franklin's marriage was a form of adultery. He never officially married his "wife," Deborah Read Franklin, who was still legally married to her first husband, a potter named John Rogers. Rogers had left her years earlier and run off to the West Indies, where it was rumored that he had died in a fight. But nobody knew for sure, and that presented a serious problem for Ben and Deborah when they decided to marry: What if Rogers came back? In those days, even unintentional bigamy was punishable by 39 lashes for both husband and wife, along with life imprisonment doing hard labor. Even if Rogers really was dead, if Franklin married Deborah he risked becoming legally obligated to repay Rogers's substantial debts.

Non-cents: In 2001 a bill was introduced in Congress to discontinue use of the penny.

• For these reasons, Ben and Deborah never formally married; instead, on September 1, 1730, they simply began presenting themselves to the community as man and wife. Such a "common-law" marriage, as it was called, was (barely) formal enough to satisfy community standards and Deborah's family, yet it spared Franklin the risk of being branded a bigamist or having to assume Rogers's debts.

What Poor Richard Said: "He that lieth down with dogs shall rise up with fleas."

What Franklin Did: Not long after he and Deborah were "married," Franklin brought home an infant son, William, that he'd fathered by another woman. Out of that one indiscretion would flow years of pain for the Franklin family: Deborah's relationship with her stepson was predictably strained; by the time he reached his twenties they barely spoke and she had taken to calling him "the greatest villain upon earth." Years later William sided with the English during the Revolutionary War, opening a breach between father and son that would never heal. When Ben Franklin died in 1790, he disinherited his son, "leaving him no more of an estate he endeavoured to deprive me of."

What Poor Richard Said: "A good Wife and Health is a Man's best Wealth."

What Franklin Did: So what thanks did Deborah get for raising Franklin's illegitimate son as her own? Not much—in addition to cheating on her throughout their long "marriage," Franklin virtually abandoned her in her old age, leaving her alone for five years while he went off to live in London from 1757 to 1762, and again in 1764, this time for more than a decade. He never returned home to visit, not even when Deborah suffered a stroke in the winter of 1768–69. When she died in 1774, she had not seen him in more than 10 years.

*   *   *

"Ben Franklin was a crafty and lecherous old hypocrite whose very statue seems to gloat on the wenches as they walk the States House yard."
                        —**William Cobbett (1763–1835), English politician**

Top-ranked democracy, worldwide: Norway. The U.S. ranked 19th.

POLITICAL ANIMALS

Think your elected representative is a turkey? You're not alone. From ancient to modern times, all kinds of critters have entered politics. And some have even been more popular than their human counterparts.

INCITATUS

The brief reign of the Roman emperor Caligula (AD 37–41) was marked by eccentric behavior (some historians call it insanity), some of which involved Incitatus, his prize stallion. Caligula was a passionate racing fan, and Incitatus was the fastest horse in the Roman Empire. Caligula came to believe that his horse was victorious because he possessed not only speed, but also a high intelligence. The emperor provided a house, furniture, and servants for Incitatus so that the horse could meet and entertain dignitaries. Sitting at Incitatus's table, senators and nobles were forced to toast his health and respectfully speak to him about state business. Declared a full citizen of Rome, Incitatus was even given the title of deputy high priest. The steed received a hefty salary for "supervising" temples built in honor of the emperor. He was even appointed senator, and was in line for more high honors when real senators—tired of their emperor's horsing around—helped assassinate Caligula in AD 41. Most historians say that Caligula's appointment of a horse to public office was a sign of his progressive mental illness, but others believe Caligula was just humiliating his enemies in the senate.

PIGASUS

During the 1968 presidential election, the United States was deeply divided over the war in Vietnam. That August, thousands of antiwar activists gathered at the Democratic National Convention in Chicago to protest. Among them were members of the Youth International Party, or "Yippies." They bought a young boar at a local farm (folk singer Phil Ochs paid for it), named him Pigasus the Immortal, and made him their candidate for president. On August 23, with great media fanfare, Yippie leader Jerry Rubin stood in front of the Chicago Civic Center and announced Pigasus's candidacy. Along with the nomination, Rubin was about to announce the pig's first press conference, where (according to

The word *candidate* comes from the Latin *candidatus*, meaning "one clad in white."

Rubin) Pigasus would not only answer reporters' questions but also demand a White House foreign policy briefing. But before Rubin could say anything, the Chicago police converged on the news conference and arrested him and his friends on charges of disorderly conduct and bringing livestock into the city. As for Pigasus, photos show policemen surrounding the captured candidate—right before they took him to the local humane society. (He was later adopted by members of the commune known as the Hog Farm.)

CACARECO

The saying that politicians need to be thick-skinned might explain why this female rhinoceros won São Paulo, Brazil's, 1958 city council election in a landslide. With a population of well over three million, the city suffered from such problems as unpaved streets, open sewers, food shortages, and rampant inflation, but officials had ignored them for years. When the city council elections were held, local college students decided to run a protest campaign and picked Cacareco, who lived in the São Paulo Zoo, as their candidate. (Part of the attraction might have been that her name means "garbage" in Portuguese.) In all, 540 candidates—including many well-known incumbents—participated in the election, but voters were so eager to embarrass the failed city government that Cacareco won easily with a spectacular 100,000 votes. And even though the city hastily disqualified her from serving, Cacareco's win made news around the world. "Better a rhinoceros than an ass," a voter explained, and the quote made *Time* magazine. Cacareco's election left a legacy: Today in Brazil, a protest vote is known as a *voto Cacareco*.

* * *

WHAT'S IN YOUR LIPSTICK?

In 2006 the U.S. Food and Drug Administration revised its rules for the manufacture of beauty products such as hair spray and lipstick. From now on, beauty companies are forbidden to use any cow brains in their products...at least from older cattle. The brain parts taken from younger cows, however, are still allowed.

Ronald Reagan was once rejected for a film role because he "didn't have the presidential look."

WHEN HARRY MET BESSIE

We often think of presidents and First Ladies as stodgy old men and women. But they too were once young—and the stories of how these power couples first got together show a human side to the presidency.

When Georgie Met Martha: In 1758 Martha Dandridge Curtis was 27 and recently widowed, and a very wealthy woman. That year George Washington, also 27 and already a colonel in the Virginia militia—and not at all wealthy—met Martha via the Virginia high-society social scene and proceeded to court her. Courtship was quick, and they were married in January 1759, in what at the time was viewed as a marriage of convenience. They were, however, happily married for 41 years. (Note: The marriage took place at the plantation that Martha owned, in what was called the "White House.")

When Johnny Met Louisa: Louisa Catherine Johnson, who was born in London, met John Quincy Adams at her home in Nantes, France, in 1779. She was 4; he was 12. Adams was traveling with his father, John Adams, who was on a diplomatic mission in Europe. The two met again in 1795 in London, when John was a minister to the Netherlands. He courted her, all the while telling her she'd have to improve herself if she was going to live up to his family's standards (his father was vice president at the time). She married him anyway, in 1797—and his family made it no secret that they disapproved of the "foreigner" in their family. Nevertheless, they were married until John Quincy Adams's death in 1848. Louisa remains the only foreign-born First Lady in U.S. history.

When Jimmy Met Ann: In the summer of 1819, James Buchanan, 28, became engaged to Ann Coleman, 23, the daughter of a wealthy iron magnate in Lancaster, Pennsylvania. He spent very little time with her during the first months of the engagement, being extremely busy at his law office, and rumors swirled that he was seeing other women and was only marrying her for her money. The rumors are believed to be untrue, but Ann took them to heart, and in November, after several distraught weeks, she wrote to him that the engagement was off. On December 9 she died of an overdose of laudanum, possibly in a suicide. Buchanan was devastated, and even more so when her family refused to allow him to see

---

Makes sense: In Kentucky it's illegal for politicians to hand out booze on Election Day.

Ann's body or attend her funeral. He disappeared for some time but eventually returned to his work in Lancaster. After Ann's death, Buchanan vowed that he would never marry. He didn't…and remains the only bachelor president in American history.

When Gracie Met Calvin: One day in 1903, Grace Anna Goodhue was watering flowers outside the Clarke School for the Deaf in Northampton, Massachusetts, where she taught. At some point, she looked up and saw a man through the open window of a boardinghouse across the street. He was shaving, his face covered with lather, and dressed in his long johns. He was also wearing a hat. Grace burst out laughing, and the man turned to look at her. That was the first meeting of Grace and Calvin Coolidge. They were married two years later.

When Harry Met Bessie: In 1890, when they were both small children, Harry Truman met Bess Wallace at the Baptist Church in Independence, Missouri. They were both attending Sunday school—he was six; she was five. Truman later wrote of their first meeting: "We made a number of new acquaintances, and I became interested in one in particular. She had golden curls and has, to this day, the most beautiful blue eyes. We went to Sunday school, public school from the fifth grade through high school, graduated in the same class, and marched down life's road together. For me she still has the blue eyes and golden hair of yesteryear." Bess and Harry were married in 1919.

When Lyndie Met Lady Bird: Lyndon Baines Johnson met Claudia "Lady Bird" Taylor in 1934, a few weeks after she'd graduated from the University of Texas. Johnson was a 26-year-old aide to Texas congressman Richard Kleberg, and was in Austin, Texas, on business. They went on a single breakfast date, at the end of which Johnson proposed marriage. She said she'd think about it. He returned to Washington, and sent her letters and telegrams every day until he returned to Austin 10 weeks later, when she accepted. "Sometimes," she later wrote about her husband, "Lyndon simply takes your breath away."

When Richie Met Pattie: Thelma "Pat" Ryan graduated from the University of Southern California in 1937 at the age of 25. She got a job as a high school teacher in Whittier, a small town not far from Los Angeles, and became a member of the amateur theatrical group the Whittier

Community Players. In 1938 Richard Nixon, a 26-year-old lawyer who had just opened a firm in nearby La Habra, joined the theater group, thinking that acquiring acting skills would help him in the courtroom. In their first performance, Nixon was cast opposite Ryan. He asked her out—and asked her to marry him on their first date. They were married three years later.

When Ronnie Met Nancy: Ronald Reagan wrote in his autobiography that he first met Nancy Davis when she came to him for help. He was president of the Screen Actors Guild, and she couldn't get a job acting in movies because another Nancy Davis's name had shown up on the Hollywood blacklist of alleged communists. But according to Jon Weiner's book *Professors, Politics, and Pop*, SAG records show that Nancy's blacklist problem occurred in 1953—a year after the Reagans were married. So how did they meet? Reagan biographer Anne Edwards says that in 1949 Nancy, who had just become an MGM contract player, told a friend of Reagan's that she wanted to meet him. The friend invited the two to a small dinner party, and the rest is history.

When Georgie Met Laura: Joe and Jan O'Neill lived in Midland, Texas, and were childhood friends of Laura Welch. In 1975 another childhood friend, George W. Bush, came back to Midland after being away for a few years. The O'Neills bugged Laura to go out with George, but she didn't want to. She later said that the O'Neills were only trying to get them together "because we were the only two people from that era in Midland who were still single." She finally agreed to meet him at a backyard barbecue in 1977, when she was 30 and he was 31. George was smitten; Laura was, too. They were married three months later.

When Barry Met Michelle. In 1989 Michelle Robinson was working at a Chicago law firm when she was assigned to mentor a summer associate from Harvard with a "strange name"—Barack Obama. Not long after, Barack, 27, asked Michelle, 25, on a date. She later admitted that she was reluctant to date one of the few black men at the large firm because it seemed "tacky." Robinson finally relented, and after dating for several months, she suggested they get married. He wasn't interested. One night in 1991, during dinner at a Chicago restaurant, she brought it up again. Again, he said no. But when dessert showed up, there was an engagement ring in a box on one of the plates. They were married in 1992.

Studies show: If an 18-year-old votes, his or her parents are also likely to.

JOE McCARTHY'S LIST

Here's an article from the book It's a Conspiracy *about one of the darkest times
in American politics. In the 1950s, Senator Joseph McCarthy had the nation
believing that Red Agents had infiltrated the U.S. government. But were
the real conspirators the Communists…or McCarthy and his allies?*

THE GREAT DIVIDE

On February 9, 1950, Joe McCarthy, a rumpled, ill-shaven junior senator from Wisconsin, made a Lincoln's Birthday speech to a Republican women's club in Wheeling, West Virginia. No one—not even McCarthy—considered it an important appearance. Yet that speech made Senator Joseph McCarthy one of the most feared men in America.

Waving a piece of paper before the group, McCarthy declared, "I have here in my hand a list of 205 names made known to the Secretary of State as being members of the Communist Party, who are nevertheless still working and shaping policy in the State Department."

Republicans had been calling Democrats Communists for years. But before this, no one had ever claimed to know exactly how many Communists were in the government. McCarthy's speech made headlines. By the time he had given a similar speech in Salt Lake City, Utah, and returned to Washington, newspapers from coast to coast had repeated the charges. The country was in an uproar. The McCarthy Era—an American Inquisition that ruined the lives of thousands of innocent citizens accused of being Communists, Communist dupes, or Communist sympathizers—had begun.

SEEING RED

McCarthy's influence grew rapidly. As the chairman of the Permanent Investigations Sub-Committee of a Senate Committee on Government Operations, he presided over a witch hunt for Communists. Fear became his most potent weapon. According to Kenneth C. Davis in the book *Don't Know Much About History*, "Many of those who came before McCarthy, as well as many who testified before the powerful House Un-American Activities Committee (HUAC), were willing to point fingers at others to save their own careers and reputations. To fight back was to be

---

The Capitol Building in Washington, D.C., is rumored to be haunted by a demonic cat.

tarred with MacCarthy's 'Communist sympathizer' brush....In this cynical atmosphere, laws of evidence and constitutional guarantees didn't apply."

For four years, McCarthy was as powerful as anyone in Washington. He forced President Eisenhower to clear appointments through him; the president even instituted loyalty programs for those working for the government to prove that he, too, was tough on Communism.

WAS IT A CONSPIRACY? #1

Did McCarthy and his cronies actually believe that there was a Communist conspiracy, or was it just an attempt to gain power? Some suspicious facts:

• Early in 1950, McCarthy told friends he needed a gimmick to get reelected. He was in political hot water with voters because he had introduced no major legislation and had not been assigned to any important committees. Newspaper correspondents in Washington had voted him "worst in the Senate."

• According to Frederick Woltman, a friend of the senator's, McCarthy had made up the number of Communists on the spur of the moment during his Lincoln's Birthday speech—and had just as promptly forgotten it. Caught off-guard by the outcry, McCarthy and his advisors wracked their brains for some lead as to what he said in the Wheeling speech. But he didn't keep a copy, and he had no notes. And his aides couldn't find anyone who remembered the exact number.

• That may be why every time McCarthy counted Communists, he came up with a different number. The day after the Wheeling speech, he changed the number from 205 to 57 "card-carrying Communists." A week later, he stated before a Senate Foreign Relations subcommittee that he knew of "81 known Communists." The number changed to 10 in open committee hearings, 116 in an executive session, 121 at the end of a four-month investigation, and 106 in a June 6 Senate speech.

• Privately, friends say McCarthy treated the list of Communists as a joke. In the book *The Nightmare Decade: The Life and Times of Senator Joe McCarthy*, Fred Cook writes, "When he was asked, 'Joe, just what did you have in your hand down there in Wheeling?' McCarthy gave his characteristic roguish grin and replied, 'An old laundry list.'"

• McCarthy was able to keep up the charade for so long because he would attack anybody who questioned his accuracy. For example: When the majority leader of the Senate, unable to get a firm number from McCarthy, asked if the newspaper accounts of his Wheeling speech were accurate, McCarthy replied indignantly, "I may say if the senator is going to make a farce of this, I will not yield to him. I shall not answer more silly questions of the Senator. This is too important, too serious a matter for that."

WAS IT A CONSPIRACY? #2

Was top lawman J. Edgar Hoover a coconspirator—even though it meant he was breaking the law? (The FBI's charter prohibits it from getting involved in domestic politics.) Evidence suggests he was. In fact, without Hoover's covert support, McCarthy couldn't have kept up his attacks. More suspicious facts:

• McCarthy and Hoover were friends. The often dined together, and played the ponies frequently.

• According to Curt Gentry in his book *J. Edgar Hoover: The Man and the Secrets,* "On returning home from his speaking tour, McCarthy called Hoover and told him he was getting a lot of attention on the Communist issue. But, he frankly admitted, he had made up the numbers as he talked…and he asked if the FBI could give him the information to back him up." William Sullivan, who later became third in command at the FBI, protested that the Bureau didn't have sufficient evidence to prove that there was even *one* Communist in the State Department.

• Hoover—completely ignoring the FBI's charter—assigned FBI agents to gather domestic intelligence on his ideological enemies, poring over hundreds of Bureau security files to help support McCarthy's charges.

• According to Gentry, Hoover did even more: "He supplied speechwriters for McCarthy…[One Hoover aide] personally took McCarthy in hand and instructed him how to release a story just before the press deadline, so that reporters wouldn't have time to ask for rebuttals. Even more importantly, he advised him to avoid the phrase 'card-carrying Communist,' which usually couldn't be proven, substituting instead 'Communist sympathizer' or 'loyalty risk,' which required only some affiliation, however slight."

• As McCarthy's star rose, Hoover helped the senator pick his staff. In fact, McCarthy hired so many ex-FBI agents that his office was reportedly nicknamed "the little FBI."

• Hoover was concerned about McCarthy's reckless charges—but not because they were untrue. A Hoover crony noted: "I've spoken to J. Edgar Hoover about McCarthy. He said the only trouble with Joe is that he's not general enough in his accusations. He'll give some number like '275 Communists.' And then the FBI has to account for them. It makes the job a whole lot tougher."

McCARTHY'S DOWNFALL

When McCarthy began attacking President Eisenhower and the U.S. Army in 1954, Hoover sensed that his own job might be in danger and ordered the FBI aides to not help the senator further. Poorly prepared, McCarthy attempted to bluff his way through televised army hearings, but this time he failed. Most Americans saw him as a bully and a liar, and the press turned on him. In December 1954, McCarthy became the fourth member in history to be censured by the U.S. Senate. In May 1957, he died of alcohol-related ailments.

DISTURBING FOOTNOTES

Apparently, McCarthy depended on his coconspirators at the FBI for more than information—he also needed their silence. Curt Gentry's extensive research suggests that:

• Hoover had several fat FBI files on McCarthy that could have destroyed his career. Much of the information they contained eventually became known: that McCarthy was a boozer and a chronic gambler; that he had exaggerated and lied about his military record during World War II; that as a Wisconsin judge he had granted "quickie divorces" for a price; and that he had used campaign contributions to speculate on the stock market.

• Gentry adds that there was another, more secret file on McCarthy that only Hoover and a handful of other agents had ever seen: "It concerned McCarthy's involvement with young girls. Very young girls…Former close personal friends of the senator were quoted in the memorandum as cautioning other friends that they should never leave McCarthy with young children, that there had been 'incidents.'"

The impact that McCarthyism had on the entertainment industry changed Hollywood forever. For that story, go to page 185.

EMPEROR NORTON

Once he was "Emperor of the United States." Now he's forgotten—swept into Uncle John's Dustbin of History.

FORGOTTEN FIGURE: Joshua Norton, a wealthy 19th-century businessman and speculator who settled in San Francisco

CLAIM TO FAME: In 1853 Norton bet his fortune on the rice market and lost it all; by 1856 he was completely bankrupt. The experience left him mentally deranged, his head filled with delusions that he was emperor of California. In 1859 Norton promoted himself to emperor of the United States, and when the Civil War seemed inevitable, he issued proclamations abolishing the U.S. Congress and dissolving the republic, and assumed the powers of the American presidency.

No one listened, of course, but as the years passed, Californians—San Franciscans especially—began to treat Norton as if he really were an emperor: Riverboat companies and even the Central Pacific Railroad gave him lifetime free passes, and the state senate set aside a special seat for him in the senate chamber. Theaters admitted him without a ticket, and audiences showed their deference by standing as the emperor entered the hall. He printed 25¢ and 50¢ banknotes…which were accepted by local businesses.

When the San Francisco Police arrested him for lunacy, the judge dressed down the officers for detaining a man who "had shed no blood, robbed no one, and despoiled no country, which is more than can be said for most fellows in the king line."

Even city hall played along, picking up the tab for Norton's 50¢-a-night "Imperial Palace" (a room in a boardinghouse), and buying him a new set of clothes from the prestigious Bullock and Jones tailors when Norton's "Imperial Wardrobe," which consisted of old military uniforms combined with a collection of crazy hats, became tattered and worn.

INTO THE DUSTBIN: Although largely forgotten today, when Emperor Norton died penniless in 1880 at the age of 61, a millionaire's club picked up the tab for his lavish imperial funeral. More than 3,000 people attended, making it one of the largest funerals ever held in San Francisco.

What's Neville Bonner's claim to fame? He became Australia's 1st Aboriginal senator in 1971.

LIBERAL JUSTICE

William O. Douglas (1898–1980) served on the Supreme Court for 40 years, longer than anyone else. He was an outspoken liberal who said what he believed and didn't care if it ruffled anyone's feathers.

"We must realize that today's Establishment is the new George III. Whether it will continue to adhere to his tactics, we do not know. If it does, the redress, honored in tradition, is also revolution."

"If Nixon is not forced to turn over tapes of his conversations with the ring of men who were conversing on their violations of the law, then liberty will soon be dead in this nation."

"At the constitutional level where we work, 90 percent of any decision is emotional. The rational part of us supplies the reasons for supporting our predilections."

"I do not know of any salvation for society except through eccentrics, misfits, dissenters, people who protest."

"There is more to the right to vote than the right to mark a piece of paper and drop it in a box or the right to pull a lever in a voting booth. It also includes the right to have the vote counted at full value without dilution or discount."

"Political or religious dissenters are the plague of every totalitarian regime."

"Communism has been so thoroughly exposed in this country that it has been crippled as a political force. Free speech has destroyed it as an effective political party."

"It is better, the Fourth Amendment teaches us, that the guilty sometimes go free than the citizens be subject to easy arrest."

"Advocacy and belief go hand in hand. For there can be no true freedom of mind if thoughts are secure only when they are pent up."

"The great postulate of our democracy is confidence in the common sense of the people and in their maturity of judgment, even on great issues—once they know the facts."

"I have the same confidence in the ability of our people to reject noxious literature as I have in their capacity to sort out the true from the false in theology, economics, or any other field."

The Democratic theme song, "Happy Days Are Here Again," comes from a movie…

MR. CONSERVATIVE

*Arizona senator Barry Goldwater was defeated in a landslide when he ran
as the Republican candidate for president in 1964. But at the same time,
he started the modern conservative movement. Often outrageously
blunt, he was widely respected as a man of honesty and principle.*

"The income tax created more criminals than any other single act of government."

"Sometimes I think this country could be better off if we would just saw off the Eastern seaboard and let it float off to sea."

"The Democrats want to save more on defense so they can spend more money to buy votes through the welfare state."

"We cannot allow the American flag to be shot at anywhere on Earth if we are to retain our respect and prestige."

"We are not far from the kind of moral decay that has brought on the fall of other nations and peoples."

"We should get back to the doctrine of brinksmanship, where everybody knows we have the power and will use it."

"If they chased every man or woman out of this town who has shacked up with somebody else or got drunk, there wouldn't be any government left in Washington."

"I don't want to see this country run by big business and big labor."

"I don't necessarily vote a straight ticket in my own state because there are sometimes Democrats out there who are better than Republicans. It's hard to believe but it's true."

"War is but an instrument of international policy."

"We can be lied to only so many times. The best thing that Nixon can do for the country is to get the hell out of the White House and get out this afternoon."

"No matter what you do, be honest. That sticks out in Washington."

FEMA FAKERS

When you're watching a press conference on the news, you'd expect the reporters to be, you know, real. But as the following story illustrates, sometimes the government spin machine spins out of control.

CULPRIT: Federal Emergency Management Agency (FEMA)
GRAND SCHEME: Still reeling from their heavily criticized response to Hurricane Katrina in 2005, FEMA officials—knowing that all eyes were upon them during the 2007 wildfire season—wanted to reassure California citizens that they had everything under control. So on the afternoon of October 23, 2007, the agency informed the major news outlets of a press conference at their Washington, D.C., office…to take place in 15 minutes. Reporters were also given a number to call, but it was a "listen only" line. During the conference (broadcast live on several cable news outlets), reporters asked Deputy Director Harvey Johnson, "Are you happy with FEMA's response so far?" He replied, "I'm very happy with FEMA's response so far." Another asked, "Do you think FEMA has learned its lesson since Katrina?" Again, Johnson answered positively. That was the way the entire briefing went—not a single tough question, such as the reports of formaldehyde being present in trailers used to shelter those who'd lost their homes.

EXPOSED! Many *actual* reporters smelled a rat, and it didn't take much digging to discover that the press conference was staffed by FEMA employees posing as reporters. When the story broke, Johnson explained that his staff was forced to pull the ruse because no real reporters had showed up (even though they were only given 15 minutes' advance notice). Plus, he said, "We pulled questions from those we had been getting from reporters earlier in the day."

OUTCOME: Everyone from the Bush White House to major media outlets was furious with FEMA's tactics. Homeland Security Chief Michael Chertoff barked, "I think it was one of the dumbest, most inappropriate things I've seen since I've been in government. I've made unambiguously clear, in Anglo-Saxon prose, that it is not to ever happen again, and there will be appropriate disciplinary action taken against those people who exhibited what I regard as extraordinarily poor judgment." In the end, a few reprimands were given, but no one was fired.

Former Doobie Brothers guitarist Jeff "Skunk" Baxter advises Congress on missile defense.

JOIN THE PARTY: THE DEMOCRATIC-REPUBLICANS

On page 49, we told you about the birth of North America's first political party: the Federalists, led by Alexander Hamilton. Here's the next part of the story.

MEETING OF THE MINDS

As Hamilton was mobilizing his people, so was Thomas Jefferson. In May 1791, he and fellow Virginian James Madison made a trip to New York to meet with State Chancellor Robert Livingston, New York governor George Clinton, and U.S. senator Aaron Burr. According to the book *The Life of the Parties* by A. James Reichley, "The meetings among the New York and Virginia leaders, however informal, were among the most fateful in American history. The first links were formed in an alliance that was to last, in one form or another, for almost 150 years and that was to be a major shaping force in national politics from the administration of Jefferson to that of Franklin Roosevelt."

Jefferson, Madison, and the others saw themselves as defenders of the new republic against Hamilton and the "monarchical Federalists." The party they formed became known as the Democratic-Republicans, or Republicans for short. Historians consider them the first opposition party in U.S. history, as well as the direct antecedent of the modern Democratic Party.

THE ALIEN AND SEDITION ACTS

The Democratic-Republicans lost their battle: Hamilton pushed his bank legislation through Congress, and President Washington signed it into law. They lost another major battle in 1792 when Governor Clinton ran against John Adams for vice president and lost. A third defeat came in 1796 when Washington declined to run for a third term as president: Jefferson ran for president against Vice President Adams…and lost by only three electoral votes.

In 1793 France—which was in the throes of its own revolution—declared war against England, giving the Federalists and Democratic-Republicans something new to disagree about. The Jeffersonian

---

The political terms "left" and "right" were coined during the French Revolution.

Republicans sided with republican France, and the Federalists sided with England. But neither side thought the United States should get involved in the war. Partisan emotions intensified in 1796, when the French began an undeclared war on American shipping as part of their war against England and refused to receive President Adams's minister to France.

Angered by the insults, the Federalists began preparing for what they thought was an imminent war with France. They tripled the size of the army, authorized the creation of the U.S. Navy (the Continental Navy had been disbanded in 1784), and then in the face of the unanimous opposition of the Democratic-Republicans in Congress, passed what became known as the Alien and Sedition Acts.

The Alien Acts said that aliens (who were assumed to have Democratic-Republican leanings) had to live in the United States for 14 years—up from 5—before they would be eligible to vote. The acts also permitted the detention of citizens of enemy nations and increased the president's power to deport "dangerous" aliens. The Sedition Act outlawed all associations whose purpose was "to oppose any measure of the government of the United States," and imposed stiff punishments for writing, printing, or saying anything against the U.S. government.

READING BETWEEN THE LINES

By the time the Alien and Sedition Acts expired or were repealed four years later, only one alien had been deported and only 10 people were convicted of sedition, including a New Jersey man who was fined $100 for publicly "wishing that a wad from the presidential saluting cannon might 'hit Adams in the ass.'"

But no one knew that back in 1798. To Jefferson and his supporters, it was obvious that the Alien Acts, and especially the Sedition Act, were targeted at them. Republicans could now be fined or jailed for speaking out against the Adams administration, and if they weren't U.S. citizens, they could even be deported.

The fact that the Sedition Act expired after the 1800 presidential election seemed to prove their suspicions that the law was intended to curb Anti-Federalist dissent. While the acts were in force, Adams and the Federalists were legally protected from Democratic-Republican criticism, but if they happened to lose the 1800 election, the expiration of the Sedition Act would leave them free to criticize the Democratic-Republicans.

U.S. gov't secrecy designations, lowest to highest: Confidential, Secret, Top Secret, Sigma 16.

There was more: The Democratic-Republicans also feared that Adams, having tripled the size of the army, would begin using it against his political opponents. As if to confirm their fears, in 1799 Adams called out federal troops to put down an anti-tax rebellion led by Pennsylvania farmers opposed to taxes levied for the anticipated war with France.

The Democratic-Republicans were convinced that if the Federalists remained in power, democracy's days were numbered, so they embarked on their strongest effort yet to capture the White House and Congress.

A TOUGH CALL

John Adams had mixed feelings about running for reelection. He hated living in Washington, D.C., and he hated being president. The president "has a very hard, laborious, and unhappy life," he warned his son John Quincy Adams. "No man who ever held the office of president would congratulate a friend on obtaining it." And now that he was completely toothless, he was incapable of making public speeches in support of his candidacy for reelection.

The only reason Adams ran at all was because he was determined to prevent Jefferson from getting the job. Adams liked Jefferson personally, but he saw himself and Jefferson as "the North and South poles of the American Revolution." He strongly disagreed with Jefferson's views on government and the Constitution, and feared that Jefferson would drag the country into a European war to defend France.

CHANGE OF FORTUNE

The Democratic-Republicans, who believed that freedom was on the line, had no such reluctance—although Jefferson, announcing that he would "stand" for election rather than "run" for it, remained at his Monticello estate during the campaign. The party fought a hard campaign for him.

On election day, Adams carried New England, and Jefferson won most of the South. New York proved to be the swing state, which helped Jefferson, because his running mate was Aaron Burr. As founder and head of the Tammany political machine in New York, Burr was able to deliver the state to Jefferson, allowing him to win the presidency with 73 electoral votes to Adams's 65. The Democratic-Republicans also won control of both houses of Congress.

FEDERALIST FAREWELL

The Federalists had accomplished much in the years following the Revolution: They had succeeded in drafting the U.S. Constitution, which strengthened the power of the federal government; they had enacted economic programs that strengthened credit and helped the economy grow.

But by 1800 their best days were behind them. "Federalism, as a political movement, was a declining force around the turn of the century," historian Paul Johnson writes in *A History of the American People*, "precisely because it was a party of the elite, without popular roots, at a time when democracy was spreading fast among the states. Adams was the last of the Federalist presidents, and he could not get himself reelected."

THE LAST STRAW

It got worse for the Federalists. They vehemently opposed the War of 1812, and in the fall of 1814, when things seemed to be going very badly for the United States, Federalist delegates from New England met secretly in Hartford, Connecticut, to draft a series of resolutions listing their grievances with the federal government, which a negotiating committee would then bring to Washington, D.C. Some of the delegates to the secret convention had even discussed seceding from the Union.

Bad timing: By the time the negotiating committee arrived in Washington to protest the war, it was not only over, it had actually ended on a positive note, thanks to General Andrew Jackson's victory in the Battle of New Orleans.

When the rest of the country learned that the Federalists had been holding secret meetings to contemplate splitting off from the rest of the country, the party's image took a pounding. "Republican orators and publicists branded the Hartford convention an act of subversion during wartime," A. James Reichley writes, "ending what was left of Federalism as a political force."

But the die was cast. In spite of themselves, the Founding Fathers had created what they most feared: political factions. The era of the two-party system in the United States had begun.

To learn about Old Hickory and the rise of the Democratic Party,
go to page 153...or else we will have to challenge you to a duel!

POLITICAL SQUIRMING

Few people have mastered the fine art of the excuse/apology as well as seasoned politicians have. Let's all watch as they try to squirm their way out of some embarrassing political predicaments.

POLITICIAN: Rep. Frank Chopp (D-WA)
OFFENSE: In 2007, during debates over whether a taxpayer-funded NASCAR raceway should be built near Seattle, a reporter asked Chopp, who opposed the raceway, if he was aware that racing legend Richard Petty was currently in town to promote it. Chopp's response: "You mean that guy who got a DUI?" Realizing his mistake, Chopp quickly started backtracking.

SQUIRM: "By the way, on that last point, I was told that—so I'm not sure. You better check to make sure it's accurate."

AFTERMATH: Not only was it inaccurate, but Petty has long advocated *against* drunk driving—he even refuses sponsorship from any company that sells alcohol. The next day, Chopp invited Petty to his office to apologize personally. Petty hadn't heard what Chopp had said; he figured the congressman was simply apologizing for his opposition. But when Petty found out later, he said, "I'm glad you didn't tell me that before because I might have went off on him. I don't drink, okay?" He then joked, "I'm not saying I don't run over people when I'm sober, though."

POLITICIAN: California governor Arnold Schwarzenegger
OFFENSE: During a closed-door policy meeting in 2006, the Governor made a few racy statements about Assemblywoman Bonnie Garcia. He joked that Garcia's "black blood" and "Latino blood" made her "very hot." The tape was leaked to the press, and Schwarzenegger's comments were printed in newspapers all over the United States, prompting this apology.

SQUIRM: "Anyone out there that feels offended by these comments, I just want to say I'm sorry. The fact is that if I would hear these kinds of comments in my house, by my kids, I would be upset, and today, when I read it in the papers, it made me cringe."

AFTERMATH: The person least upset by the comments was Garcia

Was he a D or an Arrgh? The Bahamas' 1st governor, Woodes Rogers, was a former pirate.

herself. In fact, she saw it as a compliment. "I love the governor because he is a straight talker, just like I am," she said. "Very often I tell him, 'Look, I *am* a hot-blooded Latina,' and this is kind of an inside joke that I have with him."

POLITICIAN: Tom DeLay (R-TX), House majority leader

OFFENSE: In 2005 DeLay commented on the controversial rulings of the federal judges in the case of Terri Schiavo, the brain-damaged Florida woman who spent 15 years in a persistent vegetative state and was at the center of a battle between family members over whether to maintain her life support. "We will look at an arrogant, out-of-control, unaccountable judiciary that thumbed their nose at the Congress and the president," said DeLay, who then added, "The time will come for the men responsible to answer for their behavior." Critics on both sides accused DeLay of advocating violence against the judges, prompting him to elaborate…more on the wording itself than the implications it suggested.

SQUIRM: "I said something in an inartful way. I shouldn't have said it that way, and I apologize for saying it that way. It was taken wrong. I didn't explain it or clarify my remarks, as I'm clarifying them here. I am sorry that I said it that way, and I shouldn't have."

AFTERMATH: DeLay weathered that storm, but soon found himself at the heart of another scandal—receiving gifts from a lobbyist in exchange for favorable legislation. In January 2006, he resigned from his post as House Majority Leader, and in April resigned from his seat in congress.

POLITICIAN: Ray Nagin, mayor of New Orleans

OFFENSE: During the aftermath of Hurricane Katrina, the African American mayor spoke of his plans for rebuilding his hometown. "This city will be chocolate at the end of the day," he proudly announced. "You can't have New Orleans no other way—it wouldn't be New Orleans." The remark "chocolate city" outraged not only his fellow politicians, but also many New Orleans citizens who felt it was a limited and racist portrayal. Nagin needed to save face, and quick, as he was up for reelection.

SQUIRM: "How do you make chocolate? You take dark chocolate, you mix it with white milk, and it becomes a delicious drink. That is the chocolate I am talking about. New Orleans was a chocolate city before Katrina. It is going to be a chocolate city after. How is that divisive? It is

The Nehru jacket was named after Jawaharial Nehru, India's 1st prime minister.

white and black working together and making something special."
AFTERMATH: Nagin won reelection.

POLITICIAN: Cynthia Hedge-Morrell (D), New Orleans city council-woman

OFFENSE: Late for a meeting with FEMA officials in February 2007, Hedge-Morrell checked out a government-issued SUV and sped down the highway at nearly 100 mph with the vehicle's blue lights flashing, weaving in and out of cars and driving on the shoulder. When a state trooper pulled her over, Hedge-Morrell refused to exit the vehicle, yelling, "Do you know who I am? What the hell are you stopping me for?" After waiting a few minutes for a police supervisor to show up, Hedge-Morrell was released without a speeding ticket. New Orleans citizens, still weary of their elected officials' bungled response to Hurricane Katrina, demanded that Hedge-Morrell not be given special treatment just because she's on the city council. Said Gary Russo, the driver who called 911 on the former elementary school principal, "We all have to deal with traffic, simple as that. She ain't the president."

SQUIRM: "I deeply regret the incident, and I will be a more careful driver in the future. I take responsibility for my actions, because when I taught children, I always told them to step up and take responsibility when you make a mistake. Admit what you did, and use the word 'I.'"

AFTERMATH: Hedge-Morrell was never issued a ticket, remained on the city council, and kept using the taxpayer-funded SUV (with a driver).

POLITICIAN: Former U.S. Rep. Rick Santorum (R-PA)

OFFENSE: While running for president in January 2012, Santorum was speaking at a fund-raiser in Iowa. According to the video of the event, Santorum appears to have said, "I don't want to make black people's lives better by giving them somebody else's money." His critics, including the NAACP, charged that the comment was racist because it singled out African Americans as the only ones living off the welfare state.

SQUIRM: "I looked at the video. I'm pretty confident I didn't say 'black.' What I think—I started to say a word and then sort of changed and it sort of said—'blah'—mumbled it and sort of changed my thought."

AFTERMATH: Despite a drubbing in the press—"*SANTORUM HATES BLAH PEOPLE!*"—he went on to win the Iowa caucus.

In 2008 Barack Obama had 459,000 friends on MySpace. Miley Cyrus: 552,000.

THREE NEAR MISSES

Here at the BRI, we're always amazed at the role that chance plays in life. Take these three instances, for example:

JFK'S EAGLES

In 1985 Norman Braman, owner of the NFL's Philadelphia Eagles, was visiting the U.S. Capitol when Senator Edward Kennedy told him the story of how John F. Kennedy considered buying the Eagles in October 1962. Not yet two years into his first term, JFK was already thinking about what he would do after leaving office. When he learned the Eagles were for sale, he and brother Bobby instructed Ted to go to Philadelphia to meet with the team's management and discuss a possible sale. But Ted never went, and someone else bought the Eagles. "What happened?" Braman asked. "The Cuban Missile Crisis," Ted told him.

POISONING GENERAL WASHINGTON

Phoebe Fraunces, the daughter of a New York tavernkeeper, reportedly saved the life of General George Washington after pretending to sympathize with English spies. When Thomas Hickey, a member of Washington's guard, told her to serve the general a plate of poisoned peas, she did so, and then whispered a warning to Washington. He (or she, depending on which version you read) immediately flipped the peas out the window, where some chickens ate them and died. Hickey was later executed for treason.

THE HUGHES H-1

In 1934 millionaire aviator Howard Hughes built an experimental plane called the *H-1*. In January 1937, it set a transcontinental speed record by flying at 332 mph from California to New Jersey, making it the fastest plane in the world. Hughes proposed to the U.S. Army that they base a fighter plane on the design, but they weren't interested. Japan was. Mitsubishi engineer Jiro Horikoshi designed a fighter plane that incorporated many of the *H-1*'s features: The "Zero" was the premier fighter plane of World War II. The United States and its allies didn't develop a plane that could match it until 1943.

POLITICS AS (UN)USUAL

*The most popular politicians are often the ones who seem like they're
"one of us"—ordinary people. But just like us ordinary people,
they sometimes make some very weird decisions.*

GETTING A LEG UP

Hajnal Ban, a city councilor in Logan City, Australia, always felt that at 5'0" she wasn't taken seriously, either as a lawyer or as a politician. So in 2001, she went to an orthopedic clinic in Russia and paid $40,000 to have her legs broken in four places. Then, over the course of nine months, surgeons stretched Ban's legs by a millimeter or so every day. After nearly a year of excruciating pain in a foreign hospital, Ban returned to her city council position...three inches taller.

SMOKING SECTION FOR ONE

In Australia, it's illegal for people under the age of 18 to smoke. But officials at the Department of Education of the Capital Territory (the district that includes the capital city of Canberra) have allowed a 16-year-old student at Stromlo High School not only to legally smoke, but to take cigarette breaks during her classes. The ruling was based on a doctor's recommendation that the student is "so clinically addicted to nicotine" that she can't function without constantly consuming it—and that *not* smoking would make her schoolwork suffer.

HOW STEREOTYPICAL

In 2006 Bonilyn Wilbanks-Free was the town manager (similar to a mayor) of Golden Beach, Florida, when she referred to one of her assistants as "Mammy." The assistant, whose name is Barbara Tarasenko, is African American, and Wilbanks-Free, who is white, was evidently referring to an old racial stereotype of smiling, motherly, African American maid characters. Tarasenko, visibly offended, wasn't any happier when Wilbanks-Free tried to soften her first comment by saying, "You know how much I love Aunt Jemima." A month later, Wilbanks-Free resigned her position.

The office of United States treasurer has been held by women since 1949.

DOWN-HOME COOKIN'

In 2008 a heated presidential campaign and a press hungry for human-interest stories was the perfect recipe for...well, "Recipegate." Presidential candidate John McCain and his wife Cindy—heiress to a multimillion-dollar beer distribution company—were often criticized by their opponents as being out of touch with ordinary Americans. To counter that image, the McCain campaign began posting "Cindy's McCain Family Recipes" on its website. One problem: The folksy recipes were lifted word for word from the Food Network website. After news outlets got hold of the story, the McCain campaign quickly deleted the recipes and blamed the "error" on a low-level staffer, who was later "disciplined."

BLOCKHEAD

A weird campaign ad from 2012 featured a mysterious, mustachioed man talking about why the U.S. needs Herman Cain. "We *can* do this," he says as the camera zooms in on his face. "We can take this country *back*!" Then—as the song "I Am America" swells up in the background—he takes a long drag of a cigarette and then blows the smoke at the camera. Most people thought it was a joke. It wasn't. The man was Cain's campaign manager, Mark Block. Anti-smoking groups were outraged. Block's defense: "I'm not the only one in America who smokes, for God's sake!"

A POLITICALLY CORRECT IDEA

In 2008 the Tunbridge Wells Borough Council in Kent, England, issued a ban on the term "brainstorming" because it is offensive to epileptics, whose seizures have been described by doctors as a "storm of the brain." Instead, the council held a brainstorming session for new, less-offensive terms, and came up with "thought sharing" and "blue-sky thinking."

WANDERING COMRADE

In 1995 the Russian presidential delegation made an official state visit to Washington, D.C. The Clinton administration put the party up in Blair House, where visiting dignitaries often stay. But in the middle of the night, Secret Service agents found a man standing in the middle of Pennsylvania Avenue in his underwear, extremely drunk and trying to hail a cab so he could go get a pizza. The agents returned the man to Blair House after they determined his identity: Russian president Boris Yeltsin.

Crime pays: Congress creates an average of 56 new federal crimes each year.

THE DONALD

Donald Trump may not have won himself the presidency, but he's won a place in our hearts as the most quotable wannabe-politician billionaire in history.

"In the second grade I punched my music teacher because I didn't think he knew much about music. I'm not proud of that, but it's clear that early on I had a tendency to stand up."

"You know, it really doesn't matter what the media write as long as you've got a young and beautiful piece of ass."

"I'll tell you, it's Big Business. If there is one word to describe Atlantic City, it's Big Business. Or two words—Big Business."

"There's no one my age who has accomplished more. Everyone can't be the best."

"It's a lot better to side with a winner than a loser."

"How about the guys that stand there grabbing the urinal for balance? I watch in amazement. Then they come up and say, 'I'm a big fan, can I shake your hand?' And I'm a bad guy for saying, 'Excuse me!' They were just holding the big wonger, and they want to shake your hand!"

"The worst thing a man can do is go bald. Never go bald."

"I have a great relationship with the blacks."

"Germ phobia is a problem. You have to be selective. It's pretty dangerous out there. It's like Vietnam! Dating is my personal Vietnam!"

"I like thinking big. If you're going to be thinking anything, you might as well think big."

"I think the only difference between me and the other candidates is that I'm more honest and my women are more beautiful."

"Listen, you motherf*ckers, we're going to tax you 25 percent!"
> **—on what he would say to China if elected president**

"I am the Democrats' worst nightmare."

"I'm not a schmuck. Even if the world goes to hell in a handbasket, I won't lose a penny."

If the minimum wage had risen at the same rate as CEO salaries, it would be $23 an hour.

POLITICAL TV TIMELINE

On April 30, 1939, Franklin Roosevelt became the first U.S. president to appear on TV, as part of a test broadcast from the New York World's Fair. It marked the last time a politician appeared on television without either slamming an opponent or praising himself.

1948: A few months before the November presidential election, Republican challenger Thomas Dewey was comfortably leading incumbent Harry Truman. Dewey's advisor, advertising veteran Rosser Reeves, urged Dewey to record campaign commercials to air in the competitive districts that had TV service—he could reach thousands of voters for relatively little cost. Dewey rejected the idea as "undignified" and chose to sit on his lead. Meanwhile, Truman went on a whistle-stop campaign train tour. Dewey's lead eroded and he lost the election.

1950: The first politician to truly recognize the persuasive power of filmed advertisements was, not surprisingly, a former ad executive. Running for a Senate seat in 1950, William Benton of Connecticut set up kiosks with rear-projection screens in shopping centers and on street corners to play his campaign commercials. It was more effective than buying time on broadcast television, because even voters who didn't have a TV could see his ads while shopping. Benton was elected, narrowly defeating Prescott Bush (father of future president George H.W. Bush).

1952: While Democrats were riding a wave of postwar prosperity to congressional power, Republicans hired Rosser Reeves to counter their slogan, "You never had it so good." Reeves came up with a television advertising blitz called "Eisenhower Answers America," featuring former general and presidential candidate Dwight Eisenhower taking "off-the-cuff" questions from everyday Americans (the questions were actually scripted). These were the first-ever presidential campaign ads to air in the United States. Eisenhower's opponent, Adlai Stevenson, went on television as well...with 30-minute-long speeches. They were so long and difficult to schedule that they aired far less often than Eisenhower's brief spots.

That same year, another politician altered the relationship between politics and television. Eisenhower's running mate, Richard Nixon, was

---

In 2005 Pakistan's supreme court banned citizens from making, selling, and flying kites.

accused of accepting illegal campaign contributions, so he went on TV to appeal directly to the public, saying that the only gift he'd received was a black-and-white dog named Checkers, for his children. The "Checkers Speech" was seen on TV and heard on radio by an estimated 60 million people, and elicited an outpouring of sympathy that historians say helped lock up the election for Eisenhower and Nixon.

1960: By this time, 90 percent of American households owned a TV set. Historians say that may have made the difference in the debate between presidential candidates John F. Kennedy and Richard Nixon. Kennedy was more media-savvy than Nixon—he knew enough to wear makeup before appearing on the first televised presidential debate. Nixon, on the other hand, was recovering from an illness at the time. He wore no make-up and appeared haggard compared to the confident, youthful-looking Kennedy (who was actually only four years younger). Polls indicated that people who watched the debate on TV thought Kennedy won; those who listened on the radio—a much smaller audience—declared Nixon the victor. Kennedy ultimately won the election by a hair.

1964: Although it ran only once—on NBC on September 7, 1964—the infamous "Daisy Ad," created by the Doyle Dane Bernbach agency, helped propel Lyndon Johnson to a landslide victory over Barry Goldwater in that year's presidential race. The commercial featured a little girl standing in a field plucking petals off a daisy, and culminated with a countdown and nuclear mushroom cloud, implying that Goldwater couldn't be trusted with his finger on the button of U.S. atomic weapons. ABC and CBS never aired the ad officially, but did show it in news programs—at no cost to the Johnson campaign—while reporting on the controversy.

1968: A turning point in American politics, the 1968 presidential election was the first time that the politicians themselves became highly polished products. Roger Ailes, a media consultant to three presidents and future president of Fox News, said at the time, "This is the beginning of a whole new concept. This is it. This is the way they'll be elected forevermore. The next guys up will have to be performers." Ted Rogers, media consultant for returning presidential candidate Richard Nixon, heard the message loud and clear. He recommended a full-on image makeover for Nixon—by fattening him up with "milkshakes, eggs, and butter" and

First slogan on a T-shirt: "Do It With Dewey" (for '48 pres. candidate Thomas Dewey).

ensuring plenty of rest to make Nixon look healthier. Nixon also realized the power of TV, so in addition to Rogers and Ailes, he hired a team of TV consultants, who devised a series of weekly televised sessions between Nixon and a hand-picked panel of sympathetic Republican citizens asking scripted questions. They were designed to make Nixon—who could come off as grumpy or aloof—look more informal (and, just to be safe, no close-ups of Nixon were allowed). Nixon was elected president that fall.

1976: Following the Watergate scandal that ended Nixon's presidency in 1974, conventional wisdom said that Americans were in no mood for another career politician as president. Result: The birth of the "regular guy" political advertisement. Democratic candidate Jimmy Carter, a peanut farmer and former Georgia governor, starred in his ads wearing jeans and a work shirt, standing out in the fields. Carter was elected.

1980: By 1980 Ailes's prediction regarding the power of television had come true—the winning presidential candidate was a former B-movie star and California governor Ronald Reagan. Television had played an important role. Reagan's folksy, optimistic campaign ads declared it "morning in America" and asked voters if they were "better off now than they were four years ago." He won by a landslide.

1988: With Republican vice president George H.W. Bush facing an uphill battle against the insurgent candidacy of Democratic Massachusetts governor Michael Dukakis, it was Ailes, then Bush's media consultant, who came to the rescue. Ailes approved an ad that painted Dukakis as soft on crime. It featured convicted murderer Willie Horton, who, while serving a life sentence in Massachusetts, was released on the weekend-pass program Dukakis approved—and then stabbed a man and raped his fiancée. "The only question," Ailes reportedly told Bush staffers, "is whether we depict Willie Horton with a knife in his hand or without it."

1992: For the first time in decades, the presidential race featured a viable third-party candidate: billionaire Texas businessman H. Ross Perot, running as an independent against incumbent Republican president George H.W. Bush and Democratic Arkansas governor Bill Clinton. Rather than pay for 30-second commercials, Perot harkened back to Adlai Stevenson's long-form approach and bought 30-minute chunks of network time to air

Japanese politician Matayoshi Mitsuo says he is Jesus Christ. He's never won an election.

infomercial-style programs that mapped out his plans to improve the economy. Drawing as many as 10.5 million viewers in prime time, Perot even pulled ahead of Bush and Clinton in the polls at one point. He ultimately garnered 20 percent of the vote.

1992: In the same election, television proved it had the power to pull in the youth vote. Clinton's most impactful appearance on the tube was not on CNN or any of the Big Three Networks, but on MTV. During a network-sponsored Q&A forum, Clinton was asked by a young woman to clarify an earlier statement concerning his past marijuana use in which Clinton had said, "Yes, I tried it, but I didn't like it, and I didn't inhale." The woman asked, "If you had to do it over again, would you inhale?" Clinton's off-the-cuff response: "Sure, if I could. I tried before." That kind of candor resonated with the young audience. In the November election, exit polls showed a 20 percent increase in youth turnout over the prior election, ending 20 years of declining youth turnout. Clinton later admitted that "MTV had a lot to do with the Clinton/Gore victory."

1993: In April, Clinton appeared on MTV again and, in what may be the most important fact *ever* said by any politician on television, the president divulged to the nation he preferred briefs to boxers.

2000: Many Democrats blame Al Gore's defeat to George W. Bush on the disputed Florida vote count, but in reality, the televised debates didn't do Gore any favors. For one, he loudly sighed into his microphone during Bush's answers in the first debate, earning him ridicule in the press. Like every other big-time politician since 1975, Gore was also ridiculed on *Saturday Night Live*. He actually studied tapes of the sketches to try and improve his own debate performance, but it wasn't enough.

Today: Pundits predicted that the era of political TV advertising would be replaced by Facebook, Twitter, and YouTube. In fact, Barack Obama won the 2008 election in part by using social-networking sites to attract and organize young, tech-savvy voters. But television in politics is hardly dead. Spending on political ads in the 2010 midterm elections topped $4 billion—crushing the $2.8 billion record set two years earlier. Two-thirds of that $4 billion went to television airtime. And because of SuperPACs in 2012, more money was spent on TV ads than anyone thought possible.

BEWARE THE GLITTERATI!

*Here's one from the "Only In America" files: a new kind
of political protest. But is it foolish…or fabulous?*

SHINY, UNHAPPY PEOPLE

Newt Gingrich was hit first. It happened at an event in Minnesota in May 2011 when Gingrich and his wife Callista were sitting at a table signing books. An activist named Nick Espinosa waited in line. When he got to the couple, he reached into a Cheez-It box and assaulted them with handfuls of glitter. What's Espinosa's issue? He was protesting Gingrich's anti-gay marriage stance. "Nice to live in a free country," quipped Gingrich, who brushed himself off and continued signing books.

BEGUN, THE GLITTER WARS HAVE

But the "Glitterati," as the press named them, were just getting started. Over the next year, several more glitter-carrying gay-rights activists showed up at Republican events. Mitt Romney got glitter-bombed shortly after winning the Florida primary. "I'm happy for a little celebration," he joked. "This is confetti! We just won Florida!" Minnesota governor Tim Pawlenty also got glittered; so did Rep. Michele Bachmann, Senator Ron Paul, former Bush aid Karl Rove, and Senator Rick Santorum (twice).

But as the glitter attacks intensified, so too did the outcry to stop them. "That's an assault," said Fox News host Mike Huckabee. "These people ought to be arrested!" At least one was—University of Colorado student Peter Smith spent a night in jail for glitter-bombing Romney (who was being guarded by the Secret Service at the time). Republicans got even angrier when it was revealed that Smith worked for the Colorado Democratic Party (he was fired).

What did the general public think about the attacks? A *Huffington Post* poll from February 2012 asked readers, "Do you think glitter-bombing is fabulous or foolish?" Result: 50 percent said fabulous; 50 percent said foolish. But most people agree that it's harmless—except, that is, for a Washington, D.C., optometrist named Dr. Stephen Glasser. He told *The Hill* that glitter could conceivably "get into the eyes and actually create a cut." Even worse, it could get into the nose and cause a sinus infection. Thankfully, no politicians have been seriously injured by glitter…so far.

In 2008 French pres. Nicolas Sarkozy sued the makers of a "Sarkozy voodoo doll."

FIRST LADY FIRSTS

What's tougher than being president? Being married to the president.
Yet most have handled the job with grace, dignity, and humor.
Here are some First Lady accolades both profound and silly.

First Lady: Lucy Ware Webb Hayes, wife of Rutherford B. Hayes
Notable First: The first First Lady to be called a First Lady
Background: From Martha Washington through Julie Grant, presidential wives did not have a title. In 1876 newspaper writer Mary Clemmer Ames first referred to Mrs. Hayes, wife of the 19th president, as "the First Lady" in her column "Woman's Letter from Washington."

First Lady: Frances Folsom Cleveland, wife of Grover Cleveland
Notable First: The first First Lady to be married in the White House
Background: Frances was only 21 when she married 49-year-old President Cleveland on June 2, 1886. It was the first nuptial ceremony held in the White House for a presidential couple. Mrs. Cleveland was the nation's youngest First Lady. She was also the first First Lady to give birth to a child in the White House, when her daughter Esther was born in 1893.

First Lady: Letitia Christian Tyler, first wife of John Tyler
Notable First: The first First Lady to die in the White House
Background: John Tyler became president when President William Henry Harrison died 30 days after being sworn in. Letitia Tyler had suffered a paralytic stroke several years earlier, so her duties as First Lady were actually assigned to her daughter-in-law, Priscilla Cooper Tyler. After a lengthy illness, probably tuberculosis, Letitia died in September 1842.

First Lady: Jacqueline Bouvier Kennedy, wife of John F. Kennedy
Notable First: The first (and only) First Lady to receive an Emmy Award
Background: To prod Congress into passing a bill giving permanent museum status to the White House, she conducted a tour of the mansion for television, which earned her a special Emmy.

First Lady: Helen Herron Taft, wife of William H. Taft

Notable First: The first First Lady to decree that no bald-headed waiter or butler could serve in the White House

Background: Feeling the previous occupants of the White House were too informal and lacked dignity, Helen Taft thought this rule would create a favorable impression for guests. (Not to be confused with Lou Henry Hoover, wife of the 31st president, who insisted that all butlers, waiters, and footmen must be exactly five feet, eight inches tall.)

First Lady: Eliza McCardle Johnson, wife of Andrew Johnson

Notable First: The first First Lady to teach her husband to read and write

Background: President Andrew Johnson was born into poverty. Apprenticed to a tailor at a young age, he never spent a single day in school in his entire life. In 1827, the 19-year-old tailor married 16-year-old Eliza McCardle. Every night, after supper, Mrs. Johnson taught her husband how to read and write.

First Lady: Patricia Ryan Nixon, wife of Richard M. Nixon

Notable First: The first First Lady to visit an overseas combat zone

Background: "Visit" is an overstatement. During the Nixons' 1969 trip to South Vietnam, Pat flew over the troops in an open helicopter.

First Lady: Florence Kling Harding, wife of Warren G. Harding

Notable First: The first First Lady to vote

Background: Women were granted the right to vote in August 1920—perfect timing for Florence Harding, a strong supporter of women's suffrage. A couple of months later she cast her first ballot (presumably) for her husband Warren, who won the election by a landslide.

First Lady: Michelle Obama, wife of Barack Obama

Notable First: The first First Lady to do push-ups on a talk show

Background: In 2012 Michelle appeared on *The Ellen DeGeneres Show*. While she was discussing methods to curb childhood obesity, Ellen asked, "How many push-ups can you do? I bet I can do more." Michelle took the challenge. Ellen pooped out after 20. Michelle stopped at 25…and indicated she could have done more if she wanted to.

There are more threats against the First Lady than the VP.

GOVERN-MENTAL

More strange tales from the world of public office.

LOOK BEFORE YOU LEAP

In 2009 Arizona state senator Linda Gray (R-Phoenix) received an error-ridden email from a ninth-grader complaining about the lack of state funds for education. The senator's response was harsh: "Why didn't you take to (sic) time to write an email with the proper punctuation? Your example tells me that all the money we have spent on your education shows a lack of learning on your part." Only after the letter found its way into the press did Gray find out that the student had special needs. "I wrote harsh words to her," admitted the senator, who apologized profusely. "I don't know what got into me."

STOP—IN THE NAME OF THE LAW

For years, residents of the Chicago suburb of Oak Lawn have been complaining that motorists don't come to a complete stop at stop signs. So in 2007 Mayor Dave Heilmann came up with a creative solution: He added a second, smaller octagonal sign below 50 of the town's stop signs so, for example, drivers would see:

STOP

and smell the roses

Other signs read "STOP right there, pilgrim," "STOP billion dollar fine," and "STOP in the naaaame of love." The Illinois Department of Transportation deemed the signs violations of the Federal Uniform Traffic Control Act, and threatened to withhold funds for road projects if the signs weren't removed. Heilmann complied, but complained, "I think government needs to take itself less seriously."

THE YOLK'S ON HIM

Jiří Paroubek, a Czech politician running for a seat in the European Union Parliament, was the victim of several egg attacks in 2009. At first, only a few eggs were thrown at him. But at each subsequent event, more egg-throwers showed up. Every time, Paroubek continued speaking even though his head was covered with shells and yolks. Paroubek accused

---

A can of foot powder was once elected mayor of Picoaza, Ecuador.

leaders of the rival Civic Democratic Party of secretly having their supporters throw the eggs (the Civic Democrats denied it). But Paroubek saved his harshest words for journalists who made light of his humiliation. "After the elections, I will take a basket of eggs and come to your newsroom and throw them at you," he said at a press conference. "I don't like the way you write. I will pelt you and you will see how funny it is."

PELOSI-ROLL'D

In 2009 Speaker of the House Nancy Pelosi (D-CA) posted a short video on the new Congressional YouTube Channel. It began with her two cats running around her office at the U.S. Capitol. At the 37-second mark, Pelosi pulled a popular Internet prank called "Rickrolling": The footage suddenly cut to singer Rick Astley's 1987 music video for "Never Gonna Give You Up." Many pundits derided the fact that the person second in line for the presidency was engaging in such "juvenile" behavior, but *Time* magazine wrote, "It reflects a relatively sophisticated understanding of how the modern Internet works for an elected public official."

SPACE WAR

A coveted parking space located right next to the side entrance of city hall in Oakland, California, opened up in 2008 when a councilman retired. Who would get the space? It was narrowed down to two councilwomen: Desley Brooks and Jean Quan. Their colleagues suggested they flip a coin. Quan agreed, but Brooks claimed seniority and demanded that council president Jane Brunner make the decision. After deliberating, Brunner ruled that since both women had started in 2002, both had equal seniority; they should just flip a coin. Brooks disagreed and ordered city attorney John Russo to decide. Finally, after the dispute had gone on for three months (during which time the parking space went to whoever got there first), Russo issued a five-page written opinion, concluding that the women were equally entitled to the space. His solution: Flip a coin. (Brooks won.)

*   *   *

"Politicians are the same all over. They promise to build a bridge even where there is no river."

—Nikita Khrushchev

Why wasn't Ben Franklin entrusted with writing the Declaration of Independence?...

"HAIL TO THE CHIEF"

*It's the official anthem of the president of the United States. It must, by
decree, be played every time the president arrives at a formal function.
(Uncle John wants to know how he can get his own anthem, too.)*

THE BOATING SONG

The melody to "Hail to the Chief" began as an old Scottish air by
the same name—a highlander ditty that was sung by boatmen
while rowing on the lochs. The tune was then "borrowed" in 1810 by an
English songwriter named James Sanderson, who was writing music for a
London play called *The Lady of the Lake*, based on a popular poem by Sir
Walter Scott. The play took its storyline from the legend of King Arthur,
but centered around a Scottish folk hero—the "Chief" in the updated
version of the song. The play caught on quickly in England and soon
found its way to America, where it first ran in New York City in 1812.
When the sheet music was published in Philadelphia a short time later,
a few new lyrics were added to the song by a man named L. M. Sargent,
who retitled it "Wreaths for the Chieftain." But most people simply
referred to the song by its first line: "Hail to the chief who in triumph
advances!"

BIRTHDAY MUSIC

On February 22, 1815, the song was first performed in the presence of a
president, James Madison, at a celebration commemorating George
Washington's 83rd birthday (Washington had died in 1799). The event
received so much favorable press that sales of the song's sheet music had
doubled by the next day. Thirteen years later, the still-popular tune was
played by the United States Marine Band on July 4, 1828, when President
John Quincy Adams arrived at the groundbreaking of the C&O Canal in
Maryland. By that time, hundreds of sets of lyrics had been published—
most of them satirical. But it was the catchy melody, not the words, that
people really responded to. Over the next few years, the song was played
not just for presidents but for assorted visiting dignitaries (even some
Indian chiefs were greeted with "Hail to the Chief"). It would take the
work of two First Ladies for the old boating song to be associated solely
with the *commander* in chief.

...It was feared that he would try to include a joke.

PARTYING HARD AND WALKING TALL

• Julia Gardiner Tyler, wife of President John Tyler, was a fan of the song. In 1844 she requested that the Marine Band play it whenever the president arrived at their social gatherings, of which there were many, so that the president could make a grand entrance. The band agreed, and a tradition was born.

• The next president, James K. Polk, was so short in stature and unassuming in nature that he often went completely unnoticed when he entered a room. This irritated First Lady Sarah Polk so much that she went to the conductor of the Marine Band and ordered him to play the song every time her husband arrived at any formal function. After two consecutive terms of playing "Hail to the Chief" at every presidential function, the custom was firmly in place, but it still wasn't official.

UNDIGNIFIED

Chester A. Arthur hated the song, and when he became president in 1881 he ordered John Philip Sousa, the Marine Band leader at the time, to write a new presidential anthem. Sousa got to work and presented the president with two songs, one called "Presidential Polonaise" and another called "Semper Fidelis." Arthur loved "Presidential Polonaise," and the Marine Band played it throughout his term. But the public never really took to it, and when Arthur died shortly after leaving office, the song died with him. Meanwhile, the Marine Band adopted "Semper Fidelis" (Latin for "always faithful") for their theme song. When Grover Cleveland took office in 1885, "Hail to the Chief" quietly resumed its place as the unofficial presidential entrance song. And by this point it was becoming taboo for the tune to be used to honor any other public figure.

But the song remained unofficial until President Harry Truman, a piano player and amateur musicologist, decided to research its origins in 1953. Excited by the song's storied history, Truman ordered that it be named the official theme song of the president of the United States. In 1954 the U.S. Department of Defense (because of the song's military nature) made it official—that "old Scottish boat song" had earned its place as an American institution.

THE OFFICIAL (AND NOT SO OFFICIAL) LYRICS

The words to "Hail to the Chief" have changed often over the years, but

---

1st foreign head of state to address the U.S. Congress: King Kalakaua of Hawaii (1874).

the original lyrics are credited both to Sir Walter Scott as well as to a lyricist named Albert Gamse:

Hail to the chief we have chosen for the nation,
Hail to the chief! We salute him, one and all.
Hail to the chief, as we pledge cooperation
In proud fulfillment of a great, noble call.

And over the years, many people have had fun with the words. The song has been satirized in dozens of movies and television shows, not to mention political campaigns. Here are two alternate versions from the 1996 presidential comedy film *My Fellow Americans*:

Hail to the chief, he's the chief and he needs hailing.
He is the chief so you all had better hail like crazy.
—President Russell P. Kramer (Jack Lemmon)

Hail to the chief, if you don't I'll have to kill you.
I am the chief, so you'd better watch your step, you bastards.
—President Matt Douglas (James Garner)

*   *   *

THREE OBSCURE FORMS OF GOVERNMENT

• **Diarchy:** Two people rule, usually taking position by birth and remaining until death. The tiny European principality of Andorra has a diarchy, although the diarchs are a bishop and the president of France. Ancient civilizations such as Rome and Sparta had diarchies, too.

• **Ethnocracy:** All the major leaders are of a single ethnicity, race, or religious group, and one that's in the minority. South Africa under apartheid rule is an example of this form of government.

• **Exilarchy:** A ruler called an *exilarch* is recognized as the leader of only a country's specific religious sect or ethnic group. It's largely an honorary title, and any power given to the exilarch is handed down by the country's actual leaders. One example: The Dalai Lama is an exilarch of Tibetan Buddhists, but the country is actually controlled by the Chinese government.

HEMP MADNESS, PART I

For thousands of years, hemp has been one of humanity's most versatile crops, but over the last century it has also become one of the most controversial. Here we attempt to weed out the facts from the fiction to find out why.

THE MIRACLE PLANT

As early as 6500 BC, people in what's now China utilized hemp fibers to make clothes and fishing nets. As hemp plants spread around the world, dozens of uses were found for it, from linens in ancient Greece, to the oil in da Vinci's lamp, to the sails on Christopher Columbus's ships, to the string on Benjamin Franklin's famous kite, to the pages of the Declaration of Independence. In 1791 Thomas Jefferson stated, "Hemp is of first necessity to the wealth and protection of the country."

SO WHAT HAPPENED?

American farmers followed Jefferson's advice, and by 1850 there were more than 8,000 hemp plantations nationwide producing cloth, canvas, rope, and hemp oil for lighting and heat. But hemp production had a drawback: It needed to be processed by hand, a task performed primarily by slaves. In contrast, when Eli Whitney invented the cotton gin in 1794, it became possible to process cotton into fibers via a machine, which propelled it to the top of the cloth business. And when slavery was abolished in 1865, the work force needed to process hemp diminished. Finally, the rise of petroleum-based fuels began to replace hemp oil.

Hemp almost found new life thanks to the increased need for paper products, a side effect of bigger companies, more newspapers, and committee meetings. Up until the late 1800s, most of the world's paper had been made out of hemp, but not directly. It was recycled from worn-out sails, sheets, and clothes—most of which had been originally made of hemp. All of a sudden, the need for paper products dramatically exceeded the world's supply of old rags. Paper companies found themselves with a decision to make: They could either create huge hemp farms and then wait several months for the first yields to come in—or they could simply harvest the nation's ample forests. The quicker, higher profit came from trees. So that's what they did.

IT'S A CONSPIRACY...OR IS IT?

That explains why hemp production fell out of favor in the U.S., but why is it illegal to grow without permission from the government? Because of hemp's association with another plant in the cannabis family: marijuana. But the exact reasons for the demonization of both plants have been somewhat muddied over the years. The most widely held theory says that marijuana—and hemp along with it—is illegal because of a conspiracy between businessmen and politicians. Most of the information for this comes from a sole source: *The Emperor Wears No Clothes*, written in 1973 by hemp activist Jack Herer.

Herer's villain: William Randolph Hearst. From the 1890s until his death in 1951, Hearst was one of the most powerful businessmen in America. At his peak, he owned 30 newspapers, several magazines, and even served in the U.S. Congress. According to Herer's theory, Hearst owned enormous amounts of timber-land, and stood to lose billions of dollars if hemp replaced trees as the primary source for paper. In 1918, after a new method for the machine-processing of hemp was invented, Hearst used his clout to kill the plant.

To achieve this, Herer claims, Hearst focused his "yellow journalism" on marijuana use—the thinking being that if marijuana were outlawed, then the hemp industry would go down as well. Thousands of stories about "the killer weed" appeared over the years, with sensational head-lines like "Marihuana Makes Sex Fiends of Boys in 30 Days!"

Hearst had a powerful ally in his crusade: the DuPont Company, known today as a chemical manufacturer. In the 1920s, DuPont was spending millions of dollars on research into synthetic fibers (which would eventually lead to nylon). Like Hearst, they also stood to lose billions if the hemp industry wasn't eliminated.

TAXED TO DEATH

Herer's accusations go on to say that both Hearst and DuPont exploited their long history of financial connections to the Mellon banking family. In 1930 they convinced Andrew Mellon, then the head of the U.S. Treas-ury Department, to form the Federal Bureau of Narcotics (FBN). Appoint-ed to head the department was Mellon's nephew, anti-cannabis zealot Harry J. Anslinger. Within a year, Anslinger's anti-marijuana claims had so soured public perception of the drug that it was illegal in 29 states. But

On an average day, the president of the U.S. receives 20,000 letters and emails.

that wasn't enough—marijuana needed to be illegal *everywhere*. So in 1937 Anslinger testified before Congress: "I believe in some cases one cigarette might develop a homicidal mania." Result: the "Marihuana Tax Act," which levied a $100-per-ounce tax on cannabis. Though it didn't technically outlaw it, the act effectively prohibited the cultivation of cannabis plants of any kind, including hemp.

THE REAL STORY

While Herer's book has galvanized the pro-cannabis movement, in recent years, a lot of holes have been found in his story. According to critics, the hemp industry wasn't quashed because Hearst and DuPont were threatened by it. Several of Herer's connections are tenuous at best—in reality neither company gave a lot of thought to hemp production. They were both making plenty of money. And Hearst didn't create the anti-cannabis wave; he was riding it.

Today, the more widely accepted theory is that cannabis was made illegal because of racism. In the United States at the turn of the 20th century, minorities found themselves being blamed for much of society's problems. And the popular perception was that blacks and Hispanics were the predominant users of drugs. Prohibition movements sprang up in churches, local city halls, and state capitals. By the 1910s, the majority of U.S. states had passed laws heavily taxing or outlawing heroin, opium, and cocaine, and in 1918 even alcohol was made illegal. This anti-drug sentiment continued through the 1920s and into the Depression years, when marijuana became the target of choice. And Anslinger's warnings further frightened the segregated nation.

One example of that "fright" came in 1936 when a small church group produced a low-budget film called *Tell Your Children*, which painted pot smokers as murderers and rapists. The narrator warned, "The dread marihuana may be reaching forth next for your son or daughter....or yours...or *yours*!" (The film was rediscovered in the 1970s and given a new name, *Reefer Madness*—and is now known as an unintentionally funny cult classic.)

So basically, industrial hemp has been a victim of guilt by association. But today, it's almost common knowledge that hemp and marijuana are not the same, so where are all the hemp farms?

Don't freak out, man. Part II is on page 196.

HONK IF YOU VOTED

Americans practice their First Amendment rights on their cars' rear bumpers.

My kid is an honor student
and my president is an idiot

*Be Nice to America or We'll Bring
Democracy to Your Country*

Monica Lewinsky's Ex-
Boyfriend's Wife for President

*I'll keep my Money,
my Freedom, and my Guns,
and you can keep your
"Change"*

**There Are a Lot of Pros
and Cons in Politics**

*You Can't Fix Stupid,
But You Can Vote It Out*

Don't Steal. The Government
Hates Competition

*Your Wallet—the Only Place
Democrats are Willing to Drill*

Republicans: We Work Hard
So You Don't Have To!

They Call Him "W"
So He Can Spell It

Visualize Impeachment

At Least the War on the
Middle Class is Going Well

**A Woman's Place is in
the House...and Senate**

Re-elect Gore—2004

Bipartisanship: I'll Hug Your
Elephant If You Kiss My Ass

*Smile! You're on
Homeland Security Camera!*

Politicians and Diapers
Need to Be Changed...
Often for the Same Reason

*"Stop me when you hear something
you like." —**Mitt Romney***

REPUBLICANS FOR VOLDEMORT

Palin 2012–2014 1/2

**The Constitution:
Frustrating Liberals
Since 1789**

All Politics Is Loco

Don't Blame Me, I Voted for
UNCLE JOHN!

Self-adhesive bumper stickers were invented for the 1956 U.S. presidential election.

MAHER'S BARBS

Comedian/pundit Bill Maher has an uncanny ability to offend all sides.

"The Democrats are very bad at selling their own product. The Republicans are geniuses at it. And I've said it before: A bad product well apologized for is superior in this country to a good product."

"I don't think it's ever been like this. I know there's always been a 'passionate' divide in American politics. But I don't think there's ever been a time when the two sides just have two different sets of reality."

"I saw a bag of Mr. Salty pretzels. Isn't that nerve? Everything today is 'low salt' or 'salt-free.' Here's a guy who says, 'The hell with you, I'm Mr. Salty pretzels!' Like Mr. Tar and Nicotine cigarettes, or Mr. Gristle and Hard Artery beef-steak."

"Kids, they're not easy, but there has to be some penalty for sex."

"This country loves guns; we even have salad shooters. This country thinks that salad is too peaceable, you have to find some way to shoot it."

"If a Democrat even *thinks* you're calling him liberal, he grabs an orange vest and a rifle and heads to the woods to kill something."

"I'm supposed to be all reinjected with yes-we-can fever after Obama's big healthcare speech, and it was a great speech—when Black Elvis gets jiggy with his teleprompter, there is none better. But here's the thing: Muhammad Ali also had a way with words, but it helped enormously that he could also punch guys in the face."

"We're not even No. 1 in social mobility—the American dream— the ability of one generation to do better than the next. We're tenth. That's like Sweden coming tenth in Swedish meatballs."

"If ketchup had 1/20th of the car-cinogens in a cigarette they'd rip it off the shelves tomorrow, so the government is full of sh*t when they say that they care about you."

"The problem is that the people with the most ridiculous ideas are always the people who are most certain of them."

Q: On what sitcom did Nancy Reagan tell kids to "Just Say No?" A: *Diff'rent Strokes.*

THE KING OF CANADA

There are a lot of bizarre politicians in this book.
This guy might just be the bizarrest of them all.

B LAND MASTER
William Lyon Mackenzie King was Canada's longest-serving prime minister, leading his country through most of the Great Depression and all of World War II. Born in 1874 in Kitchener, Ontario, he studied law and economics at the University of Toronto and the University of Chicago. Inspired to delve into government service by his mother's tales of his grandfather, the rebel William Lyon Mackenzie, King became an astute politician and leader who made many lasting contributions to Canadian history. But for all intents and purposes, there were two Kings.

On the surface, he was an average-looking man who favored black suits with starched white collars. By most accounts, he was "dull, reliable, and largely friendless." When speaking to the press or in Parliament, he was deliberately vague and opaque. "It was hard to pin him down, to use his own words against him…because his speeches were masterpieces of ambiguity," writes Canadian historian Pierre Berton. In short, he was a master politician and a symbol of stability.

However, the public didn't know the *real* William Lyon Mackenzie King.

MAMA'S BOY
In those days, a politician's private life really was private. Good thing for King, because behind his neutral facade, he was a first-class eccentric. He never married, and in fact, seemed terrified of all women—except his mother. No woman, notes Berton, "could hope to compare for beauty, compassion, selflessness, purity of soul with his mother, who haunted his dreams…guiding his destinies, consoling him in his darker moments, and leaving precious little time or space for a rival."

Isabel King continued to control her son even after her death. Long after she passed away, King held séances and regularly chatted with his mother's "spirit" about matters of state.

Humorist Will Rogers once served as honorary mayor of Beverly Hills.

He liked to speak with other deceased figures as well, including departed relatives and celebrities. King traveled to Europe in 1934 where he reportedly made contact with Leonardo da Vinci, Louis Pasteur, and Philip the Apostle. He also claimed to have contacted former Canadian prime minister Wilfrid Laurier, British prime minister William Gladstone, as well as Saint Luke, Saint John, and Robert Louis Stevenson.

MIXED SIGNALS

King owned a crystal ball, but that's not how he contacted the spirit world. He had a special séance table through which spirits "spoke" to him by rapping out messages that he alone could decipher. Unfortunately, the messages weren't always accurate.

On September 2, 1939—one day after Nazi Germany invaded Poland to start World War II—King held a séance in which his dead father told him that Hitler had been assassinated. The prime minister was greatly disappointed when he was informed that Hitler was very much alive.

King wasn't a great judge of character with the dead *or* the living. In fact, he vastly underestimated the dangers posed by Hitler and Mussolini. After visiting Nazi Germany in the 1930s, King decided that Hitler was okay because he shared certain personality traits with the Canadian P.M. "I am convinced Hitler is a spiritualist," King wrote. "His devotion to his mother—that Mother's spirit is, I am certain, his guide."

King also dabbled in numerology and the reading of tea leaves, and held lengthy policy chats with his dog, an Irish terrier named Pat, to whom he liked to outline issues of national importance. (It's unclear what advice, if any, Pat offered in return.) King was even known to make policy decisions based on the position of the hands of the clock.

SPILLING THE BEANS

If King had gotten his way, no one outside of his inner circle would have ever known about his bizarre spiritual life. But he made the mistake of keeping detailed diaries of his exploits. King left explicit instructions that—upon his death—his butler was to burn all of the diaries. But as the butler was about to incinerate them, he decided to take a peek inside… and then couldn't bring himself to do it. (He must have known that King's musings would someday make for great bathroom reading.) Today, the King Diaries reside in Canada's National Archives.

The U.S. Capitol Building has 365 steps—one for each day of the year.

UH, EXCUSE ME, SIR, BUT YOUR MICROPHONE IS ON

Quiet, please. It's time for open mike night at the BRI. Had these public figures known that their mikes were hot and the tape was rolling, they would have never said what they said.

SPEAKER: President Ronald Reagan

BACKGROUND: In 1984, during the height of the Cold War, Reagan took a break from his reelection campaign to do a radio interview. He thought he was doing a sound check for the crew, but was actually being broadcast live over the airwaves.

WHAT WAS SAID: "My fellow Americans, I'm pleased to tell you today that I've signed legislation that will outlaw Russia forever." [Laughter.] "We begin bombing in five minutes." [More laughter.]

REACTION: Neither Reagan nor his supporters thought it was a big deal—it just proved that the president had a sense of humor. (Reagan's staff took steps to ensure that in the future the Great Communicator would know unequivocally whether he was being broadcast.) But Democrats blasted the president as a trigger-happy madman out of touch with the severity of his "joke." The Soviets weren't amused, either. One Moscow television station wondered how much Reagan was joking, claiming that bombing Russia was his "sacred dream." The joke didn't hurt Reagan politically, though—he won that year's election by a landslide (and he never did bomb Russia).

SPEAKER: Senator John Kerry

BACKGROUND: The 2004 Democratic presidential candidate was preparing for a TV interview, but didn't know the tape was already rolling. As one of his handlers told him to "keep smiling," he made some disparaging remarks about Republicans (through smiling teeth).

WHAT WAS SAID: "Oh, don't worry, man. We're going to keep pounding, let me tell you. Just beginning the fight here. These guys are the most crooked, lying group I've ever seen."

REACTION: After learning that his remarks were recorded and played

---

Country with the consistently highest voter turnout: Italy, averaging 92.5% since 1945.

all over the news that night, Kerry stood by them, refusing to apologize. His Democratic base was proud of the tough rhetoric, but Republicans seized the opportunity to paint him as emotionally unstable and having a personal vendetta. Did that swing some voters over to Bush? We'll never know, but Kerry lost the election.

SPEAKERS: George W. Bush and Tony Blair

BACKGROUND: They were at the 2006 G8 Summit in St. Petersburg, Russia, for formal meetings on how to resolve the Middle East crisis. But what caught the media's attention was an impromptu meeting between the American president and the British prime minister. While Bush was sitting at the table eating his lunch, Blair walked up and stood behind him, and the two started to chat.

WHAT WAS SAID (excerpts):

Bush: Yo, Blair. How ya doing?

Blair: I'm just...

Bush: You're leaving?

Blair: No, no, no, not yet.

[Later...]

Bush: Who's introducing the trade?

Blair: Angela [Merkel, the German chancellor].

Bush: Tell her to call 'em [the Syrian government].

Blair: Yes.

Bush: Tell her to put them on the spot. Thanks for the sweater—it's awfully thoughtful of you.

Blair: It's a pleasure.

Bush: I know you picked it out yourself.

Blair: Oh absolutely—in fact I knitted it! [Laughter.]

Bush: I think Condi [Condoleezza Rice] is going to go pretty soon.

Blair: But that's, that's all that matters. But if you...you see it will take some time to get that together.

Bush: Yeah, yeah.

Blair: But at least it gives people...

Bush: It's a process, I agree. I told her your offer to...

Blair: Well, it's only if I mean...you know. If she's got a...or if she needs

King George III once referred to Benjamin Franklin as an "evil genius."

the ground prepared as it were. Because obviously if she goes out she's got to succeed, whereas I can go out and just talk.

Bush: You see the irony is what they need to do is get Syria, to get Hezbollah to stop doing this sh*t and it's all over.

Blair: Is this...? [Blair taps the mic on the table and the sound is cut.]

REACTION: To the British press, it confirmed, once and for all, that their prime minister was nothing more than Bush's yes-man, and that Bush, in turn, was a typical rude American who didn't even have the courtesy to stand up and formally greet his British counterpart (some of the transcript is inaudible because Bush was eating lunch and often talked with his mouth full). Said the UK's *Daily Mirror*, "Yo, Bush! Start treating our prime minister with respect!" It also referred to Blair as the "president's poodle."

SPEAKER: French president Jacques Chirac

BACKGROUND: In 2005 Chirac attended a private meeting with two other world leaders, Russian president Vladimir Putin and then-German chancellor Gerhard Schröder. At the time, London and Paris were competing for the opportunity to host the 2012 Olympic Summer Games. The meeting wasn't recorded, but the room was full of curious eavesdroppers, one of whom wrote down everything, including some harsh words Chirac had for the English.

WHAT WAS SAID: "The only thing that they have ever done for European agriculture is mad cow disease. You cannot trust people who have such bad cuisine. It is the country with the worst food after Finland."

REACTION: France and England may not be the best of friends, but they are expected at least to act civilly toward each other. So it caused quite a stir to hear the French president blatantly insult the British (and the Finns), especially in the presence of other world leaders. And the insults ended up hurting Chirac in a big way: Paris had been the frontrunner to get the Games, but two of the voting members of the International Olympic Committee were from Finland. Result: London won the bid by a narrow margin. The French still maintain that had Chirac just kept his mouth shut, Paris would have been the host.

As for the British, they took the tactful way out. A spokesman for Tony Blair responded by saying that "there are some things that are better not responded to."

Sixteen of Canada's 22 prime ministers have been lawyers.

RESIGNED IN PROTEST

Most people fantasize about quitting their job—but what about people who love what they do…but just can't remain in the position because their morals will not allow them to?

WHO: William Pitt the Younger, prime minister of Great Britain
BACKGROUND: In 1800 Pitt introduced the Emancipation of Catholics Bill, which would have ended discrimination against Catholics (they could not, for example, hold public office at the time) and strengthened Great Britain's union with Ireland.

RESIGNATION: King George III refused to accept the bill, saying it would violate the oath he took to protect the Church of England. Pitt felt equally strongly about making concessions to Catholics, so on February 16, 1801, after 18 years in power (the second-longest term in British history), Pitt resigned in protest. He remains the only prime minister in British history to resign the position this a way. (Pitt's resignation did little to help Catholics, as the issue was effectively squashed for decades. They weren't allowed to hold elected office until 1829.)

WHO: Eleanor Roosevelt, member of the Daughters of the American Revolution (DAR), and First Lady of President Franklin Roosevelt
BACKGROUND: The DAR is a historical preservation society open to women who can prove ancestral lineage to someone who aided the American Revolution. (Roosevelt had ancestors who fought in the war.) In 1939 the DAR was caught in a controversy when legendary music impresario Sol Hurok tried to book singer Marian Anderson into the organization's concert venue, Constitution Hall in Washington, D.C. DAR officials refused to allow it because Anderson was African American, and the DAR had a "whites only" performer policy.

RESIGNATION: Roosevelt very publicly resigned her DAR membership in protest. Then she used her influence to arrange for Anderson to perform on the steps of the Lincoln Memorial. More than 75,000 people attended. Chastened DAR officials apologized, and Anderson was later allowed to perform. (The "whites only" policy, however, wasn't officially rescinded until 1952.)

In '07 Wall Street's biggest firms paid $39 bil. in bonuses; shareholders lost $74 bil.

WHO: U.S. senator James A. Bayard Jr. (D-DE)

BACKGROUND: In 1864, in the midst of the Civil War, Congress passed a law requiring its members to take a greatly expanded loyalty oath, hoping to root out supporters of the Confederacy. The new oath required them to swear that they had never taken up arms against the government or supported such action in the past, and would never do so in the future.

RESIGNATION: Senator Bayard, who'd been in office since 1850, took the oath—then immediately resigned his seat. It was an insult, he said, to long-serving members of Congress. Even worse, it would make it impossible to reunite the country after the war, as no senator from the South could honestly take such an oath, given its "in the past" provision.

ON SECOND THOUGHT: When Bayard's successor died in office in 1867, Bayard was appointed to finish out the term...and he took the expanded loyalty oath. (The wartime oath was finally repealed and replaced with a much milder oath in 1884.)

WHO: Edvard Beneš, president of Czechoslovakia

BACKGROUND: In 1938 Adolf Hitler demanded that Czechoslovakia cede to Germany their western borderland, known as the Sudetenland, which was home to many ethnic Germans. Beneš, assured that he had the backing of France and the Soviet Union, refused. In September 1938, leaders of Nazi Germany, France, Britain, and Italy met in Munich—without the Czechs—and agreed that Hitler could have the Sudetenland.

RESIGNATION: On October 5, Beneš resigned in disgust. Within months, the Nazis had taken all of Czechoslovakia. Beneš formed a Czechoslovak government-in-exile in London, and in 1945, at war's end, returned to be elected the president of the country. That lasted until the takeover by communists allied with the Soviet Union in 1948—at which point Beneš resigned again. He died later that year at the age of 64.

WHO: Einar Hovdhaugen and Helge Rognlien, members of the Norwegian Nobel Prize Committee

BACKGROUND: The 1973 Nobel Peace Prize was awarded jointly to U.S. national security advisor Henry Kissinger and North Vietnamese general Le Duc Tho for having negotiated a cease-fire between North and South Vietnam in January of that year.

In ancient Greece, a man not married by the age of 30 lost his right to vote.

RESIGNATION: Hovdhaugen and Rognlien, both longtime Norwegian politicians, were so disgusted with the choice that they resigned from the Nobel committee. Why? For starters, the cease-fire had been signed in January, and the war was still raging at the time the prize was awarded—10 months later. General Tho, in fact, refused to accept his prize for just that reason. (The war actually continued for another two years.) Another reason: Kissinger, having been the main force behind America's bombing campaigns in Cambodia, seemed unworthy of a "peace" prize.

BONUS FACT: When South Vietnam fell to the North in 1975—rendering the earlier "cease-fire" meaningless—Kissinger tried to give the prize back, but the committee refused.

WHO: Jerald terHorst, press secretary to President Gerald Ford

BACKGROUND: Vice President Ford became president on August 9, 1974, after the resignation of Richard Nixon, and made terHorst, a veteran reporter for the *Detroit News*, his press secretary the same day. Rumors began swirling almost immediately that Ford was going to pardon Nixon for any crimes he may have committed in relation to the Watergate scandal. TerHorst assured reporters that there were no such plans.

RESIGNATION: A month later, Ford pardoned Nixon. TerHorst turned in his resignation the same day. "I cannot in good conscience support your decision to pardon former President Nixon even before he has been charged with the commission of any crime," he wrote in his letter of resignation. He was replaced by NBC reporter Ron Nessen. TerHorst stood by his decision to leave the post until his death in 2010 at the age of 87.

WHO: U.S. Secretary of State Cyrus Vance

BACKGROUND: On November 4, 1979, hundreds of Iranian students stormed the U.S. embassy in Tehran, taking dozens of Americans hostage. President Jimmy Carter's aides advised him to try a rescue operation. Vance was against it, insisting it was too risky to the hostages, rescuers, and American-Iranian relations. Carter went ahead and authorized Operation Eagle Claw. It was a disaster. Eight American servicemen were killed, several aircraft were lost, and no hostages were rescued.

RESIGNATION: Vance was so opposed to the rescue plan that he actually resigned on April 21, 1980, three days before the attempt (although it was kept from the public for the sake of the mission). "I know how

In 1940 Vermont's state legislature declared war on Germany...before the U.S. did.

deeply you have pondered your decision on Iran," he wrote to the president. "I wish I could support you. But for reasons we have discussed I cannot." The 52 American hostages were held for 444 days, until January 20, 1981—the day after Jimmy Carter's presidency ended. Vance served in several diplomatic positions with the United Nations over the following decades, and died in 2002 at age 84.

WHO: Bruce Boler, a water quality specialist with the EPA

BACKGROUND: Boler was assigned to southwest Florida in 2001 to assess the impact of development in and around the area's wetlands. In the course of his work he refused several permits for golf course developments because of the amount of pollutants they would discharge into sensitive wetland areas. Outraged developers funded their own "scientific" studies, which determined that developments such as golf courses were actually better for the environment than natural wetlands. Amazingly, in 2003 the EPA accepted the studies.

RESIGNATION: Boler resigned, calling the findings "absurd," and went public with the information. (He got a new job at Florida's Everglades National Park.)

WHO: Larry Ramsell, historian for the National Fresh Water Fishing Hall of Fame in Hayward, Wisconsin

BACKGROUND: In 2005 the Illinois-based World Musky Alliance (a musky is a type of fish) filed a protest with the Fishing Hall of Fame. The problem: They listed a musky caught in 1949 by one Louis Spray in Wisconsin as the largest ever caught, at 63.5 inches—and it was a lie! The Musky Alliance claimed they had photographic proof that the fish in question was only about 56.3 inches long. That meant that a 60.25-inch fish caught by Cal Johnson, also in 1949, was really the largest. In January 2006, the Fishing Hall of Fame announced that, after a long investigation, they had determined that the record would stand.

RESIGNATION: Ramsell resigned in protest. Almost nobody noticed.

*   *   *

"A man is not finished when he is defeated. He is finished when he quits."
                                                              —Richard M. Nixon

THE GREENSPAN EFFECT

*As a kid, Uncle John played a game where he'd substitute new
nouns, verbs, and other parts of speech for the ones in a given
written passage. The old ones made sense—the new ones
made him laugh. If you're having trouble getting
through your daily newspaper, give it a try.*

MAD-LIBS (AND CONS)

Trying to understand the blathering babble of a government
technocrat can be frustrating. Former federal Reserve chairman
Alan Greenspan was a prime example. A newspaper article that started
with "Alan Greenspan said today…" would easily generate the numbing
sensation of your brain being dropped into a bucket of custard.

But wait! Don't despair! The BRI has come up with a way for any
ordinary person to actually enjoy quotes from any bloviated official.

DIRECTIONS

1. Take any quote of Mr. Greenspan's, like this one:

"Spreading globalization has fostered a degree of international flexibility
that has raised the possibility of a benign resolution to the U.S. current
account imbalance."

2. Make a list of the nouns in the quote:

- globalization
- degree
- flexibility
- possibility
- resolution
- account imbalance

3. Replace them with some more interesting nouns:

- globalization—poodles
- degree—trousers
- flexibility—funkiness
- possibility—exoskeleton
- resolution—Keith Richards
- account imbalance—banana cream pie

4. Now, fixing the grammar as necessary, the quotation becomes:

It's illegal in Connecticut to play Scrabble while waiting for a politician to speak.

"Spreading poodles have fostered trousers of international funkiness that have raised the exoskeleton of a benign Keith Richards to the current U.S. banana cream pie." Isn't that better?

5. But wait—you can keep going. Make a list of the verbs in the quote and replace them with your own:
- spread—yodel
- foster—mutate
- raise—ooze

6. Now you have: "Yodeling poodles have mutated trousers of international funkiness that have oozed the exoskeleton of a benign Keith Richards to the current U.S. banana cream pie."

7. Now, the adjectives:
- international—yellow
- benign—moldy
- current—charbroiled
- U.S.—aboriginal

8. And we get: "Yodeling poodles have mutated trousers of yellow funkiness that have oozed the exoskeleton of a moldy Keith Richards to the charbroiled aboriginal banana cream pie."

YOUR TURN

Here are two more quotes that you can plug your own silly words into:

"The risk exists that, with aggregate demand exhibiting considerable momentum, output could overshoot its sustainable path, leading ultimately in the absence of countervailing monetary policy action to further upward pressure on inflation."
—Ben Bernanke, Federal Reserve chairman

"The hours of non-hours work worked by a worker in a pay reference period shall be the total of the number of hours spent by him during the pay reference period in carrying out the duties required of him under his contract to do non-hours work."

—Department of Trade and Industry's draft law for minimum wage

India has a bill of rights...for cows.

THE MAGNA CARTA

*Most people have heard of it—maybe in a ninth-grade history class
or on Jeopardy! last week. But what is it? Answer: a piece of
writing that has helped shaped governments for 800 years.*

BACKGROUND

When asked to name the most important documents in Western
civilization, historians almost always include the Magna Carta.
What's so important about it? Many people assume that this landmark
document, written in 1215, helped advance human rights and led directly
to the Declaration of Independence and the U.S. Constitution. Not
quite. The Magna Carta actually wasn't intended to help the common
man, but it did mark the first time in history that written law challenged
the absolute power of a monarch, and the first time that governments,
even kings, could be held accountable for their actions. Without that,
modern democracy would not exist.

STRUGGLE FOR THE THRONE

In 1002 Ethelred II, the Anglo-Saxon king of England, married Emma,
the daughter of the duke of Normandy (now a region of northern
France). The marriage created a blood alliance between these two king-
doms, designed to unite them against invasion by the Vikings. In 1066
the next king of England, Edward the Confessor (an Anglo-Saxon) died,
leaving no heirs. That left the door open for the *Norman* bloodline (the
one descended from Emma) to make a claim for the throne of England.
William, the duke of Normandy, invaded and conquered England.

When William (known today as William the Conqueror) officially
became king of England, he installed a *feudal* system. Norman troops who
had fought on William's side were given English lands as a reward for
their loyalty, and they became *barons*. According to the feudal system,
anyone who lived within the baron's jurisdiction was obliged to pay taxes
to the baron and serve in his militia. The barons, in turn, paid taxes to
the king.

England operated that way until 1199, when King Richard the Lionheart died and his brother, John, claimed the throne. John, the youngest

son in the royal family, actually ranked beneath his nephew, Arthur of Brittany, in the order of succession. So how did he become king? Arthur disappeared and John took the throne by force. This enraged the barons, but what could they do? They couldn't fight the king of England…or could they?

FOOL'S PARADISE

Two incidents ultimately drove the barons to challenge the king.

Royal Error #1: In 1207 John appointed the Bishop of Norwich, John de Gray, Archbishop of Canterbury, the Catholic Church's highest representative in England. Traditionally, the king consulted with the bishops of England before making that appointment…but John didn't do that. The bishops protested to Pope Innocent III, who then put his own man, Stephen Langton, in the position. Infuriated that his power had been usurped, King John banished the council of bishops from England. In retaliation, Pope Innocent III excommunicated John (and, by extension, all of England) from the Church. The barons urged John to make amends, which he did…sort of. The Pope agreed to reinstate King John (and England). His price: England itself. The Church would *own* England and John would be little more than a local governor. In addition, the Church levied a huge tax on England. Where would John get the money? From the barons.

Royal error #2: In 1206 French forces seized the region of Normandy. Because it was their ancestral homeland, the barons demanded John send troops to reclaim it. He delayed for eight years before finally leading the English army into the occupied territories himself. England lost; France kept the land.

REBELLION

Upon hearing of the defeat, the barons became furious. They banded together in 1215 (while John was traveling back from France) and decided it was time to take action against the king. Using as a basis the "Charter of Liberties," a ceremonial document issued by King Henry I at his coronation in 1100, they created a new document—one that would be legally binding. Its essence: The king's power would no longer be absolute. He would be accountable for his actions, and the barons would have a say in decision-making.

John returned to London that June to find that the barons had taken control of the city. There was only one way for the king to get his country back: submit to the barons' 63 written demands. In return, the barons offered to sign a pledge of loyalty to King John. The resultant document—all of it in Latin—was called the "Great Charter," or *Magna Carta*.

THE DOCUMENT

Most of those 63 demands relate very specifically to life in 13th-century England. One, for example, repealed a tax on loans inherited by minors; another opened up royal hunting lands to barons. But two sections had a much broader impact.

• Clause 61 called for a committee of barons that could meet at any time to overrule the king's actions, by force if necessary.

• Clause 39—the only part of the Magna Carta that could be applied to a commoner (it prevented the king from jailing anyone or seizing property without proper cause or a fair trial, also known as *habeas corpus*—translation: "you must have the body").

John wasn't about to surrender authority, even with armed barons breathing down his neck. He signed the Magna Carta just to satisfy them. (The ceremony took place on June 15, 1215, under a tree in Runnymede, a meadow in London not far from Buckingham Palace.) But as soon as the barons relinquished control of England and left London, he renounced the document and then appealed to Pope Innocent III, who technically still ruled England. The Pope declared the Magna Carta null and void.

A NEW HOPE

When the barons learned of John's treachery, they declared civil war. But the conflict was brief: King John died in 1216 and was replaced by his nine-year-old son, Henry III. The barons called a truce when the Magna Carta was reissued under Henry's name, although with sections removed, notably Clause 61, the "committee of barons" rule. In 1225 Henry (now 18 years old) pared it down to only 37 clauses. But since he respected the basics of the charter—staying out of church and baronial affairs—the relationship between the crown and the barons remained smooth. Over Henry's 56-year reign, the document's principles became part of England's legal tradition, an accepted system of assumed rights and laws commonly referred to as "English common law."

The 2008 presidential election was the 1st ever between 2 sitting U.S. senators.

COMING TO AMERICA

In 1765 England needed money to pay for the troops that protected its American colonies. Parliament decided that the colonies should foot the bill, so it passed the what was called Stamp Act, which placed a tax on written materials sold in the colonies, including newspapers, pamphlets, contracts, licenses, and playing cards. Colonists objected to being taxed by an assembly thousands of miles away in which they didn't even have a representative.

The Massachusetts Assembly declared that taxation without representation violated "the natural rights of Englishmen," by which it meant the Magna Carta, the document which had guided the moral code of governing for more than 500 years. That declaration would be the first of several colonial challenges to the English throne (culminating in the American Revolution), fueled by the Magna Carta's thesis that leaders are not above the law.

In addition to its philosophical influence, a few clauses of the Magna Carta actually became integral parts of the American governmental system. Clause 39, or *habeas corpus*, providing that arrests and trials of citizens must have merit, is found in Article One of the U.S. Constitution. And Clause 61, which called for a committee of barons to oversee the king's actions, inspired the "checks and balances" system by which the various branches of U.S. government—executive, judicial, and legislative—have oversight of each other to ensure that none of them becomes too powerful.

LASTING IMPACT

So what became of the actual physical document? There never was one "master" Magna Carta—42 copies were made and signed, one for each of the barons and two for the king. Amazingly, four of those 42 copies are still in existence today. One of them is on display at the Houses of Parliament, one is in the British Library, and one is in a cathedral in Salisbury, England. The fourth copy is usually housed at Lincoln Cathedral in Lincolnshire, but is occasionally loaned out. It was shown at the New York World's Fair in 1939 and in 2007 at the 400th anniversary celebration of Jamestown, the first English colony in North America, where it was presented as a link between the old world of England and the new world of America.

RATHERISMS

*Former CBS News anchor Dan Rather was known as a
serious journalist, but we love him for these odd phrases,
all ad-libbed during election-night coverage.*

"This race is hotter than a Times Square Rolex."

"The presidential race is swinging like Count Basie."

"This race is humming along like Ray Charles."

"Bush is sweeping through the South like a big wheel through a cotton field."

"In southern states, Bush beat Kerry like a rented mule."

"You know that old song: It's delightful, it's delicious, it's de-lovely for President Bush in most areas of the country."

"His lead is as thin as turnip soup."

"Keep in mind they are teetotally meetmortally convinced they have Ohio won."

"The reelection of Bill Clinton is as secure as a double-knot tied in wet rawhide."

"We don't know whether to wind a watch or bark at the moon."

"These returns are running like a squirrel in a cage."

"This race is as tight as a too-small bathing suit on a too-hot car ride back from the beach."

"Bush is sweeping through the South like a tornado through a trailer park."

"This race is as tight as the rusted lug nuts on a '55 Ford."

"This race is spandex-tight."

"This presidential race is shakier than cafeteria Jell-O."

"When it comes to a race like this, I'm a long-distance runner and an all-day hunter."

"The Michigan Republican primary is tighter than Willie Nelson's headband."

"His lead's thin as November ice."

"A lot of people in Washington could not be more surprised if Fidel Castro came loping through on the back of a hippopotamus this election night."

Bush's press secretary Tony Snow said "I don't know" 400 times in his 1st 6 months.

JUSTICES FOR ALL

U.S. citizens who lose a trial can appeal the decision to a higher court—sometimes all the way up to the Supreme Court, which hears fewer than 100 cases a year. Here are some of the most impactful.

MARBURY v. MADISON, 1803

Background: In 1801, just before he left office, President John Adams (a Federalist) appointed William Marbury to be the justice of the peace in Washington, D.C. Problem was, the incoming administration of Thomas Jefferson (a Republican) didn't want to give Marbury the job, and Jefferson's secretary of state, James Madison, refused to honor the appointment. Marbury sued, insisting that under the Judiciary Act of 1789 (which, among other things, gave the president the power to appoint judges and justices of the peace), he was entitled to the position.

The Decision: In 1803 the Supreme Court declared that Marbury was indeed entitled to his position, but because of several other provisions in the Judiciary Act of 1789, the court didn't have any power to enforce its ruling. It also declared that any law that contradicted the Constitution would be voided. And the 1789 law did just that because it monkeyed around with the Supreme Court's jurisdiction. That meant the entire law was unconstitutional, and thus, by default, Marbury had no right to the job. By declaring the Judiciary Act unconstitutional, the court gave itself "judicial review," which was basically "the right to declare laws unconstitutional"—and this is still the court's main role in government today.

Whatever Happened to… Marbury remained an important man in the private sector as a banker and corporate director. His home, the Forrest-Marbury House, is now the Ukrainian Embassy in Washington, D.C.

DRED SCOTT v. SANDFORD, 1857

Background: Dred Scott was a slave whose owner, John Emerson, traveled frequently. In the 1830s, Emerson took Scott to live in several northern states where slavery was prohibited. After Emerson died, Scott petitioned a court in St. Louis, Missouri, for his freedom from Emerson's widow. Because her brother, John Sanford, was managing her inheritance, Sanford's name is attached to the case. (Sanford's name was misspelled as Sandford on the court records.)

U.S. federal subsidies to corn growers amount to $40 billion per year.

The Decision: The Supreme Court declared that no person of African ancestry could become a U.S. citizen and therefore had no rights, even in states or territories that banned slavery. The court also declared that African Americans—free or enslaved—had no legal rights anywhere in the United States. The Dred Scott decision just deepened the animosity between the North and South that eventually led to the Civil War.

Whatever Happened to... Scott was sent back to the widow. She remarried, and her new husband freed Scott. He enjoyed only a few months of freedom before he died of tuberculosis. John Sanford was committed to an insane asylum before the case was settled, and died there.

PLESSY v. FERGUSON, 1896

Background: Slavery ended with the passage of the Thirteenth Amendment after the Civil War, but race was still an issue. Louisiana passed a law requiring that blacks and whites travel in separate railway cars. In 1892 Homer Plessy, who was of mixed race, was arrested when he sat in a coach reserved for whites. Lower courts convicted him, so Plessy appealed his case all the way to the Supreme Court.

The Decision: It was for this case that the justices devised the infamous phrase "separate but equal" to rationalize Louisiana's law. They declared that as long as African Americans had a coach to travel in (the "equal" part), they could be separated from white passengers. "Separate but equal" became the law of the land for more than 50 years.

Whatever Happened to... Plessy later became an insurance agent and died in 1925.

BROWN v. BOARD OF EDUCATION, 1954

Background: The father of African American student Linda Brown, a girl in Topeka, Kansas, wanted her to attend an all-white school, but she was refused admission. Her father and other like-minded parents sued and lost...sued and lost...until they reached the Supreme Court.

The Decision: In 1954 Chief Justice Earl Warren delivered the court's unanimous decision: Segregation (including "separate but equal" facilities) was damaging, unfair, and henceforth illegal.

Whatever Happened to... Linda Brown and her younger sister were only two of a dozen children in the lawsuit, but their names began with a B, so they were listed first. The Browns still live in Topeka and run an educational consulting firm.

ENGEL v. VITALE, '62; ABINGTON TOWNSHIP v. SCHEMPP, '63

Background: In both of these cases, parents of children in public schools objected to the schools' reading of prayers or Bible verses as part of the school day.

The Decision: The court found that by forcing students to pray or read the Bible, the schools were violating the First Amendment, which forbids laws that establish a government-sponsored religion or prevent the free exercise of religion. Many Americans were—and still are—opposed to the decision that seemed to "remove" prayer from public schools. However, the court did not actually ban prayer, only prayers mandated by the school authorities. Kids are still free to pray (or not pray) on their own.

Whatever Happened to... Ellery Schempp, one of the kids who rebelled against the Bible readings (he tried to read from the Koran instead, even though he wasn't Muslim), is now a noted physicist, speaker, and author.

MIRANDA v. ARIZONA, 1966

Background: In 1963 police in Phoenix, Arizona, arrested Ernesto Miranda for rape. They interrogated him until he confessed, and then demanded he write out his confession—which ultimately got Miranda convicted. His attorney appealed on the grounds that Miranda never saw a lawyer and was never even told that he *could* see a lawyer until after he confessed. In effect, the police had denied him his constitutional right to legal counsel.

The Decision: The Supreme Court ruled that the police had violated Miranda's Fifth Amendment right to avoid incriminating himself. Today, people accused of crimes have to be told they have the right to an attorney if they're going to be interrogated by the police. In fact, there's a whole list of rights, and if you've ever seen a cop show on TV, you know what they are: "You have the right to remain silent," etc. These are now known as the Miranda rights.

Whatever Happened to... Ernesto Miranda won a new trial, but a surprise witness turned up to testify against him and he was convicted again. In 1976, in a bit of irony, he got out of prison and was stabbed to death during a bar fight. The suspect was read his Miranda rights and chose to remain silent. He was released, and no one was ever charged with Miranda's murder.

ROE v. WADE, 1973

Background: Before 1973, many states had laws prohibiting abortion. Jane Roe (a pseudonym for a woman named Norma McCorvey) sued Henry Wade, a prosecuting attorney in Texas, when she was denied the right to terminate her pregnancy.

The Decision: The Supreme Court decided that Jane Roe's choice to have an abortion was protected by her Fourteenth Amendment right to privacy, and state antiabortion laws were struck down. Still, the controversy never ceased, and cases retesting the legality of abortion are still being brought before the court.

Whatever Happened to… In 1984 Norma McCorvey revealed that she was Jane Roe. The child she'd had was given up for adoption. In the 1990s, McCorvey began working for Operation Rescue, stating that she no longer believed that abortions should be legal.

BUSH v. GORE, 2000

Background: Democrat Al Gore and Republican George W. Bush ran against each other for president in 2000. The election was famously "too close to call" because of disputed results in Florida. Voters there cast six million votes, and in the end, Bush pulled ahead there by fewer than 1,800 votes. When some of Florida's counties retallied their ballots, Bush's lead shrunk to 300 votes. The Democrats pushed for a statewide recount, but the Republicans resisted. Their candidate had won, they said. Both political parties filed lawsuits, and the case quickly ended up in the hands of the Supreme Court.

The Decision: The court stopped the recount, ensuring victory for Bush. Technically, the justices were simply deciding whether to allow a recount in Florida, but in actuality, they chose who would be president. This angered Americans who believed that contested elections shouldn't be left up the Supreme Court because it will ultimately side with the candidate more aligned with the majority of justices' political leanings.

Whatever Happened to… Bush served two terms as president. Gore starred in the Oscar-winning environmental documentary *An Inconvenient Truth* in 2006, and won the Nobel Peace Prize in 2007.

There is no constitutional way to remove a Supreme Court justice for incompetence.

UNCLE JOHN'S STALL OF FAME: POLITICS EDITION

Where would a book on politics be without the toilet? Down the drain, that's where! So we decided to flush out our favorite Stall of Fame entries from past books in order to shine a light on public officials who have had the chutzpah to turn Uncle John's favorite room into a political statement. We salute you!

Honoree: Irene Smith, a member of the St. Louis Board of Aldermen in Missouri

Notable Achievement: Taking care of business…while taking care of business

True Story: In July 2001, Smith and three other lawmakers were staging a filibuster over a redistricting plan that they felt would hurt their constituents. Smith had to go to the bathroom, but the president of the board told her that if she left the room for any reason, she would lose the floor and her filibuster would end. Rather than abandon her cause, Smith held out for 40 minutes; then, when she couldn't put off nature's call any longer, "her aides surrounded her with a sheet, tablecloth, and quilt while she appeared to use a trash can to relieve herself," according to one account. "What I did behind that tablecloth was my business," she explained afterward. No word on whether Smith won her redistricting fight, but she certainly won the day—the board of aldermen adjourned without voting on the controversial plan…but not without condemning Smith. "The people in Missouri must think we're a bunch of morons," Mayor Francis Slay told reporters.

Honoree: State Senator Al Lawson of Florida

Notable Achievement: Coming up with a "pay-as-you-go" plan to help growing towns upgrade their sewer systems.

True Story: Lawson introduced a bill in 2005 that would place a tax of two cents per roll on toilet paper. The money was to be used to fund the

All in the family: President Grant appointed 13 of his relatives to federal posts.

sewer system improvements and to help fast-growing Florida communities cope with increasing demands on infrastructure. Lawson estimated the tax could raise as much as $50 million per year. "Two cents is not going to hurt families at all," he said. "People don't mind paying for it." Governor Jeb Bush would not commit one way or the other, but said that if toilet paper is taxed, people might use less of it. "That's not necessarily a good thing," said the governor.

Honorees: Li Zhaoxing, a Chinese diplomat, and Taro Aso, a Japanese diplomat

Notable Achievement: Successfully practicing "toilet diplomacy"

True Story: In Malaysia in 2006, during summit talks to improve the tense relationship between China and Japan, Aso was using the men's room when Li happened to walk in. With the press corps waiting outside, the two talked about state matters…for 20 minutes. Then they exited (one at a time) and went to their respective seats for the "formal" set of meetings. Once there, Aso announced to his colleagues, "I just met Li in the toilet and we had a good discussion." Asked later whether Aso knew that Li was already in the restroom, he dismissed it as pure coincidence, adding, "But it was awfully cold in the conference room."

Honoree: Rella Morris, mayor of Granite Falls, Washington

Notable Achievement: Being the first U.S. elected official to preside at an official function…dressed in toilet paper.

True Story: Known as the gateway to Washington's Cascade Mountains, Granite Falls became better known as "the town without a toilet" years ago when vandals blew up the town's only portable public restroom. The town went without any public facilities until the late 1990s, when Mayor Morris and the city council decided it was time for a change. They raised the $91,000 needed to build a public restroom complete with four stalls, two urinals, and sinks with infrared sensors to turn the faucets on and off.

When the restrooms were finally constructed (which took more than a year), the town celebrated with its first-ever Toilet Festival. They had an exhibition of toilet-themed art, a toilet-paper-tearing ceremony (instead of a ribbon-cutting), and a raffle to determine which lucky citizen would get to flush the first flush. Mayor Morris didn't exactly dress to the nines for the occasion, but she did dress to the two-plies, wearing a robe made of toilet paper and carrying a toilet plunger for a scepter. "This town," she told the crowd, "really knows how to potty!"

Honoree: The government of Suwon, South Korea

Notable Achievement: Using clean bathrooms as a foreign-relations tool

True Story: "In this era of globalization," declared a Suwon government official, "it is important to become the leader in the world in the cleanest bathrooms." The city has spared no expense in making that a reality. There are 580 plush public restrooms with heated toilet seats. Visitors can enjoy violin music (piped in through speakers) along with tasteful paintings and flower arrangements to keep the mood fresh. Suwon makes a little extra on the side by giving guided tours, and some well-to-do ironic hipsters even meet in the fancy bathrooms for tea.

Honoree: Lieutenant Governor Steve Windom of Alabama

Notable Achievement: Strategic use of a chamber pot to wear down his political enemies

True Story: In March 1999, Windom, a Republican, was presiding over the 35-member state legislature composed of 18 Democrats and 17 Republicans. During an important battle over senate procedures, Windom feared that if he surrendered the gavel and left the chamber for even a minute, the Democrats would take control and his party would lose the fight. So the lieutenant governor decided he wouldn't even to go out to the bathroom until the battle was won.

"Anticipating the worst," one reporter wrote, "he brought a pitcher to the chamber and conducted business—both official and personal—from behind a large podium." Two days and two 15-hour marathon sessions later, the Democrats gave in and Windom won the battle. "It takes guts to be an effective lieutenant governor," he told reporters. "It also takes a bladder of steel."

*   *   *

"A conservative, a liberal, and a moderate walk into a bar. The bartender says, 'Hi, Mitt!'"

—**Foster Friess**

Women in Switzerland did not win the right to vote until 1971.

THE MAYOR WITH TWO NAMES

Here's a strange story about a mayor who was well liked by the citizens of his small town. But they didn't know about his bizarre, secret past.

MEET DON LaROSE

In the mid-1970s, Don LaRose was a happily married man with two young daughters. A respected pastor in the town of Maine, New York, he often gave sermons warning against the evils of Satan. Then, in 1975, he suddenly vanished. Three months later, Minnesota police picked up a homeless man who said his name was Bruce Kent Williamson—but he couldn't remember much other than that. After he was checked into a mental hospital in Chicago, his memory started to come back. He said he thought his name was Don LaRose and that he'd been abducted by "Satanists" who were "determined to expunge every last bit of righteousness" from him. He said they brainwashed him with shock treatments until he believed he was a totally different person. "In truth," he said, "I'm not sure who I am." Staff were able to locate his family and send word that he was safe.

LaRose's wife went to Chicago and brought her weary husband home. Though his memory was still cloudy, he tried to pick up the pieces of his former life. In 1977 the LaRose family moved to Hammond, Indiana, and Don resumed his duties as a Baptist minister. At first, life was good. But underneath, he was a terrorized man. LaRose told local police that his Satanist abductors had caught up with him again and were threatening to make his life a "living hell if he didn't stop blaspheming Satan." The police didn't believe him. Then, in 1980, Don LaRose disappeared again.

MEET KEN WILLIAMS

A few months later, a man in his early 40s named Ken Williams arrived in northwest Arkansas. While Don LaRose had been a clean-shaven man with glasses, Ken Williams had a graying beard, bushy eyebrows, and no glasses. That was all the disguise he needed—for the next 27 years, LaRose lived as Ken Williams. After remarrying in 1986, he was once again a respected family man…but the guilt of leaving his first family haunted him. "What I had done weighed heavily on my heart and mind from the first day I rode out of Hammond," he later wrote. "What happened in 1980, whether it was right or wrong, I did because I was under threat for the safety of my family. If I'd stayed, there'd be bodies in a grave." In 21 years of marriage, he didn't even tell his second wife about his former life. Williams was appointed mayor of Centerton, Arkansas, in 2001 after the town's previous mayor resigned. He was reelected twice.

THE JIG IS UP

Williams might have continued living with his secret if he hadn't been so preoccupied with his former life. In March 2007, he created the website *DonLaRose.com*, which chronicled his former self's mysterious disappearance. One of LaRose's nephews found the site on the Internet and shared it with his family; they were amazed at how detailed it was. And then they saw the name of the site's creator: Bruce Kent Williams. It was so similar to "Bruce Kent Williamson" that they knew they'd finally found him. Not only was he not dead, not homeless, and not in a mental institution, but there he was—the *mayor* of a town. Rather than call the police, they called the *Benton County Daily Record*—and the story shocked Centerton's 5,500 citizens. At first, Williams denied it, but soon admitted to the accusations and resigned. His second wife, Pat, asked, "Who are you—Don LaRose or Ken Williams?" He replied, "I'm a little of both, I guess."

A TALE OF TWO FAMILIES

Pat Williams supported her husband: "I love him. I'll stand by him. We're in it for the duration." And many people in Centerton felt the same way. Said one citizen: "I can verify the fact that Mayor Ken Williams was always unbiased, fair in his decisions, and wise beyond his years. He is an honest gentleman."

But with Don LaRose's family, it was a different story. His first wife, who had since remarried and still lived in Indiana, refused to speak to the press about the ordeal. So did his two adult daughters. His father, 97-year-old Adam LaRose, did take questions from his hospice, and explained that he'd never gotten over the sting of being abandoned by his son: "I would love to see him again. That would be my day." LaRose has since met with some of his family, including his father. However, LaRose's 22-year-old grandson, Tony Hofstra, is skeptical: "I don't know if he's crazy or if he's lying to everybody about this Satanic attack and all these threats. I don't know if he just didn't want to pay child support and disappeared."

In August 2008, police determined that Williams had committed a crime, and he was brought up on felony forgery charges. He pleaded guilty and was sentenced to five years' probation and 100 hours of community service. "I just wanted to put the experience behind me," he said.

STILL PREACHING

Today, he runs two websites. The first, *KenWilliamsMinistries.com*, makes no mention of Don LaRose. His other site, *DonLaRose.com*, contains an eight-chapter book that Williams calls his "amazing story of survival." Is it true? No one—perhaps not even Williams himself—knows for sure (he's said that some of the details of his ordeal are still murky). Either way, it's a chilling read:

> I also have a recurring dream which is always the same, but with some variations. In each dream I am either tied to, or strapped to, a wooden chair, an arm chair or a recliner. In each dream the electrodes are attached to my head and I am begging them not to do it. And in each dream, when the switch is thrown, I scream as loudly as I possibly can because of the excruciating pain.

LINGERING QUESTIONS

• Where did he get the name Ken Williams? From a teenager who was killed in a car accident in 1958. Authorities aren't sure how LaRose was able to acquire his Social Security number.

• Were there ever any "Satanists"? Police have found no evidence of their existence outside of Williams's stories—and even those are sketchy. Shortly after his secret came out, he wrote on his website, "Since my unveiling on Wednesday, I have revised this report to delete portions of the story designed to keep people from following my trail." But now that the story has been told in media outlets all over the world, who knows if the Satanists will ever catch up to LaRose/Williams, or if they existed in the first place?

Oscar J. Dunn, a former slave, became lieutenant governor of Louisiana in 1868.

PRESIDENTIAL POT SHOTS

It's commander in chief vs. commander in chief! Take no prisoners!

"Jefferson was repulsive. Continually puling about liberty, equality, and the degrading curse of slavery, he brought his own children to the hammer, and made money of their debaucheries."

—Alexander Hamilton

"McKinley has no more backbone than a chocolate éclair."

—Theodore Roosevelt

"Why, this fellow [Ike] doesn't know any more about politics than a pig knows about Sunday."

—Harry S. Truman

"People have said that my language was bad, but Jesus! You should have heard LBJ."

—Richard Nixon

"Do you realize the responsibility I carry? I'm the only one standing between Nixon and the White House."

—John F. Kennedy

"Putting Bush and Quayle in charge of the economy is like making General Sherman the fire marshal of Atlanta."

—Bill Clinton

"Being attacked on character by Clinton is like being called ugly by a frog."

—George H. W. Bush

"When the American people cried out for economic help, Jimmy Carter took refuge behind a dictionary. Well, if it's a definition he wants, I'll give him one: Recession is when your neighbor loses his job. Depression is when you lose yours. And recovery is when Jimmy Carter loses his."

—Ronald Reagan

"I certainly don't know what Obama believes in. The only foreign policy thing I remember he said was he's going to attack Pakistan and embrace [Iranian president] Ahmadinejad."

—George W. Bush

"Part of the reason people are so intensely involved in this election is that they know that they'll be called to choose the next president. And no matter what happens, they'll be glad that George W. Bush won't be on the ballot."

—Barack Obama

The Millard Fillmore Society celebrates the insignificance of the 13th president.

HE VOODOOED THE PREZ

Maybe there's more to voodoo curses than we think…

CURSES!

In November 2006, President George W. Bush made a brief stop in Jakarta for a meeting with Indonesian president Susilo Yudhoyono. At the same exact time, an Indonesian man was slitting the throats of a goat and a snake and stabbing a crow in the chest so he could mix their blood together—with some spices and broccoli—and then drink the concoction. And whatever he couldn't drink, he smeared on his face.

Ki Gendeng Pamungkas, a well-known "black magic" practitioner in Jakarta, was performing what he said was a Voodoo ritual to curse the president and his Secret Service contingent. The ritual, he said, would put Secret Service agents into a trance, making them believe they were under attack, which would lead to chaos. As for President Bush: "My curse will make him bloat like broccoli," said Pamungkas. He added that it was sure to work, because "the devil is with me today."

VOODOO? WHO DO?

While the president never complained (publicly) of any intestinal trouble during his trip, shortly after the curse several strange incidents occurred. Voodoo or coincidence? You be the judge.

• Just hours before arriving in Jakarta, the auto-brake on *Air Force One* malfunctioned and six tires blew out as the plane was landing in Ho Chi Minh City, Vietnam (nobody was hurt).

• The next day, the presidential contingent traveled to Hawaii, where the president's travel director, Greg Pitts, 25, was mugged and beaten after leaving a nightclub in Waikiki. Newspaper reports said he was "too drunk" to describe the suspects to police.

• And across the globe, while eating at a restaurant in Argentina, the president's daughter Barbara was robbed. Someone stole her purse…right under the noses of her Secret Service guards. (The night before, another agent was involved in an altercation after a night out. Secret Service officials said it was a "mugging.")

By law, Yankee bean soup must be served in the Congressional dining room at all times.

JOIN THE PARTY: THE DEMOCRATS

*With the Federalist Party no more (page 97), a new party emerged.
And as this next chapter illustrates, corruption, partisan bickering,
and contested elections are nothing new in American politics.*

ONE-PARTY SYSTEM

After the Federalists dissolved in 1820, it seemed that American democracy might be returning to a one-party system. What prevented that from happening? The fact that four men—Secretary of War John C. Calhoun, Secretary of the Treasury William Crawford, Secretary of State John Quincy Adams, and Speaker of the House Henry Clay—all wanted to succeed Monroe as president.

Calhoun and Crawford were not above using the patronage and other perks of their offices to gain an advantage in the race. And both of them leaked details of the other's doings to news reporters. In the process, the entire Monroe administration became tainted with a reputation for corruption.

ACTION JACKSON

Many Americans were outraged by Calhoun's and Crawford's scheming. One such man was General Andrew Jackson, hero of the Battle of New Orleans in 1815 and a leader so tough that his soldiers called him "Old Hickory" after "the hardest wood in creation." As the first war hero since George Washington, Jackson was the most popular living American, and for years his admirers had urged him to run for president. For years he had turned them down.

But the corruption of the Monroe administration changed his mind. It convinced Jackson that it was "his public duty to campaign for the presidency and engage in what he called 'a general cleansing' of the federal capital," historian Paul Johnson writes in *A History of the American People*. "Jackson became the first presidential candidate to grasp with both hands what was to become the most popular campaigning theme in American history—'Turn the rascals out.'"

The speaker of the UK House of Commons must show "extreme reluctance" on taking office.

Jackson became the fifth candidate to enter the race for president in 1824. Although he was the least politically experienced of the candidates, he was the most popular man in the country. Result: On election day, Jackson won more votes and carried more states than any other candidate. But amazingly, it wasn't enough.

POLITICAL SCRAMBLING

Because the electoral college vote was split among four candidates, none of them, not even Jackson, won an absolute majority of electoral votes. According to the Twelfth Amendment to the Constitution, that meant that the House of Representatives would have to choose between the top three finishers: Jackson, Adams, and Crawford. Each state's delegation would get one vote.

Because he came in fourth, Henry Clay was excluded from consideration for the presidency. But as Speaker of the House, he was well positioned to steer it to the candidate of his choice, and his choice was John Quincy Adams. Crawford had suffered a stroke during the campaign and was in no condition to assume presidential duties, and Clay saw Jackson as "a mere military chieftain" with a bad temper and not nearly enough political experience to be president. By comparison, Adams was the Harvard-educated son of a former president, and had served stints as secretary of state and U.S. ambassador to Russia.

Clay worked hard to deliver the presidency to Adams, but when the time came to vote in the House of Representatives, he was still one vote short—he needed New York. But the New York delegation was evenly split, which, according to the rules, meant that its vote wouldn't even be counted unless someone in the delegation changed his vote.

THAT'S THE TICKET

Henry Clay put enormous pressure on an elderly New York congressman named Stephen Van Rensselaer to change his vote in favor of Adams…but Van Rensselaer couldn't make up his mind. So when the vote was called, he lowered his head, closed his eyes, and whispered a short prayer, asking for divine guidance.

When Van Rensselaer opened his eyes, the first thing he saw was a ticket for John Quincy Adams on the floor beneath his desk. That was all he needed—Van Rensselaer picked up the ticket, carried it over to the

Landlords: The federal government owns about 30% of the land in America.

ballot box, and put Adams in the White House.

Jackson, who'd won more votes and carried more states than anyone else, was convinced that he'd just been cheated out of the presidency. The Adams presidency, he charged, was the result of a "corrupt bargain": essentially Henry Clay had delivered the presidency to Adams and Adams appointed Clay secretary of state, which in those days was considered heir apparent to the presidency. Jackson and his supporters vowed to get revenge.

The Jeffersonian Republican Party was so deeply divided over the election of 1824 that it split in two. Jackson's supporters now began to refer to themselves as the "*Democratic*-Republican" Party—Democrats for short. Adams's supporters called themselves the "*National* Republicans."

The two-party system was back, this time to stay.

MUD FIGHT

What followed was one of the nastiest political battles in the history of the United States. Adams, his reputation tarnished by the charges of corruption, was determined to muddy Jackson's reputation as well. Adams's supporters attacked Jackson's military career, accusing him of misconduct during the War of 1812. They also dug up an old charge (possibly true) that he'd married his wife Rachel before her divorce from her first husband was final. That made her a bigamist, which was not only illegal but scandalous.

Nothing was sacred. Adams's people even attacked Jackson's deceased mother. The pro-Adams *National Journal* called her "a Common Prostitute, brought to this country by British soldiers! She afterwards married a *Mulatto Man*, by whom she had several children of which *General Jackson is one!*"

Jackson's forces fought back, attacking President Adams as an out-of-touch, elitist aristocrat, as well as an alcoholic and a "Sabbath-breaker" who, when he did go to church, went barefoot.

LIFE OF THE PARTY

But what really made the election of 1828 remarkable was that it was the first truly national presidential campaign. Traditionally, the slow pace of communication across the U.S. necessitated that political campaigns be

---

"I understand deficit spending. I was born in deficit spending." —Al Sharpton

run at the state and local level, with no national strategy or tactics. That began to change in 1826 when Senator Martin Van Buren, the political boss of New York known as "the Little Magician," joined forces with the Jackson camp.

Van Buren launched a centrally controlled communications strategy. The campaign formed its own newspaper, called the *United States Telegraph*, and hired a staff of writers to write pro-Jackson articles that were then published in the *Telegraph* and 50 other pro-Jackson papers around the country.

At the same time, local and state committees organized pro-Jackson dinners, barbecues, parades, and other events where local politicos would deliver stump speeches written by the national campaign. Campaign workers sang campaign songs—another innovation for 1828—planted hickory trees in town squares and along major roads, and distributed hickory brooms, hickory canes, and even hickory leaves that people could wear to show their support for Old Hickory. Then, on election day, local Jackson organizations marched their voters to the polls under banners reading "Jackson and Reform."

DEMOCRATS IN POWER

The old-fashioned Adams campaign could not match the strategy or intensity of the Jackson campaign. Old Hickory won 56 percent of the popular vote and 178 out of 261 electoral votes, including every state west of New Jersey and south of the Potomac River. "Organization is the secret of victory," one pro-Adams newspaper observed, and "by want of it, we have been overthrown."

"Jackson's victory brought a full-blown party system into existence," Arthur Schlesinger writes in *Of the People*. "Martin Van Buren was the champion of the organized party with party machinery, national conventions, and national committees, all held together by party discipline and the cult of party loyalty."

So with the Democrats firmly established, it was time for the Republicans to rise up beside them, right? Not so fast—there was another political party that vied for the top spot first. *Read about the birth of the Whigs on page 205.*

PARLIAMENTARY MANNERS

*This excerpt from the "Dear Miss Parliamentary Manners"
column in the* Canadian National Post *proves there's
more than meets the ear when politicians argue.*

GOV-SPEAK

A recent news story contended that decorum is taking a bruising in Canadian legislatures. The article quoted a cabinet minister as saying, "There is a certain level of civil discourse to be expected in the house even during heckling." How can you be civil and heckle at the same time? Actually, it's very easy to hector with ferocity and yet remain civil and mannerly—once you've mastered the subtle nuances of the parliamentary vernacular.

Expression: "My learned colleague."
Translation: "You cheese-eating throwback."

Expression: "If the honorable member will forward his request to my department, we will provide the relevant documents."
Translation: "Talk to the hand."

Expression: "I would be happy to address the member's question."
Translation: "I yearn to bleach your skull and use it on my desk as a novelty pencil holder."

Expression: "If the member had concerns, he should have made them known at the proper time."
Translation: "Your mother didn't have any complaints last night."

Expression: "Mr. Speaker, the people of Canada deserve an answer."
Translation: "Leave my mother out of this—I swear, I'll cut you!"

Expression: "I am outraged by your craven duplicity!"
Translation: "I'm not really upset; I just wanted to get on the news. Want to have dinner tonight?"

Liz who? Only 14% of Canadians polled know Queen Elizabeth II is the head of state.

VIDEO TREASURES

Politics is a mixture of drama and comedy with a splash of thriller and horror thrown in just to keep things interesting. Being political junkies ourselves, we compiled a list of well-reviewed political films you might enjoy.

BOB ROBERTS (1992) *Comedy*
Review: "Smart, funny political satire about a right-wing, folk-singing senatorial candidate who knows how to manipulate an audience—and the media." (*Leonard Maltin's Movie & Video Guide*)
Director/Star: Tim Robbins

A WORLD APART (1988) *Foreign/Drama*
Review: "Anti-apartheid struggles in the 1960s seen through the eyes of a 13-year-old South African girl whose mother is imprisoned for her support of the African National Congress. Excellently acted and moving mix of political and domestic drama." (*Halliwell's Video Guide*) **Stars:** Jodhi May, Barbara Hershey **Director:** Chris Menges

THE INTERPRETER (2005) *Thriller*
Review: "A taut and intelligent thriller, centering on an interpreter at the United Nations and a Secret Service agent. And, no, they don't have romantic chemistry: The players in a dangerous game are too busy staying alive and preventing a murder of an African dictator, once respected, now accused of genocide. The story was filmed largely on location in and around the United Nations; it's the first film given permission to do that. It adds an unstated level of authenticity." (Roger Ebert) **Stars:** Nicole Kidman, Sean Penn **Director:** Sydney Pollack

STATE OF THE UNION (1948) *Comedy*
Review: "Contemporary as ever, this literate comedy-drama casts Spencer Tracy as an industrialist who struggles to keep his integrity as he's swallowed into the political machinery of running for president. Hepburn is his wife and conscience, Lansbury a power-hungry millionairess backing the campaign. Great entertainment." (*Leonard Maltin's Movie Guide*) **Stars:** Spencer Tracy, Katharine Hepburn, Angela Lansbury **Director:** Frank Capra

---

25% of Tea Party members are either Hispanic, Asian American, or African American.

THE CANDIDATE (1972) *Drama*

Review: "A young Californian lawyer is persuaded to run for senator; in succeeding, he alienates his wife and obscures his real opinions. A rousing, doubting American political film." (*Halliwell's Film and Video Guide*)
Stars: Robert Redford, Peter Boyle **Director:** Michael Ritchie

THE WAR ROOM (1993) *Documentary*

Review: "Nominated for an Oscar for best documentary, this film follows Bill Clinton's 1992 presidential campaign staff (including James Carville and George Stephanopoulos) from the first primary to the acceptance speech. The viewer gets a firsthand look at the inner workings of a campaign, including mudslinging. Quite fascinating." (*DVD and Video Guide*)
Directors: Chris Hegedus and D.A. Pennebaker

UNDERGROUND (1995) *Foreign/Drama*

Review: "A sprawling, imaginative, and impressive work, alternately funny and dark, it won the Palme d'Or at Cannes. The film blends passion and politics as a telling reminder that beneath the bloodshed in the former Yugoslavia is a proud and defiant spirit. Recounting the history of that country, the movie spans 50 years." (*Boxoffice Magazine*) **Stars:** Miki Manojlovic, Lazar Ristovski **Director:** Emir Kusturica

THE GREAT McGINTY (1940) *Satire*

Review: "This witty political satire is about a hobo who gets hooked up with a crooked politician and rises in the political world from alderman to mayor, and finally to governor. Won an Oscar for its superlative screenplay, and has a sterling ensemble cast." (*Great Movies You've Probably Missed*) **Stars:** Brian Donlevy, Akim Tamiroff **Director:** Preston Sturges

ADVISE & CONSENT (1962) *Drama*

Review: There are recognizable projections of character assassination, McCarthy-like demagoguery, and use of the two hard-to-answer smears of this ill-natured generation: 'Are you now or were you once a homosexual and/or a communist?' Endowed with wholly capable performers, the characterizations come through with fine clarity, and the realistic settings give it a look of genuineness." (*Variety*) **Stars:** Henry Fonda, Charles Laughton **Director:** Otto Preminger

---

The UN Security Council president is rotated alphabetically by country each month.

YOUR GOVERNMENT
AT WORK

Would you believe it? Congress just gave us a $2-million grant to reprint this overspending article from Uncle John's Slightly Irregular Bathroom Reader. *Now that's a stimulus package we can believe in!*

STRESS REDUCTION

In an effort to reduce stress levels and improve the self-esteem of public housing tenants, the U.S. Department of Housing and Urban Development spent $860,000 on a "Creative Wellness" program in 2001. The plan: The government was paying to enhance the tenants' lifestyles through "aromatherapy, color therapy, and 'gemstone support' (tapping the healing powers of precious stones)."

GOVERNMENT PENSIONS

• In 1995 Illinois assemblyman Roger P. McAuliffe introduced legislation allowing police officers-turned-state representatives to collect pensions from both fields of employment. The sole beneficiary of the bill: Assemblyman Roger P. McAuliffe, a former police officer.

• Rhode Island state senator John Orabona claimed an annual pension of $106,000 when he retired in 1995, based on 79 years' worth of state service. The problem: He was 51 years old. So how did he acquire more years in pension credits than he'd been alive? Easy. He found (and exploited) a loophole in the state's pension legislation that made it possible for him to combine benefits from various jobs. (Another Orabona scam awarded government insiders pension credit toward summer jobs, such as lifeguarding.)

UNCOVERING FRAUD

A 2001 review of the Defense Contract Audit Agency revealed that the agency fabricated (and destroyed) documents in order to receive a passing grade from the IRS. The DCAA, responsible for auditing government contracts, blew 983 hours and $63,000 creating the fraudulent documents. The task was so difficult they had to call in additional auditors—for which they billed the American taxpayers $1,600 in travel expenses.

ACCURATE CENSUS REPORTING

In 2003 the U.S. Census Bureau reported that according to statistics compiled by their researchers, more than 200 people living in Indianapolis, Indiana, traveled to work by subway or ferry. One problem: There are no subways or ferries in Indianapolis.

GI BILLS

In 2002 the General Accounting Office reported finding that at least 200 U.S. Army personnel spent $38,000 on personal expenses using Defense Department–issued credit cards. According to reports, many of the charges (including "lap dancing") were made at strip clubs near military bases. Other charges: mortgage payments, racetrack betting, Internet gambling, and Elvis photos from Graceland. Further investigation revealed that many government offices abuse charge card programs. Some examples cited by the GAO: laptop computers, pet supplies, DVD players, pizzas, and $30,000 worth of Palm Pilots.

THE DEPARTMENT OF DUMPSTER DIVING

Before approving benefits, the Oregon Department of Human Services requires all welfare applicants to take an informational workshop on saving money. As part of the program, attendees received a list of 17 suggested "saving" techniques, one of which was to "check the dump and residential or business Dumpsters."

PROVIDING ROLE MODELS

In April 2000, during the late hours of an all-night session of the Massachusetts legislature, a representative in the middle of a passionate speech on gun control asked members, "Are you leaders or followers?" A chant of "We lead!" erupted from the floor, followed by shouts of "Toga! Toga!" Assistant Majority Whip Salvatore DiMasi responded with a call for "order in the Animal House." How did things get so out of control? It just so happened that a member of the legislature had sponsored a wine- and beer-tasting event in conjunction with a vote on the state budget. When voting took place, many members were already quite drunk. One representative was rumored to have had his legs shaved by his colleagues while he was passed out.

...were caught by cameras playing solitaire on their laptops.

EPA: THEN AND NOW

*This story bounces from idealism to corruption and back
to idealism so many times, it'll make your head spin.*

THERE'S SOMETHING HAPPENING HERE

The 1960s were a time of environmental awakening in the United States. People across the nation began to question the unchecked industrial progress of postwar America: Oily rivers were burning, cities were covered in smog, and factories spewed their waste into towns, lakes, rivers, and oceans.

One catalyst for this awakening was Rachel Carson's seminal 1962 book *Silent Spring*. An immediate best seller, it warned of the dangers of pollution and pesticides, particularly DDT, which was killing off numerous plant and bird species. Words such as "environmentalism" and "ecology," used almost exclusively by scientists until then, were now becoming a part of the national lexicon. The modern green movement was born.

TRICKY DICK

Even politicians started paying attention. Just days after taking office in January 1969, President Richard Nixon established the National Industrial Pollution Control Council (NIPCC). On the surface, it seemed that Nixon was genuinely concerned about the environment. But in reality, the committee was just for show—it was made up entirely of corporate executives, usually not the most ardent environmentalists. The public was skeptical.

Attempting to prove that he was indeed concerned about the planet, Nixon asked NIPCC member Roy L. Ash (founder of defense contractor Litton Industries) to chair the President's Council on Executive Organization in May 1969. Ash soon determined that the best way for the government to enact environmental change would be to combine all of the government's "green" offices, committees, and activities under the guidance of a single agency.

In late 1969, the U.S. Senate passed Senator Gaylord Nelson's (D-WI) National Environmental Policy Act (NEPA). And the NEPA wasn't just for show—it called for all federal agencies from then on to

John F. Kennedy was the first U.S. president to name a sibling to a cabinet post.

clear any projects that might impact the environment. Each and every project would have to file an "Environmental Impact Statement" and await review.

President Nixon signed the NEPA into law on January 1, 1970. A few weeks later, at his State of the Union address, he told the nation that the 1970s would be a "historic period when, by conscious choice, we transform our land into what we want it to become."

THE LOUD MINORITY

Still, many Americans didn't believe Nixon, who hadn't lived up to his campaign promise of ending major combat operations in Vietnam. Senator Nelson, after touring the U.S. to speak to college students about conservation, came up with a plan for what he later called a "huge grassroots protest over what was happening to our environment. I was satisfied that if we could tap into the environmental concerns of the general public and infuse the student anti-war energy into the environmental cause, we could generate a demonstration that would force this issue onto the political agenda. It was a big gamble, but worth a try." Nelson's gamble paid off and, on April 22, 1970—dubbed "Earth Day"—more than 20 million people across the nation gathered to demand that the government provide more than lip service when it came to clean air and water.

The success of the first Earth Day put Nixon's plans for a new agency into high gear. Under Reorganization Plan 3, issued by the president in July 1970, the United States Environmental Protection Agency would be created. Its sworn mission: "The establishment and enforcement of environmental protection standards consistent with national environmental goals."

E PLURIBUS UNUM

Specifically, the EPA would be charged with researching the adverse effects of pollution and how to reduce them. Then it would change public policy to reflect its findings. It would also, through grants and research assistance, help private organizations curb and prevent pollution. Some of the preexisting offices that were moved into the EPA's jurisdiction included the Federal Water Quality Administration (formerly an Interior Department office); the National Air Pollution Control Administration and the FDA's pesticide research division (both from Health, Education, and Welfare); and the Bureau of Radiological Health. In all, 15 programs were transferred to the EPA from other departments. President Nixon wanted the EPA to consider "air pollution, water pollution, and solid wastes as different forms of a single problem" and to develop a systematic approach to solving that problem. Congress approved Reorganization Plan 3, and on December 2, 1970, the Environmental Protection Agency officially opened.

EARLY SUCCESS

The EPA's first administrator, former assistant attorney general William Ruckelshaus, was determined to keep any conflicts of interest out of the new department. Called "Mr. Clean" by both friends and foes, he stated outright that the EPA had "no obligation to promote commerce or agriculture."

Almost immediately, Ruckelshaus set out to fix three particularly polluted cities: Cleveland, Detroit, and Atlanta. Their respective mayors were given six months to comply with pollution regulations or they would face legal repercussions. Cleveland and Detroit were accused of polluting the Lake Erie basin, while Atlanta was cited for polluting the Chattahoochee River. In the end, compliance took far longer than six months, but all three cities eventually did clean themselves up and are much cleaner today than they were in 1970.

Also on the hit list was DDT, the pesticide that helped spark the environmental movement in the first place. After seven months of intense hearings, the EPA banned most uses of DDT in 1972. The pesticide's manufacturers protested and filed suit, but the ban was held up in court.

The future looked bright. It seemed to many at the time that the nation's environmental problems could—and would—be solved by the end of the 1970s. On television, Woodsy Owl, Smokey Bear, and a crying Indian urged people to be more responsible outside. And in Washington, D.C., the EPA, for a time, was holding corporate offenders accountable. According to Ruckelshaus, "We thought we had technologies that could control pollutants, keeping them below threshold levels at a reasonable cost, and that the only things missing in the equation were national standards and a strong enforcement effort."

But it wasn't going to be that simple.

It's illegal to die in the UK House of Commons, or to enter wearing a suit of armor.

THE INDUSTRY PROTECTION AGENCY

As the 1980s began, there was less reason for optimism. The Reagan administration put environmental concerns on the back burner, and corporate interests began to take precedence over everything else. The government agency once hailed as the "good guys" had abandoned the movement that helped create it.

"In my 25 years with EPA," said whistle-blower William Sanjour in 1998,

> I have heard countless remarks and witnessed many heartless actions denigrating environmental concerns and, most particularly, community environmental activists. While for the outside world, the EPA puts on a face of concern and caring for the unfortunate victims of environmental pollution, the agency is permeated with contempt for these same people.

One of the most alarming claims made by Sanjour: In the 1980s, the EPA knew that Westinghouse was dumping its toxic waste in Bloomington, Indiana. Although concentrations of toxins in the area were more than 15 times higher than recommended levels, the public was told there was no danger (even though EPA staffers wore protective respiratory equipment at the sites). Why so hush-hush? According to the EPA, alerting the public would have "upset the negotiations" with Westinghouse. And that's just one of many similar stories that have leaked out.

RECENT VIOLATIONS

• One week after the September 11 attacks in New York City, the EPA stated that the air around Ground Zero was safe to breathe, even though it contained harmful levels of asbestos, lead, concrete, and glass fibers. Two years later, the Office of Inspector General of the EPA issued a report that stated they "did not have sufficient data and analyses to make such a blanket statement," but the White House Council on Environmental Quality "convinced the EPA to add reassuring statements and delete cautionary ones."

• In the 2000s, the EPA was criticized for overestimating gas mileage on some car models by up to 50 percent. This angered auto manufacturers who believed their rivals received unjustly high ratings. In 2006 the EPA altered the way it calculated gas mileage, resulting in lower and more accurate estimates. This angered car owners, including Toyota Prius owners who discovered that the car's 60 mpg rating had been downgraded to 45 mpg.

• In 2006 *Scientific American* claimed the EPA had dragged its feet in regulating pesticides, many of which the scientific community had already deemed dangerous. Even EPA staffers have questioned whether the agency is "too closely allied with the chemical companies and the makers and users of these pesticides."

• Two years later, the EPA dismissed neurotoxin specialist Deborah Rice from a committee that was evaluating the effects of fire-retardant chemicals. Rice had previously run afoul of the American Chemistry Council—a trade association for the chemical industry—when she claimed that a certain chemical was toxic. Now the ACC wanted to have her removed from the committee, claiming she was biased and that her inclusion "called into question the overall integrity" of the panel. The EPA caved to the pressure.

SO CAN THE EPA BE TRUSTED?

Many widely read magazines and studies quote statistics from EPA reports. But, given the agency's tumultuous history, how accurate are they? For the most part, figures on municipal waste and the like are probably on the mark. As former employee Sanjour attests, most EPA staffers just want to do their jobs. And, obviously, they work best when there's no conflict of interest. But a confidential survey of 1,600 EPA scientists revealed that more than 50 percent worry about political pressure affecting their work. Since the EPA is now heavily influenced by policy makers with little scientific knowledge, balancing the political and scientific aspects of its work has become one of the agency's biggest challenges.

But, as has been the case from the beginning, the EPA is only as effective as the current presidential administration allows it to be.

CHANGE?

Shortly after President Obama took office in 2009, he appointed Representative Henry Waxman (D-CA), a longtime environmental champion, as chairman of the House Committee on Energy and Commerce. An outspoken critic of the EPA's conflict of interest, Waxman has been hailed by the environmentalist community as the first high-level politician in a long time who has given them reason to hope.

A November 2008 *Time* magazine article covering president-elect

Obama's new energy policy stated that, "It's not yet clear how he'll act, but his renewable energy advisor Jason Grumet has said that Obama would be willing to use the EPA to directly regulate CO2—something President George W. Bush refused to do." For his part, Obama said, "I think the slow chipping away against clean air and clean water has been deeply disturbing. Much of it hasn't gone through Congress. That is something that can be changed by an administration, in part by reinvigorating the EPA, which has been demoralized."

So will the Environmental Protection Agency once again be able to protect the environment without the meddling of industry? Only time will tell.

*　　*　　*

SOME OF THE EPA'S ACCOMPLISHMENTS

1971: Banned the use of lead-based paint in toys.

1972: Banned the dumping of toxic chemicals in the ocean.

1972: In cooperation with the Canadian government, spearheaded the cleanup of the heavily polluted Great Lakes, which supplied drinking water to 25 million Americans.

1973: Began the phaseout of heavily polluting leaded gasoline.

1974: Congress passed the Safe Water Act, which allowed the EPA to regulate the quality of public drinking water.

1978: Began the phaseout of chlorofluorocarbons (CFCs), the propellant in aerosol cans that damage the ozone layer.

1980: Congress passed the EPA's Superfund initiative, which cleans up toxic waste sites. To date, the EPA has helped clean more than 1,000 formerly uninhabitable locations.

1991: Helped popularize recycling with the passage of the Federal Recycling Order, which required government offices to implement waste-reduction and recycling programs.

1996: The bald eagle, once threatened due to exposure to DDT, was removed from the endangered species list, owing in part to the EPA's ban of the pesticide in 1972.

In 1941 Winston Churchill had a heart attack while opening a window in the White House.

A VIDAL LINK WITH THE PRESIDENCY

*Best-selling author Gore Vidal (born in 1923) is famous for his
historic novels* Burr, Lincoln, *and* 1876. *He's also known for
his acid-sharp criticisms of U.S. presidents. Calling himself
the last of the "small-r republicans," here are some
of Vidal's musings on the men in the Oval Office.*

GEORGE WASHINGTON: "Washington is our first millionaire,
with no great love of the people. Of course, he acquired his fortune in the most honest way, by marrying it."

JOHN ADAMS: "On September 5, 1774, forty-five of the weightiest
colonial men formed the First Continental Congress at Philadelphia. The
weightiest of the lot was the Boston lawyer [and future president] John
Adams, known as the best-read man in Boston. Short, fat, given to bouts
of vanity that alternated with its first cousin self-pity, he was 39 years old
when he joined the Massachusetts delegation to the Congress."

THOMAS JEFFERSON: "There is a problem with Thomas Jefferson.
There always has been a problem. On the one hand, he is the voice of the
best aspect of the United States, which was the notion that every person
had life, liberty, and the inalienable rights, including the pursuit of happi-
ness, which turned out to be the joker in the deck."

ABRAHAM LINCOLN: "Lincoln, like Bismarck in Germany, took a
loosely federated nation with nothing much in common but a language
and made a centralized (eventually militarized) federal state."

THEODORE ROOSEVELT: "As president, Theodore Roosevelt spoke
loudly and carried a fair-sized stick. When Colombia wouldn't give him
the land that he needed for a canal, he helped invent Panama out of a
piece of Colombia; and got his canal."

FRANKLIN DELANO ROOSEVELT: "The best president of the 20th century was the FDR of 1933 to '37. He saved corporate capitalism. I can't say, in retrospect, this was such a good thing, but I was a kid when the Bonus Army marched on my hometown of Washington during Hoover and revolution was in the air. The next year FDR was in office."

HARRY S. TRUMAN: "Truman replaced the republic that Lincoln had thoughtfully left in place with a national security state, a militarized economy with bases on every continent. And he allowed our civil liberties to fade away. The first warning was when he required all government workers—several million people from the Post Office up to Cabinet members—to swear loyalty oaths to the republic that was no more. Pure Stalin."

JOHN F. KENNEDY: "He didn't have it. He had no plan. He was playing a game. He enjoyed the game of politics, like most of them do. There was no real substance to him. He was quite intelligent, very shrewd about people, but he liked the glamour of it all. He loved war, he had a very gung-ho attitude. I began to part company with him about the Bay of Pigs. Then we all forgave him, and he started the invasion and started to beef up the troops in Vietnam."

BILL CLINTON: "Clinton, people took seriously, because he was a wonderful speaker, he was a great explainer, he understood the economy, everybody knew that. The other presidents just went blank on the subject of economics. Clinton could lecture your ear off."

GEORGE W. BUSH: "I'm not a conspiracy theorist, I'm a conspiracy analyst. Everything the Bushites touch is screwed up. They could never have pulled off 9/11, even if they wanted to. Even if they longed to. They could step aside, though, or just go out to lunch while these terrible things were happening to the nation. I believe that of them."

BARACK OBAMA: "I was hopeful. He was the most intelligent person we've had in that position for a long time. But he's performed dreadfully as president. He has a total inability to understand military matters. He's acting as if Afghanistan is the magic talisman: Solve that and you solve terrorism. Obama would have been better off focusing on educating the American people. His problem is being overeducated. He doesn't realize how dim-witted and ignorant his audience is."

RUMORS OF MY DEATH: THOMAS JEFFERSON

While Mark Twain was visiting England in 1897, he received an inquiry from the U.S. about a report that he had died. "Rumors of my death," he cabled back, "are greatly exaggerated." He's not the only celebrity whose death has been erroneously reported. One time it even happened to the vice president of the United States.

DIRTY POLITICS

Who "Died": Vice President Thomas Jefferson

Cause of "Death": America's first really nasty presidential campaign was underway in 1800 when, on June 30, the *Baltimore American* reported that Jefferson (running against incumbent president John Adams) had died suddenly at his Virginia home. The story was confirmed the next day by the *Philadelphia True American*.

What Happened: According to Bruce Felton and Mark Fowler in their book *The Best, Worst and Most Unusual*:

> Reports of the death of the vice president elicited no statements of sympathy, no words of grief from President Adams, vice presidential candidate Charles Cotesworth Pinckney, or any other prominent Federalist politician, which is a measure of the bitterness of the campaign. On the other hand, Jefferson's friends spent July 4 in somber mourning. News traveled slowly in that era, and reports of Jefferson's death did not reach some outlying areas until the middle of July. And the truth followed about one week behind.

So what was the deal? *The Gazette of the United States* finally explained: "An old Negro slave called Thomas Jefferson, being dead at Monticello, gave rise to the report of the demise of the Vice-President—the slave having borne the name of his master."

But the whole episode "was no innocent misunderstanding," according to Felton and Fowler. "The rumors and reports were cleverly calculated to underscore Jefferson's slave-owning status, and the gossip about his affairs with black women. Had the timing been better, it might have influenced the election."

Rep. Earl Blumenauer (D-OR) founded the Bi-Partisan Congressional Bicycle Caucus.

THE PARANOID'S FIELD GUIDE TO SECRET SOCIETIES

Secret societies actually do exist. In fact, there are dozens of them, from the Freemasons to the Ku Klux Klan. But are they really responsible for the world's ills, as some people believe? Probably not, but on the other hand, you never know...

THE ILLUMINATI

Who They Are: This group was founded in 1776 by Adam Weishaupt, a Jesuit priest, in Bavaria. His mission: to advance the 18th-century ideals of revolution, social reform, and rational thought (the word *illuminati* means "the enlightened ones" in Latin). Weishaupt and his cronies were fiercely opposed by the monarchs of Europe and by the Catholic Church, which is why they had to meet and communicate in secret. German author Johann Goethe was a member. In the United States, both Benjamin Franklin and Thomas Jefferson were accused of being members and denied it, but both wrote favorably about Weishaupt and his efforts.

What They're Blamed For: This group has been associated with more conspiracy theories than any other. Considered the silent evil behind such paranoid bugaboos as One World Government and the New World Order, the Illuminati have been blamed for starting the French and Russian Revolutions, as well as both world wars, and almost every global conflict in between. They are said to use bribery, blackmail, and murder to infiltrate every level of power in society—business, banking, and government—to achieve their ultimate goal: world domination.

BILDERBERG GROUP

Who They Are: Founded in 1952 by Prince Bernhard of the Netherlands, the Bilderberg Group (named after the hotel in Oosterbeck, Holland, where the first meeting was held) was founded to promote cooperation and understanding between Western Europe and North America. To that end, leaders from both regions are invited to meet every year for off-the-record discussions on current issues. The list of attendees has included presidents (every one from Eisenhower to Clinton), British prime ministers (Lord Home, Lord Callaghan, Sir Edward Heath, Margaret Thatcher), captains of industry like Fiat's Giovanni Agnelli, and financiers like David Rockefeller. Invitees are members of the power elite in their countries, mostly rich and male. Meetings are closed. No resolutions are passed, no votes are taken, and no public statements are ever made.

What They're Blamed For: The fact that so many of the world's most powerful players refuse to disclose anything about the group's meetings strikes many outsiders as downright subversive. What are they doing? The group has been accused of handpicking Western leaders to be their puppets, pointing to circumstantial evidence like the fact that Bill Clinton was invited to attend a meeting before he became president, as was Britain's Tony Blair before he became prime minister. Conspiracy buffs have even accused the Bilderbergers of masterminding the global AIDS epidemic as a way of controlling world population to the benefit of the European/American elite.

TRILATERAL COMMISSION

Who They Are: Founded in 1973 by David Rockefeller and former National Security Council chief Zbigniew Brzezinski, this organization is composed of 350 prominent private citizens (none currently hold government positions) from Europe, North America, and Japan (the trilateral global power triangle). Like the Bilderberg Group, their stated goal is to discuss global issues and to promote understanding and cooperation. Unlike other groups, this one is more visible: It publishes reports, and members are identified. It's also more diverse, with women and ethnic groups represented. However, membership is by invitation only, usually on the recommendation of serving members, making it one of the most exclusive private clubs in the world. There are no representatives from developing nations.

What They're Blamed For: Many conspiracy theorists view the Trilateral Commission as the "sunny" face of the evil machinations of international bankers and business moguls who are working to make the world their oyster, with one financial system, one defense system, one government,

Franklin D. Roosevelt referred to World War II as "the War for Survival."...

and one religion—which they will control. Again, all members are major players in business and government. Americans of note include Bill Clinton, Jimmy Carter, Henry Kissinger, and George Bush (the elder), former Federal Reserve Chairman Paul Volcker, former Speaker of the House Tom Foley, and former U.S. Trade Representative Carla Hills, to name a few. Since there is considerable crossover between the Trilateral Commission and the Bilderberg Group, the commission is thought by some to be under the control of the Illuminati. That it is completely private, with no direct role in government (read "no accountability"), only adds fuel to the fires of suspicious minds.

SKULL & BONES SOCIETY

Who They Are: This society was founded at Yale University in 1833. Only 15 senior-year students are admitted annually; they meet twice a week in a grim, windowless building called the Tombs. Unlike most campus fraternities, Skull & Bones appears to focus on positioning its members for success after college. But no one knows for sure, because members are sworn to total secrecy for life. The names of past and current members include many of America's power elite: both George Bushes, William Howard Taft, as well as the descendants of such famous American families as the Pillsburys, Weyerhausers, Rockefellers, Vanderbilts, and Whitneys.

What They're Blamed For: What's wrong with a little good-old-boy networking? Nothing, perhaps, but Skull & Bones members have also been accused of practicing satanic rites within the walls of the Tombs. Initiation reportedly requires a pledge to lie in a coffin, confess sordid details of his sex life, and endure painful torture so that he may "die to the world, to be born again into the Order." Like the Illuminati, the Order (as it's called by its members) supposedly works to create a world controlled and ruled by the elite—members of Skull & Bones.

BOHEMIAN GROVE

Who They Are: Founded in 1872 by five *San Francisco Examiner* newsmen as a social boozing club, the Bohemian Grove has been called "one of the world's most prestigious summer camps" by *Newsweek*. Prospective members may wait up to 15 years to get in, and then have to pony up a $2,500 membership fee. The Grove itself is a 2,700-acre retreat set deep in a California redwood forest. Members' privacy is zealously guarded: No strangers are allowed near the site, and reporters are expressly forbidden

...Harry S. Truman changed it to "World War II" in 1945.

entry. The Bohemian Grove motto is from Shakespeare: "Weaving spiders come not here," a reminder that all deal-making is to be left at the gates. The members relax and entertain each other by putting on plays, lecturing on subjects of the day, and wining and dining lavishly.

So why does anyone care about the Bohemian Grove? Well, the membership is a virtual Who's Who of the most powerful people (mostly Republican) in American government and business. Members past and present include Dick Cheney, Donald Rumsfeld, Karl Rove, George W. Bush, Richard Nixon, Gerald Ford, Henry Kissinger, Caspar Weinberger, Stephen Bechtel, Joseph Coors, Alexander Haig, Ronald Reagan, and hundreds more. Critics claim there is no way men like these (no women are allowed) can hang out together and not make backroom deals.

What They're Blamed For: Conspiracy theorists claim that the Manhattan Project, which led to the atomic bomb, was set up at the Grove and that the decision to make Eisenhower the Republican presidential candidate for 1952 was hammered out between drinks on the lawn.

Darker charges have been made against the Grove as well. Members are purported to practice some odd rituals, such as wearing red hoods and marching in procession like ancient druids, chanting hymns to the Great Owl. Members say it's all in good fun, but outsiders wonder at the cultlike overtones. Outrageous rumors were rampant in the 1980s: sacrificial murders, drunken revels, even pedophilia, sodomy, kidnapping, and rape. Of course, none of this has ever been proven, but as limousines and private jets swoop into this secret enclave in the woods, the "big boys" continue to party and the rest of the world remains in the dark about just exactly what goes on.

*   *   *

POOPUS INTERRUPTUS

In May 2006, Guy Fournier, chairman of the state-run Canadian Broadcasting Corporation, appeared on the TV talk show *Tout le Monde en Parle* (*Everyone's Talking About It*). Fournier commented on the air that at his age—74—he enjoyed defecation more than lovemaking. The remark created such a public outcry that he had to resign from his job.

That's goofy: Mickey Mouse is prohibited from running for office in Comal County, TX.

WHAT CONSPIRACY?

We personally don't believe in all of these crazy conspiracy theories.
That black helicopter hovering overhead is just…sightseeing?
For hours on end? Someone go get the tin foil.

"In politics, nothing happens by accident. If it happened, you can bet it was planned that way."
—**Franklin D. Roosevelt**

"Give me control of a nation's money and I care not who makes the laws."
—**Mayer Amschel Rothschild**

"More things in politics happen by accident or exhaustion than happen by conspiracy."
—**Jeff Greenfield**

"The world is governed by people far different from those imagined by the public."
—**Benjamin Disraeli**

"The de facto censorship which leaves so many Americans functionally illiterate about the history of U.S. foreign affairs may be all the more effective because it is not official, heavy-handed or conspiratorial, but woven artlessly into the fabric of education and media. No conspiracy is needed."
—**William Blum**

"The ruling class has the schools and press under its thumb. This enables it to sway the emotions of the masses."
—**Albert Einstein**

"Anyone who knows how difficult it is to keep a secret among three men—particularly if they are married—knows how absurd is the idea of a worldwide secret conspiracy consciously controlling all mankind by its financial power, in real, clear analysis."
—**Oswald Mosley**

"I really wish there was some Big Brother conspiracy, but it's all about trying to make a dollar. If anyone doesn't think that this is about making money, then they're crazy."
—**Montel Williams**

"The real truth of the matter is that a financial element in the large centers has owned the government of the U.S. since the days of Andrew Jackson."
—**Franklin D. Roosevelt**

The '48 UN Universal Declaration of Human Rights has been translated into 321 languages.

NIXONIA

Random trivia about President Richard M. Nixon (1913–94).

• Nixon is the only person in American history to be elected to two terms as vice president and two terms as president.

• Nixon claimed to have never had a headache.

• At age three, Nixon fell from a horse-drawn carriage and was run over by a wheel, leaving him with a permanent scar on his forehead.

• During the 1960 presidential campaign, 43-year-old John F. Kennedy got a lot of attention because he was so young. But Nixon wasn't that much older—he was 47.

• Nixon's favorite lunch: cottage cheese with ketchup.

• Nixon's two favorite songs: "Mr. Bojangles" and "The Impossible Dream."

• While at Duke University Law School, Nixon had two nicknames: One was "Gloomy Gus," because he was considered a sourpuss; the other was "Iron Butt," because he studied so hard.

• His Secret Service code name: Searchlight.

• Nixon left the navy and successfully ran for Congress in 1946, won a Senate seat in 1950, and was selected to be Dwight Eisenhower's running mate in 1952. That means he was elected vice president just six years after leaving the navy.

• Nixon's mother named him after 12th-century English king Richard I (the "Lionheart").

• Most requested document at the National Archives: the 1972 photo of Elvis Presley's Oval Office visit with Nixon.

• When he went in for his annual presidential physical, Nixon would wear his hospital gown backward, with the opening in front, then walk down the hallway to startle nurses.

• Nixon's favorite TV show was *Gilligan's Island.*

• Two of his accomplishments as president: He abolished the draft and created the Environmental Protection Agency.

• Nixon appeared on the cover of *Time* magazine a record 56 times.

Studies show: *Daily Show* viewers are 20% more informed than general news viewers.

PECULIAR PARTIERS

*Think the Republicans and Democrats are weird? They got
nothing on these real (and really odd) political parties.*

PARTY: The Polish Beer Lovers' Party
COUNTRY: Poland
PLATFORM: In 1989 Poland's government abruptly switched from
communism to democracy. More than 100 political parties hastily formed,
including the Polish Beer Lovers' Party (*Polska Partia Przyjaciół Piwa,* or
PPPP). Led by satirist Janusz Rewinski, the PPPP's slogan was "It won't be
better but for sure it will be funnier." Their main objective: to encourage
the country's vodka drinkers to switch to beer (to combat alcoholism).
Partly because of the strange platform, and partly because the Polish people were so thrilled to finally be *allowed* to discuss politics at the pub, the
PPPP received 3 percent of the vote in the 1991 elections and was awarded 16 seats in Parliament. But when party members realized that they'd
have to actually *govern*—and not just talk about how great beer is—they
split off into two factions—"Large Beer" and "Small Beer"—and then dissolved as a party. But some of the PPPP's members remained in Parliament as serious politicians…who happen to enjoy beer.

PARTY: Party! Party! Party!
COUNTRY: Australia
PLATFORM: Who says a party has to win an election to change things?
This party's platform was the same as its name: "Party! Party! Party!"
Formed in 1989, the PPP received a mere 0.69 percent of the vote in the
Australian Capital Territory Legislative Assembly election. To keep simi-
lar partying parties away, the legislature passed a new law: For a party to
run a candidate, it must have at least 100 members and a constitution.

PARTY: The Miss Great Britain Party
COUNTRY: England
PLATFORM: Formed in 2008 by Robert de Keyser, chairman of the
annual Miss Great Britain beauty contest, his goal was "to appeal to the
millions of voters who have been reduced to cynical apathy by the dreary

---

First nation in the world to grant universal suffrage: New Zealand, in 1893.

and sometimes rather murky world of Westminster and Brussels. We want to bring some fun, glamour, and transparency to the political process but at the same time send the serious message that beauty does have a real power of its own to harness and create positive change." The Miss Great Britain Party ran several candidates—present and former pageant contestants—in local and regional elections. They campaigned on trivial issues, such as a "British Bank Holiday which encourages people to look fabulous for the day," along with more serious ones, such as equal pay for women. However, none of the beauties received enough votes to get elected in any of their races, and the party dissolved a year later.

PARTY: The Surprise Party
COUNTRY: United States
PLATFORM: Gracie Allen (wife of George Burns, and one of Uncle John's favorite comedians) ran for president in 1940. The Surprise Party's slogan: "Down With Common Sense!" Allen took that satirical message on a 34-city whistle-stop train tour along with her mascot—a kangaroo named Laura. Ever the innovative one, Allen claimed to have invented the sew-on campaign pin "so the voter can't change his mind." Like any good politician, she kissed babies, but refused to kiss male babies unless they were "over 21." Among her more memorable campaign promises was to make Congress work on commission. "When the country prospers," she speechified to the delighted crowds, "Congress would get 10 percent of the additional take." Of course, Allen didn't become president, but she was—surprise!—elected mayor of Monominee, Michigan (even though she wasn't on the ballot). Allen politely turned down the opportunity to serve as the town's mayor because she didn't live there.

PARTY: The Donald Duck Party
COUNTRY: Sweden
PLATFORM: The Donald Duck Party is a party of one: Bosse Persson. But what he's lacked in members (and votes), he's made up for in longevity: Persson registered the party in the 1980s, and was still running for various offices as recently as 2006. Although Persson has never received more than a handful of write-in votes, he's held strong to his two core values: free liquor for all, and higher curbs so sports car drivers can't park on the sidewalks. So if you travel to Sweden and the liquor is free and the sidewalks are high, you'll know there's a Persson responsible for that.

Number of federal employees allowed to stamp a document "Top Secret": 3,978.

TV NEWS UNFILTERED

Next time you think there's nothing on TV, remember Brian Lamb's story and spend a few minutes watching his channel. What channel? Read on.

MR. LAMB GOES TO WASHINGTON

During the Vietnam War, a young navy lieutenant from Indiana named Brian Lamb was assigned to the Pentagon press office to report troop deaths to the media. The amount of information either omitted or censored in order to paint a rosier picture of the war appalled him. "The government lied to us," he later recalled. "We just weren't getting the straight scoop."

During that time, Lamb also served as an aide in the Johnson White House. Once again he saw a huge gap between what the American people knew and what was really happening. "I got a firsthand education about how the media interacts with the government, and it led me to think that there could be a better way."

That better way was a news outlet that would report what was happening in politics—with two major differences: 1) no censorship from government; and 2) no commentary from media pundits.

FINDING AN IN

Over the next decade, as Lamb worked in various television and political jobs, he tried to drum up support for a news channel that showed gavel-to-gavel coverage of Congress. Although many people agreed that it was a good idea, it wasn't feasible. Why? The Big Three networks had cornered the market on delivering the news to the masses. And besides, all-day congressional debate wasn't exactly something the public was clamoring for. But then in the late 1970s, cable TV hit the scene. That changed everything.

Cable meant more channels, which meant Lamb now had a place to put his network. But he still needed money and—more importantly—he needed the government's permission.

• Government approval was the easy part. In 1977 Lamb met with Speaker of the House Tip O'Neill and learned that Congress had been thinking the same thing—they'd recently passed House Resolution 866,

---

In Bolivia, the voting age is 18 for married people and 21 for single people.

permitting broadcast coverage of House proceedings.

• Finding the money took a little longer. Lamb knew that trying to convince taxpayers to pay for a free government-access channel would be a tough sell, so instead he went to the CEOs of emerging cable companies around the country and asked *them* to finance the channel by setting aside a small percentage of their revenue. The response was slow at first, but after Bob Rosencrans, the CEO of Columbia Cablevision, wrote a check for $25,000, others chipped in, and Lamb found himself with $400,000.

AMERICA'S NETWORK OF RECORD
On March 19, 1979, the Cable-Satellite Public Affairs Network, or C-SPAN, with a staff of four, began cablecasting the United States House of Representatives' daily proceedings (gavel-to-gavel and without commentary) to 3.5 million households. At first it only aired from 8:00 a.m. to 5:00 p.m. on weekdays, but soon switched to 24-hour coverage, replaying the day's events in prime time. In 1980 C-SPAN added a call-in feature to give people the opportunity to ask politicians direct questions. This was the first large-scale avenue for regular citizens to speak directly to their political representatives. That year C-SPAN also received its first of many Cable Ace Awards. By 1984 it was covering every political event to which it had access, and really made its mark during the presidential campaign. While the Big Three covered the highlights, C-SPAN broadcast every minute of the Iowa caucus and both the Republican and Democratic national conventions.

THIS LAMB AIN'T NO SHEEP
Over the years, Lamb has had to remain diligent to ensure that the network's coverage remains both complete and objective. C-SPAN has never received a cent from either political party (not that they haven't offered). Corporations have also offered to pay the network substantial fees in return for displaying their logos on-screen. And on a few occasions C-SPAN has been asked to omit or edit certain sections of congressional debates that got out of hand. Lamb's response is always the same: No.

Yet while C-SPAN strives to be nonpartisan, both sides have accused the network of bias: In March 2007, conservatives accused it of catering to the left by broadcasting coverage of an anti-Iraq War march, but staying away from a smaller march in favor of the war. On the other side, liberals

Ford, Carter, Bush, and Clinton all attended the 1999 funeral of King Hussein of Jordan.

point to reports that C-SPAN's morning call-in show, *Washington Journal*, features nearly twice as many Republicans as Democrats. So does Lamb have a political bias? He won't say. "I vote in every general election, but I'm not a party member—I've never told anyone who I've voted for."

RATINGS, SHMATINGS

One way Lamb curtails the criticism is to completely ignore C-SPAN's numbers. "We don't know whether we have three viewers or three hundred thousand," he says. "It's probably a good thing, too, because then someone might be on our backs to increase the numbers, or worse, we'd stop broadcasting what deserves to be on." What is known is this: 85 million homes receive C-SPAN; 52 million people admit to being "sometime" or "regular" viewers.

And they have a lot to tune in to. Today C-SPAN consists of three separate networks, a radio station, and 17 websites. In 1996 the network added *About Books*, which gives authors exposure they couldn't get anywhere else. And even though C-SPAN is now a multimedia juggernaut, it's still a nonprofit organization and still receives its money solely from cable companies. "C-SPAN," says Lamb, "is the voice of America, with all its flaws."

WHAT'S ON C-SPAN?

Think it's just long-winded politicians speaking into microphones on the House floor? Well, most of it is, but you can also find:

• **International flair:** The often-lively proceedings of the parliaments of the United Kingdom and Canada.

• **State funerals:** Every big funeral from Richard Nixon to Rosa Parks. "Our coverage of funerals is very popular," boasts Lamb.

• **Political goofs:** Regular C-SPAN viewers see their fair share of questionable political gestures and slips of the tongue. For example, in July 2006, Senator Joe Biden of Delaware said on camera that "you cannot go into a Dunkin' Donuts or a 7-Eleven unless you have a slight Indian accent." (He later said it was a compliment.) And in July 2007, Senator Bill Nelson of Florida said on the Senate floor, "Certainly, all the intercourse that I had as a military officer was the best. But that was not the case for a lot of our returning soldiers." (He was talking about how he was treated by the public after returning home from Vietnam. We think.)

Sen. Barbara Boxer (D-CA) writes political thrillers featuring a heroic Democratic senator.

FOLLOWING PROTOCOL

When one is addressing the exalted Uncle John at official Throne Room functions,
one must first bow, then curtsy, then jump up and down for 10 seconds while
singing "Rubber Duckie." It may sound weird, but it's protocol.

INTERNATIONAL INCIDENTS

In today's jet-set culture, most heads of state lead an incredibly hectic life—trips, negotiations, press conferences, speeches, and dozens of meetings every day. All of those comings and goings present some unusual scheduling problems. For instance, what would happen if a foreign leader arrived at the White House for an official visit, and the president happened to be out playing golf? Or if the president flew to a summit meeting and the host country had forgotten to book a hotel room for him? In international relations, these embarrassing situations have to be avoided at all cost. That's why governments follow "protocol"—official procedures and rules of diplomatic conduct, right down to the minutiae of how flags are displayed, how officials are addressed, who speaks first at a ceremonial event, and whether it's proper to shake hands, bow, or salute. In the United States, there is an entire State Department division devoted to the finer points of making sure our government doesn't embarrass itself: the Office of the Chief of Protocol.

WE'RE ON A MISSION

The two most important jobs of the 64-person Office of the Chief of Protocol are 1) planning the schedules of foreign leaders visiting the president and 2) accompanying the president on his official visits abroad and coordinating all travel and meeting plans with the White House, the First Lady's staff, and the host country's officials.

But that's not all the Protocol Office does. It organizes treaty-signing ceremonies, resolves diplomatic-immunity cases, and helps foreign diplomatic missions set up their embassies in the U.S. It also plans the schedules of presidential delegations at foreign inaugurals, funerals, weddings, and similar ceremonies. It organizes swearing-in ceremonies for U.S. ambassadors and other State Department officials. It arranges the arrivals of foreign dignitaries visiting the U.S., along with any foreign journalists accompanying them. It approves the credentials of foreign ambassadors and then acts as the president's liaison to them while they're in Washington. And it plans and carries out the president's and the secretary of state's visits to the United Nations General Assembly.

In brief, the office oversees or assists with just about everything that has to do with state visits, U.S. diplomats, foreign diplomats in the U.S., and official ceremonies. Where diplomacy is concerned, it's our national concierge, party planner, travel agent, gift giver, hotelier, and mediator.

And that's still not all it does.

MANAGING THE WORLD'S MOST EXCLUSIVE HOTEL

Blair House, on Pennsylvania Avenue across the street from the Old Executive Office Building of the White House, is the president's official guesthouse for visiting heads of state and occasional domestic guests, such as presidents-elect. The Office of the Chief of Protocol maintains and manages the facility with the help of a staff (on call 24/7) that spares no effort to make each guest comfortable and provide everything he or she might need (like jelly beans for president-elect Ronald Reagan or burgers for King Hussein of Jordan).

The original building was a single townhouse constructed in 1824 by Dr. Joseph Lovell, the eighth surgeon general of the U.S. Army. In 1837 it was purchased for $6,500 by the family of Francis Preston Blair, owner of the *Washington Globe* newspaper and close friend of Andrew Jackson. The house remained in the Blair family until 1942, when the State Department bought it to provide accommodations for VIPs visiting President Roosevelt.

Today Blair House comprises the original townhouse plus three adjacent ones, which look separate from the outside but are actually connected inside—they add up to a whopping 70,000 square feet and 119 rooms. Blair House is, in fact, bigger than the White House, with 14 guest bedrooms, 9 staff bedrooms, 35 bathrooms, 4 dining rooms, many conference rooms and sitting rooms, an exercise room, a hair salon, kitchens, laundry and dry-cleaning facilities, and even a flower shop. It's decorated in the style of an elegant 19th-century home, with antiques, fine art, Oriental rugs, polished silver, and crystal chandeliers. There are about 20 official visits to Blair House per year and 50 to 100 other functions, such as receptions and meetings. While a visiting president, prime minister, or monarch is in residence, his or her national flag flies over Blair House, which becomes, in effect, an embassy of that nation.

Pop-itics: Coca-Cola has spent $31 mil. on lobbying since 1998; Pepsi, $28 mil.

The Office of the Chief of Protocol also maintains Blair House's official guest book. Some visitors simply sign their names—François Mitterand, Margaret Thatcher, or Jawaharlal Nehru, for example—but others leave messages. During the week of President Reagan's state funeral, Nancy Reagan stayed at Blair House and left this entry: "Many thanks for all your kindness and thoughtfulness at a very difficult time in our lives." Hamid Karzai, chairman of the Interim Administration of Afghanistan, was a little more informal: "Such a wonderful and pleasant stay at the homely Blair House. I will remember you guys."

THE GIFT UNIT

The Protocol Office's Gift Unit is "the central processing point for all tangible gifts received from foreign sources by employees of the Executive Branch of the Federal government." The unit keeps a detailed list of each gift, including a description, name and title of recipient, date of acceptance, estimated value, current location, name of the donor and government, and circumstances justifying acceptance. Almost all gifts are accepted because, according to official guidelines, "non-acceptance would cause embarrassment to the donor and the U.S. Government."

In 2001, for example, more than 150 gifts were received for President Bush, and hundreds more were received for the First Lady, their daughters, the vice president, the vice president's wife, and the secretaries of state, treasury, and defense, as well as dozens of other government officials. The list includes paintings, rugs, statues, books, vases, dishes, bowls, pitchers, a silver coffeepot, silver spoons, jewelry, watches, pistols, sabers, daggers, arrows, coins, plaques, carved elephant tusks, a patchwork coverlet, a drum, a briefcase, an evening purse, shawls, neckties, wine, a baseball bat, desk sets, table linens, toiletries, ornamental boxes, a silver- framed photo of Queen Elizabeth II, a silver-framed photo of the king and queen of Spain, two ceramic coffee mugs, a CD called *The Best of Western Gotaland*, a laser portrait of the president on stretch nylon fabric, a pair of brown lizard-skin boots for the First Lady, a pair of black ostrich-skin boots for the president, and an Inuit sculpture of a walrus.

What happens when someone from the Protocol Office screws up?
Or worse yet—when the president does? Find out on page 236.

Steven Spielberg donated $100,000 to the Democratic super PAC Priorities USA Action.

THE HOLLYWOOD BLACKLIST

*We told you about McCarthyism on page 89. Here's
how the "Red Scare" he created in the middle of the
20th century led to the blacklisting of hundreds
of Hollywood actors, writers, and directors.*

BETTER DEAD THAN RED

In the late 1940s, the House Un-American Activities Committee (HUAC), which had formed a decade earlier to weed out Communist infiltrators in the government, turned its attention to Hollywood.

That made life very difficult for people in the entertainment industry. Years earlier, in the 1930s, many of those artistic intellectuals had joined, or flirted with the idea of joining, the Communist Party. Why? Because back then, the United States was mired in the Great Depression and the Nazi party was rising in Germany. The basic ideals of communism—everyone working together for the common good—led many of them to believe that communism could lead to a Utopian society. However, World War II and the rise of Communist dictator Joseph Stalin changed all that. By the war's end, communism was equated with fascism. One dictator. No democracy. No utopia.

By 1947, most of Hollywood's elite had moved well beyond communism, but it didn't take much during the Red Scare to link them to it. Nearly every artist or intellectual in America at the very least knew someone who belonged to the party. So when the commie-seeking spotlight landed on Tinseltown, it found more than it was looking for.

ROUND ONE

The congressional investigation began in October 1947. The committee, headed by Representative J. Parnell Thomas (R-NJ), interviewed two groups. The so-called friendly witnesses, who were willing to testify about Communist activity, were allowed to read prepared statements and were treated with respect. They included actors Gary Cooper, Robert Taylor, Robert Montgomery, and Ronald Reagan. These witnesses also included studio heads Jack Warner, Louis B. Mayer, and Walt Disney, whose employees had recently unionized and held a strike, which, Disney told the committee, had been instigated by communists. Disney named a few of his former employees and then recommended outlawing labor unions for their "un-American tendencies."

THE HOLLYWOOD TEN

The second group were screenwriters, actors, and directors who were either alleged or admitted members of the American Communist Party. Nineteen of these "unfriendly" witnesses were subpoenaed; 11 were called to testify. German playwright and songwriter Bertolt ("Mack the Knife") Brecht was the only one of the eleven to answer any questions on the stand. He claimed he was not a Communist; but after testifying, he immediately left Hollywood to return to East Germany.

The remaining ten, mostly screenwriters, refused to testify, citing the First Amendment, which forbids Congress from infringing on the right of free speech. For refusing to divulge their political affiliations past or present, the Hollywood Ten were cited for contempt of Congress. In 1948 they were sent to prison for terms ranging from six months to one year, and fined $1,000. Who were they?

• **Alvah Bessie:** Oscar-nominated screenwriter of 1945's *Objective, Burma!*

• **Herbert Biberman:** screenwriter of *The Master Race* and husband of Gale Sondergaard, who won the first Best Supporting Actress Oscar and was also blacklisted

• **Lester Cole:** screenwriter with Alvah Bessie on *Objective, Burma!* and cofounder of the Writers Guild of America

• **Edward Dmytry:** director of *The Caine Mutiny*; Oscar-nominated for 1947's *Crossfire*

• **Ring Lardner Jr.:** screenwriter, Oscar winner for the 1942 screenplay of *Woman of the Year*

• **John Howard Lawson:** screenwriter, Oscar-nominated for 1938's *Blockade*, and cofounder of the Screen Writers Guild

• **Albert Maltz:** screenwriter, Oscar-nominated for 1945's *Pride of the Marines*

• **Samuel Ornitz:** screenwriter of 1937's *It Could Happen to You!* and cofounder of the Screen Writers Guild

In 1980 Ronald Reagan considered naming ex-president Ford as his running mate.

- **Adrian Scott:** producer of the Oscar-nominated *Crossfire* in 1947
- **Dalton Trumbo:** screenwriter, Oscar-nominated for 1940's *Kitty Foyle*

ADDING INSULT TO INJURY

The Motion Picture Association of America issued a press release known as the Waldorf Statement; it declared that the members of the Hollywood Ten would not be permitted to work in Hollywood again until they were either acquitted or purged of their contempt charges and swore that they weren't Communists. The Screen Actors Guild decided to require its officers to pledge that they weren't Communists. A few years later, in 1952, the guild additionally declared that members who hadn't been cleared of suspicion of Communist leanings by Congress could have their names stripped from previous film credits.

UNDER THE BUS

Between the first and second rounds of the HUAC hearings, Edward Dmytryk took advantage of an "escape clause": He was released early from prison when he admitted past membership in the Communist Party and agreed to cooperate with the committee. He directed three films in England while waiting to appear as a "friendly" witness. On his return in 1951, he helped incriminate several of his former colleagues. "Not a single person I named hadn't already been named at least a half-dozen times and wasn't already on he blacklist," Dmytryk said in his defense.

But the "friendliest" witness of them all was director Elia Kazan, cofounder of the Actors Studio in New York City, who had been named as a Communist during round one by studio boss Jack Warner. When Kazan first testified in January 1952, he admitted former membership in the party in the 1930s but refused to name anyone else. A few months later—after he lost the Oscar for Best Director for *A Streetcar Named Desire* and learned that he was facing the blacklist—he voluntarily testified before Congress. He named eight people who had been in his cell within the party. That included two men that Kazan himself had recruited.

Kazan's controversial decision still splits Hollywood to this day. When he received a Lifetime Achievement Award at the Oscars in 1999, he was given a standing ovation—but it was far from unanimous; a noticeable portion of the audience refused to applaud, much less stand up.

Zombie Party: An estimated 1.8 million dead Americans are registered to vote.

THE HOLLYWOOD HUNDREDS

The Hollywood Ten were the most famous members of the blacklist, but historians estimate that between 325 and 500 entertainers, directors, and screenwriters found themselves either out of work or generally unwelcome in Hollywood. Among them were entertainers John Garfield, Lee Grant, Sterling Hayden, Judy Holliday, Burgess Meredith, Zero Mostel, Paul Robeson, and Pete Seeger; writers Dashiell Hammett, Lillian Hellman, Arthur Miller, Clifford Odets, Dorothy Parker, Leo Penn (father of Sean and Chris), and Irwin Shaw; and directors Jules Dassin and Martin Ritt. At least a few of them managed to succeed elsewhere.

• Arthur Miller's 1953 play about Communist hysteria, *The Crucible*, won two Tony Awards. Miller was called to testify in 1956 but refused to name anyone, earning a contempt charge that was dismissed (which may have had something to do with his marriage to Marilyn Monroe that year).

• Writer Irwin Shaw decamped to Europe and wrote a few best-selling books (including *Rich Man, Poor Man*, which became a hit TV miniseries in 1976). He would later declare that the blacklist "only glancingly bruised" his career.

• Director Jules Dassin moved to France and made a series of films, including *Never on Sunday*, which he starred in with his wife, Melina Mercouri. (Dassin's first post-blacklist American film was 1964's *Topkapi*, which was the inspiration for the *Mission: Impossible* TV series.)

SCREENPLAY BY JOHN DOE

Some writers got around the blacklist by using pseudonyms, or fronts—fellow writers who agreed to pretend the work was theirs. Dalton Trumbo of the Hollywood Ten wrote more than a dozen screenplays between 1949 and 1958, two of which won Academy Awards: 1953's *Roman Holiday* (for which Trumbo used screenwriter Ian McLellan Hunter as a front) and 1956's *The Brave One* (for which he used the pseudonym Robert Rich).

Trumbo, with a little help from friends and admirers, was the first writer to break through the blacklist, with two 1960 productions: Director Otto Preminger hired Trumbo to write the screenplay for *Exodus*, and Kirk Douglas hired Trumbo to write *Spartacus*.

Ring Lardner Jr. kept writing, too, using fronts or writing uncredited screenplays. His first postblacklist credit was for *The Cincinnati Kid*. He would later win his second screenwriting Oscar for 1970's *MASH*.

Rep. Joe Read's (R-MT) 2012 House Bill 549 claims that global warming is...

Martin Ritt got back in the director's chair in the late 1950s. And in 1976 he produced and directed blacklisted writer Walter Bernstein's screenplay *The Front*, in which Woody Allen starred as a restaurant cashier who fronts for blacklisted writers—and eventually finds himself blacklisted, too. The movie included a few blacklisted actors, too, Zero Mostel and Herschel Bernardi among them. Bernstein got an Oscar nomination for the screenplay.

TELE-COMMIES

On June 22, 1950, *Counterattack*, an anti-Communist newsletter put out by former FBI agents, published "Red Channels: The Report of Communist Influence in Radio and Television." The report named 151 show-business people said to be "under the Communist influence," along with a brief summary of their "questionable ties," which included advocating for or working with organizations that promoted civil rights, anti-nuclear proliferation, the New Deal, and censorship.

In fact, none of the alleged activities mentioned were illegal, and few of the accusations were substantiated. But the damage was done. Within a year, most of the 151 named were fired and blacklisted in both film and TV. It's difficult to gauge just how many people were denied work in TV because of real or imagined Communist sympathies. Some of the people affected by the blacklist:

• Jazz singer Lena Horne was unable to perform in films or on TV for seven years after being named in "Red Channels" because of her involvement with the civil rights movement.

• *The Honeymooners* began as a sketch on Jackie Gleason's 1952 variety show *Cavalcade of Stars*. Actress Pert Kelton originated the role of Alice Kramden. In 1955 she was rumored to have Communist ties, so when *The Honeymooners* debuted as a stand-alone series that year, Kelton was replaced by Audrey Meadows.

• Sanka Coffee sponsored CBS's top-10 sitcom *The Goldbergs* but pulled support in 1951 because costar Philip Loeb had been listed in "Red Channels." CBS recast his character against the wishes of the show's star and creator, Gertrude Berg. Loeb never found work again, and took a fatal dose of sleeping pills in 1955.

• From 1948 to 1950, Irene Wicker hosted ABC's popular kids' show

The Singing Lady. It was canceled because Wicker was listed in "Red Channels" for having once supported a Communist candidate for office. She'd never heard of him, and *Counterattack* issued a retraction. Still, Wicker's career never recovered.

• Aaron Copland, the most prominent American composer of the mid-20th century, wrote and conducted an original piece called "Lincoln Portrait" for the Eisenhower Presidential Inaugural Concert TV special in 1953. But Copland was shunned in Hollywood because of Communist ties (he'd openly supported the Communist Party USA in the 1930s), so his segment was cut out of the special. His career later rebounded and he was awarded the Presidential Medal of Freedom in 1964.

• Tap dancer and rumored Communist sympathizer Paul Draper performed to "Yankee Doodle Dandy" on Ed Sullivan's *Toast of the Town* show in 1950. After the telecast, conservative newspaper columnists and the American Legion led a telegram- and letter-writing campaign protesting Draper's appearance. Sponsor Ford Motors forced Sullivan to issue an apology. Sullivan was so embarrassed that all future guests were screened for Communist ties by Theodore Kirkpatrick, an editor of *Counterattack*. Draper never worked in the U.S. again, and later moved to Europe.

RETURN TO REASON

Blacklisting continued throughout the 1950s, even as public sentiment turned against Senator McCarthy and *Counterattack*. In May 1954, Edward R. Murrow used an episode of his CBS news program *See It Now* to present a point-by-point critique of McCarthyism. Afterward, CBS received thousands of letters—15 to 1 in support of Murrow. Partly as a result, some blacklisted actors and writers began to find work in TV again.

The Cold War continued into the 1980s, but the Red Scare had died down and the stigma of the blacklist slipped away with it. But it had claimed many victims, including actor John Garfield, who died of a heart attack at age 39, attributed at in part to the blacklist. Sterling Hayden was another: He had named names and regretted it for the rest of his life.

*　　　*　　　*

"There has always been some kind of blacklist throughout history. But the difference is, in America they usually let you live."
—Rip Torn

Only naturalized American on the Supreme Court: Austria-born Felix Frankfurter (1939–62).

U.S. POLITICAL LISTS

Politicians make lists to keep track of their enemies. Uncle John makes lists to entertain his readers. That's why Uncle John would make a lousy politician.

3 REALITY STARS WHO RAN FOR CONGRESS IN 2010

1. Kevin Powell (*The Real World*) D-NY (lost)
2. Surya Yalamanchill (*The Apprentice*) D-OH (lost)
3. Sean Duffy (*The Real World*) R-WI (won)

8 GOV'T. SALARIES

1. Pres.: $400,000
2. V.P.: $230,700
3. Speaker of the House: $230,700
4. Cabinet: $199,700
5. Senate and House Majority and Minority Leaders: $193,400
6. Senators: $174,000
7. Reps: $174,000
8. First Lady: $0

5 PREZZY PETS

1. Tiger cub (Van Buren)
2. Billy goat (Harrison)
3. Cow (Taft)
4. Ram (Wilson)
5. Rabbit (Kennedy)

5 AMPUTEE SENATORS

1. James Henderson Berry (D-AK) lost a leg in the Civil War.
2. Max Cleland (D-GA) lost two legs and an arm in the Vietnam War.
3. Charles E. Potter (R-MI) lost both legs in World War II.
4. Dan Inouye (D-HI) lost an arm in World War II.
5. Wade Hampton (D-SC) lost a leg after falling off a mule.

8 SUPER PACS FROM 2012

1. Priorities USA Action (Obama)
2. Restore Our Future (Mitt Romney)
3. Winning Our Future (Newt Gingrich)
4. Make Us Great Again (Rick Perry)
5. Endorse Liberty (Ron Paul)
6. Red, White & Blue (Rick Santorum)
7. Americans for a Better Tomorrow, Tomorrow (Stephen Colbert)
8. The Definitely Not Coordinating with Stephen Colbert Super PAC (Jon Stewart)

6 FAVE TV SHOWS OF PRESIDENTS

1. Barack Obama: *Boardwalk Empire*
2. George W. Bush: *Biography*
3. Bill Clinton: *Tenspeed and Brownshoe*
4. Ronald Reagan: *Family Ties*
5. Gerald Ford: *Police Woman*
6. Dwight D. Eisenhower: *The Lawrence Welk Show*

President Woodrow Wilson's pet ram, Old Ike, was addicted to chewing tobacco.

MYTH-SPOKEN

*Sometimes famous political quotations were taken out
of context, were said by someone else, or were
never said at all. Here are some examples.*

Quote: "Taxation without representation is tyranny."
Supposedly Said By: James Otis, a lawyer arguing in a Boston
court against British search warrants, in 1761

Actually: For years, schoolchildren were taught that this was "the rallying cry of the American Revolution." But no one in Otis's time ever mentioned him saying it. It wasn't until 1820, almost 60 years later, that John
Adams referred to the phrase for the first time.

Quote: "There are three kinds of lies: lies, damn lies, and statistics."
Supposedly Said By: Mark Twain
Actually: Twain, one of America's most quotable writers, was quoting
someone else: Prime Minister Benjamin Disraeli of England.

Quote: "This is a great wall."
Supposedly Said By: President Richard Nixon
Actually: It's one of the lines used to denigrate Nixon…and he did say it
to Chinese officials in 1972 when he saw the Great Wall for the first
time. However, when taken in context with the rest of the sentence, it
makes more sense: "When one stands here," Nixon said, "and sees the
wall going to the peak of this mountain and realizes it runs for hundreds
of miles—as a matter of fact, thousands of miles—over the mountains and
through the valleys of this country and that it was built over 2,000 years
ago, I think you would have to conclude that this is a great wall and that
it had to be built by a great people."

Quote: "Keep the government poor and remain free."
Supposedly Said By: Justice Oliver Wendell Holmes
Actually: Ronald Reagan said it in a speech. But it wasn't written by a
speechwriter. Someone from Reagan's speechwriting office told a reporter,
"He came up with that one himself."

Britain's government buildings emit more greenhouse gases than the entire nation of Kenya.

Quote: "That government is best which governs least."

Supposedly Said By: Thomas Jefferson

Actually: William F. Buckley used this line in a 1987 column. He may have taken it from Henry David Thoreau's essay "Civil Disobedience." But Thoreau didn't attribute it. Why did Buckley attribute it to Jefferson? Who knows, but it was *first* said by the pamphleteer Thomas Paine.

Quote: "Who among us doesn't like NASCAR?"

Supposedly Said By: Presidential candidate John Kerry

Actually: This quote was well circulated during the 2004 presidential race, often used to criticize Senator Kerry (D–Mass) as out of touch and pandering to blue collar voters. Turns out that when *New York Times* columnist Maureen Dowd mocked Kerry for the quote in a March 2004 column, it was the first time the quote had appeared. Dowd made it up.

Quote: "Here I stand—warts and all."

Supposedly Said By: Oliver Cromwell

Actually: Vice President George H. W. Bush quoted this line in a 1988 campaign speech, but Cromwell (1616–58) never said it. The actual quote was "Paint me—warts and all." When the *New York Times* called Bush headquarters to question the reference, one of Bush's speechwriters claimed to have made up the quote.

Quote: "I wish I'd studied Latin at school so I could talk to you in your own language."

Supposedly Said By: Vice President Dan Quayle to a group of schoolchildren, on a tour of Latin American countries

Actually: It was invented by Democratic congresswoman Pat Schroeder as an attack on Quayle. Even though she publicly apologized to the former VP, it lives on as a "genuine quote" in popular mythology.

Quote: "I can see Russia from my house."

Supposedly Said By: Vice presidential candidate Sarah Palin

Actually: The Alaska governor was ridiculed for this quote in the 2008 election, but Tina Fey said it on *Saturday Night Live* while impersonating Palin. What Palin had really said, in defending her foreign-policy credentials, was, "You can actually see Russia from an island here in Alaska."

You've probably been wondering when eunuchs won the right to vote in India: 1994.

REAGAN'S WISDOM

They didn't call Ronald Reagan (1911–2004)
"The Great Communicator" for nothing...

"They say the world has become too complex for simple answers. They are wrong."

"We must reject the idea that every time a law is broken, society is guilty rather than the lawbreaker. It is time to restore the American precept that each individual is accountable for his actions."

"A people free to choose will always choose peace."

"Freedom must be fought for, protected, and handed on for the next generation to do the same, or one day we will spend our sunset years telling our children and our children's children what it was once like in the United States where men were free."

"To sit back hoping that someday, some way, someone will make things right is to go on feeding the crocodile, hoping he will eat you last—but eat you he will."

"We can't help everyone, but everyone can help someone."

"Peace is not the absence of conflict, it is the ability to handle conflict by peaceful means."

"Concentrated power has always been the enemy of liberty."

"We must realize that no arsenal, or no weapon in the arsenals of the world, is so formidable as the will and moral courage of free men and women. It is a weapon our adversaries do not have."

"Coercion merely captures man. Freedom captivates him."

"Information is the oxygen of the modern age. It seeps through the walls topped by barbed wire, it wafts across electrified borders."

"If you're afraid of the future, then get out of the way, stand aside. The people of this country are ready to move again."

"I never thought it was my style or the words I used that made a difference: It was the content. I wasn't a great communicator; I communicated great things."

Nancy Reagan had a part in her high school's production of *First Lady*, and...

REAGAN'S WISDOM?

…but he still had a communicator malfunction now and then.

"Well, I learned a lot—I went down to Latin America to find out from them and their views. You'd be surprised. They're all individual countries."

"You know, if I listened to Michael Dukakis long enough, I would be convinced that people are homeless and going without food and medical attention and that we've got to do something about the unemployed."

"How are you, Mr. Mayor? I'm glad to meet you. How are things in your city?"
—to Samuel Pierce, Reagan's secretary of Housing and Urban Development, during a White House reception for mayors

"Approximately 80 percent of our air pollution stems from hydrocarbons released by vegetation, so let's not go overboard in setting tough emission standards from man-made sources."

"Facts are stupid things."

"If you've seen one redwood, you've seen them all."

Ronald Reagan: My name is Ronald Reagan. What's yours?
Mike Reagan: I'm your son.
Ronald Reagan: Oh, I didn't recognize you.
—after delivering a commencement address at Mike's prep school

"The best minds are not in government. If any were, business would hire them away."

"Why should we subsidize intellectual curiosity?"

"I never drink coffee at lunch. I find it keeps me awake for the afternoon."

"We are trying to get unemployment to go up, and I think we're going to succeed."

"It's silly talking about how many years we will have to spend in the jungles of Vietnam when we could pave the whole country and put parking stripes on it and still be home by Christmas."

"I favor the Civil Rights Act of 1964, and it must be enforced at gunpoint if necessary."

…Ronald Reagan once appeared in a GE Theater production of *A Turkey for President*.

HEMP MADNESS, PART II

On page 120, you learned why hemp production fell out of favor in the United States. Here's the story of the struggle to get it growing again.

WAR HERO

In the 1930s, manufacturing hemp was still technically legal in the U.S. But few farms remained—hemp was highly taxed; the cotton, paper, and petroleum industries had taken its place; and hemp's association with marijuana hurt it even further. Besides, even cheaper plants were being imported from overseas, including "manila hemp" from the Philippines, which isn't technically hemp—it comes from the abaca plant (used to make manila envelopes).

Hemp appeared to make a comeback in 1942 when a 16-minute movie called *Hemp for Victory* was shown to U.S. farmers, urging them to grow hemp for the war effort. Who made it? The U.S. government. Were they high? No—the Japanese had captured the Philippines, cutting off the supplies of manila hemp, which was used to make cloth for parachutes and uniforms. But when the war ended, the imports resumed and hemp was dropped again, *still* a victim of its relation to marijuana.

PUBLIC ENEMY NUMBER ONE

Remember Harry Anslinger? He remained head of the Federal Bureau of Narcotics for 32 years, and never let up on the evils of marijuana and the degenerates who smoked it—even in the face of evidence that proved it wasn't really that harmful.

• In 1945 Anslinger denounced the "LaGuardia Marijuana Report" from the New York Academy of Medicine, which stated that marijuana had minimal detrimental effects and numerous beneficial ones. At Anslinger's urging, the American Medical Association described the report's findings as "gutter science."

• In 1948, at the onset of the Cold War, Anslinger changed his tune and said that pot caused people to become "pacifists"—and it would help the Communists defeat the U.S. if it was made legal.

• In 1961 President Kennedy fired Anslinger, but he wasn't in office long enough to push for any laws to change. And later in the 1960s, illegal

---

Congress has proposed 11,447 amendments to the Constitution since 1789; 27 made it.

marijuana use increased immensely and came to be associated with the youth counterculture movement.

In 1970 the Marihuana Tax Act was finally repealed, but that year's Controlled Substances Act kept marijuana use illegal and made it even more difficult to attain permission to grow industrial hemp. President Nixon had picked up where Anslinger left off—he wanted to eliminate the plant in all of its forms from U.S. soil. And then the government's "War on Drugs" efforts of the 1980s kept the campaign against pot alive. President Reagan ordered the DEA to destroy any hemp farm it found. By then, few people outside of farming even knew what hemp was.

But then, in the 1990s, public perception began to change, thanks to both the pro-hemp and pro-marijuana activists. Study after study said that marijuana is much less harmful than cocaine, heroin, and methamphetamine (though opponents warn that pot use can lead to the harder drugs). And medical marijuana is increasingly being used to ease the pain of chronic-disease sufferers.

That's promising news for the marijuana advocates, but the pro-hemp people are still trying to educate the public about the useful properties of their plant, and why it could play an important role in the 21st century. But first, there is one widely held myth about the cannabis plant that still persists.

MARIJUANA VS. INDUSTRIAL HEMP

Technically, it's not illegal to grow hemp, but you must first attain permission from the U.S. Drug Enforcement Agency, which currently is extremely difficult. Why? The DEA is concerned that hemp farmers will secretly grow pot in their fields, making it nearly impossible for DEA helicopters to spot marijuana from the air. This isn't possible, though, as marijuana and industrial hemp are planted, tended, and harvested in different ways. And neither can be grown in the same field; the plants will cross-pollinate, making them both useless for their intended purpose.

But that's not even their biggest difference. The psychosomatic agent in marijuana is the compound *delta-9 tetrahydrocannabinol* (THC). In order for the plant to be potent enough to get someone "high," it must have a THC content of 3 percent or higher. Hemp, by contrast, only has 0.5 percent or less of THC. In other words, smoking hemp to get high would be a meaningless effort. Besides, there's so much else that it *can* do.

MULTITASKER

As the drawbacks of harvesting trees and burning fossil fuels become more apparent, the better hemp production looks. It can be used to make paper, rope, netting, and clothing. Hemp is also a good food source—hemp seeds have a nutty flavor, and like nuts they're very nutritious, containing protein, omega fatty acids, and vitamins. (Hemp oil can even be made into beer.) In addition, hemp can be manufactured into plastics and construction materials. Bonus: Hemp production has a low environmental impact.

• Unlike trees, hemp grows rapidly—from seed to mature plant in 120 days—allowing for two harvests per year in some climates. It requires few, if any, pesticides, and the plants can be grown very close together, resulting in a high fiber yield per acre.

• Up to three times more paper can be produced from hemp than from trees. And tree pulp must be bleached using environmentally destructive chemicals such as chlorine. Hemp pulp can be bleached with relatively harmless hydrogen peroxide.

• Growing hemp for textiles requires much less water and fewer pesticides than cotton does. And while hemp cloth has a reputation for being rough, recent technological developments have made it much softer.

• Hemp seed oil can be used to make biofuels, similar to corn-based ethanol, but hemp, again, is a more environmentally friendly crop than corn, requiring less water and fewer pesticides.

THE GREEN MOVEMENT

Currently, hemp is legally grown in more than 30 countries, including Australia, Canada, China, Russia, the U.K., France, and Italy. The European Union even subsidizes the plant's production. In the U.S., several states issue permits allowing for the farming of industrial hemp. Not all have received permission from the DEA. Pro-hemp supporters had hoped that the restrictions would decrease during the Obama administration, but it wasn't on the president's list of priorities.

In 2010, 30 Representatives, led by Ron Paul (R-TX) and Barney Frank (D-MA), drafted a law to remove federal restrictions from hemp, but the bill went nowhere. "It's unfortunate that the federal government has stood in the way of American farmers," said Paul. So for now, hemp farmers are *still* hoping that this "miracle plant" will one day be let loose on U.S. soil. But it's up to the politicians to make that happen.

GOVERN-MENTAL

More bewildering tales from the world of politics.

SENDING A MESSAGE—GODFATHER STYLE

Pennsylvania Governor Ed Rendell was trying to convince lawmakers in 2010 to vote for his proposed natural gas extraction tax. When Representative Tim Solobay, a fellow Democrat, said he was against the tax, Rendell purchased a Tim Solobay bobblehead doll, removed the head, placed it inside a small box along with a note that urged Solobay's support, and sent it to the Representative's office. Solobay got the message—and the joke—and promised to reconsider his position. He also said the gesture was a "big hit" among Democrats. Pennsylvania Republicans, however, were less amused. A spokesman for House Minority Leader Rep. Sam Smith said, "Personally I don't see the humor in sending any sort of head to anyone. I think it is kind of sickening."

BUT NOT A DROP TO DRINK

In 2003 public officials in Hudson, New York, were required by the Americans with Disabilities Act to install handicapped-accessible water fountains in the county courthouse. Five years later, they finally got around to installing just one of the fountains…the one on the second floor. And there's no elevator in the building. County Public Works Commissioner David Robinson defended the inaccessible wheelchair-accessible water fountain, saying it's easier for people who have trouble bending (which makes no sense—the new water fountain is actually several inches *shorter* than the one on the first floor). Robinson pledged that there are "definite plans in the future" to install one of the new fountains on the ground floor.

EXOPOLITICS

In 2010 Kirsan Ilyumzhinov, the governor of the Russian region of Kalmykia, recounted this story on a Russian TV show: One day in 1997, he was reading a book at his Moscow apartment when a transparent tube appeared on his balcony. "Then I felt that someone was calling me." The next thing he knew, Ilyumzhinov was taking a tour of an alien spaceship.

Most popular reason for not voting, according to the U.S. Census: "Too busy."

The aliens spoke to him telepathically, he said, and they passed along a warning: "The day will come when they land on our planet and say: 'You have behaved poorly. Why do you wage wars? Why do you destroy each other?' Then they will pack us all into their spaceships and take us away from this place." Most people just chalked the story up as an amusing antic by the eccentric millionaire businessman. However, Andrei Lebedev, a member of Russia's parliament, didn't think it was a joke. He immediately requested that Russian president Dmitry Medvedev interrogate the governor to ensure that he didn't give the aliens any state secrets. (Results of the interrogation are unknown.)

TEXAS BANS MARRIAGE

In 2005 Texas lawmakers passed a constitutional amendment intended to outlaw gay marriage. In 2009 Texas Attorney General Barbara Ann Radnofsky pointed out a huge flaw in a 22-word phrase in Subsection B of the amendment, which reads: "This state or a political subdivision of this state may not create or recognize any legal status identical or similar to marriage." Basically, said Radnofsky, one thing that's identical to marriage is marriage itself, so in effect, no two people of any gender are legally allowed to be married in Texas. "You don't have to have a fancy law degree to read this and understand what it plainly says," she said. Currently, there are no plans to correct the phrasing, but it does call into question whether marriages of any kind that have taken place in Texas since 2005 are legal.

NICE LEGS...NOT!

Colin Hall, lord mayor of Leicester, England, was on a diet. Plus, he wasn't wearing a belt. Those two factors made for an embarrassing political predicament one morning in June 2010 when Hall was speaking to dozens of schoolchildren at a local library. After he was done thanking them, he stood up from his chair. His pants, however, did not. They fell down to his ankles, leaving his underpants exposed to the kids, who all laughed. After being ridiculed in the press, the portly mayor apologized, but also said that it was a great way to publicize his new diet. As a show of support, Labour MP Keith Vaz presented Lord Mayor Hall with a brand-new belt.

Occupy Wall Street, which spread across the U.S. in 2011, was started by Canadians.

BEAT THE PRESS

You'd think that in this world of Internet searches and instant fact-checking, it would be hard to slip a fake story into the news stream. But actually, it's pretty easy.

THIS JUST IN! "VP guns for shootout with Hillary"

THE STORY: In the early days of the 2008 presidential campaign, the *Boston Herald* published an odd news story: Vice President Dick Cheney had challenged presidential candidate Hillary Clinton to a hunting contest. According to the *Herald*, Cheney had issued the challenge during an appearance on NBC's *Meet the Press.* Then, the story went on, Clinton declined the offer, saying, "I fired a gun once, but I didn't like it, and I didn't recoil" (a joke referring to her husband's infamous "I smoked marijuana, but I didn't inhale" remark). The *Herald* story was picked up by Google News…and then by everyone else.

NEVER MIND: Apparently the editors at the *Herald* didn't bother to verify whether Cheney had recently appeared on *Meet the Press* (he hadn't). Nor did they notice that the writer listed as the original source was Andy Borowitz—a well-known comedian and satirist. Borowitz had posted the story on his blog as a joke, and was as surprised as anyone when he saw it had been picked up by the *Herald* as a real story. The *Herald*'s publisher, Kevin Convey, admitted, "We were bamboozled."

THIS JUST IN! "Stunning photos of underwater North Pole"

THE STORY: In August 2007, news sites around the globe ran a *Reuters* news-service story about how a crew of Russian deep-sea explorers had planted their flag on the seabed under the ice of the North Pole. The accompanying pictures showed the Russian submersible they'd used to find the pole.

NEVER MIND: No one in the dozens of news organizations that reran the Reuters story noticed that the photos were actually images from the movie *Titanic.* Who did notice? A 13-year-old boy from Finland, who contacted his local newspaper to inform them of the mistake. Reuters later apologized and claimed that they'd pulled the images from a Russian television broadcast that showed how such an expedition *might* look.

Reuters had incorrectly captioned the photos and sent them out to the world. The good news: A Russian submarine did actually find the underwater North Pole—just not the one in the photos.

THIS JUST IN! "Chinese rocket makes historic launch"

THE STORY: On September 25, 2008, China's official state-run news website, Xinhua.org, posted a story about the much-anticipated launch of the manned *Shenzhou 7* rocket—a mission that would feature China's first-ever space walk. The story described the launch in great detail: "The firm voice of the controller broke the silence of the whole ship. Now the target is captured 12 seconds ahead of the predicted time." The article concluded, "Warm clapping and excited cheering breaks the night sky, echoing across the silent Pacific Ocean."

NEVER MIND: Astute viewers noticed one mistake: The report was posted two days *before* the launch occurred. When pressed for an explanation, Xinhua.org blamed it on a "technical error."

THIS JUST IN! "United Airlines files for bankruptcy"

THE STORY: This headline flashed across the financial news site Bloomberg.com in September 2008. Almost immediately, United's stock began to plummet—from $12 per share down to $10, then to $8, to $3, eventually down to a penny—wiping out more than 99 percent of the stock's nearly $1 billion value. In short, the headline nearly put the already-struggling airline out of business.

NEVER MIND: The headline wasn't from that day; it was from a story that had run in 2002—six years earlier, when United *did* file for bankruptcy. (The company had since regained some of its financial footing.) The *New York Times* tried to piece together the chain of blunders: "An old *Chicago Tribune* article was posted on the website of the *South Florida Sun-Sentinel.* That article was picked up by a research firm, which then posted a link to it on a page on Bloomberg.com, which sent out a news alert." The timing couldn't have been worse. The country was in the grip of the 2008 economic crisis, and investors were jittery. When the goof was discovered, trading was temporarily halted. United's shares soon returned to their pre-panic price of $12.

In 2007 AT&T censored a live Pearl Jam webcast when they criticized Pres. Bush.

FAILED AMENDMENTS

*It's very difficult to amend the U.S. Constitution. A potential amendment
has to pass both houses of Congress with two-thirds approval, and then it
has to be approved by the legislatures of three-fourths of the states. Since
1787, only 27 amendments have been adopted. Numerous others have
been proposed...and rejected. Here are some notable rejects.*

NO FUNDS FOR CHURCHES

In 1875 President Ulysses S. Grant gave a speech endorsing the
use of federal funds to establish public schools nationwide. Maine
congressman James Blaine agreed with Grant, but not because he supported public education. He was against parochial schools—Catholic schools
(and anything Catholic) in particular. This came on the tail of a large
influx of immigrants from Ireland and Italy, two predominantly Catholic
countries, and anti-Catholic sentiment in the U.S. was high. That same
year, Blaine introduced a constitutional ban on the use of public funds for
religious-based organizations. While that may sound like part of the
debate over the separation of church and state, Blaine's real goal was to
prevent the Catholic Church from getting any tax money. (Ironically,
Blaine actively sought the Catholic vote in his 1884 run for president of
the United States, which he lost.)

NO INTERRACIAL MARRIAGE

Like many Americans in the early 1900s, Georgia congressman Seaborn
Roddenberry felt very strongly about racial integration—he was the leading Congressional advocate for segregation. After African American
boxer Jack Johnson married a white woman in 1912, creating a public
scandal, Roddenberry introduced the Anti-Miscegenation Amendment,
which would have made interracial marriage a federal crime.

NO PRESIDENTIAL TERM LIMITS

Franklin Roosevelt was elected to four presidential terms—the Constitution set no limit on the number of terms a president could serve. Prior to
that, all presidents had retired after two, a tradition started by George
Washington. But Roosevelt and his sweeping program of social welfare

---

Real newspaper headline: "Fed Chief Hints at Private Fannie."

were so hated by his Republican opposition that after he died in 1945 and Republicans gained control of Congress in 1947, they passed the 22nd Amendment, limiting the president to two terms. Since 1989, a repeal of that amendment has been proposed several times by members of Congress from both parties, as a way to continue the administrations of popular presidents.

NO AUTOMATIC CITIZENSHIP

It's set forth in the early pages of the Constitution that anyone born within the borders of the United States is automatically a United States citizen—even if they are the child of illegal immigrants. In 2003 Florida congressman Mark Foley proposed an amendment to the Constitution that would remove that stipulation. It died in committee. (Foley's career died after he was accused of having sent sexually explicit instant messages to Congressional pages.)

FEWER RESTRICTIONS TO THE PRESIDENCY

The Constitution forbids foreign-born U.S. citizens from becoming president. This was to prevent anyone from the British empire from ever seizing control of the United States. In 2003 Utah senator Orrin Hatch proposed the Equal Opportunity to Govern Amendment, which would have allowed any naturalized (foreign-born) American who'd been a legal citizen of the United States for at least 20 years to be president. It was widely seen as a way to eliminate roadblocks for California governor Arnold Schwarzenegger (who was born in Austria) in case he ever wanted to run for the country's highest office.

NO FLAG BURNING

The Flag Desecration Amendment has popped up for votes frequently since 1968. It would give Congress authority to make it illegal to burn the American flag, an act currently protected as free speech under the First Amendment. Between 1995 and 2005, six different versions of the amendment were passed by the House of Representatives, but it couldn't clear the Senate. In June 2006, the Senate voted 66–34 in favor of it…just one vote short of the two-thirds majority it needed to go on to ratification by the states. It's a good bet that the flag-burning issue will be put to yet another vote sometime in the future.

President Grover Cleveland answered the White House phone himself.

JOIN THE PARTY: THE WHIGS

In a sense, Andrew Jackson (see page 153) started two political parties: the Democrats, who loved him, and the Whigs, who hated him.

JACKSON IN OFFICE

Andrew "Old Hickory" Jackson was the most popular man in the U.S. when he won the presidency in 1828. When he left office in 1836, he was still considered the champion of the common man—if for no other reason than he angered (and impoverished) a lot of wealthy and powerful people during his two terms.

For starters, Jackson instituted a policy of filling federal government jobs by firing supporters of former president John Quincy Adams and replacing them with his own. And although he ran on an anti-corruption platform, his appointees were, as Jackson biographer Robert Remini put it, "generally wretched." One of the worst was Samuel Swartwout, a Jackson crony who was appointed to the job of collector of customs in New York. In this position, Swartwout oversaw the collection of more cash than any other government official, about $15 million a year. Swartwout absconded to Europe with more than $1.2 million of it, "more money than all the felons in the Adams administration put together," Remini writes. Adjusting for inflation, Swartwout is *still* the worst embezzler in the history of the federal government.

Jackson also managed to alienate many of his fellow Southerners. In 1832 South Carolina passed a law banning exorbitant federal tariffs, and even considered seceding from the Union. Insulted, Jackson threatened to lead an army into the state, put down the rebellion, and hang the ringleaders himself. The crisis was eventually resolved when Congress lowered the tariffs, but by then Jackson had lost a lot of support in the South.

THE BANK WAR

But what galvanized Old Hickory's opposition more than anything else was what he did to the American banking system.

Like Thomas Jefferson before him, Jackson hated banks, believing them to be corrupt institutions that enriched the wealthy and well-connected. He especially hated the Second Bank of the United States. He hated it all the more when the bank and its director, Nicholas Biddle, sided with presidential candidate Henry Clay in the election of 1832 and even offered to lend money to pro-Clay newspapers to attack Jackson.

Big mistake—Jackson was furious that the bank would try to influence the outcome of the election. "The bank is trying to kill me," he complained, "but I will kill *it*."

FROM SECOND TO NONE

When Jackson won reelection against Clay in a landslide in 1832, he set out to make good on his word. He ordered the secretary of the Treasury to pay government expenditures out of the Treasury's Second Bank accounts, while making any deposits to state banks. (Critics called them Jackson's "pet" banks.) In less than three months, the federal government's deposits to the Second Bank dwindled to almost nothing.

Biddle was determined to save his bank and believed the way to do it was by *maximizing* the economic damage from Jackson's measures. He drastically cut back on lending, prompting banks all across the country to follow suit; the panic that resulted sent the country into a recession.

Businesses in every major American city failed, throwing thousands out of work. Yet somehow, the plan backfired—Jackson's popularity actually increased, and his image grew as the protector of the common person against the greed of aristocrats and bankers. In the end, Jackson got what he wanted: the Second Bank finally collapsed in 1841.

BACKLASH

But the Bank War crystallized the political opposition to Jackson. Robert Remini writes in *The Life of Andrew Jackson*:

> The pressures of the Bank War and Jackson's imperial presidency finally brought a new party into being.... National Republicans, bank men, nullifiers, high-tariff advocates, friends of internal improvements, states' righters, and— most particularly—all those who abominated Jackson or his reforms slowly converged into a new political coalition that quite appropriately assumed the name "Whig."

The Scottish-Gaelic term *whig* was first applied to horse thieves, then to anti-royalists in the American Revolution. Now it would be used by the

Benjamin Robbins Curtis (1851) was the first Supreme Court justice with a law degree.

opponents of the tyranny of whom some called "King Andrew I."

WHAT GOES UP...

Had Jackson limited his economic meddling, perhaps the Panic of 1833–34 would have run its course without the Whigs emerging as a major political force. But he didn't.

By January 1835, he had managed to pay down the entire U.S. national debt ($60 million), and the federal government was collecting more revenues than it was spending. Jackson returned some of the surplus to the states, most of whom promptly spent it. Then, anticipating similar federal windfalls in the years to come, many states began borrowing against these future funds and spending that, too. In addition, Jackson's "pet" banks were now bulging with federal deposits, which allowed them to print and issue paper currency backed by federal monies. (In the 1830s, banks printed their own currency.) The country was soon awash with cash. Result: disaster.

The influx of so much capital into the economy led to huge inflation and soaring real-estate prices, creating a speculative economic bubble that burst in 1836 after bad weather led to crop failures throughout the U.S.

...MUST COME DOWN

As the economy began to teeter, foreign creditors started demanding payment in gold and silver out of a fear that American paper currency was losing its value. Jackson decided it would be good for the federal government to return to "sound money," too. On July 11, 1836, he ordered that all future payments for the sale of public lands (a major source of government income in the 1830s) be made in precious metals. Banknotes were no longer acceptable for these transactions, so they began to lose their value.

More bad news: A financial crisis rocked England, then the world's financial capital and a major buyer of American cotton, the country's largest export. The slump in the U.S. cotton market in turn caused the failure of hundreds of other related businesses.

"By the time Jackson retired in 1837, America was in the early stages of its biggest financial crisis to date," Paul Johnson writes in *A History of the American People*. "Far from getting back to 'sound money,' Jackson had paralyzed the system completely." Jackson's heir apparent, Martin Van Buren, managed to squeak into office in the 1836 election, partly because

---

In 2007 Pres. Chavez ordered Venezuela's clocks set back 30 min. to give people more light.

the economic crisis was just beginning and nobody knew how bad it would be. But the 1840 election would be another story.

The recession deepened into a full-blown depression that dragged on for five years, wiping out more than 600 banks and shuttering most of the factories in the East. Thousands of people lost their jobs, and food riots broke out in cities all over the nation. Van Buren never had the popularity that Jackson enjoyed, and the depression ruined his chances for reelection.

WHIGS TRIUMPHANT

In 1840 the Whigs borrowed heavily from the Jackson–Van Buren formula for victory. They put a war hero at the top of the ticket: General William Henry Harrison, who had defeated the Shawnee Indians at the Battle of Tippecanoe 30 years earlier. They staged "monster" rallies all over the country. And when a Democratic writer made the mistake of claiming that Harrison would just as soon "spend the rest of his days in a log cabin with a barrel of cider," he gave the Whigs a perfect campaign theme that they could use to distinguish their man from a sharp-dressing New York dandy like President Van Buren. Harrison rallies became "Log Cabin and Hard Cyder" rallies: Supporters built log cabins at every campaign event and served copious amounts of hard cider to the crowds.

Van Buren, vilified by the Whigs as an effete elitist who drank wine from "coolers of silver," seemed a sissy by comparison. On election day, he carried only seven states to Harrison's 19, and lost in the electoral college, 60 votes to Harrison's 234.

The Whigs also won their first majorities in both houses of Congress, and in 1840 there were Whig governors in 20 of the 26 states—not bad for a party that was barely seven years old.

WINNING THE BATTLE

The Whigs were on the brink of becoming permanently established as the second major party alongside the Democrats. But then their luck ran out.

• The 67-year-old Harrison delivered his inaugural address outdoors in the snow without wearing a hat, gloves, or overcoat. He spoke for more than an hour and a half (the longest inaugural speech in American history), contracted pneumonia, and died a month after taking office (the shortest presidency in American history).

• Vice President John Tyler, a former Democrat who joined the Whigs

What did Presidents Tyler, Fillmore, and Arthur have in common? No VP.

after falling out with Andrew Jackson, became president. But he was still a Democrat at heart, and he often vetoed Whig legislation, prompting all but one member of his cabinet to resign and splitting the Whig party in two. The Whig congressional caucus wrote Tyler out of the party.

• In 1844 the Whigs, still bitterly divided, lost the White House to Democrat James Knox Polk. In 1848 the Whigs repeated their 1840 strategy by putting a war hero at the top of the ticket—General Zachary Taylor, hero of the Mexican War—and won the White House. But on July 4, 1850, history repeated itself when President Taylor consumed large quantities of raw fruit, cabbages, and cucumbers, washed it all down with iced water…and then died from acute gastroenteritis five days later, a little more than a year into his term.

WHIGGING OUT

The Whig party was also divided over the issue of slavery. President Taylor himself had contributed to the split: As a plantation owner with more than 300 slaves, he so alienated antislavery Whigs in the north that many of them split off to form the Free Soil Party.

When Taylor died, Vice President Millard Fillmore (also a Whig) became president. He added to the controversy by signing the Fugitive Slave Law of 1850, which required the government to assist in the capture and return of runaway slaves to their owners, even in the antislavery states of the North. (Though Fillmore was personally opposed to slavery, he feared that ending it would lead to civil war, so he signed the law to cool the secessionist passions of the South.)

Historians generally credit such actions with postponing the Civil War for 10 years, but they doomed Fillmore's chances for reelection and contributed to the destruction of the Whig party. By 1848 Fillmore's hedging on slavery had cost the party support in the North; at the same time, the presence of antislavery politicians at the top of the party killed its support in the South. "Cotton Whigs," as the party's Southern faction was called, defected to the states-rights appeal of the Democratic Party. And by 1854, most antislavery "Conscience Whigs" had defected to a new party founded for the purpose of opposing slavery: the Republicans.

To read about the rise of the Republican Party, turn to page 245.

"An election is no time for a serious discussion of policy." —Canadian PM Kim Campbell

THE RIGHT STUFF

Thoughts from a conservative with a sense of humor—P. J. O'Rourke.

"Remember the battle between the generations twenty-some years ago? Remember all the screaming at the dinner table about haircuts and getting jobs and the American dream? Well, our parents won. They're out there living the American dream on some damned golf course, and we're stuck with the jobs and haircuts."

"Seriousness is stupidity sent to college."

"Every government is a parliament of whores. The trouble is, in a democracy the whores are us."

"A number of…remarkable things show up in holiday dinners, such as…pies made out of something called 'mince,' although if anyone has ever seen a mince in its natural state he did not live to tell about it."

"There's one…terrifying fact about old people: I'm going to be one soon."

"Everybody knows how to raise children, except the people who have them."

"You can't shame or humiliate modern celebrities. What used to be called shame and humiliation is now called publicity."

"A fruit is a vegetable with looks and money. Plus, if you let fruit rot, it turns into wine, something Brussels sprouts never do."

"Feminism is the result of a few ignorant and literal-minded women letting the cat out of the bag about which is the superior sex."

"The sport of skiing consists of wearing three thousand dollars' worth of clothes and equipment and driving two hundred miles in the snow in order to stand around at a bar and get drunk."

"Politicians are interested in people. Not that this is always a virtue. Dogs are interested in fleas."

"I like to do my principal research in bars, where people are more likely to tell the truth or, at least, lie less convincingly than they do in briefings and books."

The Oval Office in the White House is only 22 feet long.

CONGRESSIONAL BRIEFS

Now we step back and let some of our fellow political media outlets describe the follies and flubs all too common on Capitol Hill.

BUT IT'S DEFINITELY NOT BRAIN SURGERY

"At a press briefing, Senate Majority Leader Thomas Daschle (D-SD) lit into President Bush's plans for a space-based missile-defense system, saying that committing billions of dollars 'to a concept that may or may not be practical or doable is something that I am mystified by.' But as his mystification intensified, Daschle said. 'It just seems like common sense. I mean, this isn't—this isn't rocket science here.' Daschle quickly caught his mistake, as the room erupted in laughter. 'Now that I think about, it *is* rocket science."

—Roll Call

SHAMELESS EXPLOITATION

"A controversy started September 11 when Brian Kerns (R-IN) gave the *Indianapolis Star* a harrowing account of watching a hijacked plane slam into the Pentagon during his commute on George Washington Memorial Parkway. 'I'm in shock,' he said. 'I still can't believe it. I drove into the office and told my staff to go home.' The *Indianapolis Star* reported, however, that the plane in question never flew over the Parkway. And an American Legion official said he remembers being in Kerns's office with the congressman when networks reported the Pentagon attack. Kerns's response when pressed on whether he was mistaken about what he saw: 'Who knows?'"

—Associated Press

DON'T QUIT YOUR DAY JOB

"Concerned that 'the pickup owners of this nation might get screwed in all this gas-guzzler talk about SUVs and vans,' Senator Zell Miller (D-GA) introduced an amendment to keep pickup fuel economy requirements at 20.7 mpg. He also co-wrote, sang, and recorded a song called

---

Congress is one of the few workplaces in the U.S. where it's still legal to smoke indoors.

'The Talking Pickup Truck Blues.' A sample of the lyrics: 'Sure, an SUV is classy travel, / But it ain't much good for haulin' gravel, / Or hay or seed or bovine feces. / So please, don't make my pickup truck an endangered species.'"

—**Fox News**

POLITICAL THEATER OF THE ABSURD

"In 2001 House Speaker Dennis Hastert (R-IL) held a press conference surrounded by a group of hard hat–wearing 'working Americans.' But the 'workers' were really lobbyists in disguise. The conference was called to pass off the trillion-dollar Bush tax cut as a boon for the working class. According to a memo sent to the lobbyists, 'The Speaker's office was very clear in saying that they do not need people in suits. If people want to participate, they must be DRESSED DOWN, and appear to be REAL WORKER types.'"

—*Common Dreams*

IN THE DOGHOUSE

In January 2011, Senator Barbara Mikulski (D-MD) "stood in front of the cameras and assembled reporters in a Senate gallery, flapping her arms and belting out a stadium favorite of Baltimore Ravens fans: 'Who let the dogs out? Who, who? Who, who?' Why? She was celebrating. She had just won a Super Bowl bet with New York senators Charles Schumer and Hillary Clinton."

—**Capital News Service**

TOOT-TOOT

"Patrick Kennedy (D-RI) was accused of causing $28,000 in damage to a rented yacht on a Y2K booze cruise. He later appeared at a political roast dressed in a sailor suit and capped off the evening by singing 'Patrick the Sailor Man.' At the same roast, the admitted former cokehead joked about Senator Lincoln Chafee (R-RI), another admitted former cokehead: 'Now when I hear someone talking about a Rhode Island politician whose father was a senator and who got to Washington on his family name, used cocaine, and wasn't very smart, I know there is only a 50-50 chance it's me.'"

—*Mother Jones*

At 310,000 words, Alabama's state constitution is the longest in the world.

IT'S A CONSPIRACY!

*More unbelievable conspiracy theories from
the world of politics and government.*

THEORY: The government released a video game that was really
an experimental mind-control device.
THE STORY: In 1981 a game called Polybius showed up in a few
arcades in Portland, Oregon. Unlike the two-dimensional, graphically
simple games of the era (Pac-Man and Space Invaders, for example),
Polybius featured rotating 3-D images and strobe lights. Many people
played this alluring game, yet no one remembers it. Why? The combination of spatial focus and strobe lights caused brain damage. Many players
suffered amnesia, insomnia, and nightmares. At the peak of the game's
popularity, arcade owners noticed mysterious men in black suits who
came to collect data from Polybius machines. They were from the military—Polybius was being used to test mind-control techniques. After a
few weeks, Polybius vanished from the arcades forever.

THE TRUTH: In 1980 Sinnescholsen, a small German video game
maker, created Polybius, a disorienting game that simulated 3-D graph-
ics. But arcade owners weren't interested: They said it was too new and
too weird to be commercially viable. So Sinnescholsen decided to test-
market the game in six arcades in Portland, Oregon. The owners were
right—the game bombed. But one 13-year-old boy who played the game
suffered a seizure from it. Sinnescholsen employees flew to Portland and
immediately removed the game from the arcades (explaining the "men in
black"). Faced with possible scandal, the company dissolved. The legend
probably took off because one of Polybius's designers was Ed Rottberg,
also the creator of Battlezone, a video game used by the U.S. government
to train army recruits.

THEORY: The U.S. Food and Drug Administration (FDA) is attempting
to turn American males into homosexuals by convincing them to eat
more soy, which triggers homosexuality.
THE STORY: While the FDA claims that a diet rich in soy protein
reduces the risk of cancer and heart disease, the agency knows the real

truth about soy: It's extremely high in estrogen. Result: Babies who are fed soy formula grow up to have sexual-development problems. In men, the estrogen-rich soy delays puberty and shrinks the genitals. In women, it speeds up puberty and enlarges the uterus. These malformations, along with the estrogen, "feminize" the brain, making men more likely to become homosexual.

THE TRUTH: The theory can be traced back to a column written by Jim Rutz in 2006. He outlines his case against soy but doesn't cite any specific research, instead saying "research in 2000" shows that soy leads to thyroid problems but doesn't divulge who conducted the research. Rutz also said that "leukemia went up 27 percent in one year," without mentioning which year. Hormone imbalances were proven not to have anything to do with sexual orientation in a 1984 Columbia University study. Soy does contain trace elements of estrogen, but not enough to cause sexual deformation. As for the left-wing conspiracy in the FDA, that's unlikely because the agency's leadership is appointed by the president. So from 2000 to 2008—when the conspiracy theory was in full swing—the FDA was headed by a Republican.

THEORY: Astronauts have never been back to the Moon since the 1969 landing because they were scared away by an alien spacecraft base.

THE STORY: Plans to inhabit, mine, and colonize the Moon were thwarted once Neil Armstrong and Buzz Aldrin visited the lunar surface. There was more than rocks and dust there: There was a massive Moon city and UFO base being used by aliens to spy on Earth. Ham radio operators claim to have eavesdropped on *Apollo 11*'s communications with NASA and report that Armstrong said, "You wouldn't believe it! I'm telling you there are other spacecraft out there, lined up on the far side of the crater edge. They're on the Moon watching us!" All witnesses have since been put under a strict gag order by the U.S. government to keep quiet about it…or else.

THE TRUTH: All other "evidence" aside, there's one major hole in this theory: Humans haven't been scared off of the Moon by aliens; in fact, we've been back a lot. From 1969 to 1972, U.S. astronauts visited the Moon six more times, all without extraterrestrial encounters. And several unmanned probes have since mapped and photographed the entire surface of our celestial neighbor. The only evidence of civilization is the stuff that earthlings have left there.

In 2007 the British government approved a request to create human-pig hybrids.

THE PLOT AGAINST FDR

Conspiracy theories are fun to read about because they're usually so bizarre that they couldn't possibly be true. What's even more fun is a conspiracy that's not a theory at all. Here's one that actually happened.

ALL THE RAGE IN EUROPE

In the 1930s, many Western countries suffered severe economic depressions. The need to prevent unrest and establish control was so desperate that in Italy, Germany, and Spain, military-backed coups installed fascist governments. In that system a centralized government, led by a sole dictator, holds all the power and the individual citizen has little recourse. Fascist governments readily use force to quell what they perceive as threats, such as labor unions. Some notable fascist dictators of the 1930s: Benito Mussolini in Italy, Francisco Franco in Spain, and Adolf Hitler in Germany.

In another country, a fascist coup was attempted not by the military, but by a group of powerful businessmen and politicians. They wanted to overthrow the democratically elected head of state through blackmail and threats of violence—and then replace him with a puppet dictator who would serve their interests. That country was the United States.

RAW DEAL?

Franklin D. Roosevelt was elected president in 1932 largely on the basis of his New Deal, a far-reaching series of reforms designed to stimulate the economy out of the Great Depression (see page 61). Roosevelt's plans weren't universally popular—giving control of economic matters to the government instead of business in a free-market economy was viewed by many as communism, especially Social Security, which was perceived as the needy getting "something for nothing."

But the crux of the New Deal was job creation. Roosevelt proposed more than 10 new government agencies such as the Works Progress Administration, the Civilian Conservation Corps, the Civil Works Administration, and the Tennessee Valley Authority, that would over-see construction and beautification projects and generate millions of new jobs.

What's the #1 source of revenue for the U.S. government? Individual income tax.

THE PLOT BEGINS

Business leaders were especially opposed to the National Recovery Administration, which set minimum wages and reduced the workweek, even in the private sector. Accustomed to paying their workers whatever they wanted (for as much work as they wanted), barons of industry stood to lose millions.

A group of anti-Roosevelt business leaders and politicians (Democrats and Republicans) formed an organization in 1933 called the American Liberty League (ALL), dedicated to "fostering the right to work, earn, save, and acquire property." In other words, they advocated individual wealth-building and villainized welfare. The ALL was so dedicated to that goal that it would do whatever was necessary to secure their wealth. That included staging a militia-backed coup to force Roosevelt out of office and replace him with a pro-business dictator.

BUSINESS CLASS

In June 1933, a number of ALL members met to discuss the specifics of removing Roosevelt. Among those reported to be in attendance were:

• Irénée Du Pont, president of the DuPont chemical company

• Dean Acheson, the undersecretary of the Treasury, a position to which he was appointed by Roosevelt

• Al Smith, the 1928 Democratic presidential candidate

• Grayson Murphy, a board member of several companies, including Goodyear, Bethlehem Steel, and the J. P. Morgan & Co. banking conglomerate

• Robert Clark, one of Wall Street's wealthiest investors

• William Doyle, commander of the Massachusetts department of the American Legion, a veterans' service and political organization. The 300,000 Massachusetts members were almost exclusively veterans of World War I.

• Gerald MacGuire, a bonds investor as well as the commander of the Connecticut department of the American Legion

• Prescott Bush, an influential banker and a board member of several corporations. (Later, Bush became a Republican senator from Connecticut from 1952 to 1962, and was the father of George H. W. Bush, and grandfather of George W. Bush.)

The president of the United States has a secret zip code for receiving personal mail.

The plan: The group would force Roosevelt to create a new cabinet position called the secretary of general affairs, which would be filled by a person of the ALL's choosing. Next, they'd force Roosevelt to admit to the public that he had been crippled by polio (a fact not widely known because he was rarely photographed in his wheelchair). They'd hoped that the disclosure that the president couldn't walk or even stand without assistance would destroy the people's trust in his ability to pull the country out of its economic mess, and the backlash would force Roosevelt to shift authority to the secretary of general affairs.

In all likelihood, of course, Roosevelt would refuse to meet the ALL's demands to create the new position, confess his condition, and transfer power. Part two of the plan: If Roosevelt refused, Doyle and MacGuire would activate their American Legion brigades to form a militia of more than 500,000 who would then storm Washington, D.C., and take power by force.

THE BUTLER DID IT

For the American people and 500,000 soldiers to go along with a plan to depose a president, the ALL knew that whoever they chose to be the secretary of general affairs would have to be popular with both the military and the general public. So, acting on behalf of the plotters, MacGuire approached Smedley Butler, a major general in the Marine Corps and the most decorated marine in history at that point. Butler was as loved by the military and respected by the general public just as later generals Dwight Eisenhower, Douglas MacArthur, and Colin Powell would be. That's because in 1932, when World War I veterans marched on Washington to lobby Congress over still-unpaid combat bonuses from 15 years earlier, Butler publicly supported them and even gave a speech encouraging them to fight for what was rightfully theirs.

CLANDESTINE MEETING

MacGuire visited Butler at his home in Newton Square, Pennsylvania, in June 1933. They met for just 30 minutes, but MacGuire gave him the complete details of the plot, including the names of those involved and a promise of $3 million in financial support. Butler asked MacGuire why something as drastic as a coup was necessary. MacGuire said that it was because Roosevelt's social programs proved he was a Communist. "We need a fascist government in this country to save the nation from the

---

Of the careers Americans view as having the highest prestige, politician didn't make the list.

Communists who want to tear it down and wreck all that we have built," Butler later said MacGuire told him.

Butler agreed and told MacGuire he was in...except that he really wasn't. What the ALL members hadn't taken into consideration was that the combat bonus protests of the previous summer, which had made Butler beloved among soldiers, ended when President Herbert Hoover sent in the cavalry to break it up. Butler was so appalled by this treatment of the veterans that he renounced Hoover and the Republican Party, became a Democrat, and had actively campaigned for Roosevelt in the 1932 election.

PLOTLESS

After speaking with MacGuire, Butler promptly reported the meeting and the brewing fascist coup to the McCormack-Dickstein Committee, the congressional committee in charge of investigating threats to the government, such as fascist coups. (In the 1940s, the committee would try to root out Communists under a different name: the House Un-American Activities Committee.)

Butler gave his testimony to the committee between July and November 1934. Nearly all of the conspirators Butler named were asked to testify. But since they weren't subpoenaed, merely asked, they never showed up. The only exception was Gerald MacGuire, and he denied everything. In its final report, the committee officially stated that it believed Butler:

> Your committee received evidence showing that certain persons had made an attempt to establish a fascist government in this country. There is no question that these attempts were discussed, were planned, and might have been placed in execution when and if the financial backers deemed it expedient. This committee received evidence from Maj. Gen. Smedley D. Butler (retired), who testified before the committee as to conversations with one Gerald C. MacGuire in which the latter is alleged to have suggested the formation of a fascist army under the leadership of General Butler.

But the findings—and Butler's credibility—were undercut when the report was released to the public with the names of the conspirators blacked out. The names were never officially released, and no one associated with the "plot" was ever held accountable.

Sarah Palin won "Miss Congeniality" at the '84 Miss Alaska pageant (but came in 2nd).

COUP DE-TAH-TAH

So why didn't the federal government prosecute the plotters? At the time, Roosevelt was trying hard to get his New Deal programs passed through Congress. Releasing the names of the government officials and appointees involved would have undermined Roosevelt's authority and made him look like a weak leader. In fact, many believe that it was President Roosevelt himself who suggested that the McCormack-Dickstein Committee withhold the conspirators' names and not pursue charges…provided the plotters agreed to stop speaking out publicly against his social and relief programs.

The compromised report, coupled with the altogether absurd nature of the idea of a fascist coup in America (even if it was true), led to little media coverage. The *New York Times* and *Time* magazine reported on the committee's findings, but dismissed Butler's claims as rumor and hearsay.

How serious were the conspirators? The idea never got past the planning stages, and the conspirators may have met only that once. When news that Butler had turned informant got out, the plot crumbled. But the group did have one "backup" plan—shortly after MacGuire met with Butler, MacGuire also approached James Van Zandt, the head of the Veterans of Foreign Wars office, and offered him the position of secretary of general affairs should Butler decline. After Butler revealed the plot to the congressional committee, Van Zandt told reporters his story, lending Butler's story some credence, but that's as far as it went.

IRONIC POSTSCRIPT

The American Liberty League, in addition to proposing fascist coups, operated as a legitimate pro-capitalist organization. It folded in 1940. That same year, Franklin Roosevelt was elected to his record third presidential term. Roosevelt was reelected again in 1944, but in the same national election, Republicans took control of Congress from the Democrats, gaining a majority in both the Senate and the House. After Roosevelt's death five months later, the conservative government was eager to start anew, and in 1951 passed the 22nd Amendment to the Constitution, which limited future presidents to two terms. Why? Many senators and representatives feared that a president who held office for too long could become a dictator.

How many vice presidents became president because the president died? Eight.

DELUSIONS OF GRANDEUR

*Uncle John, our Lord of Porcelain and Grand Master of Flushery,
thinks that it's funny how dictators give themselves long,
flowery titles describing their amazing greatness.*

DICTATOR: Jean-Bédel Bokassa
POSITION: President of the Central African Republic
(1966–76), emperor of Central Africa (1976–79)
OFFICIAL TITLE: "His Imperial Majesty, Bokassa the First, Emperor of
Central Africa by the will of the Central African people, united within
the national political party, the Movement for the Social Evolution of
Black Africa"

DICTATOR: Enver Hoxha
POSITION: Secretary of the Albanian Labour Party (1941–85)
OFFICIAL TITLE: "Comrade-Chairman-Prime Minister-Foreign Minis-
ter-Minister of War and Commander-in-Chief of the People's Army"

DICTATOR: Idi Amin
POSITION: President of Uganda (1971–79)
OFFICIAL TITLE: "His Excellency President for Life, Field Marshal Al
Hadji Doctor Idi Amin Dada, VC, DSO, MC, Lord of the Beasts of the
Earth and Fishes of the Sea and Conqueror of the British Empire in
Africa in General and Uganda in Particular and the Most Ubiquitous of
all King of Scotland dictators"

DICTATOR: Joseph-Désiré Mobutu
POSITION: President of Zaire (1965–97)
OFFICIAL TITLE: "Mobutu Sese Seko," which means "the all-powerful
warrior who, because of his endurance and inflexible will to win, will go
from conquest to conquest, leaving fire in his wake!"

First American to vote from space: Astronaut John Blaha, in 1997.

DICTATOR: Francisco Macias Nguema
POSITION: President of Equatorial Guinea (1968–79)
OFFICIAL TITLE: "Unique Miracle, Grand Master of Education, Science, and Culture"

DICTATOR: Teodoro Obiang Nguema Mbasogo
POSITION: President of Equatorial Guinea (1979–present)
OFFICIAL TITLE: "Gentleman of the Great Island of Bioko, Annobón and Río Muni"

DICTATOR: Yahya Jammeh
POSITION: President of Gambia (1994–present)
OFFICIAL TITLE: "His Excellency the President Sheikh Professor al-Haji Doctor Yahya Abdul-Azziz Jemus Junkung Jammeh Naasiru Deen"

DICTATOR: Muammar al-Gaddafi
POSITION: President of Libya (1969–2011)
OFFICIAL TITLE: "Brother Leader, Guide of the First of September Great Revolution of the Socialist People's Libyan Arab Jamahiriya"

DICTATOR: Kim Jong-Il
POSITION: Supreme Leader of North Korea (1994–2012)
OFFICIAL TITLES: North Korea's state-controlled media were extremely gracious toward Kim. They most commonly referred to him to as "Great Leader," but other titles that were seen in print include:

• "Dear Leader, who is a perfect incarnation of the appearance that a leader should have"
• "Sun of the Communist Future"
• "Shining Star of Paektu Mountain"
• "Guarantee of the Fatherland's Unification"
• "Invincible and Iron-Willed Commander"
• "Guiding Star of the 21st Century"
• "Highest Incarnation of the Revolutionary Comradely Love"
• "Glorious General, Who Descended From Heaven"

As president, Andrew Jackson broke 93 treaties with Native Americans.

UNSUNG ECO-HEROES IN GOVERNMENT

A few years ago, when we put together Uncle John's Certified Organic Bathroom Reader, *we discovered that the U.S. government and the environment have had a love-hate relationship. Here are three politicians who made a big difference for their biggest constituent: planet Earth.*

HUGH HAMMOND BENNETT (1881–1960)

Claim to Fame: The father of soil conservation

Life Story: After spending two decades as a surveyor and scientist in the U.S. and South America, in 1928 Bennett authored a USDA bulletin called "Soil Erosion: A National Menace." He warned that irresponsible farming techniques were allowing soil to erode and be swept away by wind.

In April 1935, as Bennett was testifying before Congress, nature provided a frightening visual aid to prove his point: A massive dust storm that had started in the Great Plains had now reached all the way to Washington, where it blacked out the midday sun. "This, gentlemen," said Bennett as he pointed out the windows, "is what I have been talking about." Shortly after, Congress passed the Soil Conversation Act and Bennett spent the next 17 years as chief of the USDA's Soil Conservation Service—now known as the Natural Resources Conservation Service.

At first, farmers were apprehensive about someone from Washington telling them how to farm, but Bennett toured extensively, giving lectures on how conserving the soil would save their farms from a future dust bowl. Today, farmers consider him a hero.

Environmental Statement: "Almost invariably, conservation farming—which, after all, is common-sense farming with scientific methods—begins to show results the very first years it is applied."

MURRAY BOOKCHIN (1921–2006)

Claim to Fame: Author, pioneer of the green movement

Life Story: Born in New York to Russian immigrants, Bookchin spent a few years in the American Communist Youth Movement before becoming disillusioned with the authoritarian policies of Stalin in the 1930s. After that, he bounced around from libertarianism to anarchism to socialism, but he made his greatest impact as a conservationist. Writing 27 books under several pseudonyms, Bookchin was among the first to speak out against chemical food additives and toxic pesticides, and to advocate for the use of alternative energy sources. One of his most important works, *Our Synthetic Environment* (written under the pen name Lewis Herber), was released in 1962, six months before Rachel Carson's influential book *Silent Spring*, which many people credit with starting the modern environmental movement. Were it not for Bookchin's need to keep a low profile (his political leanings made him unpopular in some circles), he would most likely be as famous as Carson.

In 1974 Bookchin founded Vermont's Institute for Social Ecology. He later played a significant role in organizing the Green Party. In 1992 London's *Independent* named Bookchin "the foremost Green philosopher of the age."

Environmental Statement: "The great project of our time must be to open the other eye: to see all-sidedly and wholly, to heal and transcend the cleavage between humanity and nature that came with early wisdom."

RUSSELL E. TRAIN (1920–)

Claim to Fame: The "Conservative Conservationist"

Life Story: Train began his professional life as a government attorney. But it wasn't until he was in his 40s that the lifelong Republican realized his true calling as a conservationist. He founded the African Wildlife Leadership Foundation in 1961, and in 1968 was appointed to the National Water Commission by President Johnson.

The following year, President Nixon gave Train a challenging job: dealing with the growing number of controversial environmental issues, including the highly debated Trans-Alaska Oil Pipeline. Train persuaded Congress to create the Council on Environmental Quality, which focused on identifying the most important environmental problems and creating federal policies to find solutions. While Train headed the CEQ, he helped standardize the catalytic converter in automobiles to reach the Clean Air Act's emission reductions. He also spearheaded the Toxic Substances Control Act, which regulated new and existing chemicals, and the National

---

In 1990 France's gov't created a new cabinet position: the Ministry of Rock 'n' Roll.

Pollutant Discharge Elimination System, a part of the Clean Water Act. Often disagreeing with Nixon's opinions, Train pushed for increasing government involvement in conserving energy and reducing water pollution. He was head of the EPA from 1973 to '77 before going on to serve as the president and chairman of the World Wildlife Fund. Later, he was named chairman of the National Commission on the Environment.

And he's still speaking out for conservation. In 2010 Train wrote an open letter to Senate leaders urging them not weaken the government's Clean Air Act, which some Republican lawmakers had proposed. He warned that "overturning science in favor of political considerations" could weaken the EPA and have a negative impact on the air we breathe.

Environmental Statement: "The Golden Rule says, 'Thou shalt do unto others what you would have them do unto you.' To my way of thinking, those others include the whole community of this Earth, all the living things—and inanimate as well—and we damage that extraordinary structure at our peril."

*   *   *

GO, BALLOONS!

Don Mischer, the producer of the 2004 Democratic National Convention in Boston, really wanted all of the balloons to drop on cue. When they didn't, here's what a live microphone caught him saying.

"Go, balloons. I don't see anything happening. Go, balloons. Go, balloons. Go, balloons. Stand by, confetti. Keep coming, balloons. More balloons. Bring them. Balloons, balloons, balloons! More balloons. Tons of them. Bring them down. Let them all come. No confetti. No confetti yet. All right. Go, balloons. Go, balloons. We're getting more balloons. All balloons. All balloons should be going. Come on, guys! Let's move it! We need more balloons. I want all balloons to go. Go, confetti. Go, confetti. Go, confetti. I want more balloons. What's happening to the balloons? We need more balloons. We need all of them coming down. Go, balloons. Balloons! What's happening, balloons? There's not enough coming down! All balloons! Why the hell is nothing falling? What the (censored) are you guys doing up there? We want more balloons coming down! More balloons! More balloons!"

IRONIC, ISN'T IT?

All politics is ironic. After all, these public "servants"
try to pretend they will "serve" you as long as you
elect them as your "leader." Here are some
more examples of irony in government.

DETAILS, DETAILS...

Florida's secretary of state, Katherine Harris, became famous during the 2000 presidential election as the person in charge of the disputed Florida ballot count. In the 2004 local election in her hometown of Longboat Key, Florida, Harris was informed that her vote would not be counted. Why? Because she had turned in an invalid ballot. (She forgot to sign it.)

DO UNTO OTHERS...

In 1998 former White House aide Linda Tripp made national headlines for her part in the Monica Lewinsky scandal. It was Tripp who had secretly taped private telephone conversations in which Lewinsky revealed intimate details of her affair with President Clinton. Tripp then gave the tapes to the special prosecutor, ultimately leading to Clinton's impeachment. Five years later, Tripp won a $595,000 settlement against the Pentagon...for violating her privacy. Details of her life, including when she was arrested as a teenager, had been leaked to the media after she turned over the tapes.

AN IRONY OF ORWELLIAN MAGNITUDE

In his 1949 novel *1984*, George Orwell foretold of a dark future in which England would be ruled by "Big Brother," a government which constantly spies on its citizens to keep them in line. In England today, there are a reported 4.2 million closed-circuit cameras watching the people. But one neighborhood in London is leading all of the others: On a single block in Canonbury Square in Islington, North London, there are 32 cameras trained on the streets, alleys, an even on peoples' properties. One of Canonbury Square's biggest claims to fame: George Orwell lived there while he was writing *1984*.

In Waterbury, VT, politicians are prohibited from "telling lies or fabricating stories."

BORN IN THE "U.S.A."

In the 2008 U.S. presidential election, questions of citizenship dogged one of the candidates. Barack Obama? Well, yes, but he wasn't the only one. As Obama's critics were accusing him of actually being born in Kenya (thus making him ineligible for the job), John McCain's citizenship was also called into question. Why? He was born in South America. So why was McCain eligible for the presidency? Because he was born on a U.S. military base to two American citizens in the Panama Canal Zone. (Had McCain won, would he have been challenged by rivals to produce a birth certificate?)

THE BIG AND THE SMALL OF IT

On paper, Republicans are for "small government," and Democrats are for "big government." In reality, it hasn't quite worked out that way. Based on data gathered from 1976 to 2010, the three GOP presidents in that span—Reagan and the two Bushes—increased the federal workforce by 261,000 employees. The three Dems—Carter, Clinton, and Obama—actually reduced the federal workforce by 304,000 employees.

MORE GOVERNMENTAL IRONY

• In 2000 an 87-year-old man dropped dead while standing in line at a government office in Bogotá, Colombia. He was there to apply for a government certificate to prove that he was still alive.

• In 1919 *The New York Times* commissioned a poll asking people who they thought were the ten most important living Americans. Herbert Hoover won first place. Franklin Roosevelt, then assistant secretary of the navy, saw the poll and wrote to a colleague: "Herbert Hoover is certainly a winner, and we could make him President of the United States." Ironically, after a less-than-stellar presidency by Hoover, Roosevelt took over and became one of the most important Americans of the 20th century.

• In January 2000, a Florida teacher gave his 70 seventh-grade students a simple assignment—write a letter to their elected representative. Purpose: To demonstrate that "their opinions matter." As of the end of the school year, not one of the 70 students had received a reply.

• Vice President Joe Biden attended a meeting in 2011 with the new Government Accountability and Transparency Board. However, reporters were banned from attending the closed-door "transparency" meeting.

Mark it down: 1835 was the first and (so far) last time that the U.S. gov't was debt-free.

THE RANKIN FILE

This political pioneer was first and foremost a woman of conscience, whatever the consequence. Whether or not you agree with Jeanette Rankin, you've got to admire her spirit.

HEAR HER ROAR

In November 1916, a short, feisty suffragette from Missoula, Montana, named Jeanette Rankin beat seven male rivals to become the first woman ever elected to the United States Congress. And that made her the first woman ever elected to a national legislature in any Western democracy. "I knew the women would stand behind me," she said when she took office, "and I am deeply conscious of the responsibility before me. I will not only represent the women of Montana, but also the women of the country, and I have plenty of work cut out for me."

Born in 1880, Rankin was an excellent student who graduated from the University of Montana. After that, she worked as a teacher, seamstress, and a social worker. Then, at age 30, Rankin took up politics when she joined in the fight for the women's right to vote in Montana. "Men and women are like right and left hands," she declared. "It doesn't make sense not to use both." And when Montana women were granted the right to vote in 1914, Rankin decided to run for Congress. With her brother Wellington as her campaign manager, she was triumphant and took her seat in the House of Representatives on April 2, 1917.

STANDING ALONE

Not surprisingly, Rankin was not welcomed to Congress with open arms. And it wasn't just the men who shunned her: The congressional wives proved to be very unfriendly. Why? They were reportedly afraid that she'd have designs on their husbands. Plus, the U.S. Capitol at that time had no bathrooms for women—there'd never been a need. To make matters worse, four days after she took her seat in Congress, Rankin made the extremely unpopular decision to vote *against* America's entry into World War I (the vote was 373–50). It is customary to vote without comment, but Rankin broke with tradition, announcing dramatically, "I want to stand behind my country, but I cannot vote for war."

In 1923 the U.S. Attorney General declared it legal for women to wear trousers.

Rankin championed many causes during her two years in Congress: women's rights, birth control, equal pay, and child welfare. In 1919 she proudly introduced the Susan B. Anthony Amendment, which gave women the right to vote, on the floor of the House; it passed and was ratified by the country as the 19th Amendment to the Constitution. "If I am remembered for no other act," she later said, "I want to be remembered as the only woman who ever voted to give women the right to vote."

THE WAR ROOM

The ratification of the 19th Amendment was a triumph for Rankin and the suffrage movement. But her earlier anti-war vote had sealed her political fate. When she ran for the Senate in the next election, she was soundly defeated. Yet that loss only fueled her fire. For the next two decades, Rankin worked for the Women's International League for Peace and Freedom and the National Conference for the Prevention of War. She saw war as a terrible waste and was fond of saying, "You can no more win a war than win an earthquake."

In 1940, when she was nearly 60, Rankin made her second successful run for Congress on the slogan "Prepare to the limit for defense; keep our men out of Europe." Then, in 1941, the Japanese bombed Pearl Harbor. The next day, President Franklin Delano Roosevelt asked Congress to declare war on Japan. Despite pressure from the president, Congress, and her family, Rankin cast the lone dissenting vote in the legislature, explaining, "As a woman I can't go to war. And I refuse to send someone else." Her vote caused a near-riot in the House chamber. She was showered with boos from the angry crowd in the gallery and had to hide in a phone booth until the Capitol police escorted her out. Jeanette Rankin holds the historical distinction of being the only member of Congress to vote against both world wars.

STICKING TO HER BELIEFS

Though Jeanette Rankin never ran for public office again, she continued to work for peace for the rest of her life. In 1968 at the age of 88, when the United States was sending soldiers to fight in Vietnam, she led the Jeannette Rankin Brigade—5,000 women in black—in a silent protest march on Washington, D.C.

Shortly before Rankin passed away at 92, she said, "If I had my life to live over, I'd do it all the same. Only this time I'd be nastier!"

Only U.S. president known to have seen a psychiatrist: Richard Nixon.

POISONOUS PUNDITS

Now it's time to take the gloves off.

"Fox News is worse for our society than Al Qaeda. It's as dangerous as the Ku Klux Klan ever was."
—**Keith Olbermann**

"President Obama's speeches are all fake and they say nothing. Cotton candy for stupid people. But you, Glenn Beck, you are a thinker. Just like me, you are unbiased. You are simply seeking truth, like me."
—**Victoria Jackson**

"When I see a 9/11 victim family on television, I'm like, 'Oh shut up.' I'm so sick of them because they're always complaining."
—**Glenn Beck**

"I have good news to report. Glenn Beck appears closer to suicide. I'm hoping that he does it on camera."
—**Mike Malloy**

"If I lived in Massachusetts, I'd try to vote ten times. Yeah that's right, I would cheat to keep those bastards out. I really would. Because that's exactly what those Republicans are."
—**Ed Schutlz**

"It just took a few shootings at Kent State to shut that down for good."
—**Ann Coulter, on how to deal with Occupy Wall Street**

"Obama's got a healthcare logo that's right out of Hitler's playbook, who, like Obama, also ruled by dictate."
—**Rush Limbaugh**

"George Bush giving tax cuts is like Jim Jones giving Kool-Aid: It tastes good but it'll kill you."
—**Al Sharpton**

"I'll tell you who should be tortured and killed at Guantanamo: every filthy Democrat in the U.S. Congress."
—**Sean Hannity**

"Democrats need to push their agenda while their boot is on the neck of the greedy, poisonous old reptile."
—**Bill Maher**

"If I could strangle [my critics] and not go to hell and get executed, I would. But I can't."
—**Bill O'Reilly**

Scholars who holler: The term *pundit* comes from the Hindu word for "scholar."

ELECTION FOLLIES

*Because presidential campaigns all seem to have their own official
"campaign songs," we thought it would be fun to assign
some song lyrics to these strange election stories.*

HE'S A REAL NOWHERE MAN

Randy Wooten, a karaoke bar owner and mayoral candidate from Waldenburg, Arkansas (pop. 80), cried foul when he was told that he didn't receive a single vote in the 2006 election. He knew that he got at least *one*—his own. Wooten also claimed that "about eight or nine" of his friends voted for him, too, which would have made it a close election, as only 36 votes were cast. Wooten's wife said that she voted for him, too, and she blames the city's brand-new touch-screen voting machines for the screwup. "When you touched one name, it would jump to the next. If you didn't touch it just right, exactly where you were supposed to, it would jump. It makes you wonder about all of them." After a recount—which he lost—Wooten said he was done with politics, adding, "After a while, it just gets tiresome."

GROUND CONTROL TO MAJOR TOM

Visitors to the reelection website of Jyrki Kasvi, a member of parliament in Finland, can read about his platform in Finnish, Swedish, English... and Klingon. "Some people say that combining *Star Trek* and politics is blasphemy," Kasvi said, but he did it to show that "politicians can laugh at themselves." He wasn't able to post a direct translation, however, as there are no Klingon words for "tolerance" or "green" (Kasvi is a member of the Green League). He won the race.

SIGN, SIGN, EVERYWHERE A SIGN

On the morning of the Fitchburg, Wisconsin, mayoral election in 2007, incumbent Tom Clauder was driving past city hall in his pickup truck when he saw a woman pulling one of his campaign signs out of the ground. Angry, he made a U-turn and chased the woman as she drove away. Clauder got right on the sign-puller's tail and followed her through an adjoining parking lot. Both drivers called the police. It turned out that the woman was Jessica Nytes, the wife of Jeff Nytes, the opposing mayoral

---

The only house the queen of England is forbidden to enter: the House of Commons.

candidate. Nytes claimed that his wife yanked the sign because, according to campaign rules, signs are supposed to be at least 33 feet from the center of the highway, and this one wasn't. She was simply performing a "public service," Nytes said. Clauder told reporters that the sign-pulling incident was "low, really low," while Nytes countered that as many as 50 of *his* roadside campaign signs had been stolen in the week leading up to the election. Most experts say that yard signs have little effect on local elections. Either way, Clauder won by a significant margin.

WE ARE THE WORLD

While traveling across the United States in May 2004, President Bush's campaign bus proudly displayed a large sign that read: "Yes, America can!" The statement—which reaffirmed Bush's pledge to keep jobs in the United States—was called into question when reporters discovered that the bus was actually manufactured by Prevost Car, an auto company based in Canada, which is jointly owned by Volvo (based in Sweden) and Henley's Group PLC (from England). When asked at a press conference for an explanation, a Bush campaign spokesman assured reporters that "many of the bus's components are American-made."

SATURDAY NIGHT'S ALL RIGHT FOR FIGHTING

While debating an election reform bill in Taiwan's parliament in May 2007, dozens of lawmakers from opposing parties started fighting each other. They sprayed their rivals with water, threw punches, and even hurled their shoes at each other. And this was not an isolated incident—there have been many such brawls in Taiwan's parliament since the 1980s. It turned out, though, that the battles aren't as fierce as they look. In fact, they're staged specifically for media coverage. Lawmakers will call each other the night before and plan it out, including asking each other to wear soft running shoes to work (so the kicks don't hurt as much). Opposing party members have even been spotted having drinks together after the melees. Why do they do it? To prove to their constituents that they will fight for them. "They just want to steal the spotlight going into the primaries," said People First Party member Lee Hung-chun, who is ashamed of the tactic. "Parliament," he argues, "should be a sacred and noble place."

Of 13,000 Romney ads that aired in the '12 Florida primaries, 92% were negative. (He won.)

MORE PECULIAR PARTIERS

We're thinking of starting our own political party here at the BRI. Why? Because none of those "serious" politicians ever speak up about the need for better bathroom reading. Okay, we're kidding...but are these people?

PARTY: Guns and Dope Party
COUNTRY: United States
PLATFORM: Founded by conspiracy theorist Robert Anton Wilson, this party's platform is similar to the Libertarian party, which strongly supports personal freedoms, including gun ownership and legalized drugs. The difference: The Guns and Dope Party advocates that supporters vote for themselves as write-in candidates in every election, and wants to replace one-third of Congress with ostriches.

PARTY: Extreme Wrestling Party
COUNTRY: Canada
PLATFORM: This party was formed in Newfoundland in 1999 (a year after former pro wrestler Jesse Ventura's became Minnesota's governor). Party leader Quentin Barboni took control when he beat 11 other wrestlers in a "battle royale" match. Despite the ridiculous setup, the Extreme Wrestling Party had serious platforms, including easing gun control laws to help struggling indigenous seal hunters, and getting Canada out of NATO. The party failed to win any seats and disbanded in 2000.

PARTY: Two-Tailed Dog Party
COUNTRY: Hungary
PLATFORM: The party is "led" by a two-tailed puppy named Istvan Nagy, which is a common, generic Hungarian name (like John Smith). Why run a dog for office? Because something so cute couldn't be dishonest. In the 2006 federal election, the party promised eternal life, world peace, two sunsets a day, one-day workweeks, free beer, less gravity, and the construction of a mountain on the Great Hungarian Plain.

South Korea's president serves one 5-year term; additional terms are not permitted.

PARTY: McGillicuddy Serious Party
COUNTRY: New Zealand
PLATFORM: Formed by a group of comedians and street musicians, this party ran candidates in every federal election in New Zealand from 1984 to 1999. Among the group's aims were to institute a Scottish monarchy in New Zealand, replace paper money with chocolate, raise the school graduation age to 65, and lower the speed of light to 60 mph. McGillicuddy Serious also wanted to restrict voting rights among humans to women under the age of 18, but wanted to extend the rights to hedgehogs and trees.

PARTY: Absolutely Absurd Party
COUNTRY: Canada
PLATFORM: AAP advocates want to lower the legal voting age to 14 because "when was the last time a 14-year-old started a war?" Among the party's other ideas: The candidate coming in dead last wins the election; parliament seats should be won in a raffle, and the Department of Defense should be replaced with a team of Rock, Paper, Scissors experts.

PARTY: Church of the Militant Elvis Party
COUNTRY: England
PLATFORM: This political group, founded in 2001 by "Lord Biro," wants to overthrow capitalism. Reason: Capitalism leads to a free media, which Biro blames for turning Elvis Presley into a fat, drug-addicted shadow of his former slim self.

PARTY: Official Monster Raving Loony Party
COUNTRY: England
PLATFORM: Founded in 1983 by a musician called "Screaming Lord Sutch," the party seriously calls for redistribution of wealth and food for the poor, but also advocates for a few very bizarre principles. For example, the OMRLP was against England adopting the euro—they wanted Europe to adopt the English pound (and also wanted to introduce a 99-pence coin to "save on change"). Amazingly, some of the OMRLP's policies have actually been adopted as laws, including lowering the voting age to 18 and issuing passports to pets.

George Bush, Dick Cheney, and Don Rumsfeld all have slime-mold beetles named for them.

COBURN'S WASTEBOOK

*His fellow lawmakers call him "Dr. No." Why? Senator Tom Coburn (R-OK)
loves to vote against anything he deems has wasteful spending. Each year,
Coburn releases his "Wastebook"—citing the 100 most blatant examples
of unnecessary government grants. Here are some examples from 2011.*

• $113,227 for a video game preservation center in New York.

• $550,000 for a documentary about the influence of rock 'n' roll on the collapse of the USSR.

• $48,700 to promote Hawaii's chocolate industry.

• $60,000 to conduct an inventory of Henderson, Nevada's trees.

• $764,825 to study how college students use mobile devices for social networking.

• $75,000 to promote the role Michigan plays in producing Christmas trees.

• $15.3 million for the infamous Bridge to Nowhere in Alaska, including "more than a million dollars just to pay for staff to promote one of the bridges."

• $120 million worth of benefit checks sent to deceased government employees.

• $6,279 for 13 snow-cone machines for the Department of Homeland Security…to help promote homeland security.

• $350,000 to support an International Art Exhibition in Venice, Italy.

• $18 million to improve the environment in China.

• $10 million to produce a version of *Sesame Street* in Pakistan.

• $610,908 to conduct a survey to find out how happy people are in other countries.

• $765,828 to build an International House of Pancakes near Capitol Hill.

• "Perhaps there was no bigger waste of the taxpayer's money in 2011 than Congress itself," said Coburn. "The dismal 9 percent approval rating, the lowest ever recorded, would indicate the vast majority of Americans agree."

1st Afr. American elected to the Senate by popular vote: Edward Brooke (R-MA) in 1967.

MORE DUBYA

President George W. Bush continues his war on…the English language!

"I will have a foreign-handed foreign policy."

"The California crunch really is the result of not enough power-generating plants and then not enough power to power the power of generating plants."

"I haven't had a chance to ask the questioners the questions they've been questioning."

"I know how hard it is for you to put food on your family."

"That's George Washington, the first president. The interesting thing about him is that I read four books about him last year. Isn't that interesting?"
—to a German reporter

"I am mindful of the difference between the executive branch and the legislative branch. I assured all four of these leaders that I know the difference, and that difference is they pass the laws and I execute them."

"So long as I'm the president, my measure of success is victory—and success."

"Families is where our nation finds hope, where wings take dream."

"Saddam Hussein was a state sponsor of terror. In other words, the government had declared, 'You are a state sponsor of terror.'"

"He can't take the high horse and then claim the low road."

"I'm mindful not only of preserving executive powers for myself, but for my predecessors as well."

"Anyone engaging in illegal financial transactions will be caught and persecuted."

"They misunderestimated me."

"Thank you, your Holiness. Awesome speech."
—to Pope Benedict

"I can press when there needs to be pressed; I can hold hands when there needs to be—hold hands."

"You never know what your history is going to be like until long after you're gone."

When asked in '10 what he missed most about the presidency, Bush said, "Being pampered."

PROTOCOL GAFFES

In the world of international diplomacy there are mistakes, and then there are gaffes—moments of minor screwed-up protocol (see page 182). Real mistakes rock foreign policy and can have worldwide repercussions, sometimes for decades (such as the Bay of Pigs invasion). Minor protocol gaffes generally make headlines for a few days and then go away... until they appear in Uncle John's Bathroom Reader.

AGE BEFORE BEAUTY

In 1977 President Jimmy Carter was riding in an elevator with Chief of Protocol (and former child movie star) Shirley Temple Black. When the elevator stopped, Black stepped aside and said, "After you, Mr. President." That was correct protocol, but Carter felt it was ungentlemanly for him to leave the elevator before Black. After the two argued about it for a while, an aide finally pushed them both off the elevator at the same time.

BOW TO YOUR BIG-EARED LEADER

In 1981 Leonore Annenberg, President Reagan's chief of protocol, made a small curtsy to England's visiting Prince Charles. Oops! The chief of protocol should have known that one of the rules of U.S. protocol is that no American is supposed to bend a knee to anyone.

GANDHI, KING OF JORDAN

When Indian prime minister Rajiv Gandhi was in the U.S. on an official visit in 1985, President Ronald Reagan held a 30-minute one-on-one talk with him. "They really hit it off," one White House official reported. "It was a warm, cordial session." The gaffe? At the end of the meeting, Gandhi tactfully pointed out that none of the points the president had made had anything to do with India. Reagan had in fact studied and repeated notes that related to the king of Jordan.

PROTOCOL—CHUNKY STYLE

While on a 12-day trip through the western Pacific in 1992, President George H. W. Bush came down with an intestinal flu. He carried on with his schedule anyway, but he still wasn't feeling well at a state dinner in the

---

FDR once caused an international incident when he sent a destroyer...

home of Japanese prime minister Kiichi Miyazawa…and threw up all over himself. The prime minister held Bush's head in his lap until the president had recovered sufficiently to walk to his limo for a speedy return to the guest suite at Akasaka Palace. For the short walk, Mr. Bush wore a green overcoat given to him by a Secret Service agent to cover up the unsightly mess on his suit. The incident inspired the birth of a new Japanese verb: *bushusuru*—to "do a Bush," or "to commit an instance of embarrassing public vomiting."

THOU SHALT NOT MIX UP THE COMMANDMENTS

In 2007 President George W. Bush visited the Vatican. One of the gifts he gave Pope Benedict XVI was a walking stick with the Ten Commandments carved into it…except it was the Protestant version of the Ten Commandments, which are slightly different from the Catholic version.

WE'RE NOT IN KANSAS ANYMORE

In 2009 President Barack Obama presented British prime minister Gordon Brown with a 25-DVD box set of classic American films collected especially for the occasion by the American Film Institute. A few days later, Brown sat down to watch *Psycho*, but was disappointed to find that the U.S.-made DVDs wouldn't play in his British DVD player. (One British reader wrote in to the *Guardian* to ask if the movie *Clueless* was included in the box set. It wasn't.)

ROYALLY TOASTED

President Obama was back in England in 2011 and managed to make an even bigger protocol gaffe. At an official function with the royal family, the president stood up, raised his glass, and declared, "And now I propose a toast to the queen." And then he paused. Once the orchestra heard the "Q" word, that was their cue to start playing "God Save the Queen." Protocol dictates that no one speaks during the song, but Obama kept talking, giving his toast over top of the music. The royals in attendance remained stoic, while the queen gave Obama a very bemused look. Still, he kept talking. After the toast ended and no one took a drink, Obama stood there awkwardly waiting for the song to finish. Once it finally did, everyone took a drink and Obama sheepishly sat down. Obama later joked to British prime minister Gordon Brown: "I thought it was a soundtrack, like in the movies." Brown joked, "Nice voice-over."

THE CHEMTRAILS CONSPIRACY

*What's crazier? That some people actually believe the United States
government is purposely spraying caustic chemicals into the air?
Or that those people have evidence to back up their claims?*

THE UNFRIENDLY SKIES

In May 2000, an anonymous letter started making the rounds on the Internet. Here's an excerpt:

I work for an airline in upper management levels. I will not say which airline. I wish I could document everything, but to do so would result in possible physical harm to me. Airline companies in America have been participating in something called "Project Cloverleaf" for a few years now. They told us that the government was going to pay our airline, along with others, to release special chemicals from commercial aircraft. When asked what the chemicals were, they told us that information was given on a need-to-know basis and we weren't cleared for it. They told us the chemicals were harmless, but the program was of such importance that it needed to be done at any cost. The public doesn't need to know what's going on, but that this program is in their best interests.

The unknown writer went on to say that Project Cloverleaf made use of a "Powder Contrail Generation Apparatus," which was attached to the planes.

By the time the letter appeared, discussion of "chemtrails" had already become a fixture on late-night radio talk shows, in alternative magazines, and online. Dozens of conspiracy websites reported (and still report) that, far from being harmless, chemtrails are something to be very afraid of. But what are they?

LINE UP

If you look up when a jet plane passes overhead, you'll often see a white plume that looks like a chalk mark in the sky. That's called a *contrail*, short for "condensation trail." A contrail forms when water vapor around the exhaust from a jet plane flying above 30,000 feet freezes. Sometimes, though, planes leave behind trails that are thicker, longer, and longer-lasting. These, according to conspiracy theorists, are "chemical trails," or *chemtrails*. Here's how they say you can tell the difference:

• Contrails are visible about one wingspan's distance behind a jet plane. Chemtrails are directly behind a plane, with no gap between the plane and the trail.

• Contrails form straight lines. Chemtrails crisscross the sky in zigzag patterns that often form a large grid.

• Contrails last for moments and then dissipate. Chemtrails last for hours and leave behind a hazy stain in the sky.

Contrails are basically just water vapor—an incidental by-product of regular aircraft. But chemtrails, say the conspiracies, contain a mixture of pesticides and heavy metals, such as barium and aluminum. They're dispensed by either passenger jets or unmarked planes that fly repeatedly over the same area, at lower-than-normal altitudes. Once in the sky, chemtrails are supposedly heated by super-powerful radar or microwaves, creating chemical fibers known as "angel hair" that fall to the ground in a toxic mist.

COUGH, COUGH

So why are these dastardly doses of death being dumped on us? There are several theories.

Population control: It's a part of the Illuminati's "New World Order Depopulation Agenda," the aim of which is to kill off masses of undesirable people, or at least render them sterile so they can't multiply. (This is occurring in North America and Western Europe—but not in China because that nation, according to the theory, "is being groomed by the NWO to replace the United States as the leading nation of the world, both economically and militarily.")

Urban unrest: Some conspiracy theorists claim that spraying chemtrails over low-income inner-city neighborhoods has resulted in increased outbreaks of violence and crime, causing unrest in the cities, which will eventually lead to chaos. (No word on what kind of outcome that chaos is supposed to lead to.)

Weapons testing: The military is using chemtrails to test out various forms of biological warfare—and U.S. citizens are the guinea pigs.

There is no limit to the amount of time the U.S. Senate can debate a bill.

Weather control: Imagine one country threatening another country with "Surrender—or you won't see any rain for 20 years!" Chemtrails may be the means to achieve this.

Environmental aid: Another theory is far less grim. Chemtrails were designed to stop global warming by increasing what's called "global dimming." Believers point to physicist Dr. Edward Teller, known as the "Father of the Hydrogen Bomb" and also the father of the "Star Wars" missile defense program. In 1997 Teller wrote in the *Wall Street Journal* that the same chemicals used in topical sunscreen could be used to block the harmful atmospheric rays that cause global warming and that passenger jets are perfectly suited to disperse them into the atmosphere. Interestingly, chemtrails started appearing in much greater numbers shortly after Teller's article was published.

HAARP ATTACK

At the heart of the chemtrails controversy is the U.S. Air Force project HAARP (High Frequency Active Aural Research Project) in Alaska. According to its website, HAARP is an unclassified research project that studies the ionosphere and radio science. Conspiracy theorists, however, say this is a ruse. They claim the classified mission of HAARP is to establish a massive radar grid that combines electromagnetic waves with chemtrails in order to spread the chemicals across the world's atmosphere, giving the American military-industrial complex control over everything from the weather, to enhanced surveillance, to mind control.

To back up their claims, they exhibit a 1996 research study published by the USAF called "Weather as a Force Multiplier: Owning the Weather in 2025." The unclassified report was produced by students, faculty, and scientists from academic branches of the air force. They were challenged to imagine a set of fictional scenarios set 30 years in the future and what possible responses the military might have. These scenarios describe using weather modification to achieve "battlespace dominance" by enhancing precipitation (making rain), inducing drought, generating cloud cover, and disrupting satellite communications and radar.

THE RAINMAKERS

Government control of the weather is not a new concept. During World War II, attempts were made to combine chemical agents with cloud seeding, and during the Vietnam War covert cloud-seeding operations tried to make enough rain to muddy jungle trails and hinder the movements of enemy soldiers. These operations were exposed in the late 1960s, and by the early 1970s the U.S. Senate called for an international treaty against weather manipulation. They got one: The United Nations Convention on the Prohibition of Any Hostile Use of Environmental Modification Technique, which was ratified by the U.S. and 30 other nations, entered into effect in 1978.

DEATH RAY 2000!

But just because something is illegal, does that mean the government won't do it? Carolyn Williams Palit, a Texas woman in her 50s, believes that not only is the government continuing to spread chemicals in the atmosphere, but that they're actually weapons:

> It involves the combination of chemtrails for creating an atmosphere that will support electromagnetic waves, ground-based electromagnetic field oscillators called "gyrotrons," and ionospheric heaters. They spray barium powders and let it photoionize from the ultraviolet light of the sun. Then they make an aluminum-plasma generated by "zapping" the metal cations that are in the spray with either electromagnetics from HAARP, the gyrotron system on the ground [the Ground Wave Emergency Network], or space-based lasers. The barium makes the aluminum-plasma more particulate dense. This means they can make a denser plasma than they normally could from just ionizing the atmosphere or the air. More density [more particles] means that these particles are colliding into each other and will become more charged. What they are ultimately trying to do up there is create charged-particle, plasma beam weapons.

Palit believes we are victims of "state-sponsored torture" and that the U.S. Congress is knowingly using American tax dollars to fund it.

THE OFFICIAL RESPONSE

In response to Palit, her followers, and the other conspiracy theorists, NASA, the USAF, the EPA, and the NOAA (National Oceanic and Atmospheric Administration) have all released rebuttals, explaining that chemtrails are nothing more than really big contrails, caused by various atmospheric, weather, and air traffic conditions.

In their "Aircraft Contrails Factsheet," the agencies explained the difference between short-lived contrails and persistent contrails—the ones most likely to be mistaken for chemtrails. The photographs in the pamphlet show the crisscrossing patterns and grids that chemtrail believers so often point to as proof that the lines are not contrails. In 2005 the USAF released their own "Contrails Facts," a long, exhaustive document that goes into infinite detail about contrails, and debunks chemtrails, calling them a "hoax."

The air force didn't do themselves any favors by using the word "hoax"; that just stoked the conspiratorial fires, as people started picking apart every word in the air force's explanation as proof of just the opposite. "The latest line of attack would earn approval from George Orwell himself," wrote one website. "Chemtrails are now counted by our children in staged 'educational' events. These events serve the purpose of indoctrination into an Orwellian world that declares the operations to be 'normal.' It is a world in which there is no need to question this authority."

PROTECT YOURSELF

So if you believe the government, then you have nothing to worry about. But if you *don't* believe the government, is there anything you can do? One option is to construct your own "Chembuster"—a device that will "absorb bad energy and release good energy." To build one (you can find directions online), combine aluminum shavings, magnets, crystals, and copper pipes with epoxy or polyester resin in a large bucket. Use a dowsing rod to find a good spot to place your bucket, apply "psychic insights," and voilà, the chemtrails will no longer affect you because the Chembuster is "transmuting the atmospheric orgone energy envelope from a polarity that allows chemtrails to persist, to another orgone polarity, which will cause chemtrails to disperse."

There. Now you can breathe easy!

*　　　*　　　*

MR. AND MRS. BULL

In 2009 the Florida state senate was debating enforcement of bestiality laws, and the subject turned to animal husbandry—which simply means the breeding and raising of livestock. Democratic senator Larcenia Bullard, however, thought that it meant…well, something else, and blurted out, "People are actually taking these animals as *husbands*?!"

Branching out: 15 U.S. senators have gone on to be elected president.

HIS ROTUNDITY

Recently, we've had "Tricky Dick," "Slick Willie," "Shrub," and "Nobama," which are pretty tame compared to some of these other mean nicknames for American presidents.

Little Jemmy: James Madison was the shortest president, just 5'4" (average height of a male American at the time: 5'8"), which explains the "little." "Jemmy" was a nickname commonly given to children and babies named James (like Jimmy). The name implied that Madison was a toddler, and not a man.

General Mum: General William Henry Harrison, hero of the Battle of Tippecanoe, was elected in 1840 and died after only a month in office. He caught a cold while delivering a three-hour inaugural address in freezing temperatures; the cold developed into pneumonia, which killed him. Ironically, his nickname during the election campaign was "General Mum" because, like any savvy politician, he avoided addressing any definitive opinions on controversial issues.

His Accidency: When William Henry Harrison died, Vice President John Tyler ascended to the presidency.

The Negro President: Given to Thomas Jefferson following the election of 1800, which he won thanks to "the three-fifths compromise," which counted slaves as three-fifths a person for population purposes. That, in turn, gave greater representation to slaveholding states in determining electoral vote distribution, allowing Jefferson, of Virginia, to defeat New Englander John Adams.

The Fainting General: While fighting in the Mexican-American War in 1848, future president Franklin Pierce was on a horse when it was startled by exploding artillery. The horse tossed him forward onto the pommel of his saddle, which was driven into his groin. The injury was so painful that Pierce fainted and remained passed out, lying on the battlefield for the rest of the day.

Queen Victoria in Riding Breeches: Rutherford B. Hayes and his wife,

"Lemonade" Lucy Hayes, were ardent teetotalers. It wasn't very macho for a man to abstain from alcohol—or smoking, as Hayes also did—earning him this emasculating nickname. (Why "riding breeches"? Hayes was a cavalry soldier in the Civil War.)

The Walrus: Chester Alan Arthur sported a large handlebar mustache, and he was fairly overweight, both of which made him look like a walrus.

Uncle Jumbo: It's a fat joke. By the time he was running for reelection in 1892, Grover Cleveland's weight had risen to 250 pounds. Some newspapers called him "Uncle Jumbo." Others favored "the Stuffed Prophet" and "the Elephantine Economist."

His Rotundity: Another fat joke. It's what detractors called the overweight second president, John Adams, who was also accused of being pompous. (When Washington was president, Adams proposed calling him "His Majesty" or "His High Mightiness.")

Ronnie Raygun: President Ronald Reagan proposed the multibillion-dollar weapons defense system called the Strategic Defense Initiative, which would use orbiting structures in space to shoot down Soviet-launched nuclear missiles. SDI was perceived as so bizarre and impractical that it was called "Star Wars," earning Reagan this sci-fi nickname.

President Hardly: A play on the name of Warren G. Harding and his work ethic—he reportedly left most of the day-to-day work of his office to advisers.

Kid Gloves: Benjamin Harrison suffered from various skin problems, particularly infections on his hands, and often wore gloves during the frequent outbreaks. Other nickname: "The Human Iceberg" because, although he was a gifted orator, he tended to be cold and aloof in person.

That Man in the White House: This may be the harshest nickname for a president. So far, at least three have been given the label: Barack Obama, because some of his critics suggested he wasn't actually born in the U.S. George W. Bush's opponents labeled him "Commander-in-Thief" after the disputed 2000 election. And Franklin Roosevelt was called "that man in the White House" by opponents who were so disgusted with his social-welfare agenda that they couldn't even bring themselves to say his name.

Filmmaker Michael Moore was once the youngest elected official in the U.S....

JOIN THE PARTY: THE REPUBLICANS

*Now that you know where the Democrats came from (page 205),
let's venture across the aisle for the story of the GOP.*

THE GREAT DIVIDE

By the time Zachary Taylor, a Whig, was elected president in 1848, the U.S. was deeply divided on the issue of slavery. Southerners wanted to extend it into new western territories as they were admitted to the Union. The North was just as determined to confine slavery to the states where it was already entrenched. Nobody knew how to abolish slavery entirely without starting a civil war.

Taylor's election only made matters worse: He owned 300 slaves, so even though he'd kept a low profile on the issue during the election, it was clear where he stood. The idea of a proslavery Whig president was more than the antislavery Whigs could take. Rather than support Taylor, these Conscience Whigs split from the party to join the Barnburners, an antislavery faction of New York Democrats. Together, they then merged with abolitionists called the "Liberty Party" to form the Free Soil Party. Their presidential candidate: ex-president Martin Van Buren.

Taylor managed to win, anyway, thanks in large part to slavery supporters who hoped his administration would be strongly proslavery. They were wrong. When California applied for admission to the Union as a free state, Taylor agreed and asked Congress to admit it immediately. One problem: Admitting California as a free state would upset the even balance of free and slave states, putting the free states in the majority.

DRAWING THE LINE

If California were admitted as a free state, it would also upset the tradition set by the Missouri Compromise of 1820, banning slavery in the new territories north of latitude 36°30', but permitting it below that line. (Missouri is above the line, but the compromise allowed it to enter the Union as a slave state.) Technically this rule only applied to territories that were part of the Louisiana Purchase; California wasn't one of them.

But Southerners wanted the line to apply anyway, which would have made slavery legal in southern California. They were furious when President Taylor supported the admission of the entire territory as a free state. When these so-called "die-hard" Southerners threatened to secede because of it, Taylor, a retired army general, responded by promising to personally lead the army against any state that tried to secede.

WAR POSTPONED

California's admission never led to civil war, mostly because Taylor died from indigestion barely a year into his presidency. His successor, Millard Fillmore (also a Whig), was willing to compromise. With Fillmore's encouragement, Senator Henry Clay of Kentucky pushed through Congress the Compromise of 1850, consisting of five measures:

> 1. A new Fugitive Slave Law got the federal government more directly involved in the capture and return of slaves who escaped into free states.

> 2. Buying and selling slaves was abolished within the city limits of Washington, D.C. (People in D.C. could still *own* slaves, they just couldn't buy or sell them there.)

> 3. California was admitted as a free state, ending the equal balance of slave and free states in the Union.

> 4. The land east of California was divided into the Utah and New Mexico Territories, with their final status as free or slave territories intentionally left vague. It was still possible that both might choose to become slave states. Meanwhile, slaveholders and abolitionists were free to settle in these territories.

> 5. The border between Texas (a slave state) and Mexico was formalized.

ONE STEP FORWARD, TWO STEPS BACK

The Compromise of 1850, intended to cool passions between North and South, worked…for a while. But as time passed, two of the five provisions in the compromise made things even worse than they already were.

The Fugitive Slave Act compelled federal marshals to assist in capturing slaves even if they opposed slavery. The marshals faced fines of up to

$1,000—a lot of money in the 1850s—if they failed to do so. If a slave escaped while in their custody, *they* were liable for the full value of the slave. And for the first time, anyone who assisted a slave trying to escape could be fined and even jailed for up to six months. Fugitive slaves were denied a trial by jury and were not allowed to testify on their own behalf. The Fugitive Slave Act, designed to help Southern slave owners, only served to turn many Northerners even more vehemently against slavery.

But what really inflamed passions was the unresolved status of the Utah and New Mexico territories, and the admission of California as a free state on the grounds that that was what Californians wanted. Letting citizens of a territory organize themselves as they saw fit sounds reasonable enough, but "popular sovereignty," as its supporters called it (opponents called it "squatter sovereignty"), proved to be very problematic.

Popular sovereignty undermined an important premise of the Missouri Compromise, which was that *Congress,* not the people, had the power to ban slavery. If California, New Mexico, and Utah could decide for themselves, didn't that mean that *all* new territories would have that right?

THE KANSAS-NEBRASKA ACT

Tensions escalated dramatically in 1854 when Senator Stephen A. Douglas of Illinois introduced legislation opening much of the Indian Territory to white settlers. Called the Kansas-Nebraska Act, the legislation carved two new territories—Kansas and Nebraska—from land previously used to relocate Native American tribes that had been forcibly moved from their ancestral lands east of the Mississippi River.

Both Kansas and Nebraska were part of the Louisiana Purchase. Both were entirely above latitude 36°30', and according to the Missouri Compromise that meant that slavery was outlawed. But Douglas was determined to apply popular sovereignty to the new territories, giving settlers the right to decide the slavery question for themselves.

Douglas wasn't motivated by a desire to expand slavery—he wanted to get a northern transcontinental railroad built from Chicago (in his home state) to the Pacific. Running the tracks through Nebraska made the most sense, but to do that he needed to set up a new territory, and to do *that* he needed the support of the South. They weren't about to let another free territory evolve into another free state, so Douglas appeased them by applying the principle of popular sovereignty.

THEM'S FIGHTIN' WORDS

Initially Douglas had only wanted to organize one territory—Nebraska. But Southerners had insisted on two, so Douglas proposed organizing both Nebraska and Kansas, applying the principle of popular sovereignty to both. Even that wasn't enough: Southerners in Congress wanted the language of the bill to specifically repeal the Missouri Compromise.

Douglas resisted at first, but then he and the Southerners, all Democrats, agreed to let President Franklin Pierce, also a Democrat, decide: Pierce sided with the South.

The Kansas-Nebraska Act infuriated Northerners, who for more than 30 years had viewed the 36°30' line as sacred. The act "took us by surprise," an Illinois Whig named Abraham Lincoln wrote later. "We were thunderstruck and stunned." But Douglas rammed the bill through both houses of Congress, and in May 1854, President Pierce signed it into law.

What followed in the Kansas Territory was four years of violence as both sides of the slavery issue rushed settlers there to claim the territory for their side. In May 1856, proslavery raiders sacked the town of Lawrence; three days later, a Connecticut abolitionist named John Brown attacked some slavery supporters at Pottawatomie Creek, killing five. More than 200 people were killed in this mini civil war.

OUT WITH THE OLD

Another casualty of the Kansas-Nebraska Act: President Pierce. The Democrats didn't even bother to nominate him for a second term. He just served out the rest of his term and then went home. The Whig party was another casualty. Already damaged by the fight over the Compromise of 1850, it collapsed when antislavery Conscience Whigs bolted the party. By the end of 1854, the party was over.

So where did the Conscience Whigs go? Many joined with other antislavery elements to form a brand-new party that made its priority the opposition to slavery in new territories. Drawing inspiration from the Jeffersonian Republicans, the group named itself the Republican Party.

GREAT SCOTT

Also destroyed by the Kansas-Nebraska Act was Stephen A. Douglas's bid for the presidency in 1856. The struggle had generated so much controversy that the Democrats passed on his candidacy and instead nominated

33% of former Congress members hire on with lobbying firms.

former Secretary of State James Buchanan. What made Buchanan such an attractive candidate? According to historian David Herbert Donald, he "had the inestimable blessing of having been out of the country, as minister of Great Britain, during the controversy over the Kansas-Nebraska Act." The Republicans nominated former California senator John C. Frémont as their candidate. Buchanan won, but Frémont made an impressive showing, winning 11 states.

Just two days after Buchanan was inaugurated as president, the Supreme Court handed down its infamous *Dred Scott* decision. Years earlier, Scott, a slave, had been taken by his owner, a U.S. Army surgeon, to live in Illinois and the Wisconsin Territory, both of which outlawed slavery. Scott sued for his freedom, arguing that living where slavery was banned had made him a free man.

The Supreme Court disagreed, finding that as a Negro, Scott was not an American citizen to begin with and thus had no right to sue in federal court. And even if he did, the chief justice argued, *any* laws excluding slavery from U.S. territories were unconstitutional, because they violated the Fifth Amendment by depriving slave owners of their property without due process of law. "The right of property in a slave," he wrote, "is distinctly and expressly affirmed in the Constitution." Suddenly, it seemed as if every state in the Union might become a slave state.

THE FREEPORT FUMBLE

For many Americans, Dred Scott was the final straw. It seemed impossible that the North and the South could remain together as a country. Even Lincoln observed (in a debate with Stephen A. Douglas the following year): "This government cannot endure permanently half slave and half free."

Lincoln was challenging Douglas for his seat in the U.S. Senate, and it was during the second of their seven debates that Douglas ruined his last chance to win the presidency. In Freeport, Illinois, on August 27, 1858, Lincoln challenged Douglas to reconcile popular sovereignty with the *Dred Scott* decision: If antislavery laws were unconstitutional, how were anti-slavery settlers supposed to ban slavery?

Douglas replied that if settlers refused to legislate a local "slave code" (local regulations that protected the rights of slave owners), slave owners would not bring their slaves into the territory because their property rights were not guaranteed.

First American president to visit Europe while in office: Woodrow Wilson, in 1918.

Douglas's "Freeport Doctrine," as it became known, did little to appease Northerners and it cost him nearly all of his support in the South. He still managed to win the 1860 Democratic nomination for president, but Southern Democrats were so angry with him that, rather than support him, they split off from the party and nominated their own candidate, John C. Breckinridge.

AND THE WINNER IS...

Abraham Lincoln, who'd just lost the race for Senate, became the Republican nominee for president. The Republican Party was barely six years old, but slavery was such a powerful issue—and Douglas's Freeport Doctrine such a huge blunder—that Douglas and Breckinridge split the Democratic vote... and Lincoln, a brand-new Republican, won.

But "it was ominous," David Herbert Donald writes, "that Lincoln had received *not a single vote* in 10 of the Southern states."

Lincoln was elected president on November 6, 1860; barely a month later, South Carolina seceded from the Union, and by the time Lincoln was sworn into office on March 4, 1861, Mississippi, Florida, Alabama, Georgia, Louisiana, and Texas had also seceded. The first shots of the Civil War were just five weeks away.

With the secession of the Southern states (and all of the Southern Democrats), the Republican Party was left in full control of the federal government. As the Civil War dragged on year after year, it seemed that Lincoln's reelection was doomed and that General George McClellan, a Northern Democrat running as a peace candidate, would defeat him. But the tide of the war eventually turned in the North's favor, and in 1864 Lincoln was reelected with 55 percent of the popular vote. The Civil War finally ended on April 9, 1865; Lincoln was assassinated five days later.

THE RISE OF THE REPUBLICANS

Victory in the Civil War ushered in an era of Republican domination that lasted until the Great Depression of the early 1930s: Of the 18 presidential elections held between 1860 and 1932, the Republicans won 14.

Born in an era of terrible crisis that threatened to destroy the Union, the Republican Party managed to save the Union and, in the process, established itself in very short order as one of the great political parties in American history.

The *Chicago Times* on Lincoln's Gettysburg Address: "silly, flat, dishwatery utterances."

THE BIG SWITCHEROONY

You may be asking yourself: Aren't the Democrats the liberal ones, and the Republicans the social conservatives? Political parties switch ideologies more often than you might think, and in this case, the Democrats and Republicans remained set in their 19th-century platforms until the late 1920s. Then the Great Depression hit. President Franklin Roosevelt, a Democrat, believed the way out of it was via government intervention—more social programs and more safety nets. The Republicans back then, like now, believed that free market capitalism would get the country going again. But it was the practices of Wall Street executives, most of whom were Republicans, that caused the financial collapse that led to the Great Depression. Result: Most Americans blamed the hard times on the Republicans, and because of Roosevelt's growing popularity, the power in the executive *and* legislative branches went mostly to the Democrats—and stayed with them through World War II.

Result: The Republicans were once again the opposition party, and they needed numbers, so they set their sights on the South, seeking votes by promising a smaller, less intrusive government and, more importantly, states' rights. The civil rights movement was just getting going, so by catering to the disenfranchised "Dixiecrats" who feared a larger government would take away their freedoms, a shift occurred. By the 1960s, the party started by Abraham Lincoln that had brought about the end of slavery was now the same party associated with opposing civil rights.

Are the parties switching ideologies again today? Will a third party ever make headway in America? As that debate picks up steam, it's uncertain where the parties will align themselves as the 21st century unfolds.

* * *

I AM BARACK OBAMA

In 2008 Alexandre Jacinto decided to run for a seat on the town council in Petrolina, Brazil. Brazilian election law allows candidates to use any name they want, so Jacinto ran as "Barack Obama." "I read a book about Obama's rise," Jacinto said, "a poor, simple man who became a senator. My aim too is to get to the top—the presidency." He wasn't the only one: Five other candidates around the country also chose that name. So there just may be a "President Barack Obama" of Brazil someday.

In McCook, NB, voters are prohibited from visiting the polls on roller-skates.

THE 🐴 AND THE 🐘

The origins of two party animals.

FIRST CAME THE DONKEY

Andrew Jackson was a jackass. The slave-owning, Indian-displacing Democrat embraced that image—even though his Republican opponents were using it to deride him in the 1828 presidential election. Out of spite, Jackson added a jackass to his campaign posters. The image stuck with Old Hickory until his death in 1837. That year, a political cartoon called "A Modern Baalim and His Ass" (by a cartoonist whose name has been lost to history) was the first one to use a donkey to represent the entire Democratic Party. Then it faded from use.

The donkey symbol would have most likely died out completely had it not been resurrected 30 years later by Thomas Nast, an influential political cartoonist for *Harper's Weekly*. A liberal Republican (before the parties switched ideologies), Nast used a menagerie of animals in his cartoons. For instance, Democrats also became foxes and two-headed tigers, but it was the donkey that the party would eventually adopt as its mascot…even though it was originally meant as an insult.

THEN CAME THE ELEPHANT

Although an elephant was first used in a cartoon to describe Republicans in 1860, it was Nast who popularized that symbol as well. In 1874 he took issue with *New York Herald* editors who were running alarmist editorials that charged Republican president Ulysses S. Grant with "Caesarism." Rumors abounded that Grant would run for a third term in 1876, which, even though it was legal at the time, was severly frowned upon. (And the rumors were false.) Nast was a close friend of Grant's, so in the cartoon he depicted the *Herald* as an ass in lion's clothing who "roamed about in the forest and amused himself by frightening all the foolish animals." One of the frightened animals was an elephant, which Nash labeled "the Republican Vote." Nast and his contemporaries kept that image alive, as well as the Democrats' donkey. By 1900 both animals were firmly entrenched in American politics.

Nast-y Fact: Thomas Nast was also responsible for two other pieces of Americana—Uncle Sam's goatee and Santa Claus's plump belly.

No one knows the exact origin of the Republican nickname "Grand Old Party."

GOVSPEAK

More "wit" from the public sector.

"Eight more days, and I can start telling the truth again."

—Sen. Chris Dodd (D-CT), a week before an election

"As the hobbits are going up Mount Doom, the Eye of Mordor is being drawn somewhere else. It's being drawn to Iraq, and it's not being drawn to the U.S. You know what? I want to keep it on Iraq. I don't want the Eye to come back here to the United States."

—Sen. Rick Santorum (R-PA)

"UPS and FedEx are doing just fine, right? It's the Post Office that's always having problems."

—President Barack Obama, countering his own argument for government-run healthcare

"When I was on my way to the podium a gentleman stopped me and said I was as good a politician as I was an actor. What a cheap shot."

—Gov. Arnold Schwarzenegger

"Did the training wheels fall off?"

—Sen. John Kerry (D-MA), after President George W. Bush crashed his mountain bike

"I know you believe you understand what you think I said, but I am not sure you realize that what you heard is not what I meant."

—Fed chairman Alan Greenspan, before a Congressional committee

"Every American should have above-average income, and my administration is going to see they get it."

—President Bill Clinton

"Lawrence Welk is a wonderful man. He used to be, or was, or, wherever he is now, bless him."

—President George H. W. Bush

"I was provided with additional input that was radically different from the truth. I assisted in furthering that version."

—Oliver North, on his role in the Iran-Contra affair

"The more we remove penalties for being a bum, the more bumism is going to blossom."

—Sen. Jesse Helms (R-NC), on welfare

"Everything has been said, but not everyone has said it yet."

—Rep. Morris Udall (D-AZ)

60% of Americans can name the Three Stooges; 17% can name 3 Supreme Court justices.

ABNORMAL ACTIVISTS

Most protests are pretty dull: A group of people march somewhere, hold up
signs, yell things, and maybe the police come. In our book The World's
Gone Crazy, *we set out to find demonstrators who have a little more*
pizzazz—like squirting a cop with milk...straight from the cow.

PINK DAWN

The Problem: For seven years, a two-story-tall pink flamingo (made of chicken wire and pink bedsheets) attached to an outside wall above the Cafe Hon in Baltimore, Maryland, was a local attraction. But in October 2009, cafe owner Denise Whiting was surprised to get a notice from the city saying that she would be charged an annual fee of $800 because she didn't have a permit for the large outdoor display. Whiting was furious: "It really has become a hallmark of Baltimore." Instead of paying the fee, Whiting removed the flamingo. Citizens and business owners were outraged that the city would crack down so hard on such a favorite local landmark. Then DJs at a local radio station, 98 Rock, got an idea.

The Protest: On the rainy morning of October 27, workers arriving at city hall were greeted by hundreds of fake pink flamingos sticking up out of the lawn "in silent protest."

Did It Work? With a crowd gathering outside, Mayor Sheila Dixon went out to the flamingo field and talked to Whiting. The mayor agreed to reduce the fee to $400 and promised to promote local businesses with new signs on the freeway. Whiting paid the fee and, a few weeks later, built a new giant flamingo—this one made of fiberglass. Said Mayor Dixon: "I hope that Flamingogate will now be behind us."

A DROP IN THE BUCKET

The Problem: European dairy farmers' operating costs have been steadily rising in recent years. But with supplies up and demand down, they've had to sell their dairy products at lower prices. For years farmers have been pressing the European Union Farm Commission to set minimum prices, but their requests have been repeatedly denied.

The Protest: In October 2009, more than 2,500 angry farmers drove their tractors to EU headquarters in Brussels, Belgium, and proceeded to

---

Victoria Clafin Woodhull, the 1st female U.S. pres. candidate, ran in 1872. (She lost.)

dump millions of gallons of milk and thousands of pounds of eggs and manure into the streets. Armored police arrived and formed a riot line to push the protesters back. During the struggle, a farmer grabbed hold of one of his cows' udders, pointed a teat toward the officers, squeezed, and sprayed milk at them (it traveled an impressive 15 feet). The cops blocked the milk with their riot shields, but the cow broke free from the farmer's grasp and chased a bystander down the sidewalk. It took the efforts of several farmers and police officers to apprehend the cow. Meanwhile, the protest continued.

Did It Work? So far, no. The EU Farm Commission insists that it can't control how much retailers charge. Expect more milk protests in the future.

600 CHEEKS AGREE

The Problem: In the summer of 2009, citizens in the Canadian town of Sarnia, on the shore of Lake Huron, were outraged to see, day after day, a large, wing-shaped balloon floating 1,000 feet above the lake. The balloon, which was monitored by a U.S. defense contractor, carried a surveillance camera capable of reading the name of a boat from nine miles away. According to the U.S. Department of Homeland Security, it was only there to monitor shipping traffic. Sarnia's citizens, including the mayor, complained to the Canadian government that it was an invasion of their privacy. "The U.S. has no right to spy on us!" said one local. But there was little the Canadian government could do because, technically, the balloon was hovering over U.S. waters.

The Protest: An estimated 300 Sarnians decided to make a statement that their government couldn't: They marched down to the waterfront, dropped their pants, and mooned the balloon.

Did It Work? The mooning turned out to be a moot point. Why? The balloon wasn't even in the sky that day (it had been knocked down by a storm a week earlier). But protesters agreed that baring their behinds was a "symbolic measure." And after the balloon was repaired, it was relocated…to the skies above Afghanistan.

THE BUILDING BLOCKS OF CHANGE

The Problem: In 2006 the German power company E.ON announced plans to build a coal-fired power plant in the English town of Kingsnorth. Despite charges that the plant would "emit more greenhouse gases than the entire country of Ghana," construction crews got to work, with a planned completion date of 2012. As part of a public-relations campaign, E.ON built a small-scale Lego replica of the plant in the Legoland theme park in Windsor, England. Located close to the Lego Big Ben and Lego Westminster Abbey, the Lego model of the power plant stood four feet high, and its giant smokestack even emitted steam.

The Protests: On July 8, 2008, museum attendees were surprised to see six tiny Lego protesters "climbing" the smokestack, followed by the unrolling of a banner hung from the top of the power plant that read "Stop Climate Change." Tiny Lego police dotted the scene around the smokestack, along with a Lego police helicopter.

The museum wasn't the only place activists infiltrated that day; all over the UK, thousands of people gathered to protest against the power company and the government. Naked environmentalists (real people, not Legos) scaled the walls of E.ON's corporate offices, a group blockaded a biofuel depot in Essex, and dozens of activists lay down in a pool of oil in front of the Royal Bank of Scotland to stage a "die-in."

Did It Work? Maybe. A year later, E.ON announced that the power plant would be delayed until 2016. It wasn't due to the protests, said a company spokesman, but because "electricity demand has fallen during the global recession."

SLAVES TO FASHION

The Problem: Sir Phillip Green is one of England's richest men, thanks to TopShop, his successful chain of retail clothing stores. According to a 2007 article in London's *Times Online*, "Factories owned by Green, worth nearly £5 billion, employ hundreds of workers from Sri Lanka, India, and Bangladesh in Mauritius, where they labor for up to 12 hours a day, six days a week." Reportedly, the workers were paid only a few cents per day.

The Protest: On December 5, 2008, dozens of activists wearing Santa Claus suits marched to the front of TopShop's flagship store in London. There, they treated holiday shoppers to "A TopShop Christmas Carol," a skit that parodied the Dickens classic, with Green as Scrooge. The real Green tried to have the protest disrupted, but the police let the show continue. After the play, the Santas, carrying heavy sacks and signs reading "End Slave Labor," marched to TopShop's corporate headquarters and dumped the contents of the sacks—thousands of signatures from people

---

Only 17% of Americans can identify Andrew Jackson as the man on the $20 bill.

urging Green to treat his workforce more fairly.

Did It Work? Not really. Green claimed that he would "address the matter," but he has repeatedly refused to join the Ethical Trading Initiative, an "an alliance of companies, trade unions, and voluntary organizations working in partnership to improve the lives of workers across the globe."

EAT YOUR HEART OUT

The Problem: In 2009 the European Union imposed a ban on importing most Canadian seal products on the grounds that Inuit hunters, who provided the raw material, were "inhumanely killing seals." The Inuits claimed that they'd been humanely—and sustainably—killing seals for thousands of years. Joining in the debate was Michaëlle Jean, who served as Canada's governor general, a largely ceremonial position appointed by Britain's Queen Elizabeth II. Many wondered whether she would side with Europe or with Canada.

The Protest: Jean made a surprise appearance at an Inuit community festival in Rankin Inlet, Nunavut. With cameras rolling, "Her Excellency" brandished a traditional Inuit *ulu* blade, crouched over a freshly killed seal, and began to skin it. Then she pulled out a chunk of the seal's heart, held it up for all to see…and took a bite out of it. "It tastes like sushi," she said.

Did It Work? The European Union upheld the ban. When asked to comment about whether Jean's gesture had helped or hurt the Inuits' cause, an EU spokesperson said it was "too bizarre to acknowledge."

*   *   *

PALIN-DROMES

Yo, boy! These poli-palindromes read the same forward and backward!

- Slapdash, self-royal Clinton's not nil. Clay or flesh, sad pals?
  - Rail, rotund Al Gore: hero, glad nut, or liar?
    - Media harass Sarah? Aid 'em!
      - Star Comedy by Democrats
        - No 'X' in Nixon?
        - Rise to vote, sir!

Presidential candidate who ran the most times: Socialist Norman Thomas, with 6 tries.

BREAKING THE CODE

In its early days, Hollywood didn't have much content regulation. There were no ratings and few rules about what could appear on the screen. Then a government bureaucrat named Will Hays made a code.

UNHOLY-WOOD

Maybe it was Fatty Arbuckle's scandalous murder trial in 1921, or the explicit drug use portrayed in the 1923 film *Human Wreckage*. Or maybe it was the nudity in the 1925 films *Ben-Hur* and *Bright Lights*. No one movie or event can be blamed for Washington's growing unease with what was happening in Hollywood. In the late 1920s, movies and movie stars were increasingly seen as immoral, something from which the masses needed protection.

To circumvent possible government legislation—and to assure an uneasy public—the studios turned to a body they had created in 1922, the Motion Picture Producers and Distributors of America (MPPDA). This association was set up so the studios could police themselves and avoid any government intrusion on their business. Politician Will Hays had been put in charge, although the position didn't have much real power. But he did have some impressive credentials—he was postmaster general for President Harding as well as former Republican National Committee chairman—which probably helped to justify his $100,000 salary.

CODE? WHAT CODE?

Even though a code was written by 1930, the MPPDA had no real authority. And that's the way Hollywood wanted it: They could pay lip service to conservative groups, while keeping their movies profitable—and filled with sex and violence. The 1932 film *Red-Headed Woman* caused much controversy: It featured a sultry Jean Harlow having an affair with a married man, shooting her own husband and getting away with it, and then gambling with another lover. Religious organizations and women's groups were horrified at the movie's overt sexuality, disregard for class distinctions, and unpunished immorality.

Other films, such as 1933's *Mayor of Hell*, brought up race and class issues: James Cagney's character leads a "socialist revolution" in a boy's reform school by overthrowing the warden, during which a young African American boy comforts a terrified white schoolmate.

Another controversial film, 1932's *Freaks*, was cast with members of real sideshow acts and tried to shed light on shunned elements of society and their community. The movie had a healthy dose of what was then considered "deviant" sexuality: A woman tries to seduce a midget; a Siamese twin "feels" a kiss given to her sister; and a transvestite makes a pass at the Strong Man.

CRACKING DOWN

But Hollywood would soon learn it couldn't ignore its rules forever. A powerful Catholic group, the Legion of Decency, finally threatened to stage massive boycotts of films that failed to meet the Hays code, which would have severely hurt the film industry's bottom line. So in 1934 the major studios shrewdly decided that every film they paid for would adhere to the code, and they gave Will Hays the power to make sure everyone else followed suit. The studios had a monopoly on the movie theaters, and without Hays's approval, a movie couldn't open in any of them.

Noting in the preamble that movies "may be directly responsible for spiritual or moral progress, for higher types of social life, and for much correct thinking," the code stressed that audiences should never sympathize with "crime, wrongdoing, evil, or sin." Certain sinful elements, such as adultery and seduction, could be suggested only when necessary for the plot; other things were strictly forbidden. The sexual no-no's:

- Excessive and lustful kissing
- Suggestive postures and gestures
- Sex perversion (homosexuality)
- White slavery (prostitution of white women)
- Miscegenation (interracial romances)
- Sex hygiene and venereal diseases
- Scenes of actual childbirth
- Complete nudity

The rules for violence were a little more lax, requiring that murders simply not "inspire imitation," and that crimes such as "safe-cracking" and the "dynamiting of trains" not be shown in detail (in case anyone was taking notes). And the "principle of compensating values" ruled that villains could commit crimes as long as they were punished.

Yet Hays didn't stop with just sex and violence—the code had a series of regulations on a wide range of other topics. No bad words or religious profanity were allowed; costumes that might have overexposed dancers' bodies were not allowed; ministers could not be villains or even "comic characters"; and the American flag always had to be treated respectfully. But there were a few odd things that the code did allow, as long as they were done in "good taste," including the "branding of people or animals," "actual hangings," and the "sale of women."

CHIPPING AWAY AT THE CODE

Most filmmakers hated the regulations, and skirmishes often broke out. The most famous was in 1938 when David O. Selznick fought the Hays office over Rhett Butler's classic line in *Gone With the Wind*, "Frankly my dear, I don't give a damn." The problem was that it was already in the best-selling book, and the public expected it to be in the film. Selznick finally compromised—he used the line and paid a fine of $5,000.

Howard Hughes defied the Hays code in 1943 with his movie *The Outlaw*, which featured well-endowed newcomer Jane Russell. Having completed the film in 1941, Hughes battled the censors for two years over its sexual content, finally premiering it in a San Francisco theater without the Hays stamp of approval. (At the end of each screening, Hughes had Jane Russell and a costar act out a 20-minute scene that had been cut at the request of the Hays office.) The movie had been banned in New York, causing Hughes to shelve it for three more years. When it was rereleased in 1946, the owner of the theater was arrested; Hughes filed, and lost, a $1 million suit against the Motion Picture Association of America (the new name of the MPPDA). But the movie was taken on the road and shown throughout the country as Hughes continued to fight. His persistence finally paid off: By 1947 *The Outlaw* was no longer banned.

It wasn't until the 1950s that the code began to crack. Battles over content actually became an important marketing tool: Director Otto Preminger used the Hays code to drum up publicity for 1953's *The Moon Is Blue*. The code met its end in the liberal 1960s, with its influx of unregulated foreign films and loosening of obscenity laws. Instead of censoring films, a rating system was created in 1968 that warned people what was already in the films. The Hays code of 1930 was no more.

June 18, 1873: Susan B. Anthony was fined $100 for attempting to vote for president.

POLITICAL ANIMALS

A few more "tails" of elected officials who weren't quite human.

BOSTON CURTIS

On September 13, 1938, in the small town of Milton, Washington, 52 citizens voted for Boston Curtis to serve as their Republican precinct committee member. Curtis hadn't bothered to campaign, but because he ran unopposed, he won 52 to 0. When results of the election were announced, the town was shocked to learn that they'd voted for a mule. Milton's mayor, Kenneth "Catsup" Simmons (a Democrat), was the mastermind behind the election. He'd brought Boston to the courthouse, inked one of his hooves, and used the mule's hoofprint as a signature for all the legal documents needed to register a candidate. Boston was registered as "Boston Curtis" because he belonged to Mrs. Charles Curtis, who lived in town. Simmons told the press (including *Time* magazine) that he ran Boston to make a serious point: Primary elections were a problem because voters often didn't even know who they were voting for. But people who knew the mayor claimed that he'd also done it to trick the town's Republicans into voting for an animal that resembled the donkey—the mascot of the Democratic Party.

TIAO

The chimpanzee known as Tiao ("Big Uncle") was a big attraction at the Rio de Janeiro Zoo. He was famous for his bad temper; if anyone got too close to Tiao—be they staff, zoo guests, or even visiting dignitaries—he would spit and throw excrement at them. Perfect temperament for political office, right? That's what a group of activists, led by the comedy team Casseta & Planeta, thought when they ran Tiao for mayor of Rio in 1988. Under the banner of the newly formed Banana Party, Tiao's slogan was "Vote Monkey—Get Monkey." More than 400,000 Brazilians, who were fed up with the corruption at Rio's city hall, voted Monkey, but Tiao came in third in the election. When the chimpanzee died in 1996, Rio's (human) mayor declared a weeklong mourning period.

BOSCO

If animals can run for office—and win—what happens when they actually

---

A 1977 Supreme Court ruling deemed it unconstitutional to ban lawyers from advertising.

get to serve out their terms? The answer lies in the hamlet of Sunol, a tiny rural community located east of San Francisco. In 1981 two locals were arguing over which of them would make a better mayor and decided to hold an unofficial election to settle the dispute. Another local, Brad Leber, entered his dog Bosco, a Labrador-Rottweiler mutt, who ran as a "Puplican" with the platform of "A bone in every dish, a cat in every tree, and a fire hydrant on every street corner." When all the votes were counted, Bosco was the new honorary mayor.

In 1981 few people, even in San Francisco, knew much about Sunol. That changed after Bosco's election made world news. The Chinese newspaper *People's Daily* reported that Bosco was proof that Western democracy was a failed system—it couldn't even distinguish between people and dogs. Sunol residents, now the focus of international controversy, retorted that the newspaper had no sense of humor. Bosco served the community, mainly by being himself. Residents enjoyed "bribing" the mayor with beef jerky or ice cream. Tourists were encouraged to pet him. He made the spotlight again when he appeared on *The Third Degree*, a TV game show where celebrity panelists tried to guess his occupation (they failed). And the national media—including Tom Brokaw of NBC—would sometimes meet with Bosco for an "interview." Bosco was such a success that Sunolians reelected him six times. He was mayor until 1994, when he died at age 15. He is memorialized in the Sunol restaurant Bosco's Bones & Brew, where a life-size replica stands atop the bar and dispenses beer with a lift of its leg.

LLAMAS AND DONKEYS AND GOATS (OH, MY!)

Four-legged mayors have presided over several cities across the U.S.

• Clay Henry III was the third generation of goats to be mayor of Lajitas, Texas. His judgment may not have been sound, though, because Clay III reportedly drank 30 to 40 beers every day. (Really.)

• A donkey named Paco Bell outcampaigned a llama to remain the mayor of Florissant, Colorado.

• Rabbit Hash, Kentucky, elected a dog named Junior Cochran as its mayor. Twice. (He beat out another dog and a donkey.)

• A goat named Opie won the 2004 mayoral election in Anza, California. "Opie stands for why so many people moved out here," said one local resident. "We don't want some human sitting on a throne."

Jefferson, Lincoln, and Grant all filed for bankruptcy at one point of their lives.

THE SECRET HITLER FILES

There's nothing funny about Adolf Hitler, but he is endlessly fascinating.
Since the U.S. Congress passed the Nazi War Crimes Disclosure Act
in 1998, almost 3 million classified files have been opened to the
public—including a 1942 secret profile of Hitler compiled by
the Office of Strategic Services (OSS). Some excerpts.

PERSONAL APPEARANCE

- "Hitler never allows anyone to see him while he is naked or bathing. He refuses to use colognes or scents of any sort on his body."

- "No matter how warm he feels, Hitler will never take off his coat in public."

- "In 1923 Nazi press secretary Dr. Sedgwick tried to convince Hitler to get rid of his trademark mustache or grow it normally. Hitler answered: 'Do not worry about my mustache. If it is not the fashion now, it will be later because I wear it!'"

SOCIAL BEHAVIOR

- "While dining with others, Hitler will allow the conversation to linger on general topics, but after a couple of hours he will inevitably begin one of his many monologues. These speeches are flawless from start to finish because he rehearses them any time he gets a moment."

- "His favorite topics include: 'When I was a soldier,' 'When I was in Vienna,' 'When I was in prison,' and 'When I was the leader in the early days of the party.'"

- "If Hitler begins speaking about Wagner and the opera, no one dares interrupt him. He will often sermonize on this topic until his audience falls asleep."

PERSONAL HABITS

- "Hitler has no interest in sports or games of any kind and never exercised, except for an occasional walk."

Pres. who vetoed the most bills: Franklin D. Roosevelt (635). Least: George W. Bush (12).

• "He paces frequently inside rooms, always to the same tune that he whistles to himself and always diagonally across the room, from corner to corner."

• "He always rides in an open car for parades regardless of the weather, and expects the same of his entire staff, telling them: 'We are not bourgeois, but soldiers.'"

• "Hitler's handwriting is impeccable. When famous psychologist Carl Jung saw Hitler's handwriting in 1937, he remarked, 'Behind this handwriting I recognize the typical characteristics of a man with essentially feminine instincts.'"

ENTERTAINMENT

• "Hitler loves the circus. He takes real pleasure in the idea that underpaid performers are risking their lives to please him."

• "He went to the circus on several occasions in 1933 and sent extremely expensive chocolates and flowers to the female performers. Hitler even remembered their names and would worry about them and their families in the event of an accident."

• "He isn't interested in wild animal acts, unless there is a woman in danger."

• "Nearly every night Hitler will see a movie in his private theatre, mainly foreign films that are banned to the German public. He loves comedies and will often laugh merrily at Jewish comedians. Hitler even liked a few Jewish singers, but after hearing them he would remark that it was too bad he or she wasn't an Aryan."

• "Hitler's staff secretly made films for him of the torture and execution of political prisoners, which he very much enjoyed viewing. His executive assistants also secure pornographic pictures and movies for him."

• "He loves newsreels—especially when he is in them."

• "He adores gypsy music, Wagner's operas, and especially American college football marches and alma maters."

• "To excite the masses, he uses American college football–style music during his speeches." His rallying cry—'Sieg heil!'—was even modeled after the cheering techniques used by American football cheerleaders."

By law, information collected in a U.S. Census must remain confidential for 72 years.

WORLD POLITICS 101

Keeping up with world events can be a full-time job. Those of us who just like to peruse the morning paper over coffee and a doughnut can find ourselves confused by international news—there is such variety in the different types of government from country to country... what does it all mean? Here are some of the basics.

THE SKY IS FALLING

Imagine waking up one morning to newspaper headlines announcing that the United States government had collapsed and that the president and the entire cabinet were stepping down and calling for new elections. It would be frightening. You'd probably expect chaos and lawlessness to follow. You might even wish you'd listened to your crazy neighbor—the one with the stockpile of ammunition and canned goods.

Well, in parliamentary democracies, governments "collapse" all the time—it happened, for example, in Canada in 2006. All it means is that the dominant political party lost control of the legislature. There are almost 200 countries in the world, and each one of them has a government that is organized at least a little bit differently from all the rest. The terminology that reporters use to describe what is going on in the world doesn't always make sense to people who are familiar with only one system. So, for the discerning bathroom reader, here's a social-studies primer to help simplify the world beat.

TYRANTS AND KINGS

Most countries have some form of representative government, in which voters elect politicians to represent them in a legislative assembly. That doesn't mean that they are always full democracies, just that some kind of political representation is built into the system. The least-representative governments: countries such as China, Cuba, Syria, Vietnam, and North Korea, where only a single political party is allowed to participate.

Along with undemocratic, single-party systems, there are still a few absolute monarchies left in the world—among them Saudi Arabia, Qatar, and Swaziland—where a hereditary king (or, in Qatar's case, an *emir*) has complete control over the government.

There are also many countries where the mechanisms of representative government are mostly for show and the real power is a military *junta* (Myanmar and Fiji), or a president without a strong legislature to check his power (Robert Mugabe in Zimbabwe, for example).

THE FREE WORLD

Representative governments tend to fall into two basic categories: *parliamentary* and *presidential*. The biggest difference between the two has to do with what civics textbooks call "separation of powers." Under a presidential system (used in countries as varied as the U.S., Mexico, Brazil, Afghanistan, Cameroon, Sudan, and the Philippines), the executive branch of government is completely separate from the legislative branch. In the U.S., this means that the president holds power independently of Congress.

In a parliamentary government (like those in the UK, Canada, Australia, Italy, Israel, most of Europe, India, Japan, and Cambodia, among others), the executive and legislative branches are combined. The executive (usually called the prime minister) is the leader of the legislative assembly (parliament). Think of the prime minister as a combination of the president of the United States and the Speaker of the House.

The prime minister is also selected differently from a president. A president is elected directly by the voting public to serve a fixed term in office (in the U.S., four years; in Mexico, six). Under a parliamentary system, citizens don't get to vote for prime minister—not directly, anyway. The voters elect members of Parliament (MPs), and the leader of the party that wins the most seats becomes prime minister.

PARTY TIME

Not only is a prime minister not directly elected by popular vote, he or she usually doesn't serve a fixed term in office. No one in a parliamentary system does—general elections aren't held on a fixed schedule. In Canada and the UK, elections are traditionally held at least once every five years, but there isn't even a written rule that requires it.

So how does the system work? The head of the dominant political party becomes prime minister, and must then "form a government." To American ears that probably sounds like what the Founding Fathers did back in the 1780s, but it's actually closer to what a president does during his first few weeks in office. Primarily, it involves assigning key cabinet positions to the appropriate politicians.

The original U.S. Mint was the first federal building erected by the U.S. gov't.

The tricky part is that it's more difficult to form a government at some times than at others. In the UK, there are two main political parties (Labour and the Conservative, or Tory, party), and one of them usually wins an absolute majority in Parliament. They are then able to form what is called a "majority government." This means, in effect, that the majority party can run the government however it pleases without too much interference from the opposition.

In Canada, the last two elections have resulted in what is called a "minority government." There are four political parties represented in the Parliament of Canada, but two of them (the Conservatives and the Liberals) held more than 70 percent of the seats as of 2008. The Conservatives had more seats than the Liberals, but not enough to constitute a majority. Because of this, the government of Prime Minister Stephen Harper had to make policy compromises and court the votes of MPs from the other three parties in order to get anything done.

MULTIPARTISAN

Some countries have so many parties that there's *never* a majority government. The Israeli *Knesset* is a good example: Israel uses a proportional representation system in which citizens cast their votes for a party rather than for an individual candidate. The parties are then assigned seats in the legislature based on the percentage of the popular vote they received. In Israel, any party that gets at least 2 percent of the vote gains seats. And in the 2003 and 2006 elections, the 120 Knesset seats were divided between 12 parties. (Many more were on the ballot but fell short of the 2 percent threshold for representation.) The party that "won" the 2006 elections controls less than 25 percent of the legislature. In a situation like this, government-forming becomes a trickier business. The leader of the party that gets the most votes becomes prime minister, and attempts to form a government by piecing together a coalition of smaller parties. Together, such an association can vote as a majority block, but, not surprisingly, these coalitions can be hard to hold together.

WHEN GOVERNMENTS COLLAPSE

Coalition governments last until the least-satisfied party involved decides to withdraw its support. This usually means that the prime minister no longer controls enough votes to get anything done. When this happens, most parliaments will hold a "vote of no confidence" in the prime minister, and the government is said to have "collapsed." In most cases, this leads to the dissolution of parliament and a new round of general elections.

Several European governments collapsed in 2008. Belgium's prime minister resigned when the five-party coalition government he'd spent nine months building was unable to work together on key issues facing the country. In Austria, an uncomfortable alliance between the two dominant parties ended when one of them pulled out of the governing coalition in a bid to force new elections. And in Italy, the 20-month-old Prodi government lost a vote of no confidence and was replaced by a new coalition headed by former prime minister Silvio Berlusconi.

LAME DUCKS AND MIDTERM ELECTIONS

Majority governments are more stable than coalitions and are usually able to call elections at a time that is politically advantageous for them—when they think they stand a good chance of retaining power. Sometimes, a prime minister can even step down and be replaced without new elections being held. This happened recently in the UK in 2008, when Tony Blair resigned as head of the Labour Party. Because the party still controlled Parliament, they simply chose a new party leader (Gordon Brown), who then became the new prime minister.

To understand how this differs from a presidential system, compare it with what was going on in the U.S. in 2006: The Democrats took control of Congress—despite the fact that there was still a Republican president in office with two years left in his term. Under a parliamentary system, this couldn't happen, because whoever controls the legislative branch of the government (parliament) also controls the executive (the prime minister).

MINISTERIAL VS. PRESIDENTIAL

Both systems have their pros and cons. Advocates of parliamentary democracy point out that it is more responsive to social and economic changes. If a prime minister makes an unpopular decision and loses his base of support, he faces a swift removal from office—unlike the American president, who can lose both popular and congressional support and still serve out the remainder of his term. On the other hand, in situations where coalitions are difficult to build and maintain, critics charge that parliamentary governments can be unstable. Italy is the most common example of this: Since becoming a parliamentary republic at the end of World War II, Italy had 62 governments in as many years. That doesn't mean there is no functional government in Italy, just that there is a high turnover rate at the prime minister's office. (They're still a highly developed modern democracy with the seventh-largest economy in the world.)

The relative stability of a fixed-term presidential system has shortcomings, too. In the U.S., five of the last seven presidents have been forced to work with a Congress controlled by the opposition party. Critics complain that partisan bickering in such situations can lead to legislative gridlock—as it did in 1995, when the Republican-controlled Congress and the Democrat president Bill Clinton couldn't agree on a budget and the federal government actually shut down all nonessential services for 26 days.

GOD SAVE THE QUEEN

The boundaries that define president and parliament can get even fuzzier. Some presidential governments also have a prime minister (such as France, Egypt, South Korea, and Russia), and some parliamentary governments also have a president (Germany, India, Italy, Ethiopia, and Bangladesh).

And then there's the queen of England. The U.K. is a constitutional monarchy, which means that it is has a democratic government that evolved over time out of an absolute monarchy. Over hundreds of years, the kings and queens of England gradually lost their political power to parliament. Today, the queen is a figurehead—she plays the same role in former British colonies like Canada and Australia—though she does so through an appointed governor-general who acts as her representative. The emperor of Japan has a similar job in his country.

READ WITH CARE

So when you read the paper or listen to the news, remember that no two governments are exactly alike, and that the word "government" itself can have multiple meanings depending on the political system being described. Kings, queens, presidents, and prime ministers play different roles in different countries, and "democracy" comes in different shades. The easiest way to understand international news stories is to check a current almanac or the Internet for background information on a given country. Give it a try and impress (or annoy) your friends with your informed observations about the state of the world. Oh, and vote for Uncle John for president in the next election (if there is one).

Why didn't Maryland secede from the Union in 1865? Lincoln had its legislators arrested.

SENATE SCUFFLES

The U.S. Senate is supposed to be a temple of decorum where political leaders can debate the great issues of the day with dignity and mutual respect, but...

HOT FOOTE

In 1850 the issue of slavery had turned the Senate into a hotbed of emotion. Vice President Millard Fillmore worried publicly that "a slight attack, even an insinuation, often provokes a more severe retort, which brings out a more disorderly reply, each Senator feeling a justification in the previous aggression." He promised, in his role as president of the Senate, to act at the first hint of disorder to prevent any conflict from getting out of hand.

Two weeks later, his worst fears came true when Missouri senator Thomas Hart Benton got into a nasty argument with Mississippi senator Henry Foote over a simple point of order. Benton, a bull of a man, charged up the aisle at Foote; the diminutive Foote drew a pistol. "Let him fire!" Benton yelled. "Stand out of the way and let the assassin fire!" Fortunately, he didn't—a disaster was avoided when the Senate quickly adopted a motion to adjourn.

PAIN BY CANE

On May 22, 1856, South Carolina's senator Andrew Butler was ridiculed on the Senate floor by antislavery advocate Charles Sumner of Massachusetts during a debate over whether Kansas should be admitted to the Union as a slave or free state. During his speech, entitled "The Crime Against Kansas," Sumner accused Butler of leading the effort to spread slavery to Kansas, for Butler, he said, had taken "a mistress, who, though ugly to others, is always lovely to him...I mean, the harlot, Slavery."

Butler's response is not recorded, but by all accounts Sumner concluded his speech and the day's session continued. Meanwhile in the House of Representatives, Butler's cousin, Congressman Preston Brooks, was preparing his own response to what he considered a grievous slander against a kinsman and fellow Southerner. Moments after the Senate adjourned for the day, Butler grabbed a cane and strode into the Senate

---

At least 37 BBC TV executives earn more than the British prime minister.

chamber. Sumner was sitting at his desk putting stamps on copies of his speech to send to constituents. Slamming his metal-tipped cane onto the unsuspecting Sumner's head, Brooks proceeded to beat the helpless man viciously. Then he turned on his heels and walked out.

To their partisans, each man became an instant hero. The stunned and bloodied Sumner was carried away by friends. It took him months to recover from his wounds, but he returned to the Senate and served another 18 years. As for Brooks, he survived a Senate censure vote and was even reelected to office, but died six months later at the age of 37.

DEATH BY DUEL

In 1859 Senator David Broderick of California, a power broker in the Democratic Party's antislavery faction, was challenged to a duel by political enemy and proslavery activist David Terry, California's chief justice. They met at dawn at Lake Merced, south of San Francisco. Broderick had the first shot, but when his gun misfired, Terry calmly put a bullet through Broderick's chest. Broderick now has the unique distinction of being the only U.S. senator to be killed in a duel while in office. Terry was tried for murder and acquitted, and three years later he joined the Confederate army. In 1889 the elderly Terry was gunned down by the Supreme Court justice Stephen Fields's bodyguard after Terry confronted Field in a train station restaurant and slapped him.

SCORE ONE FOR THE SENATOR

Over the years more than a few senators have been attacked by disgruntled constituents, but it's much less common to hear that an actual sitting senator was the one to start the fight. It happened in 1917 when a war protester named Alexander Bannwart and two other men confronted Massachusetts senator Henry Cabot Lodge in his office. They wanted to urge Senator Lodge to vote "no" on the upcoming resolution to enter World War I. Bannwart and Lodge argued. The words "coward" and "liar" were spoken. All of a sudden, the 67-year-old senator rose up and decked the 36-year-old pacifist...and laid him out cold. The protester was arrested, but Lodge said he was too busy to press charges. Two days later, Lodge voted with the majority of his fellow senators to go to war. Bannwart later caught the patriotic fever gripping the nation and, after announcing that he'd changed his mind, he enlisted in the army.

U.$. Congre$$: 42% of representatives and 67% of senators are millionaires.

DEMS AND REPUBS

The fundamental differences between America's two major parties.

"Republicans have nothing but bad ideas, and Democrats have no ideas."
—**Lewis Black**

"Conservatives tend to see the world in black and white terms, good and evil. Liberals see grays."
—**Bill O'Reilly**

"A conservative is a man who wants the rules changed so no one can make a pile the way he did."
—**Everett Dirksen**

"A conservative is a liberal who got mugged the night before."
—**Frank Rizzo**

"Liberals feel unworthy of their possessions. Conservatives feel they deserve everything they've stolen."
—**Mort Sahl**

"Republicans believe every day is the 4th of July. Democrats believe every day is April 15."
—**Ronald Reagan**

"If the Republicans will stop telling lies about the Democrats, we will stop telling the truth about them."
—**Adlai Stevenson**

"My grandmother's brain was dead, but her heart was still beating. It was the first time we ever had a Democrat in the family."
—**Emo Phillips**

"Republicans study the financial pages. Democrats put them in the bottom of the bird cage."
—**Will Stanton**

"I never say 'Democrats' and 'Republicans.' It's 'liberals' and 'Americans.'"
—**James Watt, interior secretary in the Reagan administration**

"You have to have been a Republican to know how good it is to be a Democrat."
—**Jacqueline Kennedy**

"Democrats say government will make you smarter, taller, richer, and remove the crabgrass on your lawn. Republicans say government doesn't work, and then they get elected and prove it."
—**P. J. O'Rourke**

"Liberal and conservative have lost their meaning in America. I represent the distracted center."
—**Jon Stewart**

"Republican" and "Democrat" are both towns in North Carolina.

YOUR GOVERNMENT AT WORK

Some more examples of the ways politicians are ensuring that your tax dollars are being well spent on…

NONBINDING RESOLUTIONS
In 2007 the *Tennessean* newspaper discovered that 42 percent of all measures filed in the Tennessee state legislature were nonbinding resolutions with no force of law. Among the resolutions: one lauding Tennessee native Justin Timberlake and another celebrating religious freedom in Turkey (the Turkey measure passed; Timberlake's failed). The paper singled out one representative, Tom DuBois, who "introduced 167 congratulations, memorials, and proposals to rename stretches of highway." In all, the resolutions cost Tennessee taxpayers $70,000.

NONEXISTENT ORGANIZATIONS
• Congressman John Murtha (D-PA) drafted a bill in 2007 which included an earmark appropriating $1 million for the "Center for Instrumented Critical Infrastructure" (CICI). According to research by Congressman Jeff Flake (R-AZ), there is no such center. He confronted Democrats about it on the House floor, but none of them had heard of the CICI, either. Still, they voted down Flake's measure to strike the funds. It was later revealed that the $1 million was actually slated to go to a consulting firm called Concurrent Technologies Corporation, whose CEO had donated $7,000 to Murtha's campaign.

• In 2002 the U.S. Department of Education granted $55,000 in student loans for three students to attend the "Y'Hica Institute" in London, England. One problem: Neither the institute nor the students were real. They were created by a congressional investigation team that was testing the DOE's verification policy. It failed.

NONEXISTENT AIRLINE PASSENGERS
A 2005 government audit discovered that between 1997 and 2003, the

U.S. Defense Department spent more than $108 million on 270,000 airline tickets…which they never used. In 27,000 instances, they even paid *twice*, by first paying for the unused tickets and then reimbursing the employees who were supposed to have used them. The Government Accountability Office blamed the "glitches" on the failure of department personnel to notify the travel office when tickets weren't used.

JUNK FOOD

Promoting healthy eating is one of the foundations of British Columbia premier Gordon Campbell's government. It came as a surprise, then, when reports surfaced that Campbell's Liberal MLAs (Members of the Legislative Assembly)—along with the civil servants who work for them—used government-issued credit cards to buy nearly $85,000 worth of pizza in the fiscal year 2005–06. It was also revealed that the Ministry of Children and Families spent $20,000 on doughnuts.

CAR SERVICES

To transport its city engineers to on-site inspections, the New York City government leases 107 SUVs, some of them at a cost of $4,000 per month—the same amount it would cost to rent a luxurious Bentley. An investigation by local news station WCBS discovered that these "official use only" SUVs were rarely put to official use. The news prompted the city comptroller's office to perform an audit, which uncovered even more troubling facts: Many of the city employees who were using the SUVs as personal vehicles had either suspended licenses or DUI convictions…or both. Total annual cost of the cars: $1.4 million.

COMMENCEMENT ADDRESSES

Montana governor Brian Schweitzer gave the graduation commencement address at Froid High School in 2007, which had a graduating class of… one. The Democratic governor, along with his entire entourage, traveled to Froid (pop. 195) to speak to Valedictorian Roxie Britton, the only member of her graduating class. Schweitzer gave a passionate speech to Britton (along with a small, enthusiastic crowd), where he spoke about reducing the need for foreign oil and using more alternative energy. He ended his speech by calling on the class of 2007 (Britton) to "look toward the future with a positive attitude."

After George W. Bush's 2004 reelection victory, Canada's immigration website…

WAR PLAN RED

When this bizarre story surfaced a few years ago, it reminded us of this quote, attributed to Warren G. Harding: "I can take care of my enemies all right. But my damn friends—they're the ones that keep me walking the floors at night."

NORTHERN EXPOSURE

If you had to invade another country, how would you do it? Believe it or not, the United States military spent a lot of time pondering that question in the late 1920s, when it came up with a plan to invade its closest neighbor, Canada.

There was certainly a precedent for the two nations battling it out. The Continental Army invaded Canada during the American Revolution, and the U.S. Army made repeated incursions during the War of 1812. In 1839 the state of Maine only narrowly avoided a shooting war with the province of New Brunswick over a border dispute. Then, in 1866, about 800 Irish-American members of a group called the Fenian Brotherhood tried to occupy part of Canada for the purpose of using it as a bargaining chip to force Great Britain to grant independence to Ireland. (They were quickly driven back across the U.S. border.)

That last invasion had an upside for Canadians: It convinced the last holdouts in the independent provinces of New Brunswick, Nova Scotia, Ontario, and Quebec that they'd be better able to defend themselves against the *next* invasion if they banded together to form the Dominion of Canada, which they did on July 1, 1867.

TO THE DRAWING BOARD

Of course, these skirmishes paled in comparison to World War I, which raged from 1914 to 1918. The war, which was precipitated by the assassination of Archduke Ferdinand of Austria, caught most of the belligerents by surprise. It also lasted longer and was far more costly in blood and treasure than anyone ever dreamed a war could be. None of the nations that fought in it wanted to be caught off guard again; many began planning for whatever war might be lurking around the corner. America's military brass drafted a whole series of color-coded war plans to cover just about every conceivable scenario: War Plan Black was a plan for war with

Germany; War Plan Orange dealt with Japan, a rapidly growing power in the Pacific. Other colors included Green (Mexico), Gold (France), Brown (the Philippines), and Yellow (China). There was even a War Plan Indigo, in case the United States had to invade Iceland, and War Plan White, which dealt with civil unrest within America's own borders.

THE CANADIAN STATES OF AMERICA

War Plan Red was the U.S. military's plan for going to war with the British Empire, in the unlikely event that Britain (code name: Red) decided to "eliminate [the United States] as an economic and commercial rival." Since Canada (code name: Crimson) was part of the empire and shared a 5,527-mile border with the U.S., much of the plan dealt with invading Canada and knocking it out of action before the British could use it as a staging ground for attacks on the U.S.

Here's how the invasion of Canada would have gone:

• The United States (code name: Blue) would attack and occupy Halifax, Nova Scotia, Canada's largest Atlantic port. The attack wold deny Britain access to the rail and road links it would need to land troops in Canada and disperse them across the country.

• Next, the U.S. Army would attack across the border along three fronts: Troops would attack from either Vancouver or New York to occupy Montreal and Quebec City; from Michigan into Ontario; and from North Dakota into Manitoba. Meanwhile, the U.S. Navy would take control of the Great Lakes. The effects of these attacks would be to seize Canada's industrial heartland while preventing similar attacks on the U.S., and to further disrupt the movement of Canadian troops from one part of the country to another.

• Troops would cross from Washington into British Columbia and seize Vancouver, Canada's largest Pacific port. The U.S. Navy would blockade the port of Prince Rupert, 460 miles to the north.

Once the crisis passed and relations between America, Canada, and Great Britain returned to normal, the U.S. troops would be withdrawn from Canadian territory, right? No—"Blue intentions are to hold in perpetuity all Crimson and Red territory gained," the military planners wrote. "The policy will be to prepare the provinces and territories of Crimson and Red to become states and territories of the Blue union upon the declaration of peace."

U.S. Rep. Justin Amash's (R-MI) father lived in a Palestinian refugee camp as a child.

THE FOG OF WAR(S)

So how serious was the United States considering invading Canada? In all probability, not very. War Plan Red doesn't go into nearly as much detail as War Plan Black (Germany) or War Plan Orange (Japan), which military planners correctly assumed were much more significant threats. The intent of other color-coded plans may have been to make war plans involving Germany and Japan seem less controversial. Why all of the subterfuge? After the horrors of World War I, in which nearly 10 million soldiers died, many people concluded that planning for wars only made them more likely.

The U.S. military didn't feel this way, of course, and one way they may have gotten around public opinion was to come up with all kinds of improbable war plans to make the *real* plans seem more palatable. The military felt that a public that would not have tolerated the idea of preparing for war with Germany and Japan would be less alarmed by the idea of the United States preparing for war with Germany, Canada, Iceland, Jamaica, Monaco, and Andorra.

WHAT'S GOOD FOR THE GOOSE...

Any sting Canadians may have felt when War Plan Red was declassified in 1974 was offset by the knowledge that Canada had drafted its own plans for invading the United States, and had done so several years before War Plan Red was approved in 1930. Defense Scheme No. 1, as it was called, was created in 1921 by James Sutherland "Buster" Brown, Canada's director of military operations and intelligence. In many respects, it was the opposite of War Plan Red: In the event that an American attack was imminent, Canadian forces would strike first, attacking and occupying key cities such as Albany, Minneapolis, and Seattle.

Unlike with War Plan Red, these cities wouldn't be annexed or even occupied for any longer than was absolutely necessary. The idea was to knock the U.S. off balance, then retreat back into Canada, blowing up bridges and destroying roads and railroads along the way in the hopes of delaying the inevitable American counterattack until British reinforcements arrived. The plan received mixed reviews from the Canadian military: One general called it a "fantastic desperate plan that just might have worked"; other officers thought Brown was nuts. Defense Scheme No. 1 remained on the books until 1928, when it was scrapped as impractical.

Calvin Coolidge was the last American president to write his own speeches.

SNAKES AND RAPPERS

When politicians and citizens mix it up, things can get ugly.

FISTS ON A PLANE

It was a case of he said/he said after an altercation in economy class between former Massachusetts governor Mitt Romney and Grammy-nominated rapper Sky Blu (real name: Skyler Gordy, the nephew of Motown founder Berry Gordy). Both were returning to Los Angeles after attending the 2010 Winter Olympics in Vancouver, British Columbia. While the plane was still at the airport, taxiing for takeoff, Sky Blu reclined his seatback. Romney was sitting behind him. According to Sky Blu, Governor Romney sternly ordered the rapper to put up his seat. Sky Blu ignored him. Romney asked again. Then, according to Sky Blu, Romney grabbed his shoulder in a "Vulcan grip." Sky Blu stood up, turned around, and raised his fists. "I didn't take it any further than that," he later said. "The man assaulted me. I was protecting myself." A Romney spokesperson said that the rapper actually did take a swing at the politician. Whether he did or not, Romney's wife screamed, the flight crew intervened, and the plane returned to the gate, where police took Sky Blu into custody. Romney didn't press charges; Sky Blu was released and caught a later flight home. He later said that if Romney had simply asked him nicely, he would have put up his seat.

SNAKE ATTACK!

In 2011 town officials in Harraiya, India, denied a permit to Hakkul the snake charmer. He needed one to set up a snake sanctuary. (He captures snakes in people's homes but doesn't have enough room to keep them at his own house.) Hakkul had been granted a permit at the regional level, but the local offices in Harraiya kept holding back his application until certain "fees" could be paid; they basically bribed Hakkul for money he didn't have. That's when the old, bearded snake charmer and a throng of his supporters entered the offices carrying several sacks of snakes—including poisonous spitting cobras—and let them go. Workers scattered and jumped up on tables while the snakes slithered to and fro. By the time game officials arrived to remove the snakes, Hakkul was gone. And not all of the snakes were captured. (No word on whether he got his permit.)

State Rep. Steve Holland (D-MS) tried to rename the Gulf of Mexico the "Gulf of America."

VOTE FOR ME!

Do political campaigns bring out the best in people? Apparently not.

GRASSROOTS CAMPAIGN

In 2005 Edward Forchion, also known as "Weedman," ran for governor of New Jersey on the slogan "Take a Toke, Then Vote!" The self-proclaimed leader of the "Marijuana Party," Forchion had also run in 1998. About the 2005 campaign he said, "It's a whole angrier thing." He was angry because he'd spent five months in jail in 2002 for filming a TV ad promoting the legalization of marijuana, which prosecutors said was a violation of his parole. (He was on parole after serving 16 months for distribution of marijuana.) After a federal judge finally freed Forchion, finding that the arrest had violated his right to free speech, Forchion wanted revenge. "My whole reason for running for office is to specifically give the finger to the attorney general," he said. (Forchion got 8,271 votes, coming in sixth out of 10 candidates.)

CANDIDATE FROM CELL BLOCK C

In November 2005, Randy Logan Hale won one of three available seats for the Romoland School District board in Riverside, California. People in the district were confused: They had never seen Hale at any board meetings, and he hadn't attended any of the candidate events, either. A call to his wife, Penny, cleared it up: He was in jail. The school board candidate had been incarcerated since September for parole violations stemming from a 1998 spousal-abuse conviction. Penny Hale said that her husband had run for a school board seat because "he cares about kids." When he won, she said, "He'll be glad." But you have to be a registered voter to run for office, and convicted felons aren't allowed to vote. In May 2006, Hale was charged with perjury, forgery, and voter fraud.

HEART OF THE MATTER

When California farmer and businessman Tom Berryhill entered the Republican primary for assemblyman in 2006, he probably didn't expect his "heart" to be questioned quite the way it was. His opponent, former Modesto city councilman Bill Conrad, sent out a mailer with the red-lettered headline "Tom Berryhill doesn't have the HEART for State

---

Duh! Bill Clinton's 1992 presidential campaign slogan: "It's the Economy, Stupid."

Assembly." What was he referring to? The fact that Berryhill was a heart transplant recipient. Conrad's letter continued with "Heart Transplant Facts":

- The Average Lifespan of a Heart Transplant recipient is seven years. (Berryhill's heart transplant was six years ago.)
- Heart Transplant patients take anti-rejection medications for life, which weaken the immune system making the recipient more susceptible to illness and death.
- Severe stress SIGNIFICANTLY shortens the life expectancy of Heart Transplant recipients.

The ad continued, "Can you imagine the costs to taxpayers for a special election when poor health renders him unable to fulfill the duties of office?" The letter was condemned, mocked, ridiculed, and lambasted by the press (and voters in the district). "He's set a new low," said Berryhill. "This is the type of thing that keeps good people from running for office." (Berryhill won, and served until 2010, when he retired.)

MORALLY BANKRUPT

In 2006 Arizona resident Mike Harris argued in court that child-support payments to his ex-wife were putting him "near bankruptcy." The judge cut the payments in half, from $2,000 per month to $1,000. But just months after the case, Harris, a candidate for Arizona governor, somehow found his finances improved—he donated $100,000 of his own money to his campaign. Questioned by reporters, Harris said he was simply doing better…but he wouldn't be increasing his payments to his ex-wife.

OTHER STANDOUTS

- George W. Bush didn't win in 2004. Neither did John Kerry. Who did? Green Party presidential candidate David Cobb. According to survey of dentists conducted by the California Dental Association, Cobb had the "most attractive" and "most trustworthy" smile.

- In 2006 Republican congresswoman Marilyn Musgrave of Colorado received an unusual "gift" at her office. The package, wrapped in one of the reelection campaign mailers that had been sent to her constituents, was full of dog poop. Using the address on the mailer, police tracked the package to Kathleen Ensz, a prominent local Democratic Party official, who was cited for criminal use of a noxious substance (the dog poop).

When Victor Biaka Boda, an Ivory Coast senator, disappeared in 1950,…

LINCOLNSPIRACY?

John Wilkes Booth killed the 16th president...or did he?

BACKGROUND
On April 14, 1865, President Lincoln was shot while watching a play at Ford's Theatre in Washington, D.C. The country was thrown for a loop: No American president had ever been assassinated. John Wilkes Booth, a young actor with Confederate sympathies, was witnessed pulling the trigger. As it is with many sudden, tragic events, the conspiracy theories abounded. Here are a few that circulated in the weeks and months after Lincoln's death.

CONSPIRACY THEORY: Vice President Andrew Johnson, next in line to the presidency and a Southerner, hired John Wilkes Booth to assassinate Lincoln.

THE STORY: On the afternoon of April 14, 1865, Booth stopped by the Kirkwood House, a Washington hotel where Johnson kept an office. Johnson was out, so Booth left a note (later found by Johnson's secretary William Browning). Why would an assassin want to meet with the vice president? To coordinate final details, such as Lincoln's whereabouts for that night. While Johnson was military governor of Tennessee in 1862, he and Booth had mistresses who happened to be sisters, and were often seen together. The relationship grew over their mutual hatred of Lincoln, whose death fulfilled both men's ambitions: fame for Booth, the presidency for Johnson.

THE TRUTH: Browning really did find a note, and Booth and Johnson really did know each other in Tennessee. The theory spread because Northern congressmen hated Johnson. Booth may have been just stopping by to see a friend, albeit a curiously well-connected friend...but no one knows for sure.

CONSPIRACY THEORY: Mrs. Lincoln shot Mr. Lincoln.

THE STORY: The Rothschilds, a European banking family, wanted Lincoln dead for two reasons: 1) He was going to shut down their money-printing bank in favor of a federally backed currency; and 2) he'd sired an

---

...it was widely assumed that he was eaten by his constituents.

illegitimate child with a Rothschild. They planned to kidnap Lincoln from Ford's Theatre, drug him, and leave him on a ship at sea for several days. When Lincoln returned, the baby scandal would force him to resign and abandon his currency plan. The kidnapper they supposedly hired was Mary Todd Lincoln's opium dealer, who also happened to be John Wilkes Booth's theatrical stand-in. But as "Booth" arrived, Todd, who was high on opium, shot Lincoln because she'd just found out about the illegitimate child. The fake Booth panicked and escaped. The real Booth changed his name and went into hiding.

THE TRUTH: Rumors about Mrs. Lincoln's involvement began when she didn't show up at her husband's funeral. But it's not because she was a murderer: She was simply overwrought. The Rothschilds were a very powerful banking family in Europe, but they never had any money-printing operations in the United States (although at the time, individual banks often did print their own money). There is no doubt that Booth pulled the trigger. Witnesses saw him enter the box, and because Mrs. Lincoln was sitting next to the president, she couldn't have shot him in the back of the head.

CONSPIRACY THEORY: The Catholic Church killed Lincoln.

THE STORY: In 1856 Lincoln, then a lawyer in Illinois, represented an ex-priest in a slander case over a claim that the Vatican planned to take over the United States. The Vatican was livid that their plot had been exposed. They decided to kill Lincoln, which would throw the country, still fragile after the Civil War, into chaos and allow for an easy takeover. The church also planned to stack the odds by importing millions of Catholic immigrants from Ireland, Germany, and France. Former Confederate president (and secret Vatican puppet) Jefferson Davis offered a $1 million reward to anyone willing to pull the trigger on Lincoln. The man who stepped up: John Wilkes Booth, who had spent three years in Rome learning assassination techniques from the Jesuits.

THE TRUTH: The theory was spread by Charles Chiniquy—the ex-priest Lincoln defended in 1856. The church had excommunicated Chiniquy because he'd had an affair with a teenage girl. After Lincoln died, Chiniquy published a book outlining the Catholic Church's "plan" to take over the United States and fill it with Catholic immigrants—indicative of both the anti-immigration and anti-Catholic sentiments of the time.

POLITICS AS (UN)USUAL

One last round of political mayhem.

HE REALLY KICKED A HOME RUN!

Vice President Joe Biden's blatant attempt to pander to San Francisco's voters backfired in January 2012 when he boasted to a crowd of potential donors: "And the Giants are going to the Super Bowl!" Biden got booed. Why? He got the team name right, just the wrong sport…and the wrong city. The New York *football* Giants were going to the Super Bowl, not the San Francisco *baseball* Giants (who were in their offseason). Adding insult to gaffe: The night before, the Giants had achieved their Super Bowl berth…by beating the San Francisco Forty-Niners.

VOTE SHMOTE

Lisa Osborn of Burton, Michigan, lost her bid for a spot on the board of education by one vote—her own. Why? She attended her son's baseball game that day, and figured she had enough supporters to carry her in the election. She would have won with one more vote. "It was a dumb move," said Osborn.

SHOULD HAVE SETTLED

In 2008 the city of Bridgewater, New Jersey, charged a resident named Tom Coulter $5.00 for a CD recording of a public council meeting. After Coulter paid, he felt he should only have to pay for the actual cost of the disc itself, which was 96 cents, so he asked the city to return the balance. The city refused, so Coulter took them to court. City leaders could have settled, but decided to fight. They lost. In the end, Bridgewater spent $17,500 on legal fees and Coulter's court costs…and still had to refund him his $4.04.

MACARONI AND KNEES

State senator Ralph Shortey (R-OK) drafted legislation in 2012 that would make it illegal for food manufacturers to "make or sell food or other products that contain aborted human fetuses." What's his beef? "People are thinking that this has to do with fetuses being chopped up and put in our burritos," said Shortey. "That's not the case. It's beyond that." He drafted the bill after reading online reports by a pro-life group which accused food

---

Presidential salaries: Washington, $25K. Clinton, $200K. Bush and Obama, $400K.

companies of adding embryonic stem cells to "enhance the flavor" of their products. The companies all denied this, and there is no evidence that anyone has done this. Critics pointed out that the bill is unnecessary because cannibalism is *already* a federal crime—including embryonic stem cells. Some critics charged that there was more to it than even that. Shortey's bill, if passed, would also make it illegal for people to "consume" anything that's made with stem cells, even if it's contained in medicine. According to political columnist Stephen Foster Jr., it's a clever political ploy: "On the one hand, if Democrats vote in favor of the bill, Republicans will have succeeded in banning embryonic stem cell research and treatments. On the other hand, if Democrats vote against it, Republicans will accuse Democrats of wanting to eat fetuses."

ROADHOUSE OF COMMONS

In 2012 members of the British Parliament got into a drunken brawl at a pub located inside the House of Commons. "It was like the Wild West in there," said an MP who witnessed the fracas. Exact details were murky because most of the patrons were quite drunk, but it appears that Labour MP Eric Joyce, 51, was "dancing erratically" and loudly complaining about "too many Tories" in the pub. Then Joyce went ballistic and started knocking over chairs and throwing drinks at the Tories, one of whom was Conservative MP Stuart Andrew, 40, who bore the brunt of Joyce's wrath. "Poor Stuart was just having a quiet pint and minding his own business and Eric headbutted him," said another MP. Police arrived and arrested Joyce; he was suspended from the Labour Party the next day.

HUH?

Huh Kyung Young has run for president of South Korea four times, all unsuccessfully. He is the head of the Democratic Republican Party, which is not represented in South Korea's parliament. Why? Well, for starters, Huh claims to have an IQ of 430. He also claims he can heal people's cancer simply by looking into their eyes (in "0.1 seconds" no less). Huh, who's in his 60s, is running on a world peace platform. His big idea: Move the UN headquarters from New York to the demilitarized zone that separates the two Koreas. From there, he says, he will "unify the world." But if Huh never makes it to the presidency, at least he has his world record to fall back on: "I am so popular that I get several phone calls every second from my fans. I am thinking of reporting myself to Guinness World

---

Records as the man who receives the largest number of phone calls in the world."

MADDOWNED

Just when we thought that the news outlets have learned their lesson about reporting satirical news items as fact, MSNBC's Rachel Maddow did just that: In 2011 she criticized a conservative organization called ChristWire for "begging" former VP candidate Sarah Palin to "speak out publicly and forcibly for an American-led invasion to protect our interests in North Africa." Had Maddow checked ChristWire a bit further, she would have realized it was a fake site. Other claims made by the site: Xbox video games are terrorist training tools; Japanese scientists plan to take over the world with evil robot babies; and Bill Murray is a "murderer of lambs." Maddow later apologized for not verifying the source. "Props to them for a brilliant piece of satire." She then added, "And shame on us for believing them."

A KILLER MISTAKE

When Congresswoman Michele Bachman (R-MN) kicked off her presidential campaign in 2011, she did so from Waterloo, Iowa. "John Wayne was from Waterloo," she boasted in her speech. "That's the kind of spirit that I have, too!" One problem: It was John Wayne *Gacy* who was from Waterloo—a serial killer who murdered 33 people. John Wayne the movie star was from another town on the other side of Iowa.

THE GULLIBLE INTELLIGENCE AGENCY

Two years after the September 11, 2001, terror attacks, Dennis Montgomery, a 57-year-old software developer, offered the CIA a way to catch al-Qaeda. He told them he'd developed software at his Nevada company that could un-scramble terrorist messages hidden among the pixels on Al Jazeera's news channel. The CIA awarded Montgomery $20 million in government contracts without even testing the software. It turned out to be completely bogus—Montgomery was simply a tech geek trying to con the government. He wasn't prosecuted, and all information regarding the incident has been classified to avoid any further embarrassment to the CIA.

...President Truman's health plan. The firm invented the phrase "socialized medicine."

FINAL THOUGHTS

Just in case you're not completely disillusioned with the political machine...

"The best argument against democracy is a five-minute conversation with the average voter."
—**Winston Churchill**

"Elections and politicians are in place in order to give Americans the illusion that they have freedom of choice. You don't really have choice in this country."
—**George Carlin**

"When government accepts responsibility for people, then people no longer take responsibility for themselves."
—**George Pataki**

"The harder you try to suppress the truth, the more inevitable it is that it will find a way to come out."
—**Arianna Huffington**

"Too often we enjoy the comfort of opinion without the discomfort of thought."
—**John F. Kennedy**

"Creative semantics is the key to contemporary government; it consists of talking in strange tongues lest the public learn the inevitable inconveniently early."
—**George Will**

"Instead of just being dazzled by these corporate mega-mergers, there should be a nagging voice in all of us asking: Is democracy going to be bought up too?"
—**Thomas Friedman**

"People don't care if politicians attack each other with untrue stories. They figure if you don't want to get hurt, you shouldn't have filed for office. They figure whatever happens to us, our lives will be better than theirs."
—**Bill Clinton**

"Everybody knows politics is a contact sport."
—**Barack Obama**

"Political language—and with variations this is true of all political parties—is designed to make lies sound truthful and murder respectable, and to give an appearance of solidity to pure wind."
—**George Orwell**

"Any nation that can survive what we have lately in the way of government is on the high road to permanent glory."
—**Molly Ivins**

Think your vote doesn't count? Officially, in 2000 Bush beat Gore by 537 votes.